BABY
BROTHER'S
BLUES

BABY BROTHER'S BLUES

a novel

PEARL CLEAGE

ONE WORLD
BALLANTINE BOOKS • NEW YORK

Copyright © 2006 by Pearl Cleage

Published in the United States by One World Books, an imprint of The Random House Publishing Group, a division of Random House, Inc., New York.

Grateful acknowledgment is made to Jessica Care Moore for permission to reprint "Armageddon Love" from *The Alphabet Verses The Ghetto* by Jessica Care Moore, copyright © 2003 by Moore Black Press. Reprinted by permission of Jessica Care Moore.

ONE WORLD is a registered trademark and the One World colophon is a trademark of Random House, Inc.

ISBN 0-345-48110-0

Printed in the United States of America on acid-free paper

www.oneworldbooks.net

2   4   6   8   9   7   5   3   1

First Edition

Book design by Susan Turner

For Zaron W. Burnett, Jr.,
the one and only

ARMAGEDDON LOVE

if the sky falls
and covers us
like an ocean
if the sun turns
cold and light
abandons our
hearts i would
wrap my arms
around the space
left behind and
know it was you

JESSICA CARE MOORE
The Alphabet Verses The Ghetto (2002)

I think that if Black men can acknowledge the sins of our fathers and can work to correct the effects of them and not repeat the sins, if we can do those things, then life in the Black community will be just the most peaceful thing in the world. If we fix ourselves, everything else will fall in line like a linchpin. I think we have to straighten out the misbehavin' men.

ZARON W. BURNETT JR.
Interview in *Gender Talk*
by Johnnetta Betsch Cole
and Beverly Guy-Sheftall (2003)

ACKNOWLEDGMENTS

I thank my daughter Deignan Cleage Lomax, for being such a great friend, great daughter, great mother. I thank my grandchildren, Michael and Chloe, for the pure pleasure of having them in my life. I thank my sister, Kristin Cleage Williams; Jim Williams; and their children and grands. I thank my friends and neighbors for their love and support, especially Cecelia Corbin Hunter, Ingrid Saunders Jones, Shirley C. Franklin, Ray and Marilyn Cox, Art and Jeanette Cummings, Walt and Lynn Huntley, A.B. and Karen Spellman, Lynette Lapeyrolerie, Zaron W. Burnett, III, Don Bryan, Johnsie Broadway Burnett, Doug and Pat Burnett, Pam and Nyla Burnette, Granville Edward Freeman Dennis, Brother Kefing, Kenny Leon, Donald P. Stone, Jimmy Lee Tarver, Valerie Jackson, Ayisha Jeffries, Helen and Gary Richter, Tayari Jones, Andrea Hairston, and Maria Broom. Thanks also to the Shrine of the Black Madonna and MEDU Bookstores, *Booking Matters* magazine, published by Shunda and Jamill Leigh, Paschal's Restaurant, and ROOTS International. Thanks also to Howard Rosenstone, Denise Stinson, and Nancy Miller for taking care of business. I also send greetings to my friend, the late, great Bill Bagwell, wherever he may be.

BABY
BROTHER'S
BLUES

BABY
BROTHER'S
BLUES

1

Regina was waiting for Blue. To the untrained eye, she looked like any other attractive, energetic black woman in her midthirties, going about her normal Saturday tasks. She stopped at the drugstore for some mouthwash, bought fifty of the James Baldwin commemorative stamps at the post office, had a long lunch at the Soul Vegetarian restaurant. Adrift in an afternoon of waiting, Regina was looking for something, anything, to distract her from counting the hours as they passed at their usual speed, although she could have sworn they were barely crawling by.

It had started last night. As she watched her husband pull on his black cashmere coat and reach for his perfectly blocked homburg, she was suddenly afraid of where he was going and what he might do when he got there.

"Blue," she said softly, "I don't think I can do this anymore."

Her timing was terrible. He had already uttered the phrase that served as their signal to announce the always surreal moment when her husband left their house, got into a big, black Lincoln with General Richardson, and disappeared into the night. What he did in these moments he did without the sanction of anyone or anything, other than his absolute confidence in the accuracy of his own moral compass and the trust and permission of the people who protected him with their loyalty, their gratitude, and their silence.

Her words floated there between them. Blue, his hand already on the doorknob, stopped to look at her standing nervously in the darkened hallway. Even in the low light, she could see his eyes gleaming, blue as a clear mountain stream, fathoms deep and ancient. She shivered. After two years of marriage, the always unexpected color of her husband's otherworldly eyes still surprised her, twinkling like sapphires in his dark brown face.

Although he had his mother's high cheekbones and his father's lean, compact physique, Blue was the only one in his family with those eyes. Speculation about where they came from had poisoned his father against his mother, although she was innocent of any infidelity. Many years later, after her aunt Abbie predicted correctly that Regina would come to Atlanta and fall in love with a man "who had the ocean in his eyes," Blue confirmed Abbie's theory that his eyes were a way to be sure that in this lifetime, unlike the last two when they had missed each other by a hair, Regina couldn't walk past him without noticing. This time around, that would have been impossible.

At this moment, her husband's blue eyes were dark pools, magical and mysterious, full of questions she had to answer.

"Can't do what, baby?" His voice was gentle, but she knew that General was already waiting for Blue out front. This was no time to talk.

Regina spread her arms wide, palms up, and looked at him helplessly. "*This*. You know, *this.*"

His eyes softened a little, but he didn't come toward her. She felt time passing, but Blue seemed not to notice. She had never seen him become impatient and he didn't now. Regina, however, was increasingly uncomfortable. The idea startled her. She was never uncomfortable around Blue. How could she be? He knew her thoughts almost before she did. She had even accused him of mind reading once or twice, and he hadn't denied it. But she didn't want him to read her mind tonight. There were some things that deserved a moment all their own. A moment not already weighted down by midnight comings and going, and cars with tinted windows, and drivers who waited out front with the motor running.

"Sometimes I worry, that's all." She walked up to him and kissed his cheek softly. He smelled like citrus.

He smiled at her, his eyes now the turquoise of the Caribbean Sea on a perfect Jamaica day.

He put his arms around her and kissed her so long and slow and deep, she felt her knees tremble. "Don't worry," he said, putting on his hat and opening the door.

"Be careful."

"Careful as I can." And he was gone.

That was when she started waiting, thirty-six hours twenty-eight minutes and thirty-two seconds ago, which was a lot of waiting, even for Regina. Lately, things had been peaceful and she wanted them to stay that way. Before the current calm descended, there had been a year of barely controlled chaos following the disappearance of two of the surrounding neighborhood's worst predators, a pimp who called himself King James, and his half-witted henchman, known appropriately as DooDoo. Their thuggish followers had made several angry incursions into West End, the area that her husband had taken under his protective wing before Regina ever met him, and where they now lived quietly in a beautifully restored Victorian house with a huge vegetable garden out back and roses out front that seemed to bloom all year long.

Blue's reaction to these brutal attacks on the peace, which usually involved violence against women and children, was immediate and, she suspected, sometimes fatal. It wasn't something they talked about anymore. What was there to say? Regina had married Blue Hamilton knowing exactly who and what he was. His entrance into her life had been so accurately predicted by her aunt, the self-proclaimed "postmenopausal visionary adviser," that when he walked out of the bright blue front door of one of the many apartment buildings he owned in West End, she recognized him with a jolt of physical desire and emotional memory that made her blush like a schoolgirl.

Later, as they got to know each other, he had told her in all seriousness about what he perceived as his failure in a past life to lead his people when he was their emperor. If that wasn't enough for her to consider, he movingly described her role in the women's resistance to his regime's corruption. His words triggered a flood of her own blood memories and made her know that he was telling the truth.

Blue's acceptance of the responsibility the neighborhood had informally conferred upon him a decade ago as their de facto godfather grew as much out of his desire to atone for his empire's past-life crimes against women as it did out of his need to provide the leadership and focus West End required. Like most African American urban neighborhoods, the community's biggest challenges were youthful predators, middle-aged desperadoes, wannabe gangsters of all ages, and domestic bullies who preyed upon the women and children trying desperately to love them.

In response to these ever-present threats, what Blue promised was that in the twenty-odd square blocks under his control, women would be safe, men would be sane, and children would act like they had some sense. It was a peaceful oasis in a sea of neighborhoods plagued by guns and crack, desperation and despair. Part of what Regina loved and respected about Blue was his willingness to provide protection for ordinary black folks who only wanted to go to work when they could find it, raise their children once they had them, pay their bills as close to on time as possible, and grow old in peace in the little houses they had paid for in exchange for all the hard work that defined their lives.

The only problem arose when Regina took a good long look at exactly *how* Blue was able to do all that. How was one man—even one as smart and strong and charismatic as her husband—able to keep the streets so peaceful that women walked unescorted and unafraid to the twenty-four-hour beauty shop and there hadn't been a rape in ten years? It was a legitimate question, and Regina was a smart woman. She knew the answer.

In the interest of her own peace of mind, she tried not to think about it too specifically. She didn't ask Blue any questions to which she didn't really want answers, and he didn't volunteer information that might be more than a loving wife needed to know about her loving husband in the general ebb and flow of their everyday lives. Blue's other role was something separate and they both knew it. To minimize the strangeness of the transition moments, they had developed a kind of verbal shorthand. When he stepped into his other role, he would simply say he had "business to attend to," a phrase he never used any other time. She would tell him to be careful.

"Careful as I can," he would always say. "Careful as I can."

Sometimes his business took only a few hours. Other times he was gone overnight, and once or twice longer. Those were the worst times. Those endless hours gave her too much time to imagine that he had come to harm. She closed her eyes, banishing the thought, suddenly panicked at sending out such negative energy into the universe that something evil might turn in her husband's direction.

Regina took a deep breath and tried to calm down. She watched a movie on television, perused a magazine or two, flipped through the pages of a new novel she had been curious about. Finally, around hour forty-two, she went upstairs and pulled her favorite rocking chair up to the bedroom window. It was September and the nights were just starting to cool off from an August that had alternated between one-hundred-degree sunshine and monsoon-force rains that overwhelmed the city's aging infrastructure and made many of Atlanta's thoroughfares fast-flowing rivers of rainwater and big-city rubbish.

Tonight, there was no rain in sight and none predicted. Just the barest suggestion of a chill. Regina wrapped her gray shawl around her shoulders and decided to stop pretending she wasn't waiting for Blue. There was no reason to pretend anything. There wasn't even anyone around to pretend *to*, unless she counted the baby. *The baby.* She loved the sound of the words in her head, even though she had yet to speak them out loud. Her doctor had confirmed what her home pregnancy test had told her. She was ecstatic, but before she could tell Blue, he had said he had "business to attend to," and all bets were off. She was going to have her husband's child and he didn't even know it yet. Too busy saving the world to hear the big news!

Regina tried to work up some indignation, but she couldn't. Blue wasn't off somewhere "saving the world." He was securing this one small spot on the map for his wife, and soon, for his child. He was doing what a man was supposed to do if he was really a man, and if he was anything at all, her husband was one hundred percent man. If she had anything to say about it, this baby would grow up proud to call Blue Hamilton Daddy.

"Don't worry, baby," Regina whispered, wrapping her arms around her body and rocking the chair slowly. "Daddy's on his way home right now. I can almost feel it, can't you?"

Outside in the street, an old man and woman strolled by, arm in arm, laughing and talking easily, their strides in perfect sync like they had been walking together for more years than they had walked apart. Regina watched them unobserved from the darkened window, and as she did, the man stopped suddenly, leaned over, and kissed the woman right in the middle of whatever story she was telling.

"You're crazy!" Regina heard the woman say, and the man beside her didn't deny it.

"If I'm crazy for kissin' my own wife, then send my black ass to the asylum and I won't even be mad!"

The woman shushed him gently, laughing. Regina smiled to herself as they continued down the street and out of sight. She was happy that they still made each other laugh and that they lived in a place where they could take that laughter out for an evening stroll unmolested. They could walk at midnight if they wanted to and be as safe as if it was high noon. Six blocks away that would be impossible. The presence of predators was too real and too dangerous. But in West End, there was still time and space for lovers, and Regina knew who they had to thank for that.

She pulled her shawl a little tighter around her body. "Don't worry, baby," she whispered again. "Daddy's on his way."

2

Wesley "Baby Brother" Jamerson had made an art form of avoiding responsibility. The sorry state of his life, to hear him tell it, was the result of racism, his father, his mother, his sister, his teachers, preachers, counselors, confidants, and co-conspirators of all kinds who spent their time trying to make sure a brother couldn't catch a break. The fact that he had been jobless, homeless, addicted, and incarcerated, all before he hit twenty-one, was not evidence of any lack of discipline on his part, but simply proof of the effectiveness of the plot against him.

He should have known better than to come to D.C. in the first place. His sister was the queen of the uptight, judgmental bitches. They hadn't even talked for almost two years. He must have been out of his mind from the acid that Marine with the bum leg had given him on the plane. No other way to explain the decision to show up at his sister's door, looking for some open arms.

Most of the other guys on the flight were wounded, being sent to Germany to continue their recoveries or, like him, on temporary family leave. When Wesley told the Marine in the seat beside him that he had five days to get home, bury his mother, and get back to his outfit in Fallujah, the stranger shook his head sympathetically and handed Wesley a small tab of LSD.

"That's a lot of shit to deal with for a five-day pass," he said. "This will help you keep things in perspective."

A product of the blunt, crack, Xstasy generation, Wesley turned the tab over in his hand. He had always been curious about acid, but his friends called LSD and mushrooms "hippy shit." They were content to confine their drug explorations to questions like: How much high-quality marijuana could a human being smoke and still function? Or: Was it really possible to smoke crack without getting addicted? Or: Does it really make an erection last longer if you sprinkle some coke on your penis before you have sex?

Wesley had considered all those questions ad infinitum, alone and in the company of other truth seekers. In the process, he had smoked more than his share of marijuana, good and bad, snorted and smoked a little coke when he was around somebody who had it and was willing to share, but he had never dropped acid.

"Should I do it now or wait until we get there?" Baby Brother asked.

The guy shrugged, his overly bright eyes indicating he had already begun his trip. "Suit yourself. Takes about an hour to kick in and then you're on your own."

He smiled beatifically at Wesley and turned to contemplate the expanse of bright blue sky outside his window. Wesley decided to do it right then. He needed something to take the edge off. He wasn't worried about a bad trip, that bane of the amateur drug user's existence. The guy beside him looked serene. Besides, Wesley had been in hell for the last four months, doing things and seeing things that were surely worse than any bad drug trip.

The worst this stuff could do was give him some new nightmares, and that might not be such a bad thing. He was tired of the old ones. Tired of going to sleep every night and seeing the faces of the dead babies and terrified old people, the weeping women in all that black shit they always wore. Tired of hearing the anguished screams of his wounded buddies all day, and then again all night. Anything was better than that. He put the tab under his tongue the way he had heard you were supposed to, laid his head back against the hard seat, and closed his eyes.

He woke up when they landed in Germany seventeen hours later, feeling high in a way he had never felt before, but relaxed in a way he'd thought he would never feel again. He turned to thank the Marine, but the guy had already gotten off the plane and disappeared, taking his cane, his backpack, and Wesley's wallet with him. *More shit luck!* He had borrowed two hundred dollars from his buddies for the trip and now he was flat broke. He knew he could stay on the base once he got to D.C., but what was the point of coming all this way to spend the night around the same bunch of farting hard legs he's just left in Iraq?

If he told the army he'd lost his ID, they'd replace it, but not the money. He would have to chalk that up to his own stupidity and make the best of it. That's when he thought about his sister. He was prepared to let bygones be bygones if she was. He now understood that Cassie only meant to help him stay out of jail when she signed the papers for him to go into the army, but at the time, he was furious, blaming everyone from his sister to his girl-friend for the fact that he'd been caught selling dope to middle-school kids on the playground.

The judge was unimpressed with his self-righteous wrath and told him he had two choices. Two years in the army, or ten years in jail without pos-sibility of parole. He was only seventeen, so as his legal guardian, Cassie had to sign for him. She wept when she handed the papers back to the judge, but Wesley blamed her for not getting him a better lawyer, for not in-terceding more forcefully with the cops, for not being in his corner *when the shit came down.*

Cass had not even been aware of her baby brother's existence before her father's deathbed confession that he had fathered a son, her brother, with a young faculty member he met at UC Berkeley on one of his many lecture tours. Her mother, he assured her, had gone to her grave with no knowledge of her husband's bastard child, although he had named the boy Wesley Jamerson Jr. Stunned, Cass had finally agreed to her father's plea that she look out for Wesley, who was only fourteen.

At the time, she was a twenty-four-year-old grad student with a part-time job, a steady beau, and no responsibility for anyone but herself. Within three months, Wesley had been kicked out of boarding school and had come to live with her, an angry ball of misdirected adolescent rage that sucked the positive energy out of every room he entered and replaced it with the sound of gangsta rap and the smell of cheap marijuana. Inquiries as to the identity, whereabouts, and responsibilities of his mother drew only the vaguest, increasingly hostile answers until she realized he had no idea where his mother was. She had simply abandoned him when he got too hard to handle.

Once Cass understood his situation, she felt a sudden wave of sympathy for her baby brother. She dismissed his past disciplinary problems and brushes with juvenile authorities as the not-unexpected result of his parents' weird response to his very existence. She dedicated herself to trying to make a home where he would feel wanted, acknowledged, and affirmed. Within six months, he had been kicked out of two more private schools and picked up for truancy twice from the public one she had managed to get him into in the middle of the academic year.

His book bag always contained more drugs than books and his explanation was always the same: "Somebody put that stuff in there to get me in trouble!" Her efforts to enlist his help in creating the peaceful, nurturing home she'd fantasized about met with a stone wall of defiant resistance. By the time he was seventeen, his cherubic face and bad behavior had earned him a place in a second-rate street gang where his moniker was "Baby Brother." One day, he demanded that Cass address him that way at home, too. Without looking up from the book she was reading, Cass told him to go to hell.

"You first," he said, grabbing his backpack and heading out the door.

The next day, he was picked up at Ralph Bunche Middle School selling kids two joints for a dollar. When the principal called the police, they found twenty-six dollars in the pocket of Baby Brother's Sean John jeans and it wasn't even lunchtime. In his chambers after the hearing, the judge told Cass he admired her struggle to help her brother get on the straight and narrow, but that given the options, the army was the only real chance the boy had to turn his life around.

"It'll make a man out of him," the judge said, thrusting the enlistment papers at Cass and glowering at Baby Brother, slouched in his chair like he was too bored even to sit up straight. "Or it will kill him. Your choice, young man. Make the right one."

Once he shipped out, Baby Brother spent months blaming Cass for the chain of events that landed him in Iraq. For a long time, almost a year, he had refused her phone calls and returned her Christmas and birthday packages that followed him from basic training, to a few weeks of specialized combat training, and on to Fallujah. After a while, the packages stopped coming, and he told himself he didn't care. It was Cass's fault he was even in this hellhole. What was a care package of snack food and tube socks going to do to make that better?

Their estrangement was so complete, he didn't even know she was married until he used the change he had in his pocket to catch the metro to the stop nearest the house where he hoped she still lived. She couldn't still be mad. She had sent all those packages, hadn't she? That must mean she still loved him and would be overjoyed that he had shown up unexpectedly on her doorstep, *right?*

He rang the bell and stepped back, trying to arrange his face into an ingratiating smile. Suddenly a big, angry stranger opened the door to his sister's house and frowned down at him.

"I don't believe this," the stranger said. "You've got a hell of a nerve showing up here. We didn't know if you were alive or dead."

Baby Brother was taken aback and a little intimidated. He didn't even know this guy's name and the man was already pissed. He decided the best defense was a big, bold, blustery offense. "I'm looking for my sister, *motherfucker.* Who the fuck are you?"

"I'm her husband, *motherfucker,* that's who I am." The big man let it sink in while he looked at Baby Brother with undisguised contempt. "And I know all about you. I know what you put her through before you disappeared, and if you came here because you think you can do it again, let me tell you one thing."

He stepped through the front door, and even in his shirtsleeves, he looked fit and muscular. Baby Brother tried to stand tall, hoping his military uniform gave the illusion that his five-foot-seven was really six-foot-two.

"If I ever see you around here again, or hear about you trying to contact my wife in any way, I'm not going to call the police or your commanding officer. I'll come looking for you myself!"

The guy looked at Baby Brother like he expected a response. When he didn't get one, he frowned. "Are we clear?"

Baby Brother looked up into his brother-in-law's angry face. He looked familiar in a weird way. *Had he met this guy before?* He wondered if Cassie had told him about the money he stole from her, or the time he got them thrown out of their apartment for fighting with the landlord, or how he ran up her credit cards to ten grand, or the time she paid for his fifteen-year-old girlfriend to have an abortion and went with her to the clinic when Baby Brother said he wasn't going. He wondered if Cassie had told her husband about the couple of times he had shoved her around, or that one time he had slapped her when she kept nagging him about school just before he got arrested for the last time and she signed the army papers. She'd still had the black eye when they went to court, so that day she kept her sunglasses on most of the time.

Court! All of a sudden he remembered where he had seen this face before. *Cassie had married the fucking judge!*

"We clear, *Your Honor*," Baby Brother said as he headed down the front steps to let the guy know he recognized him, too. At the sidewalk, he turned back with a sneer. "And you tell my sister I said she ain't got to worry. I won't be back."

The judge looked at him, then slowly shook his head. "You young-bloods think the world owes you a living, *and for what?* You're mad at your mamas, mad at your daddies, mad at the women foolish enough to have your children. Always crying the blues. People died to make a place for you and you don't have the good sense and discipline to step up and claim it. I'm sick of you, and I'm sick of your bullshit blues. Now get the hell out of my face and *grow the fuck up!*"

Baby Brother didn't know what to say to that, so he walked on down the street. When he got to the corner, he looked back, but the porch was empty. *Now what?* It was after six and people on the street were hurrying home from work or segueing into evening activities that did not include any more time in the unseasonable chill than necessary. Baby Brother saw his options narrowing down to a series of unappealing choices.

He turned up the collar on his uniform jacket and cursed himself for not bringing a coat. It had been 114 degrees when he left Iraq. The idea of carrying a heavy coat hadn't crossed his mind. All he knew was that an aunt in California he didn't know he had, contacted him to say that his mother had died, they were having a memorial service in D.C. in a week, and if he wanted to come, he was invited.

Of course, he applied for emergency leave to attend the funeral. Every day away from the murderous mayhem of this insane war was a day when the chances of living through it went up astronomically. Besides, he was really in need of some R&R. He figured he'd go to D.C., rent a motel room with the money he'd borrowed, score some weed, hook up with his buddies from the old gang, if any of them were still around, and forget about Iraq for three days.

The idea of actually going to his mother's funeral never crossed his mind. She had been dead to him since she sent him to his dad and disappeared. It was still hard for him to believe she had been able to toss him out of her life so easily. When he was little, she'd doted on him, gave him anything he asked for, and excused his misbehavior as growing pains. But when he got older, she stopped thinking he was her very own gift from God. She tried to establish some rules, but by that time, he was too used to having his own way to give it up easily and no amount of punishment seemed to make any difference.

In desperation, she had demanded that his father take responsibility, threatening him vaguely with disclosure of their affair if he did not. Professor Jamerson had reluctantly agreed to handle his son. When his mother announced she was sending him back east to live, Wesley had imagined a new beginning with the man who had given him his name, but little else. Unfortunately, that wasn't what his father had in mind. Sticking him in first one private school and then another, Dr. Jameson saw his son once a year, on Christmas, and never invited him home. Letters from his mother were few and far between and finally stopped coming all together. Angry and emotionally abandoned, Baby Brother plunged into adolescence with a chip on his shoulder and a determination to show the world that he was tough enough to handle whatever came his way.

Less than five years later, he had burned every bridge almost before he crossed it and found himself in the middle of a war he didn't understand any better than he had understood his life back in the States. He shivered in the cold wind. *When the hell was he going to catch a damn break?* Awash in self-pity, he didn't even see the man who walked by him, turned around, and then called his name.

"Wes Jamerson?"

Baby Brother turned around and saw the grinning face of a buddy he hadn't seen since the lucky motherfucker finally got shipped home for good. He grinned back.

"Is that really Jive Time Jason Harris, the ladies' pet and the punk's regret?"

"Live and in the flesh." Jason laughed and embraced Baby Brother with real affection.

Baby Brother clocked his friend's expensive shoes and stylish overcoat. He couldn't remember what Jason's job had been before the war. Whatever it was, he must be good at it. Jason looked like a businessman or a highly placed political operative.

"What are you doing here, man? When the hell you get out?"

"I didn't. I just came home to bury my mother."

"Oh, hey, man, I'm sorry to hear it. Rest in peace and all that, you know?"

"Thanks, man. It's cool, but thanks." Baby Brother didn't want to talk about his mother. He wanted to see if Jason could put him up for the night, point him toward some pussy, and front him the money to buy it, but he didn't know how to ask. Squatting on an Iraqi rooftop, waiting for a home-made rocket to light your ass up, you can ask a nigga for anything, Baby Brother thought, and if he can, he'll give it to you. But back in the world, things were different. Saying hello on the street was one thing. A few drinks to catch up was expected. But an overnight guest who had probably seen you at your worst—violent and kill crazy, or crying like a little bitch— that was a judgment call. Only time would tell if the brotherly bonds they'd forged under fire would hold up a few blocks from DuPont Circle.

"So you already been to the church or whatever?" Jason said, sound-ing restrained out of respect.

"That's where I'm coming from," Baby Brother lied. "She was cre-mated."

He didn't know why he added the unnecessary embellishment, except the moment seemed to require a little more detail to be convincing. The wind was kicking up again and the chill went through his uniform like a thousand tiny knives. He shivered again and Jason saw it.

"Hey, man, you been walking around all day without a coat on?"

"I'm out of the habit," Baby Brother said.

"I heard that! What was it over there when you left?"

"One hundred and fourteen."

"Damn!" Jason winced and shook his head. "That's brutal!"

"Almost as brutal as this hawk whistling up my ass," Baby Brother said with another shiver. "Listen, it's good to see you, man, but I'm looking for a warm bar with a cold beer."

"Fuck that," Jason said, suddenly animated again. "I live two blocks from here. I got beer and a little weed left over from New Year's Eve."

"Now you're talkin'," Baby Brother said, relief flooding his body. "I wasn't sure you'd still be smoking. You look like a damn congressman or some shit."

"Don't knock it," Jason said, leading the way. "If that idiot we got in the White House can be elected president, all things are possible."

"Yeah, well, you better get in line behind that African nigga from Chicago. You know the white folks ain't got room for both y'all!"

"Fuck you, nigga." Jason laughed. "You ain't changed a damn bit."

And I hope you haven't either, Baby Brother thought. *I hope you haven't either.*

3

Abbie Allen Browning needed a world atlas. She had to find Preston-pans. She needed to see it on a map to believe that it really existed. She had been reading a news account in the Atlanta paper of a town in Scotland that had decided to mark Halloween by officially pardoning eighty-one people—*and their cats*—executed centuries ago for being witches. The town, the name of which was Prestonpans, had recorded the largest number of witch executions in all of Scotland, which had a grand total of more than three thousand five hundred, mainly women and children, not to mention countless cats, usually black.

The report quoted a historian who presented evidence in support of the pardons by saying, "It's too late to apologize, but it's sort of symbolic recognition that these people were put to death for hysterical ignorance and paranoia."

The words leaped out at Abbie. Reading them, she couldn't help but recognize that these same two emotions were visible everywhere in her own country these days. Hate crimes were on the rise from sea to shining sea as frightened, angry people took out their frustrations on anybody who didn't look, talk, think, eat, or have sex in what was deemed an acceptable fashion. In Prestonpans, they had called them witches and burned them alive or tied heavy stones to their feet and drowned them or hanged them by the neck until they died and the community could breath a sigh of relief that evil had been defeated, at least in their small, Scottish corner of the world.

That's why Abbie had to see it on the map. She needed some information about the town's topography, its climate, its crops. She needed some specifics in order to convince herself that it must have been something in the water or the air that made the people of Prestonpans act in such barbarous fashion toward their neighbors. She needed to convince herself that the hysterical ignorance and paranoia were theirs alone and could never manifest themselves in Washington, where she lived, or Atlanta, where her niece Regina lived with her husband, or here on Tybee Island, where she was a frequent guest at their beach house and where she was now rummaging more and more frantically through the bookshelves looking for an atlas.

How could Blue overlook such a household necessity? Abbie thought maybe she should call her friend Peachy and see if he had one, but then he'd think she expected him to bring it out to the island, and he'd already been by that morning with a bag of oranges, which were her favorite fruit, a dozen green Granny Smith apples, and a bunch of ripe bananas that couldn't have looked fresher if he'd picked them in his garden like he did the tomatoes he'd brought the day before.

Abbie enjoyed Peachy. He was a regular visitor, but he never just hung around. He respected her need for solitude and, by doing so, increased her pleasure in his company. There had always been strong sexual energy between Abbie and Peachy, from the first time they met in D.C. right before Blue and Regina's wedding, but after five years of celibacy, Abbie was not in any hurry to initiate sex. She really liked Peachy, and if there was any possibility that sex would tip some invisible balance toward weirdness, it was fine with her if they continued to be what they were—good friends.

She decided not to call and ask him to find her an atlas. She'd thought enough about the fate of the Scottish witches for one day. She stood up and stretched. It felt good to relieve some of the tension in her back. She brought her arms down slowly and rolled forward until her palms were resting on the floor in front of her. She smiled to herself. Abbie worked hard to maintain her strength and flexibility. Most sixty-year-old women hadn't touched their toes in thirty years. Abbie did it every day at least twice. *Sixty ain't twenty*, she thought, smiling to herself, *but it ain't half-bad.*

She had just put the last of the scattered books back in place and decided to watch the sunset from the widow's walk at the top of house, when the phone rang. The caller ID showed Peachy's number.

"I was just thinking about you," she said, skipping hello. "Were your ears burning?"

"I thought that only happened if you were talking about me."

"Six of one, half a dozen of the other," she said. "Aren't you going to ask me what I was thinking?"

"I'm pretty sure you're about to tell me."

"I was wondering if you had a world atlas."

"Planning a trip?"

She was pleased to hear concern about the edges of his voice. "I've been reading about witches," she said. "Do you know there's a town in Scotland where they killed eighty-one people for being *witches.* I want to look the place up, but there are no maps over here."

"Witches?"

"Witches. Killed their cats, too."

"Their cats? For what?"

"For being witches."

"Can cats be witches?"

"Can *people?*"

"Is that a trick question?" There was a smile in his voice.

"I'm not a witch!"

"I didn't say you were," he said gently, "but you admit that you're different. You got magic. You see visions. You brought Blue and Regina together across at least two past lifetimes that we know of and you can read people's minds."

He was right. If she had lived in Prestonpans, she would almost certainly have been branded a witch, cat or no cat.

"What's the name of that town again?"

"Prestonpans," she said. "It's in Scotland."

"Well, they sound like some pretty stupid people to me. Let's never go there."

She laughed at the practicality of his suggestion. "Why didn't I think of that?"

"Because then you wouldn't need me." He didn't wait for her to confirm that. "I went fishing this afternoon. I've got a pretty little sea bass in the cooler that's too big for me to eat alone. I'd be prepared to cook it if you're open to some company for dinner."

"I'd love some company," she said. "If you hurry, you can catch the sunset."

"Where are you going to watch it?"

Sometimes she walked to the curve in the beach where the freighters turn up into the mouth of the Savannah River, but not today. "On the roof. Come on up when you get here."

"I'm on my way."

She went to the refrigerator, took out a bottle of champagne, and filled a silver bucket with ice. She placed it on a tray with two glasses and carried it upstairs and out the door that led to the house's uppermost deck. It was really too big to be called a widow's walk, but that's what they called it anyway. She guessed it was just tradition, but the sound of it always made her a little sad. Abbie was glad Peachy was coming. She needed some company to help her stop thinking about witches and widows.

Putting the tray down on a small table between a pair of white wicker rockers, Abbie went back inside to wash her face and slip into one of the ankle-length skirts she favored these days. They tended to be made of colorful, gauzy fabrics that rippled in the breezes off the ocean like they had just fluttered in from the Caribbean and smelled, of course, of patchouli, her favorite scent. She chose a lime-green skirt and a bright yellow top, slipped on a pair of small silver hoop earrings, unlocked the sliding-glass door downstairs, and went back outside to wait for Peachy.

Sitting down in one of the rockers, she closed her eyes, took a deep breath, and made a decision. It was time to talk to Peachy about sex. After all, she had never intended to be celibate. Menopause had driven her to it. She found the hot flashes distressingly public manifestations of a very private rite of passage. She hated being in the midst of a discussion concerning something totally nonmenopause-related and feeling her face flush bright pink as rivulets of sweat rolled down her scalp like she was walking in the rain.

The person with whom she had been engaged in conversation would suddenly look concerned or embarrassed and then ask if she was feeling all right. At that point, she'd mop her brow and say something like: "It's just a hot flash. Please go on with what you were saying about the role of the full moon in the tomb architecture of ancient Egypt." But the moment was gone. And that was only the tip of the iceberg. There were also drenching night sweats, unexpected weight gain, and vaginal dryness, which was every bit as unappealing as it sounded.

After several embarrassing exchanges, Abbie realized her gentlemen friends were simply not up to the complex task of making love to a post-menopausal woman. They were, in fact, responding like frightened school-boys, terrified of the mirror her body provided to their post-middle-aged mortality. Sex became an awkward exchange of compromises, denials, and fallback positions that bore little resemblance to the sweat-drenched, passion-filled exchanges she was used to. Distressed and confused, she finally made a conscious decision to be celibate until she could figure it all out. Now, five years later, she wasn't sure she was ready to sleep with Peachy yet, but she was ready to admit she had been *thinking* about it. *One small step for womankind . . .*

She heard him turn into the driveway just as she was about to resign herself to the fact that he was going to miss the sunset. She smiled to herself. *Who was she talking about anyway?* Peachy Nolan was famous for being in the right place at the right time. He had once done sixty-eight one-nighters in a row and never been late to a single gig. *Why would he start now?*

4

General Richardson glanced in the rearview mirror at his friend sitting in the backseat of the car as they sped through the Georgia night. In all the years of their association, he had kept only one secret from Blue. In principle, he knew it was wrong, but he didn't feel like anybody could hold this one lapse against him once they heard the whole story. How are you supposed to tell a man you started having sex with his mama when you were eighteen and that the two of you kept doing it until she died twenty years later, and neither one of you ever told a living soul? General and Blue were like brothers, but even brotherly love goes only so far.

He had wanted to tell Blue. They had both wanted to, but Juanita had been so nervous about how her son might react that she could never quite bring herself to do it. Then she got sick and all bets were off. He had still wanted to tell Blue what had been going on, but Juanita begged him to respect her wishes and keep their secret, and General said he would. He was still keeping it.

Not long before she died, they had the house at Tybee to themselves for a few days. They had been sitting on the deck, holding hands while they watched the tide coming in, when he asked her if she believed in the past lives Blue was always talking about. She smiled and turned her face to him. She was so thin now. General could carry her in his arms like a child.

"I hope it's true, you know?" she said. "I'd love to bump up on you again next time around."

He grinned and squeezed her hand.

"Do you believe it?" she asked.

"I'm not sure," he said, *wanting* to believe it, but not sure he really did. "Blue ain't been wrong about much else I can remember."

She laughed softly. "He was always so sure about everything. Even when he was a little kid, remember? He just *knew*."

"I don't know what to believe," General said. "But how about if it's true, you send me a sign?"

"A sign?"

He nodded. "You know, from *over there*, so I'll know you're okay and that you miss me."

She closed her eyes. "I already miss you, baby."

"That's why you've got to send me a sign," he said, terrified he had depressed or frightened her. They had talked frankly about death enough for him to know she wasn't scared of it. Just not quite ready to go yet, that's all. He touched Juanita's cheek. "What do you say, sweet thing?"

She opened her eyes then and turned back to him, her smile the only thing in her face that hadn't changed. It was as radiant as ever. Her eyes were as bright.

"All right," she said. "You got a deal."

He smiled back. "So what kind of sign are you going to send me?"

"I don't know yet," she said. "Does it matter?"

"Sure it does," he said. "What if I don't recognize you?"

"You'll recognize me. You just keep looking until you find me."

He promised he would. Later, when the cancer had taken everything she had and then some, Juanita reminded him of that promise. She made him swear he wouldn't dismiss or ignore any sign that seemed to mean she was calling to him from *out there*.

"If you think it's me, *it's me*," she said urgently. "Even if it's something weird, *it's me!*"

He promised never to ignore a sign. He would have promised her anything, *done* anything, to soothe her pain for a minute. He had never seen a person who wanted to live as badly as Juanita did. She fought so long and so hard, he had started to believe it when she said she might still beat the cancer. But she didn't.

General and Blue had no need to try to articulate their loss to each other. They simply said their private good-byes and scattered her ashes at sea on a day as beautiful as she was. As they headed the boat back in, General sat alone in the bow, already watching for any sign of her return. That was ten years ago.

For the first few years after her death, General had driven himself crazy. Juanita's death left a hole in his life so big he was afraid he might fall in and die of loneliness. He searched for any clue that their love lived on. He dreamed about her, and even in his dreams, he begged her to come back. But during all those terrible years, there was nothing he could really claim as a sign. He never stopped looking, but deep down, he began to believe that while he had done his dying beloved a great kindness by concocting the plan for after-life contact, no communication was forthcoming.

Then tonight, in the most unlikely place imaginable, *there it was*. It was all he could do to walk away, but his commitment to Blue was absolute. How could he say, *I'm late picking you up because I saw the sign I been waiting for on a stripper's ass and I had to check it out?*

It had been a fluke that General was even in Montre's. He didn't usually do business at strip joints, but the owner had been ducking him and an unexpected drop-by was always effective in bringing people to the table. Johnny had greeted General at the door with a shit-eating grin on his face and a bunch of bad explanations for equally bad behavior. General let him squirm long enough to make the point, then accepted the offer of a bottle of *real* champagne, instead of the *rotgut* they routinely offered their customers, to put the cherry on top of Johnny's profuse apology.

As the relieved man had scurried off to fetch the bottle from his private stash, General settled himself at the owner's table. He had about twenty minutes to kill before he was expected at Blue's. He wouldn't disrespect Johnny by declining a glass of Moët, but that was all. One glass, and he was out the door. He didn't give a damn about champagne anyway. Juanita had been crazy about champagne cocktails. She had said she liked it because it was a ladies' drink.

He didn't want to think about Juanita sitting in a crummy joint like Montre's. Her memory deserved better. He looked around for his reluctant host. If Johnny didn't hurry up, he was going to have to leave without a toast to seal their deal. Just before he got up to go, a naked young woman stopped in front of his chair, smiling. She was more attractive than the girls they usually got in a place like this and something about her looked vaguely familiar. She had just come off the stage and was sweating a little.

"Lap dance?"

Her body was perfectly proportioned and her skin was smooth and unmarked. Her teeth were white and her eyes showed none of the artificial brightness of too many drugs. In a profession whose low end is full of desperate women with stretch marks, scars, and plenty of attitude, this girl was clearly different. She was fine as hell. Wishing he had more time, he glanced at his watch.

She smiled and licked her lips, showing a small pink tongue. "It ain't got to take long if you in a hurry, baby. Best ten dollars you gonna spend tonight."

He happened to know that a lap dance at Montre's was only five dollars, but he admired her hustle. This girl was worth more than five bucks and she clearly knew it. He reached into his pocket and peeled off a hundred-dollar bill. Her big brown eyes widened like a child's.

"I'm in a hurry tonight," he said, handing her the money. "Maybe next time I come in, you can dance for me."

"For a hundred bucks, we can dance all night," she said, rewarding him with a big smile. "Thanks, baby."

"You're welcome."

"Don't be a stranger." She was already heading for another table, but moving slowly to make sure he got an eyeful of her beautiful behind, of which she was justifiably proud.

She didn't need to worry. His eyes were glued to the small, heart-shaped birthmark that she carried at the small of her back just before the billowy curve of her hips. *There it was!* A birthmark identical to the one Juanita had in exactly the same spot! He couldn't believe his eyes, but he had to have a closer look. She was turning her smile toward a table full of men clutching five-dollar bills.

"*Hey!*"

She looked back over her shoulder and he beckoned to her. The table that had been eagerly anticipating her arrival protested her sudden change in direction as she headed back to General. "Hey, girl!" the boldest one called out. "You see we holdin' good money over here, don't you?"

"You ain't holding much of it," she said, knowing whatever General wanted would be more interesting and certainly more lucrative than anything those guys had in mind.

General watched her heading back his way slowly, taking her time. Her breasts swayed provocatively, but what he wanted to see was behind her.

"Change your mind about that dance?"

"What's that on your back?" he said, his voice gruff with emotions he didn't want to share.

"It's a birthmark," she said. "You want to touch it?"

She turned her back to him again, bent over slightly at the waist, and jiggled her behind at an alarming rate of speed. He couldn't take his eyes off the birthmark. It was exactly like Juanita's, but this girl's energetic shaking of her rump made it impossible to look as closely as he wanted to, even though he was staring.

"You can kiss it if you want," she whispered over her shoulder.

"What?"

"Go on and kiss it if you want."

Blue's voice spoke sharply from the front seat and startled General out of the memory.

"That's our turn coming up!"

General realized he had been flying down the two-lane blacktop. The speedometer said sixty, and in these little towns around Atlanta, that was a guaranteed ticket. With all the emphasis on homeland security, maybe even a search. He eased his foot off the gas and made the turn, still going faster than he should have.

"You with me, brother?" Blue said quietly. General knew it was a serious question. This was no time to be distracted. He had promised Juanita he'd keep an eye out for signs, but he'd also promised to look out for her only son, especially on nights like this.

"I'm cool," General said. "Let's do this."

5

F or the first time in a long time, Brandi Harris had something to look
forward to. She was sneaking a cigarette in the tiny, airless dressing
room before she had to go back out there, but she was thinking about General. He had "I'll be back" written all over his face. She didn't think he'd
recognized her, but that was cool. That was the whole point of being in this
hellhole, to stay under radar. She wondered what he had been doing here,
talking to that fool Johnny. Guys like General didn't make a point of coming in places like this.

Montre's was not what you would call a class act. It was a no-frills
neighborhood strip joint that catered to workingmen looking for the cheap
thrill offered by a five-dollar lap dance, or wannabe gangsters whose fortunes were invested in sneakers, not stocks. The whiskey was watered, the
beer was cheap, and the dancers had seen better days. It was not the kind
of establishment that Brandi was used to working in. She had been stripping since she was fourteen, flashing a fake ID and flaunting a body that
looked like it *should* have been over eighteen even if it was still under the
legal limit.

She had started out in places worse than Montre's. No stages. No pole.

Just the dancers right on the flat floor, hoping the patrons would throw some dollar bills her way and stop trying to touch her. Touching was against the law, but some of these clubs didn't give a damn. A lap dance could become a hand job for a few dollars more, and a guy with fifty bucks could probably find somebody willing to do just about anything he could think up.

Brandi wasn't down for all that. She was a dancer and she was good at it. By the time she was sixteen, men were throwing five-dollar bills at her and she was able to move up to a classier place that had a tiny, dimly lit private room for anything more serious than a lap dance. At the new club, there was a small stage with a ramp that ran out into the audience and a gleaming silver pole. Brandi had no experience with pole dancing, but one of the other girls showed her the basics and told her to improvise.

"What you worried about?" she said. "With the body you got, all you gotta do is grin and shake that ass."

Brandi liked the pole and she got good at it. She would slither and slide around it, loving the cool feel of the metal between her thighs and the whoops of the men watching as she slowly turned herself upside down, spread her legs wide, and *shook that ass* for all it was worth. That's when men started throwing tens, but Brandi still wanted more. Neighborhood clubs were fine, but she wanted access to the places where the celebrities and athletes went to party. Where you might see Ludacris or Usher or Sleepy Brown at a table down front. Where Ray Lewis might pull up in a stretch limo the night before the Super Bowl, or Allen Iverson might stop in when the Sixers came to town.

Brandi was looking for the big time, and as soon as she turned eighteen, she found it. A club near the airport put out the word that they needed experienced dancers and she went over to check it out. Their setup impressed her. A large main floor had tables for fifty or sixty people, two stages, and a bar that could easily accommodate twenty or thirty more. The DJ booth was a tiny cubicle of light with an amazing array of machines that made sure the music kept *bangin'*, and the dancers could even change in a clean, well-lit dressing room with mirrors everywhere. Brandi had worked at one place where the dancers had to just go into the bathroom, take off their street clothes, and get to work. That made her feel cheap. This made her feel classy.

At her interview, the manager, a tall, thin black man who had a nervous habit of looking over his shoulder every few minutes, made it clear that none of the dancers were required to have sex with customers, but that sometimes they had some very special people coming through who took a liking to one dancer or another. In those cases, the manager would discreetly let the girl know what was up and she was free to take the customer to the VIP room and work out an arrangement that was mutually satisfactory. On those occasions, the girls who said yes to these special requests were expected to kick back 25 percent of what they made to the manager and keep the rest.

"We have standard rates," he said, showing Brandi the lushly appointed VIP room with its leather couches and deep-pile carpeting. In the corner was a pole like the ones downstairs. "One of the other girls will tell you how much for whatever it is you do extra."

"I do that," Brandi said, pointing at the pole.

"That's not extra," the manager said. "Every other bitch on the block can work a pole."

"Can they work it good enough to make you come just by watching?"

He stopped and looked at her. She didn't blink.

"Show me," he said, flopping down in the chair closest to the pole and hitting a switch that filled the room with the sound of Lil' John and the East Side Boys. Brandi dropped her purse, kicked off her boots, and slid her jeans down over her hips. She had deliberately worn a bright red G-string for this audition, and under her tight white T-shirt, her breasts were bare.

The manager watched her with a bored expression. He had seen so many naked women, it took a lot to impress him. She strolled over to the pole slowly, reached out and encircled it with her arm, and then leaned over to lick it like an all-day sucker. The manager was watching her pointy pink tongue just the way she knew he would. This was her shot at getting to the next level and she was ready. More than ready. She hooked her leg around the pole and began her routine. By the time she finished, the manager's eyes were glazed. She grinned at him and he grinned back.

"Close enough, baby," he said, unzipping his fly. "Now come on over here and finish me off."

After that, Brandi became a regular in the VIP room. Sometimes she had sex with the guys, sometimes she just danced for them, but she was making plenty of money either way. As required, she kicked back to the manager, and after that first time, he never requested sex from her again. He had a serious lady friend who popped in frequently, unannounced, and she did not play. The rumor was that once she found her man having sex with a dancer who should have known better. Miss Girl pulled a razor, cut the girl's butt up so bad she couldn't work anymore, and told her the next time she'd get her face.

The girl left town, and after that, the manager couldn't even pay any of the other women to have sex with him. They were more scared of his girlfriend than they were of being broke or fired. Disappointed, but undaunted, he contented himself with the new girls who hadn't heard the story yet. Brandi didn't care. She had traded what she had for what she wanted, and from where she stood, this job was well worth a onetime afternoon quickie with the boss. She'd have given up more, but she was glad she didn't have to. Her future looked nothing but bright.

After two years at the club, she had started working with the manager selling a little coke to her regulars. She knew he was involved with some shady characters, but all she ever did was sell what he gave her. Who he got it from was none of her business, until he double-crossed a hard-eyed man with no sense of humor who tortured him for two days before putting a bullet in his brain and coming to look for Brandi. She gave him what she was holding and told him everything she knew, which wasn't much. The hard-eyed man took pity on her, decided on rape instead of murder, and told her to get her fine ass out of what was now his club.

Terrified, she hid out with her cousin Madonna for a couple of weeks to regroup. The problem was, her cousin lived in West End, and once you crossed that boundary, you were subject to the absolute rule of Blue Hamilton. That was fine for some people, but if she wanted somebody to tell her what to do, she'd get married. It wasn't that Brandi didn't understand the whole godfather thing. She respected Mr. Blue, she really did. It was just that she preferred to take her chances on the outside, where things were a little looser when it came to how you made your money.

She had to lay low long enough to let that hard-eyed guy forget about her. She knew it wouldn't be forever, but for now, the high-end clubs were off-limits. That was a *real* problem. All she knew how to do for money was dance. She couldn't mooch off Madonna much longer and she sure didn't want to become a full-time prostitute. She was down to her last ten bucks when she saw a "Dancers Wanted" sign in the window at Montre's, four whole blocks over the West End line. It wasn't what she wanted, but she needed the job and they said she could start that night. So she did.

Eight months later, she was still there. She was counting the days until a year had passed and Hard Eye would have moved on to mess with some other unfortunate soul. She still swabbed down the pole with an antibacterial wipe before she got on it, even though the other dancers bitched about her thinking "her pussy must be made of gold or somethin'." Most of all, she still couldn't believe how cheap the patrons of this place were, and how much *shakin'* and *grinnin'* they expected before they would part with their little sweaty George Washingtons.

But that was about to change. She could feel it. General Richardson didn't remember her, but she knew exactly who he was. She had met him when Mr. Blue had helped Madonna handle a problem she was having with that fool King James. They didn't actually meet, per se. General was just there in the room when Brandi told Mr. Blue what was going on and asked him to help her cousin, who was afraid for her life and hiding out at her mama's house.

Blue said he would help and there'd been no more trouble, so there was no reason for Brandi to go back to his place of business. Sometimes when she went to the twenty-four-hour beauty salon in West End, she'd see General driving that big black Lincoln around and think that was the kind of man she needed. Somebody who could take her places, spend some money on her. She'd never even been to Vegas and she was almost twenty-five years old!

She wished she had spoken to him that night at Mr. Blue's after she got through talking about Madonna, but she hadn't had a chance to make any introductions. She'd told herself back then that if she ever ran into him again, she'd get in his face until he sat up and took notice. Well, she thought to herself with a smile, she sure did that. She didn't know what it was about that damn mark on her ass that got his attention, but when she asked him if he wanted to kiss it, he looked like he had seen a ghost, handed her another hundred-dollar bill, and left. That was a total of two hundred dollars and he'd never laid a hand on her. She didn't make that much for having sex. *Not that she was hookin'!* There were just times when a girl had to do what she had to do to make ends meet. Brandi was tired of that kind of life. She knew she could do better and she knew General could help her do it. All she had to do was *grin and shake that ass.* Just like always.

She snubbed out her cigarette, pinched her nipples to life, and headed back out to the pole.

6

This was not Blue's favorite part of the life he had chosen, but this was the essence of it. It was his willingness to do what had to be done that made it possible for him to impose order on one small southwest Atlanta neighborhood. He used to say this life was chosen for him, as if he had no choice in the matter, but that wasn't exactly true. Nothing happened to Blue Hamilton by accident or coincidence. His lives—this one, and the others he could remember—were ruled by the same vast organizing principle that connected all things to one another and to themselves in one endless cycle of birth, life, death, and rebirth.

His lives were no more or less extraordinary than anyone else's. The extraordinary thing about Blue was that he remembered them. He carried forward clear memories of where he had been and what he had done. He knew there was still penance to be done and scores to be settled that went back centuries, crossed oceans, survived slavery, and now brought him to West End to try to make some sense of himself and his people.

In the front seat, General kept his eyes on the two-lane blacktop, looking for landmarks. As they passed an abandoned Shell station, he slowed the car and glanced in the rearview mirror. Blue met his eyes and nodded.

General turned the big Lincoln left and eased it down the unpaved stretch that would dead-end at the trailer where the man they were looking for was hiding.

"Cut the lights," Blue said.

General's immediate obedience to the command plunged the narrow road into sudden darkness. Without being asked, he lowered the windows so they could hear anything out of the ordinary and popped the locks on all four doors while they were still too far away for the dull thump to alert a careful listener. As was his habit, Blue was dressed in a black cashmere overcoat and a dark suit. His one concession to the mission that brought them to this place was replacing his customary white shirt and dark tie with a black turtleneck sweater. His dark clothing and the Africa-dark skin of his high-cheekboned face made him almost invisible against the car's ebony interior. Only his startlingly unexpected blue eyes were visible as he slowly pulled on a pair of tight black leather gloves.

At the end of the road, the trailer came into view, a pitiful wreck of a hideout, perched precariously on a foundation of the same crumbling gray cinder blocks that supported the rusty shell of a pickup truck that had been parked there long enough to have kudzu creeping along its front and rear bumpers like a country lake lapping gently at the edges of an abandoned rowboat. There were lights on inside, and in the stillness, they could hear the television blaring *Monday Night football.* General eased the car to a stop and cut the motor. For a minute, neither man moved. From the trailer's open windows came the sound of televised cheering as some NFL gladiator broke for daylight.

Blue wondered if the man inside was alone. There were no cars around to indicate company, but Blue never made assumptions based on such a cursory review of the possibilities. Such hideouts were often visited by the loser friends of the loser fugitive who was squatting temporarily on his way to oblivion. Sometimes, these men on the run were also able to tap the sympathies of desperate women. Blue had no desire to interrupt a sexual encounter that had nothing to recommend it for a spectator or a participant.

The sounds of the game were the only thing disturbing the deserted patch of pine trees. They had found the spot on a tip from somebody who had decided this guy's crimes warranted breaking the street code that held a snitch to be only one small step above a child molester. The fugitive had abused his wife for years, sending her to the emergency room with a variety of broken bones, two concussions, and one near-fatal miscarriage brought about by being kicked in the stomach repeatedly during her seventh month of pregnancy.

When he attacked their ten-year-old daughter in a drunken frenzy, his wife finally found the courage to move into a safe house in West End with her children. This placed her under Blue's protection. At that point, General had gone to see the guy to make sure he understood that her safety was no longer simply her personal concern. He communicated Blue's policy regarding violence against women and children and told the guy not to come anywhere near West End.

Two weeks later, the guy called to beg his wife's forgiveness, told her he had found God and was a changed man. He was sorry for the things he had done and only wanted a chance to apologize to her, face-to-face, and beg her forgiveness. Relieved, but worried, she told him to meet her at a busy restaurant around the corner from the West End News. Shamefaced, he told her he was not allowed in West End and suggested they meet at their old apartment, where he was still staying. When she hesitated, he began to cry and beg her to trust him. The sound of his racking sobs touched her heart and she agreed to meet him the next day at noon.

When she arrived, he attacked her, gagged her, stripped her naked, tied her spread-eagled to the bed they had shared as husband and wife, then raped her with a broom handle and cut off her nipples with a kitchen knife. The cops who found the body the next day told Blue it was the worst thing they had ever seen. She left behind five children, all fathered by the murderer, who fled for his life. Three days later, when he showed up at his buddy's trailer, with a long story about his *bitch wife* putting him out *over some bullshit*, he still had her blood on his clothes. Pretending not to see the stains, the buddy allowed the murderer to crash and the next day headed for West End to give Blue Hamilton the information he was looking for all over the neighborhood. Friendship was one thing, but this guy was just plain wrong.

General waited patiently for Blue to give him the signal. In this moment, patience was more than a virtue. It was a necessity. A male figure passed in front of the window, turned on the light in the kitchen, grabbed a beer, popped the top, and shuffled back to the television. He was clearly in the trailer alone.

Glancing in the rearview mirror, General again met Blue's eyes. In the gloom, they glittered, hard and cold like sapphires. General slid his hand into his overcoat pocket and felt the familiar weight of the gun in his hand.

"All right." Blue's voice had the low rumble of thunder in the far distance. "It's time."

7

I n the beginning, they had ridden in the front seat together, but General felt Blue should sit in the back. "How they gonna know you're a star if you don't act like one?" was how he explained it to Blue.

After that, Blue sat in back and General drove. The arrangement suited them both. It gave Blue a chance to be alone with his thoughts and General an unobstructed view of what was going on around them at any given moment.

"You need to stop anywhere?" General asked as he headed the big Lincoln back onto the interstate.

"No," Blue said quietly. "Let's just go on to the house."

That was fine with General. He trusted Blue to make all the decisions on nights like this. He never questioned or second-guessed his friend's judgment. He did what he was asked to do. General was a soldier and they were at war. What he and Blue had done tonight was just part of what it took to win.

The two men had been friends since elementary school, back when everybody still called General by his given name, James. They had grown up on the same block; learned to ride the same bike; lost their virginity (with different girls on different nights) in the backseat of the same used

Chevrolet. Blue had started calling him General in the ninth grade because whenever they got to the playground, James always took charge of whatever game they were playing. Everybody laughed at first, but the name stuck.

Although General was two years older, they were as close as brothers, and when Blue had his first hit record at sixteen and needed to go on the road to promote it, of course General offered to drive him around to all the little clubs that were clamoring for him to perform. That trip turned into another and another and pretty soon it was a full-time job. General never looked back. The clubs were paying good money and General could always make the owners give up what they owed. As Blue's road manager, by then he was legally armed. It was a cash business, and the law acknowledged the need for protection of assets. He spent a lot of time at the firing range until he got good at it, but he'd never had to shoot anybody about their money. The *killin' shit* came later. But on the road? *Plenty pussy, plenty cash,* and a friend who was more like a brother to share the adventure. Even at the time, General knew this would be the period they'd look back on as "the good old days," and he enjoyed every bit of it.

So did Blue. He was singing better and better and the women in the audience were acting like he was all five of the Temptations in their prime. Women would rush the stage and toss their panties and fall out and Blue would just smile and keep on singing. He wore sunglasses during most of the show. Blue knew the women wanted to see his famous blue eyes, but he didn't want people to be so busy staring they didn't hear the music. He'd take the glasses off for the last number and the women would go crazy.

General knew Blue's eyes had been a real source of friction between Juanita and her husband. Old Man Hamilton wanted to know how his son showed up with what he always called "those damn cat eyes" when nobody on either side of their families had eyes that looked like that. Juanita, who had always been completely faithful to her husband, more out of fear than love, had no satisfactory explanation. Blue's father would watch Atlanta's café au lait political elite on the nightly news and snarl, "Is that him? Is that the li'l nigga's daddy?" while the light-eyed, light-skinned politico in question prattled on, innocent and oblivious to the crime with which he was being charged.

"You his daddy." Juanita would sigh. "You know you his daddy."

"Where he get them eyes from then?"

"Dr. Cox says sometimes it just happens. One of us probably got some white folks back up in our family tree and—"

"That's bullshit," he'd growl, and click off the set. The sudden silence enveloped them like a fog and she knew what was coming next.

Left to his own devices, General suspected that Blue had concocted the story of past lives to explain those unexplainable eyes. Growing up around Blue, General had ample opportunity as a child to stare at his friend's eyes without drawing his ire. At fifteen, you can't gaze into your boy's eyes and say: "Damn, brother, you got some amazing eyes, you know it?" But at five, you can say: "Hey, did you know your eyes look like a cat-eye marble?" and your friend can say "yeah" in the same way Halle Berry's kindergarten classmates must have said: "Wow, Halle, did you know you look like a fairy princess?" And she must have smiled and said: "Thanks. I know."

"You ever think about what might have happened if you had taken Jasmine up on her offer to move to Florida?" Blue said suddenly from the backseat as if they had been in the midst of a conversation about girlfriends past.

Jasmine was a beautiful woman General had met when her daughter, Zora, was a freshman student at Spelman. They hit it off until one night he had to leave her to *take care of some business* and she figured out his role in Blue's life. The very next day, she told him she couldn't love a gangster, even a *righteous* gangster, but if he wanted to go into the motel business, she was looking for a partner for a place she'd owned with her husband before he died.

Blue's question was so unexpected, General's eyes flickered to the mirror to see if there might be a clue as to what had prompted it. Blue was looking out the window, although there was nothing much to see other than the darkness.

"Nah, man," he said, passing a big UPS truck. "I can't live at no beach. Too much sand all over the place. Last time I went down there, we were out walking and it was romantic as hell, stars out and shit, and we started fooling around right there on the beach instead of acting like we had some sense and going back to the house. By the time we were done, I had sand all up my ass. No, thanks."

"You're supposed to put a blanket down."

Blue had been giving General advice about women all their lives, even though General rarely took it. After he fell in love with Juanita, most of the escapades he shared with Blue were fantasies and tall tales. He couldn't just stop talking about women all of a sudden. That would have raised Blue's suspicions immediately. So he made up stories or pretended to have long-term relationships with women he actually saw only once or twice.

"I'll try to remember that next time," General said. "What made you ask me about Florida? You offering me early retirement?"

"You ready for it?"

The conversation had taken a strange turn and General wondered if his lack of focus earlier had bothered Blue more than it needed to. Everything had gone smoothly and they were headed home. There was no cause for concern.

"I'm ready for whatever," General said, exiting at Cascade Road and heading for West End. "Just like always."

"Good," Blue said. "I'm going to hold you to it."

Just like always, General thought.

They were just a few blocks away from the tree-lined street where Blue and Regina lived. When he pulled the car up out front, General knew she'd be in the window, waiting for her husband. He never understood how she always managed to be there when they pulled up on these nights. Blue never called her on the way and she couldn't possibly sit there twenty-four hours a day, *just in case.*

Or maybe she could. After a couple of lifetimes, a day or two here and there probably doesn't make a whole hell of a lot of difference. An ordinary day was twenty-four hours, but eternity time was probably something else all together.

8

Just as General had predicted, Regina was sitting in the window when the big car glided around the corner, came to a stop in front of the house and cut its lights. The smoky, tinted windows didn't let her see who was inside and her heart fluttered a little bit in spite of her best efforts to think only positive thoughts and banish from her mind even the possibility that things had not gone as planned. The driver's-side door opened and General stepped out with the grace that always reminded her of a tiger: large and dangerous.

"Please, God," she whispered. "Please."

General opened the back passenger door and her husband stepped from the car into the darkness. Regina's eyes filled with tears of relief, but she quickly blinked them back. Blue said a few quiet words to General, who nodded and got back into the car. Only then did Blue look up to where she was sitting in the darkened window. He raised his hand in a small wave of reassurance. She raised her hand, too, and he disappeared into the small apartment that was one of the features that had sold them on this house.

That was the last she would see of Blue until morning. Although she longed to run outside and throw herself into his arms, she knew better. This was the hardest part of the complicated ritual they had concocted, but she had to respect it. She never knew the details of where he went or exactly what happened when he got there. She didn't want to know. Early on, she had told him she admired what he was doing, but confessed almost apologetically that it frightened her. That's when he promised to do everything he could to keep those parts of his life separate from his life as her lover, then her husband, and, one day, the father of her children. That's why she couldn't see him until morning.

At first, she had argued against the self-imposed separation, but he had gently insisted. As she tried to talk him out of it, something in his eyes flashed, something that let her know there were parts of him not meant for her to see. *Ever.* She had felt a small chill at the back of her neck and agreed to his suggestion, which was this: They were allowed only a wave when he first returned home from these missions. Then he would disappear into another part of the house until morning, when she would literally wake up and smell the coffee. She would then slip on a robe and go downstairs to the kitchen, where Blue would be scrambling eggs or mixing up a batch of waffles from scratch or frying bacon and handing her a mimosa like any other attentive husband who intended to woo his wife with breakfast before taking her back to bed for a more private welcome-home celebration.

Suddenly Regina was exhausted. She yawned wide like a tired toddler, brushed her teeth, and slipped into bed. Outside, she knew General was sitting in the front seat of the Lincoln with the window cracked, only the glowing tip of his cigarette visible in the darkness. On these strange nights, he was always there, just in case trouble had followed Blue home. In the morning, he would be gone.

9

Blue waited until he heard Regina running a bath at just before six the next morning before slipping on a pair of white silk pajama bottoms and heading for the kitchen. At six feet even, Blue was not a big man, but his slender body was strong and supple and his powerful arms were proof of his improbable prowess as a deep-sea fisherman, a hobby he and Peachy had enjoyed for years. Keenly aware that his enemies were always watching him for any signs of mental or physical weakness, he made sure there were none. Ever.

By the time his wife came downstairs twenty minutes later, preparations for her favorite breakfast were well under way: fresh-squeezed orange juice, almond waffles with real maple syrup, grits (because she loved the way he made them with just enough cheese for the flavor), and a cup of coffee. She was glowing from her bath and smelling like the sweetness he always tasted when he kissed her. It was all he could do not to sweep her up in his arms and ravish her right there in the middle of the kitchen floor.

She grinned at him and walked into his arms, pressing her body into his and kissing him like that ravishing idea had crossed her mind, too.

"Welcome home," she whispered.

"You okay, baby?" he said softly, leaning back to look at her.

In his dark brown face, his eyes were as peaceful as a mountain lake, clear blue without a touch of turbulence or danger. She searched in vain for anything that frightened or confused her. Standing in the circle of his smoothly muscular arms, fairly bursting with her good news, she knew there was only one answer to his question.

"I'm fine. You?"

He nodded and she tilted her head a little to kiss him again. His closely clipped mustache tickled her nose and his full, soft lips pressed against hers with a mixture of desire and restraint that she found irresistible.

"Are you hungry?" he said, when they came up for air.

She couldn't hold it any longer. The words came singing out of her mouth. "I'm *pregnant!*"

Blue wanted it to be true so badly, he was afraid at first he might have heard her wrong. *"Pregnant?"* He heard his own voice like that of a stranger.

Regina nodded. "You're going to be a daddy, Mr. Hamilton. Can you handle it?"

"Oh yeah," he said, grinning from ear to ear, wondering what he had done right in all those lifetimes to deserve a woman like this. *"Oh yeah!"*

He couldn't stop smiling and neither could she.

"I love you," she said softly.

"I love you, too," he said, holding her face in his hands.

"Is it selfish to bring a child into this mean old world?" She was smiling, but he knew she was serious.

"It's absolutely required," he said, kissing the tip of her nose. "This calls for a toast. Can you drink champagne?"

She shook her head. "How about orange juice?"

"Coming right up." He filled her glass and one for himself. "Did they give you a date?"

"March twenty-third," she said. "Give or take."

He laughed. "Give or take what?"

"Good Lord willing and the creek don't rise."

"Now you sound like Miss Abbie," he said. "Have you told her?"

"No, my darling, you're the first," she said, raising her glass, and he did, too. "To Baby Hamilton. *Welcome to the world!*"

They clinked their glasses and sipped the chilled juice like it was the finest champagne. A thought occurred to him and he smiled gently at Regina.

"Is this what you were trying to tell me last night?" he said.

She nodded and her eyes suddenly filled up with tears.

"I'm so sorry, baby," he said, setting their glasses down and gathering her up in his arms again. "Please forgive me."

"Forgive you for what?" she said, sniffling a little against his neck. "I was the one who broke the rules."

"For being a man who has to have those kinds of rules."

"But *why* do you have to?" she said, leaning back to look into his face. "Why can't somebody else do it for a while?"

"Gina," he said gently, "it's not something I do. It's who I am. It's something I carry with me. *Inside.*"

He took her hand and placed it flat against his bare chest. Smooth as black velvet, his skin was warm beneath her palm. She could feel his heart beat: slow, calm, steady.

"I'm carrying our baby," she said. "Doesn't that change things?"

"It changes everything," he said. "I've never had a child before."

She was surprised. She knew he'd had no children this time around, but she had never imagined that in all those ancient kingdoms and Harlem hideouts that were the settings of Blue's past lives, no woman had presented him with a child of his own.

"*Never?*"

He shook his head as he guided her over to the kitchen table and pulled out two chairs. He sat down across from Regina and took her hands in his. The plain gold bands they had chosen gleamed.

"Never. This one is my very first."

This pleased her so deeply, she thought she might cry again. *If this is what raging hormones feel like,* she thought, *it's going to be a very damp nine months.*

"Mine, too," she said.

He nodded. "I know."

They just sat there looking at each other for a few minutes and then she took another deep breath.

"Blue?"

"Yes?"

"What if I asked you to reconsider?"

"Reconsider what, baby?"

She shrugged helplessly, searching for the words that would convince him. "What you do. Who you are *this* time. In *this* place." She was getting closer to her real feelings and she rushed on before she could censor herself. "I know you were an emperor before, but that was then and this is now, *southwest Atlanta,* not Carthage, and you don't have to take responsibility for everybody. Can't you just take responsibility for *us?*"

He looked at her. "Just us?"

She nodded, took his hand, and pressed it against her stomach. "Just us."

He nodded, too, like he was considering the question. "And by *just us,* you mean you and me and our baby?"

She was practically holding her breath. "Yes."

"And Miss Abbie?"

That went without saying. Her, Blue, the baby, and Abbie. How much trouble could the four of them get into?

"Of course."

"And Aretha?"

He had taken Aretha under her wing when she had first arrived in Atlanta from her tiny Michigan hometown, on her own for the first time and green as grass. No way Blue was ever going to abandon his role as her godfather.

"And Aretha."

He nodded again, slowly. "And Joyce Ann?"

Joyce Ann, at almost three, called him "Daddy Blue," and brought a smile to his face that was hers alone.

"Yes. Joyce Ann comes with Aretha."

This conversation was no longer going the way she hoped it would and Regina knew it. Blue was who he was, *kid on the way or no kid on the way.* He wasn't going to change, not even for her.

She sighed and surrendered. "Sometimes I just wish we could live somewhere where somebody else could make it safe."

"And who would that somebody be?"

"Anybody but you," Regina said. "Why can't General do it?"

"Some things are worth killing over. Some things aren't. General can't always tell the difference."

"Are you going to tell the baby what you do?"

"I'll tell our baby the truth in all things."

Regina raised her eyebrows. "Past lives, too?"

"Of course."

He said it so calmly. She wondered what a child would say if their father told the tales Blue had told her. There was no way to know and no one to ask.

"It'll be easier if the baby has your eyes."

"Easier for who?" Blue smiled.

"Easier for the kid to understand who you are," she said.

"That won't be hard to understand," he said. "I'm just Daddy."

She leaned in for a kiss and suddenly wasn't as hungry for breakfast as she'd thought. "Let's eat later."

"All right." His eyes were twinkling as he slipped an arm around her waist and led her back to bed.

"I don't really want you to change," she said as they started up the stairs.

"I know."

At the top of the stairs she stopped. "Yes, I do."

He kissed her again, laughing softly. "I know that, too."

"Oh, you know everything!"

"Not everything," he said. "But I know what I know."

"Do you know me?" Regina untied her robe and let it fall to the bedroom floor in a jumble of pale pink satin.

"I'm working on it." He ran his hands slowly down her back, lingered over her hips.

She grinned and felt herself already melting under his hands. "Don't stop, okay?"

"Not a chance," he said.

"You promise?"

"Oh yeah," he whispered, his mouth against her belly and moving south. "I promise."

10

L ee Kilgore had a bad feeling. For a cop, intuition is sometimes the difference between life and death, so there was no way she was going to
ignore it. Standing in the living room of her twelfth-floor condo, she
watched the cars snaking down Seventeenth Street and knew that it was
time to make a move. All she had to do now was get Bob Watson to understand that. Lee was tired of the cocaine business. Her active involvement
over the past six years had been a fluke, not part of any long-term strategy.
Captain Kilgore had plans, big plans, but none of them included time
served for drug trafficking.

The thought made her give a little involuntary shudder as she moved
away from the window to pour herself another glass of Merlot. If her
grandfather had even suspected that the money she used those last two
years before he died to provide him with such exquisite care was coming
from the sale of drugs, he would have moved out of that beautiful Buckhead nursing home and caught the bus back to Macon. She never told him
how much it was costing to keep him where he was. Instead, she convinced
Poppy that she was using her pitiful little patrolman's salary to keep him in
a place where his room smelled like soap and shaving lotion instead of piss
and poverty.

Lee figured she owed him that much. He had raised her without complaint after her drug-addicted parents disappeared into Atlanta when she was eight years old. For a while, they would call, promising to return soon and wheedling money from Poppy. When he stopped sending cash, they stopped calling. For a few years, her mother sent birthday cards that arrived weeks late, but Lee never saw either one of them again. If it hadn't been for Poppy, she didn't know what she would have done.

When she graduated from high school with straight A's and a full scholarship to Georgia Tech, his proud face in the crowd at the ceremony was all the family she needed. He put her on the bus to Atlanta, told her to be careful and not forget the things he had taught her. She promised to visit as often as she could, kissed his cheek, and set off to make her own way.

At first she came home once a month, rain or shine. College was harder and lonelier than she'd thought it would be and she needed her grandfather's calm reassurances that she was more than up to the task. As she got more comfortable in her new environment and explored the city, her visits to Macon became less and less frequent. She tried not to miss Christmas and Poppy's birthday, but it was harder and harder to leave her new life to check in with her old one.

After graduation, she spent a year buried in the bureaucracy of the city of Atlanta's planning department and then, on a whim, responded to a police recruitment poster and found her true calling. Lee loved everything about being a cop. She was already in great physical shape, and never having been abused, she had no fear of men. Skeptical at first because at a slender five-foot-five, she looked sexy, not scary in her uniform, her fellow officers soon came to respect her courage and quick thinking under pressure.

Lee was savvy, street-smart, and tireless. Her goal was to be the chief of police before she turned forty and she knew how to do her job and let other people do theirs. When she began her rapid rise through the ranks of the department, no one was surprised. They knew she was a star on the horizon and it wouldn't hurt to be able to say they *knew her when.*

When she joined the force, Lee hadn't been looking to get involved in the cocaine business. Her rookie assignment was to a precinct notorious for the Wild West atmosphere created by the constantly warring gangs and their endless struggles to control the lucrative drug trade. Shoot-outs and beat-downs occurred in broad daylight and people were increasingly afraid of being caught in the cross fire. Her first week on the job, a seventeen-year-old dealer had used a fifteen-month-old baby as a human shield and the child was shot and killed. Lee's beleaguered sergeant wanted action, and he told Lee it was her job to make it happen.

Lee wanted action, too. Her long-term ambition required the cleanup of this precinct to be a success story, not an embarrassment. So she sat down with T. G. Thomas, the smartest of the gang leaders, and explained to him that he had a new partner. As his partner, Lee promised to create a space for him to move around in where business could be done with a minimum of disruption to community life. Distribution points would be controlled and dealers would stay away from schools, residential areas, and main thoroughfares.

There would be no more shoot-outs, she explained. It wouldn't be necessary. The leadership of the other gangs, as well as their soldiers, were being warned to clear out or face her wrath. Lee wasn't naïve enough to think she could eradicate the drug trade, but she intended to stop the casual violence that surrounded it. T.G., who couldn't have been more than twenty-five, agreed to her proposal and they shook hands. She declined his offer of a share of the proceeds, reminding him that she was still a cop and that if he didn't hold up his end of the bargain, she'd put his ass *under* the jail.

Lee knew Poppy would have called it a deal with the devil, but she was realistic. She didn't need to fix things permanently. She just needed to keep her precinct quiet until she could make her bones and move on. After that, the community was on its own again. Somebody else would have to figure out how to keep the peace.

Her strategy worked like a charm. Within days, Lee had arrested five dealers and intimidated the rest. Things started to quiet down. People returned to their porches and playgrounds, avoiding the designated spots the dealers now claimed and keeping one eye out for the ever present pit bulls. Lee nipped any renegade activity in the bud. In a month, things were going so smoothly her sergeant commended her and Bob Watson called to invite her to lunch.

That was almost five years ago. The partnership she had forged with Bob had served them both well. Of all her mentors, Bob had been the most useful, as well as the one she considered most nearly her equal in intelligence, emotional complexity, and sexual stamina. Only the sex had been a surprise. His other qualities were part of why she had been curious about him long before their involvement in the city's active cocaine trade brought them together.

She knew who he was, of course. He was well respected, professionally and personally, and had been on a first-name basis with every Atlanta mayor since Maynard Jackson took office as the first African American to hold the seat in 1973. His special interest was the ongoing gentrification of some of the city's most run-down neighborhoods, including Lee's precinct. Bob expressed his desire to talk with her about the vital role public safety played in his revitalization efforts. They chatted easily throughout the meal. Over coffee, Bob casually complimented her on forging the deal with T. G. Thomas that had returned peace to the precinct. Until that moment, she was unaware that Bob and T.G. even knew each other.

"How do you know Mr. Thomas?" Lee said.

"We've been in business together for ten years. He was fifteen when I made an investment in him. He was ready to go off on his own and he needed capital."

Bob made it sound like T.G. was going to open a shoe store and had needed a small business loan.

"I don't know what Mr. Thomas told you, but all I'm interested in is making it safe for innocent people to walk down the street."

Bob nodded slowly. "I understand completely and I share that goal."

"Good."

"Now, shall we talk about money? I'm prepared to make you a very handsome offer for your continued cooperation."

Lee put down her coffee. "What makes you think I won't arrest you?"

Bob smiled. "Because you're ambitious. You want to move ahead in the big city and you know there's a place here for somebody like you."

Flattered, but wary, Lee didn't return the smile. "You don't know me."

"Oh, yes I do," Bob said, sounding strangely seductive. "You're smart. You're talented and you're very photogenic. You can go all the way in this town, but you're missing one thing that is critical to your success."

"What's that?"

"A mentor. A person who can show you the ropes, begin to introduce you around, give you the road map."

She knew he was telling the truth. Having Bob in her corner would be invaluable. With her hard work and discipline and his contacts, she might make chief before she was thirty-five. Plus, he was very attractive, even if he was old enough to be her father.

"What's in it for you?" she said.

"A way to nurture the kind of young talent that Atlanta needs and a way to show my appreciation for your assistance in my business ventures with Mr. Thomas." He smiled at her again. "If you won't take money, you'll have to take me."

This time, she smiled back, realizing her life was about to change. "All right," she said. "I will."

"Good," he said. "Before we move on, let me say this once more and I'll let it go. If you ever want to take me up on my original offer of a cut of the proceeds, all you have to do is pick up the phone and I'll handle it personally."

"I think I've made the best deal," she said. "Now, when do I get a look at that road map?"

Bob was as good as his word and their preservation/public-safety partnership gave them a reason to be seen together without generating the gossip on which Atlanta thrives. Lee was promoted to sergeant, T.G. continued to obey the rules, and things seemed to be falling into place on all fronts. Then her cousin called to tell Lee that Poppy had had a stroke. She hung up the phone, jumped in her car, and headed for Macon.

Her first stop was the hospital where her grandfather lay unconscious, looking so frail his appearance frightened her. The doctor told her that in addition to the stroke, which seemed to have occurred more than two days before, although he had been admitted only last night, Poppy was suffering from malnutrition and dehydration. Lee was shocked, then angry. She had been sending money regularly to a young cousin who had moved in when Poppy became too frail to live alone. Where was that money going if not to care for her grandfather?

It didn't take long to find out. Her first look at the house told her all she needed to know. Even without the gray pallor or the constant shifting of his bugged-out eyes, she would have known he was a crackhead. The house was a wreck. He had moved his girlfriend in, a young white woman whose disfiguring facial scars were a result of the meth-lab fire that had killed her two-year-old when her last boyfriend's trailer blew up. Her four-year-old had been with his daddy, so he survived and was now living in Poppy's house, too.

When she opened the refrigerator, all that was inside were two bottles of cheap beer, a jug of Coca-Cola, and an open package of bologna. Neither her cousin nor his girlfriend seemed to understand why she was so angry.

"Where you get off actin' like you lovin' the old man so much?" the girl snarled. "I been livin' here six months, and this is the first I seen of you."

Lee wanted to slap the woman across her smart mouth, but it was true. She hadn't been there for Poppy when he needed her. Awash in sudden guilt, she walked out the front door without another word, stopped at the hospital long enough to tell them she'd be back as soon her grandfather could be released, and headed back to Atlanta to make the necessary arrangements.

Every place she called was expensive. The ones that were in her price range were overcrowded, smelly, and depressing. At the last place on her list, she seemed to be the only one bothered by the roaches that were everywhere. She cut the tour short and called Bob on her cellphone. He arrived at her apartment less than an hour later with twenty-five thousand dollars in cash. She told him it was a loan and she told herself it was a loan, but week after week, she accepted the envelopes he offered, and after a while, they didn't discuss it anymore. Not even when Poppy died two years later and Lee no longer had to pay almost thirty thousand dollars a month for his care. She had rationalized it by telling herself that there had been no cocaine-related murders in her precinct for almost five years, but she knew that was no excuse for what she was doing. Not anymore. She also knew she had enjoyed a long streak of good luck in a very risky business and every gambler knows the odds are always with the house.

It was clear that Bob didn't want the hassle of breaking in a new cop to run street interference for him, but Lee knew it wouldn't be difficult. Somebody always had bills to pay, or a kid on the way to college, or a taste for the high life. She hoped Bob wouldn't get ugly about her decision, but ultimately, his displeasure wouldn't matter. Bob wasn't the first mentor to have outlived his usefulness. The challenge was to find a way to dissolve their partnership with the least amount of acrimony so everybody could move on without leaving any bad feelings behind.

Lee smiled and sipped her wine. The bad feeling had now been replaced with a new sense of calm and clarity. She already had an appointment with Precious Hargrove that she'd been trying to schedule for a month. Lee knew that meeting was going to be the first step into the next phase of her life. Senator Hargrove was the future. Bob Watson was the past. Too bad he didn't know it yet, she thought, closing the drapes and picking up the remote control. She sank down into the cushions of her cream-colored couch and clicked the television into life. *How could he know it?* He had no frame of reference. Women didn't leave men like Bob. He left them. Finding himself standing all alone with his dick in his hand would be a new experience, she thought, smiling at the image.

She had to admit she'd miss the sex, but not enough to miss the boat. Bob was good, but not that good.

11

K wame Hargrove was pissed. It wasn't his daughter's fault that her mother was acting like a spoiled brat again, but it was taking all Daddy's patience not to be short with Joyce Ann, age two and a half going on twenty, who was chattering away about what adventures she'd had today in the preschool world. Normally, he loved sharing this end-of-the-day time with his daughter, but tonight Joyce Ann was supposed to be her mother's responsibility, not her daddy's. Except it was now the appointed hour, and Mommy was *missing in action.*

Taking a deep breath, he tried to focus on what his daughter was saying. Joyce Ann was his heart, a sweet-natured little angel who seemed unaffected by the increasing tension between her parents. Kwame had been present at her birth and cut the surprisingly spongy umbilical cord in one swift move that made his daughter an independent human being. It had been a profound moment. He had felt like he should apologize for separating her from her mother. He knew it was a mean old world, and once you're out in it, you're on your own.

Joyce Ann's birth was the culmination of what could only be described as a whirlwind year, filled with courtship, marriage, pregnancy, and birth, not necessarily in that order. Only two short years before, he had planned to take his newly minted Howard University architectural degree and accept a job at a firm in Washington, D.C. His mother had, of course, hoped he'd come back to Atlanta after he finished school, but as he tried to explain, there was no way to escape her shadow if he stayed in his hometown forever. In D.C., he could carve out his own place to be his own man. Kwame didn't want being Precious Hargrove's son to be his only claim to fame. She said she understood. To further mollify her, he agreed to spend the summer helping her get ready for the governor's race. In the fall, he'd planned to return to D.C. permanently.

Then he started dating Aretha, and everything changed. He couldn't get enough of her. She was a working artist whose passionate paintings and dramatic, oversize photographs were already drawing national attention. Kwame had met her once or twice before, but she had been five years younger than he was. At seventeen, that had made a difference. At twenty-six, it didn't. She fascinated him and he pursued her like a love-struck teenager.

At first he thought it was just a lucky coincidence that brought this beautiful young woman into his orbit so often he began to dress a little more carefully when he went out in anticipation of seeing her. West End is a small, fairly self-contained community, and Aretha walked or rode her bike everywhere, but after he bumped into her three times in one week, he began to realize their meetings were more than mere happenstance.

The idea flattered him immensely and he began to imagine making love to her. She was undeniably beautiful and naturally sexy. She was tall and strong without looking too hard or sinewy. She had flawless skin and her big brown eyes looked even bigger because of her close-cropped natural hair. Her breasts were always bouncing because of her long-legged stride and her hips were gracefully curvaceous.

What if she had shown up three times because she was looking for him? Did that mean she wanted him, too? He looked at himself in the mirror and liked what he saw. More than that, he liked whatever it was *she* saw. Maybe this beautiful, sensual creature was a gift from the gods to reward him for being a dutiful son. If that was the case, denying their generosity would almost certainly piss them off, which is never a good thing.

One afternoon when they ran into each other again at the West End

Newsstand, she invited him to come by her studio and see some of the new photographs she had been taking around the neighborhood. He immediately said yes and ordered them two cappuccinos to go, along with his copy of *The Washington Post.* As they strolled back to her place, Kwame was watching the way her earrings sparkled against the smooth skin of her long neck. He wanted to kiss her throat at the point right above her collarbone, before her neck flowed into the gentle slope of her shoulders.

She lived and worked in an apartment owned by Blue Hamilton, her godfather, whom Kwame had known all his life. Blue had allowed Aretha to paint the door of the building where she lived turquoise to ward off what she called "the evil eye." She assured him this was an accepted form of household protection in many North African countries. Blue said he didn't believe in the evil eye, but if she wanted to paint it, *fine.* So she did. Kwame didn't know much about the evil eye either, but by the time they walked the short distance to her apartment and passed through that blue door, they had stopped talking, allowing the sexual sparks between them to crackle and pop on their own like the last log on the campfire. They never got to the cappuccinos, though neither one seemed to mind.

Afterward, Aretha would tell Kwame she remembered music on that walk from the West End News. He would tell her he didn't remember music, only that the whole neighborhood smelled like roses. It was the sexiest safe sex he'd ever had, and from then on, she didn't have to just happen to be passing by. They spent every waking moment together, and a lot of sleeping ones, too, curled up in each other's arms as new lovers often do in the rush of those first few perfect days and endless nights. Then they got pregnant and the world turned upside down.

He'd hoped things would get better once Joyce Ann was in preschool, but they got worse. Aretha spent every possible minute at her studio while everything else in their lives, in his opinion, was going straight to hell. He had bent over backward to accommodate her for months, but not tonight! Tonight he had a dinner engagement and he wasn't going to miss it while Aretha continued to play the tormented artiste. He had picked up Joyce Ann at day care, as agreed, and arrived home with plenty of time to shower and change before seven o'clock. The only problem was, Aretha wasn't there. The house was dark and empty. He flipped on the kitchen light switch. Beside him, his daughter struggled to unzip her jacket.

"Need help, Daddy," she said, tugging gently on his shirtsleeve.

His mind racing, he helped her take off her coat, gave her some apple juice, turned the television to the Disney Channel, and dialed Aretha's studio phone. It rang six times before she answered.

"Hello?" Her voice sounded distant and distracted.

"You okay?" he said, wanting to eliminate the possibility of an unexpected mishap like a flat tire or a broken leg before inquiring as to why the hell she had taken it upon herself to change the plan she had agreed to three weeks before. He was still trying to understand how a woman with no paying job and a kid in day care from nine to five could even *have* an evening schedule that required clearing. After all, it was his salary that paid the bills.

But he knew better than to bring that up. They were both well aware of the fact that her godfather's money had paid for the comprehensive inventory of West End land and housing stock that was Kwame's only project. When completed, it would not only give Blue a plan for the future growth and development of the area, it would make Kwame's reputation as an innovative voice in his highly competitive field. Blue was paying him top dollar, so he couldn't complain, but in the quiet moments when his wife and daughter were asleep, he would sit in the house his mother had given them for a wedding gift and know at the center of his soul that this was not the life he wanted. At those moments, he felt a helplessness and despair unlike any he had known before and he seriously doubted that he would ever be happy again.

"I'm fine." Aretha sounded annoyed. "Well, I'm not really fine, but I'm not physically hurt or anything, if that's what you mean."

He took a deep breath and watched his daughter staring at a video of a little girl who used to be Denise Huxtable's daughter on the old *Cosby Show* and was now a very grown-up eighteen and a Disney Channel favorite. Sipping her apple juice contentedly, Joyce Ann watched the screen. She was standing too close, but Kwame didn't have the energy to tell her to move back. When she noticed her father looking in her direction, she smiled and pointed at the screen.

"Beyoncé," she said, clear as a bell. "See Beyoncé, Daddy?"

He nodded and tried to focus through his rising anger. "What I mean is, I have an appointment at seven, remember?"

"What time is it?"

The question infuriated him, but he was determined to keep the anger out of his voice. "It's ten to six."

"I'll be home by six-thirty."

"I have to take a shower, Aretha. Joyce Ann has to eat."

His wife was silent on the other end of the phone. He didn't have time for this nonsense.

"You didn't ask me why I wasn't fine," she said in a strange little voice somewhere between a whisper and a whine.

"Look, Ree." He didn't care how exasperated she sounded. That was nothing compared to how *he* felt. "If you're having some kind of artistic epiphany and can't get here, I'll have to get a sitter, so cut to the chase, okay? What's up?"

There was a long pause. "Why don't you just ask Teddy to come by the house?"

He looked around the kitchen, with a day's worth of dirty dishes still in the sink, toys scattered everywhere, and no sign of dinner on the way. "That's not a good idea."

"Why isn't it?"

He didn't want to argue with her. That's all they seemed to do lately. The only thing they agreed on these days was how much they loved Joyce Ann. Beyond that, everything seemed to be up for grabs.

"I've got to hang up now, Aretha. Maybe I can still get my mom to come over."

"Great," Aretha said, sounding relieved, like his desperate suggestion actually constituted a mutually satisfactory plan. "Why don't you ask her if Joyce Ann can spend the night?"

"*What?*"

"I've got to go. I'll be home late." She hung up without saying good-bye.

Kwame was so angry, he was shaking. His wife clearly had lost her mind, and now she was well on the way to making him lose his. *What the hell was he doing here?* Sometimes he thought she had tricked him by getting pregnant in the first place. It sure hadn't been part of his plan. No way he meant to live his life in the same neighborhood where he had spent his childhood. And he never meant to be working exclusively for Blue Hamilton, either, and arguing with his crazy-ass wife about whose turn it was to feed the kid.

He was clutching the phone so hard it felt like he might crush it. *He wanted to crush it!* Without knowing he was going to, Kwame drew back and flung the phone across the room as hard as he could. It hit the opposite wall with a loud plastic *pow* and scattered its electronic innards all over the less-than-spotless kitchen floor. He stood there watching the pieces rolling around at his feet and felt the anger leaving his body like a whoosh of bad air. The sound of his daughter's surprised little voice behind him turned him toward her.

"Daddy break it?"

He plastered a reassuring parental grin across his face, scooped her up in his arms, and kissed her chubby cheeks. She smelled like apple juice. "Yes, baby, Daddy broke it. Now Daddy's going to sweep it up and make you some dinner, okay?"

"Okay." She smiled at him, wiggled out of his arms, and went back to her cartoons, confident that he had things under control, which, of course, he didn't. He swept up the pieces of the kitchen phone and opened the cupboard to survey the variety of single-serving microwavable foods that were the basis of his daughter's diet these days. Aretha had never been much of a cook, but now it was getting ridiculous. He grabbed a can of pasta shaped like the letters of the alphabet, popped the top, and stuck it in the microwave for ninety seconds, just as he heard his cellphone ring.

It was playing "Fire," an old-school song by the Ohio Players. The tune let him know it was his mother calling. He had programmed the same song into her phone for his calls, startling her more staid constituents from time to time when she forgot to put it on vibrate before a meeting. Kwame was one of the few people who knew that under her carefully cultivated professional veneer, State Senator Precious Hargrove was a true *funkateer.* When he'd chosen that identifying ring for her, he knew it would show her that he remembered all those Friday nights when he was a little boy and she was a hardworking, housebound single mother who sometimes longed for a night out with loud friends and loud music and no babysitter to pay extra when she came home a little late.

Even as a child, Kwame suspected that she was lonely, but she never took it out on him. She'd just put on the Ohio Players and dance around the living room with her son as if there was no other place she'd rather be. Kwame had loved it. The sound of the music, his mother's laughter when he showed off his disco moves, the way she smelled like vanilla when she tucked him in, listened to him say his prayers, kissed him good night, and tiptoed out to do whatever helped her make it through the rest of those long nights.

Kwame grabbed his jacket and fumbled for the phone before it could go to voice mail. "Mom?"

"Hey, sweetie," she said cheerfully. "Where are you? On your way to meet the Big Shot for drinks?"

Precious didn't like Kwame's friend Teddy. She thought he was pretentious and arrogant. She had once said Teddy represented all the worst things about light-skinned Negroes, including their infuriating sense of entitlement, *just for being light*. At this point, though, Kwame didn't care what she thought as long as she could babysit.

"I'm still at home with Joyce Ann. Aretha's at her studio and she's running late."

"Want me to sit?" Precious said before Kwame could even make the request. She loved spending time with her only grandchild, and as busy as her schedule was these days, she never passed up an opportunity like this one. "I just finished my last meeting of the day. A good one, too."

Relief flooded through Kwame's body. He still had to shower and change to get to the restaurant by seven. "Tell me later, Mom." He cut her off before she started a story he didn't have time to listen to right then. "How soon can you get here?"

The microwave dinged loudly.

"Fifteen minutes?"

"Bless you!"

Joyce Ann appeared in the kitchen door. "Dinner ready?"

"Let me speak to my granddaughter," Precious said, hearing the child's voice.

"Speak to her in person when you get here," Kwame said. "She's having her dinner."

"I'm on my way."

Kwame clicked off the phone and turned to his daughter with a smile that said all was right with the world again. "We're saved, Little Bit," he said, lifting her into her high chair and clicking the tray into place. "Mommy's *cuckoo*, but Granny's on the way!"

"Cuckoo train," his daughter sang out. "Mommy's on the cuckoo train!"

He laughed, even though he hoped his precocious daughter wouldn't share the joke with her mother. Somehow, he didn't think Aretha would find it funny.

12

By the time Kwame arrived at Paschal's twenty minutes after the agreed-upon hour, Teddy had already taken a booth in the back of the restaurant and ordered a soul-food feast. Kwame was so surprised, he forgot to be disappointed in the change of his unspoken plan for the evening. He had wanted to have drinks with Teddy here and then cook a meal for the two of them at his newly renovated loft space. Last time Teddy's travels had brought him through Atlanta three months earlier, the place was a raw shell. It had since taken shape under Kwame's careful design and construction. He'd even brought in some basic furnishings just for this occasion to give Teddy the full effect of his efforts. He was looking forward to a chance to show off the place. Other than the guys who had helped him with the parts of the renovation he couldn't do alone, Teddy would be the first person allowed inside.

Kwame wondered, with a sudden pang of guilt, what Aretha would say if she knew he had bought and refurbished a space she didn't even know existed. He had intended to tell her when he first started looking around for what he told himself were investment opportunities. But when he found a place he really liked outside of West End, he knew she would object, so he didn't mention it. After all, they had a modern marriage with separate bank accounts. He was making enough money to cover it, so the whole thing was really none of her business. Why should he tell her? He needed a private space, a place where he could just be alone with his thoughts and his dreams. A place where he could bring a friend for dinner and drinks without having to be anybody but himself. Nobody's husband. Nobody's father. Nobody's son. Just *Kwame*.

The person who knew that Kwame better than anyone was Teddy Rogers. They had been friends since Teddy came to speak on a panel at Howard University when Kwame was a senior in the school of architecture. Although just a few years older than the students he was addressing, Teddy had already opened his own firm and was billing over three million dollars a year.

His fellow students were only half listening, but Kwame looked at Teddy and saw his future; a bright, young black man, polished, articulate, ambitious, Morehouse undergrad, Yale architecture degree with high honors. In addition to all that, Teddy had great contacts in both the government and corporate worlds and a confidence that was contagious. Kwame had learned the art of networking at his mother's knee and he recognized an opportunity when he saw one. He waited until the program was over and then went up to introduce himself.

Teddy had been wearing a beautiful blue suit that complemented his slight frame. Kwame suspected those shoulders were the result of artful tailoring as much as hours at the gym. He told Teddy he appreciated his take on doing business with municipal governments and asked if he could have a copy of the remarks to share with his mother, who was an elected official herself and would probably find them interesting. Teddy apologized for not having a prepared text, explaining that he enjoyed the challenge of speaking off-the-cuff, and invited Kwame to dinner.

By the time they finished their coffee, Teddy had become both a mentor and a friend. Two weeks later, they became lovers. It was, in fact, Teddy's generous offer of a place in his firm that Kwame had to turn down when Aretha wouldn't consider moving to D.C. She had told him he didn't have to marry her. She wanted a baby, she said, and she had a strong—*what did she call it? A sisterhood support network?* She'd be fine having the baby without him if that's what he wanted.

Like that was a possibility. It was his fault as much as hers and he was going to be an honorable man, no matter what. His father had told his mother to have an abortion and disappeared when she refused. He wasn't going to be that kind of daddy. He called Teddy in D.C. and told him he couldn't take his offer because he was getting married and moving back to Atlanta.

Teddy, being Teddy, didn't beat around the bush. "Is she pregnant?"

"Yes," Kwame said, feeling like a high-school boy confessing to his father.

"Is this what you want?"

The question was so unexpected, he'd almost answered it honestly, but he didn't have to. The hesitation told Teddy everything he needed to know.

"Yes." Kwame said the lie softly, like it pained him to have to tell it.

"I see. Does she know about you?"

"Of course not."

"Are you going to tell her?"

"Did you tell Genevive?"

"Genevive is from Northampton. Everybody she knows is bisexual."

"Even her husband?"

"We're not talking about me, brother, but I guess in a way we are. Long-distance relationships are always difficult."

"Everything is difficult."

"No, it's not," Teddy said soothingly. "The fact of the matter is, everything is disarmingly simple. This isn't a problem. I'm in and out of Atlanta all the time. We'll meet, we'll have drinks, we'll talk. We'll be two good friends with hot wives at home who sometimes meet for dinner when business brings us together."

"Sounds like a plan," Kwame said, relief flooding his body as he realized his friend wasn't going to judge him harshly for making a mess.

Teddy chuckled on the other end of the line. "Admit it. A part of you wanted this to happen. A beautiful wife. A cute kid. You want that respectable Atlanta *lifestyle.*" Teddy's sarcastic tone caressed the words contemptuously. "In D.C. you'd be an outlaw, undefined, making yourself up as you go along, as *Miss* James Baldwin put it so succinctly."

"Fuck you."

"*Claim your dreams, brother!*" Teddy said cheerfully. "Just play safe and don't get caught with your pants down."

"I'll do my best," Kwame said.

After the wedding, Teddy had been as good as his word. Business brought them together once or twice a month. They'd meet at whatever restaurant was currently the place to see and be seen and then let the evening proceed at its own pace, but what Kwame saw before him tonight was a first. *Teddy was eating pork chops!*

On all the times before this one, Kwame had never seen a morsel of meat pass his friend's lips. After his wife's dramatic conversion to a strict vegetarian regimen six years before on the promise of perfect skin and eternal life, Teddy had been strongly urged to follow the same path. At first he refused. The idea of life without even the possibility of a steak in it was inconceivable to him. It was only when his wife made it clear that sex with a nonvegetarian would be considered unclean by those adhering to her particular discipline that Teddy reluctantly became a vegan, too.

How, then, was Kwame to explain the two giant, center-cut pork chops on the plate in front of his friend? Not to mention a liberal assortment of side dishes, including macaroni and cheese, candied yams, and collard greens cooked in the traditional Southern style with some ham hocks thrown in to sweeten the pot.

Terry wiped his mouth and stood up as Kwame approached so they could engage in that handshake, chest-bumping thing that brothers use for greetings in the ritualized way Italian men sometimes kiss each other on both cheeks to say hello. Kwame slid into the booth across from Teddy, who grinned over the meal he was in the midst of enjoying.

"Sorry I had to start without you, brother," he said. "I've been on Genevive's damn diet for so long, when I came in here and smelled this outstanding soul food, I had to have it, man. I was powerless to resist the lure of Paschal's world-famous pork chops."

"Paschal's is famous for their chicken," Kwame said, relieved and happy finally to be sitting across from his friend. Precious had Joyce Ann until morning and Aretha could go to hell for all he cared. He was out for the evening and the first thing he needed was a beer.

"That's only because whoever took the damn survey didn't taste the pork chops," Teddy said as the white-jacketed server glided over to the booth. Kwame order a Heineken.

"You're not eating?" Teddy said as the waiter headed to the bar. Kwame leaned back and spread his long arms out on the back of the black leatherette booth. His friend looked good. At thirty-five, Teddy already had a sprinkling of what he called "distinguished grays," but otherwise he hadn't changed. Still handsome. Still curious. Still Teddy.

"Actually, I'm sorry you got dinner," Kwame said. "I wanted to cook for you at the place so you could see it."

Teddy smiled. "So if you don't cook, I can't see it anyway?"

Kwame smiled back and tried to relax. His mind was still racing from the mad rush to get here. Calm down, he chided himself. Everything's cool. This is what you've been missing. *Just let it happen.* Isn't that what Teddy used to tell him at first whenever he'd get tense. *Just relax and let it happen.*

"On my best day," Kwame said, "I can't compete with Mr. Paschal's kitchen."

"Genevive wouldn't fuck me for a month if she knew I was eating all this pork," Teddy said, taking another bite of the succulent chops.

"Does her guru know that the bodily fluid in question is protein-rich and fat-free?"

Teddy snorted contemptuously and smeared butter on a huge slab of corn bread. "Last time I ate some barbecue, I didn't get any head for two weeks. Finally, I asked her what she was so worried about. She never swallows anyway."

Kwame couldn't imagine Teddy's slender, elegant wife having any kind of sex, much less *oral sex.* He gave the obligatory chuckle to indicate he understood the many challenges of dealing with a beautiful, high-strung wife and watched the young server pour his beer carefully down the side of a tall, frosted glass to discourage foam. Kwame took a long swallow of the icy brew and felt it cool his throat and erase any remaining bad temper. He sighed out loud.

"Sounds like you needed that one. Rough day?"

"They're all rough, brother."

Teddy put down his fork and took a sip of his iced tea. "Okay. Here's how we're going to do this one. I'm going to finish my dinner before it gets cold. Since it's rude to talk and eat at the same time, although most Negroes think it's required, that leaves the floor open for you to tell me what's on your mind, unimpeded by my probing questions, on-the-spot analysis, and other friendly distractions from your narrative, which I'm guessing is pretty much on the negative side, right?"

Kwame didn't want to admit that his outlook was "on the negative side," but his friend was correct.

"I just feel like I'm stuck," he said. "Like I'm going to be thirty in two years and my life is flying by without me."

Teddy nodded and picked up his fork. "Start there."

Kwame looked confused. "Where?"

"With being stuck." Teddy popped another piece of pork chop into his mouth, followed by a forkful of greens.

Kwame took another sip of cold beer. He didn't know where to begin. Teddy chewed slowly, appreciatively, waiting for Kwame to fill the conversational void with his tale of woe. Kwame, still silent, took another swallow of beer. He was waiting, too, although he couldn't have told you for what.

Teddy smiled encouragingly. "Don't sweat it like that, man. In lieu of other jumping-off points, we can always start with my favorite state senator, your mama and my biggest fan. How's Miss Precious doing?"

"She's doing fine," Kwame said, relieved at a question he could answer directly. "The only guy who had a chance to beat her in the mayor's race head-to-head just got indicted for money laundering. She's a shoo-in."

"Good for her," Teddy said. He knew Precious didn't like him, but he admired her accomplishments anyway.

"So that can't be the problem. Even a moody fuck like you must know that puts you in the catbird seat."

Kwame snorted. "So far, all my mother's political connections have gotten me is a contract with Blue Hamilton."

"You could do a lot worse," Teddy said, savoring his macaroni and cheese. "West End is an architect's dream laboratory. It needs *everything* and any idea you come up with will be fully funded by your current employer, a progressive sort of guy, who has an overall vision of a peaceful paradise for black folks right here in southwest Atlanta. What's not to love?"

Kwame sat back and shook his head as Teddy polished off the second pork chop. "Why does it sound so much more fabulous when you describe it than when I do?"

"That's my great gift, remember?" Teddy said. "I see you more clearly than you see yourself."

"Well," said Kwame, "what do you see?"

"I see an unsatisfied mind, a restless spirit, and a lot of sexual tension," Teddy said as easily as he could have outlined the current weather conditions.

Kwame sat back and tried to smile, but succeeded only in looking like the beer had given him gas. "All that and you haven't even finished your cobbler."

"That's because you're ruining my appetite with this 'I'm stuck' crap. Just tell me one thing, and *don't bullshit a bullshitter.* Is my description pretty close?"

An unsatisfied mind, a restless spirit, and a lot of sexual tension. Kwame had to admit that pretty much summed up his current sorry state.

"Too close for comfort."

"Well, this is your lucky day. Sit back, relax, and let Dr. Feelgood cure your doldrums for you."

"Heal me if you can, brother." Kwame had to smile at Teddy calling himself Dr. Feelgood. "But I warn you, this shit is serious."

"What if I was to tell you that Bob Watson is interested in you?"

"Say what?"

In his dreams, Kwame had imagined having lunch one day with Watson at some exclusive Atlanta watering hole or other, just to shoot the shit about being an architect in Atlanta and making it work. This was not a dream he had shared with his mother. Precious found Watson almost as much of a disgrace to the café au lait crowd as she did Teddy. She accepted campaign contributions from him, but never solicited his support. Kwame could only imagine her reaction to his dream of one day working for Watson's firm.

Suddenly a sickening thought occurred to him. *What if Watson's interest wasn't professional, but personal?*

"Interested in me *how?*"

Teddy chuckled. "Down, boy. Bob Watson is an old-fashioned cock hound. He thinks being on the down low means you've been eating a lot of pussy."

Kwame laughed, but he was glad. All he needed was to run into Bob Watson at one of these Atlanta clubs on *DL night.* It wasn't even a question of being *outed.* If they were both there, neither one could mention it to outsiders. Teddy said it was sort of like the Mafia. If everybody's a killer, nobody goes to the police. It was more a question of his own expectations, and maybe even a little hero worship. Kwame wanted Bob Watson to be who he appeared to be; a happily heterosexual, extremely successful businessman whose closet housed nothing more complicated than a few whispering ghosts of long-forgotten mistresses and a succession of interchangeable lovers under the age of thirty-five.

"I ran into him at LaGuardia two days ago," Teddy was saying. "We were waiting out bad weather, so we had time to have a drink and catch up."

"Is that when he asked you about me?" Just the idea that his name had passed Bob Watson's lips was thrilling.

"He didn't ask me about you specifically. Give me a little credit here for representing your interests."

Kwame grinned. "You know I appreciate it, brother. Go on."

"What he said was he had an opening for a bright young architect with a strong planning background. I told him he had one of the best right in his own backyard."

"You said one of the best?"

"That's a direct quote," Teddy said, finally pushing his plate and wiping his mouth one final time with the white linen napkin. "Here's his card."

Teddy reached into the pocket of his perfectly tailored suit, pulled out a creamy white business card, and handed it across the table to Kwame. The clutter of cellphone, office, and home phone, e-mail address, street address, sky pager, and title all had been eliminated in favor of two words, *Robert Watson*, and one ten-digit number.

"So what happens now?"

"What happens now is he'll call you next week to set up an appointment. Knowing Bob, he'll probably take you to lunch, pick your brain for a while, and offer you the job."

That scenario was even better than Kwame's dream. Even in his subconscious, he had not been bold enough to fabricate a job offer. "Just like that?"

The card felt smooth between his fingers.

Teddy grinned. "Well, I did have my office send him a true and impressive list of your many accomplishments, along with my strongest possible personal endorsement. That ought to get the ball rolling."

Kwame wanted to jump across the table and hug Teddy. "Well, I owe you one, man. This could be just the break I need."

Teddy shook his head slowly and looked at Kwame. "You don't owe me anything. This is all about how qualified *you* are. You'd be a big asset to any firm and the only reason you can't see it is because your Atlanta sojourn has wreaked havoc with your self-confidence."

"You think so?"

Teddy was not known for being a flatterer. "I know so. Bob Watson isn't doing you any favors. He's interested in you because you represent his big three."

"What big three?" Kwame was still loving the words *Bob Watson's interested in you.*

"Smart, talented, and photogenic."

Kwame laughed. "*Photogenic?* That's pretty superficial."

"Not really. Intelligence and talent are always a winning combination, and as far as being superficial, it's a media world, brother. What are you gonna do?"

Kwame tucked the card in his pocket.

Teddy kept talking. "Plus, don't overlook the fact that your ever-lovin' mama is going to be the mayor as sure as I'm sitting here. Bob Watson is nobody's fool. Hiring her son couldn't be bad for business."

Kwame bristled. "I would hate to think he's only interested in me because he wants to get close to my mother."

"This is Atlanta, brother," Teddy said, grinning. "Everybody wants something from you, so get that self-righteous tone out of your voice and figure out what you want from them. At least that way, you'll be trading even."

Kwame wanted to argue as Teddy signaled their server, but what was the point? He knew as well as anyone that Atlanta was as cutthroat as New York or L.A. It just had a bigger smile and a whole lot more Southern charm.

"You know I met Bob when he was on the faculty at Yale," Teddy said, pulling a platinum American Express card out of his black Coach wallet and handing it to their server. "I introduced him to Marian."

Marian was Bob Watson's brittle, beautiful second wife. Kwame couldn't help but smile.

"What?"

"Nothing." Kwame shook his head. "You're just such a bourgie bastard, that's all. You probably met her at Martha's Vineyard."

"Exactly. That's where they grow women like that." Teddy signed the check, left a generous tip, and then looked across the table at Kwame. "So, I've eaten my way out of the possibility of sex with my wife until the pork passes out of my system, settled your damn future, and tipped the waiter more than he deserved. Are you going to show me your place or not?"

"Absolutely," said Kwame, sliding out of the booth. "It's about ten minutes away, just over the line."

Teddy chuckled as they headed for the door.

"What?"

"Nothing. Just the way you said that. *It's just over the line.* That Hamilton Negro has got a serious hold on y'all."

You have no idea, Kwame thought, opening the door for Teddy and glad all over again for a night outside the gates of Hamilton city. He wondered what Blue's reaction would be to his deception of Aretha. All the possibilities were too scary to consider, so he pushed them to the back of his mind. At this moment, there was no fear greater than the possibility that his friend would suddenly change his mind, feign fatigue, and go back to his hotel to crash without having sex. As keyed up as he was, such a move was guaranteed to send Kwame out into the clubs alone, searching for the satisfaction he found only in the places he never meant to go to, but that always felt like home once he got there.

"Shall I ride with you?" Teddy said casually, but his voice was suddenly thick with the same possibilities that were dancing around in Kwame's head.

"Sure," Aretha's husband said, popping the locks on his gray Honda and sliding in behind the wheel as Teddy leaned in the passenger door, grinning at Joyce Ann's car seat strapped securely in the back. "I don't have to ride in the baby seat, do I?"

"The only thing you got to worry about riding is me."

Teddy laughed out loud and swung his long legs into the car. "And just think, you used to be afraid of phone sex," he said as Kwame backed out of the Paschal's lot and headed for Nelson Street.

"I used to be afraid of a lot of things."

Teddy laid his hand on Kwame's knee. Most of the old warehouses in the area were still being renovated and at night the urban pioneers still went home to their suburbs and their dreams of a life without the endless Atlanta rush hour. For now, Kwame and Teddy had the neighborhood to themselves. The dark streets they were traveling were empty at just after nine o'clock. At a deserted corner with an endless red light, Teddy's hand moved up slowly.

Without waiting for the light to change, Kwame turned down a narrow street that ran behind his building. Knowing nobody ever walked there at night, he pulled the car over and stopped.

"What are you afraid of now?" Teddy said.

"Shut up," Kwame growled, his excitement almost unbearable as he put the car in park and turned off the lights.

Teddy didn't hesitate, knowing his friend's answer to the question. In this moment, Joyce Ann's daddy was fearless.

13

It was almost eleven o'clock by the time Aretha left her studio and stepped outside. The big blue front door clicked shut behind her and she turned to look at it before she started down the walk and headed for home. Pulling her jacket around her shoulders, she saw that the door needed a little touching up. She had done the door project when she was only eighteen. Five years later, the paint was looking a little less vibrant, a little less like something special, and more like just another fading front door.

Aretha frowned at her own carelessness. A neglected *anti-evil-eye device* was worse than no attempt at all. Maybe that was why her life was falling apart. What had happened? Everything had been so good, and then all of a sudden it wasn't. Or had it been all of a sudden? Had there been signs all along that she had missed? What if in her mad rush to be with this man, she had ignored the warnings like the people always do in the horror movies even though there is blood seeping through the wallpaper and strange noises emanating from behind the wine cellar's locked door? Maybe that's the power of really great sex, she thought. It clouds your vision until all you want is *more*.

Crossing at the corner, Aretha tried to remember the last time she and Kwame had had great sex. She felt herself wanting to modify the definition of *great* so that she could count a few recent exchanges that had showed promise, but had never achieved anything approaching the sweating, straining, licking, lifting, groaning *grindingness* that distinguishes great sex from the simply adequate, where everybody gets off, but the earth does not move.

It had been more than a year, but Aretha wasn't sure how much more. Could it really be *two* years? Since before Joyce Ann was born? She couldn't remember. At this point, she couldn't even remember if she had stopped wanting to, or he had, but the reality was that sex had become an every-other-week, *what-the-hell* kind of exchange. Admitting the sorry state of her sex life made Aretha feel sad and her feet slowed down without her realizing it. The end-of-summer wind in the trees was a soft whispering sound above her head.

She had read about relationships where people were sexually obsessed with each other, but she'd never been in one until Kwame. Her fear of AIDS and pregnancy had made her vigilant since she'd become sexually active her junior year in high school. It had been great curiosity, not a great love affair, that led her to bestow the onetime gift of her virginity on a shy young man who afterward sculpted her nude body in stone in such loving detail that she blushed seeing it in the gallery as part of his senior show.

Between that first fumbling effort, complete with slippery, uncooperative condoms and a final verdict of close but no cigar in the female-orgasm department, and her first unforgettable night with Kwame, Aretha had had two other lovers. Both possessed abundant energy and an openness to new ideas that matched her own. She became proficient at role-playing and was delighted to discover the utterly safe, totally dependable pleasures of mutual masturbation.

But being with Kwame back then had been different. She had realized that she didn't want to be creative anymore. She had wanted to experience sex the old-fashioned, preplague way with no latex anywhere in sight. She realized she had never had unprotected sex, and in that sense, *she was still a virgin.*

The thought excited Aretha so much she knew she had to plan for the next moment when she would be wrapped in Kwame's arms and her hormones would take over. At that moment, she knew safe sex would be just one more thing to think about tomorrow. She had scheduled an HIV test in the hope that her willingness to take one would prompt him to do the same.

Once they were both certified HIV-free and monogamous, they could pick a birth-control method and let nature take its course.

When she'd shared her results with Kwame a few nights later, he laughed. She was confused until he reached into his pocket and pulled out his own test results, dated the same day as hers. They both took this as a sign of mutual devotion and celebrated with an absolutely amazing weekend of unprotected sex in every possible permutation. Of course, she got pregnant. That was when everything changed.

Aretha tried to shake off the feelings her thoughts were stirring up. Her worries were spoiling her walk home. It was only five blocks between her studio and their house. The streets were lined with beautiful old trees and lovingly restored Victorians whose peaked roofs and gingerbread-house affectations recalled an era of porch swings and high-button shoes and family dinners nightly at six when Daddy came home from work.

That's not the way it works anymore, Aretha thought, wondering if those women with husbands and fathers and brothers and sons had figured out something that continued to elude her. Had they found a way to be wives and mothers and lovers and friends? Had they juggled their disparate selves without complaint, made their lovely homes havens of domestic bliss, and, in the process, earned their husbands' love and their children's devotion?

Aretha didn't believe it for a second. It probably had been just as hard for them as it was for her. Maybe that's just the way it is, she thought, turning the corner onto her street. What was the old R&B song her dad used to play all the time? *That's the way of the world?*

She didn't know if this thought comforted or depressed her. What she did know was that when she opened her back door the house was empty. It was midnight.

14

Zora Evans got on the northbound train to New York City at eight o'clock. By nine-fifteen, she had eaten a delicious dinner of roast chicken and mashed potatoes and shared a heartbreaking conversation about the war with a couple from Slidell, Louisiana, whose only son was currently serving in Iraq. When she told them she was a student at Spelman College on her way to D.C. for a meeting with other student activists who were questioning the war, the father leaned across the small dining-car table as if he had a secret he wanted to share.

Taking a deep breath, he assured her that his son was not a coward, but lately the boy's letters had become increasingly desperate. The last few had so upset his mother that they were on their way to see their congressman to demand some answers. The woman was thin and sallow with a pinched, worried expression that softened only when she showed Zora a photograph of her son, a freckle-faced redhead with big ears and the barest suggestion of a mustache.

They hugged her at the end of the meal and told her they knew their son and the other boys and girls over there would appreciate what she was doing and to keep up the good work. She watched them walking out of the dining car, holding on to the seat backs to keep from stumbling as the train rocked its way toward their nation's capital city, and rededicated herself to being a force for peace in the world.

When she got back to her little roomette, Zora pulled out her pajamas, brushed her teeth, splashed some water on her face, hung her clothes on a hanger in the narrow closet, and slipped into the bed that John, the sleeping-car attendant, had made up while she was at dinner. Train travel was too slow for most people, but she loved it. Something about being on the train made her feel connected to America in a way she rarely did at any other time. She propped herself up on the two pillows in their crisp white cases that John had stacked neatly at the head of the bed and smiled to herself as she pulled out the letter that had arrived at her apartment this morning. The pale violet paper smelled like violets, too, and her mother's slightly loopy handwriting filled the page completely.

Dearest Girl of my heart, her mother wrote in silver ink:

I'm so happy that you are going to be a part of this gathering of young people who are going to stop the war and change the world. I'm proud of you, baby. As you know, D.C. can be a strange and terrifying place sometimes with all the weird energy and habitual lying that goes on there every day the goddess sends sunshine. So I thought as you start your trip, it couldn't hurt to focus a little energy on keeping you safe and peaceful in an environment that is usually neither.

Zora loved her mother's letters and she always obeyed the handwritten instructions that came with them.

This particular spell does not require an audible, as the football guys say. Just put your hand over your heart to affirm that you will be fully present in the moment, thank the goddess for this journey, and bring back tales of Amazonian adventures to tell your mama! Listen hard! Think hard! Speak up! Be safe! (If you have sex, that is, which is not required!!) Love you madly!

Zora carefully refolded her mother's letter, put it under her pillow, and turned out the light in her tiny sleeper. She snuggled down under the thin, pink blanket the railroad provided, glad she'd brought her favorite flannel pajamas to keep her cozy. Suddenly the train rounded a gentle curve of the track and the full moon came into view outside her window. It looked so big and impossibly bright she almost felt like she could reach out and touch it. She could just imagine her mother, wrapped up in her favorite shawl, standing on the porch, soaking up the moonbeams and whispering her favorite prayer into the wind.

Zora laid her hand on her heart like she used to when she was a Brownie scout and they were ready to take the Brownie oath, but this time she wasn't going to pledge or promise anything. She was simply going to share the prayer her mother had told her would suffice even if she never learned another.

"Thank you," she whispered softly, watching the moonlit countryside flying by outside her window and realizing that even though she was on her way to talk about protest marches and petition drives, she had never felt more like an American in her life. She knew she was earning her membership in a long line of outspoken women and passionately committed men who understood that loving your country meant speaking up as loudly when it was wrong as you cheered when it was right. She was grateful for the chance to be in their number.

"Thank you," she whispered one more time, and then she slept.

15

Baby Brother was feeling no pain. He had drained three Heinekens, smoked two joints, and was watching Jason roll another. The wide-screen television blasted the latest rap videos from BET, at Baby Brother's request, and his friend knew a twenty-four-hour place around the corner that would deliver what he described as top-quality Thai food whenever they wanted dinner. All they needed now was some women. Baby Brother hadn't had sex since he'd gone to Iraq eight months ago. The locals were off-limits unless you had a death wish, and while there were always a lot of female soldiers around, most were too busy concentrating on staying alive to consider having sex. There was a lot of masturbating going on, and, in a pinch, there was always some guy who was open to oral sex if you knew how to keep quiet about it afterward.

Those guys always told themselves it wasn't about being gay. It was just about finding a way to relieve the almost unbearable tension they were under twenty-four hours a day, *every* day. Nobody needed to explain. For Baby Brother, one mouth was as good as another. When he closed his eyes, he could imagine it was a beautiful woman on her knees with her head in his lap, instead of a frightened young soldier, a long way from home.

That was how it had been with him and Jason, although as he looked around at his friend's nicely furnished apartment with its leather couches and glittering electronic gadgets, it was hard to believe those moments had ever passed between them. Tonight, Jason was eager to catch up on the news of the guys in their outfit, good and bad, and prepared to give a friend a place to crash, but nothing in his manner suggested anything more. That was fine with Baby Brother. The war was the war, but back on the mainland, that *fag shit* wasn't part of the program.

On the big screen, a dancer was shaking her behind and smiling over her shoulder like she shared the viewer's presumed pleasure in her ability to jiggle first one cheek and then the other in perfect time to the song's thumping bass line. On either side of her, young black men in baggy jeans and oversize white T-shirts, flashing diamond-encrusted gold teeth, pulled off crisp new bills from a roll of hundreds and tossed them in her direction while leering into the camera.

Baby Brother missed the life he'd had before the army. He missed the clubs and the women, *the fellas* and the drugs. Sometimes he even missed his old hardheaded sister. He'd had a good life and had thrown it all away for nothing. All those people who kept telling him he had a great future ahead of him might have been right after all. He wondered if it was too late for him to go back and mend some of those bridges he'd been so quick to burn. It hadn't gotten him very far, he had to admit. The truth was, he might not live to see twenty, fighting a war he didn't understand against some people he wasn't even mad at.

He drained his beer as Jason twisted up the ends of the joint and flipped it to Baby Brother.

"Fire that shit up and I'll get us another couple of beers."

"Cool." Baby Brother did as he was told and inhaled deeply, letting the acrid smoke fill his lungs. Vietnam vets were always talking about the amazing dope they had smoked over there. No such luck in this war. He had heard there was lots of heroin in Afghanistan, but in Iraq, there were no drugs on the base or on the street. Where that Marine had scored LSD was a mystery.

Jason handed him another cold beer, took a long swallow of his own, and picked up the remote. "I have to cut away to the news, brother. Part of my job is to brief the boss in the morning on who said what about who else. In this town, all that shit changes so fast, you better pay attention if you're going to keep up."

"No problem," said Baby Brother, passing the joint and listening to his stomach rumbling. "Where's the menu for that Thai place?"

"Next to the refrigerator."

Jason was an associate with a big D.C. lobbying firm and he was eager to make up the time he'd lost in the army, when his reserve unit was called up for active duty, by being the best junior executive they'd ever had. At twenty-eight, Jason was ambitious, attractive, and hardworking. He was on his way up the ladder, but he knew it would take a lot of work. That's why his love life was, as he put it, *shot to shit.*

"Women don't want to come second to a brother's job," he explained. "But they want that bling bling lifestyle, so what are you supposed to do?"

"Lie to them," Baby Brother said. "Tell them you are whoever and whatever they want you to be to get that pussy."

"That ain't me, man," Jason said, laughing at his friend's directness. "I'm not trying to trick anybody out of anything. I'm looking for a voluntary exchange."

Before Baby Brother could respond, their attention was drawn to the story that led the news. An Arabic-language website had broadcast a video of a suicide bomber packing his trunk with explosives, driving down the busy highway to his destination outside the American green zone, and detonating a blast that killed a dozen people and sent a huge fireball leaping into the air. The size of it and the absolute premeditation of the act rendered them both speechless.

Baby Brother set down his beer and leaned back against the soft leather of the couch. Jason quickly changed the channel back to BET, regretting the intrusion of the grim reality to which his buddy was returning in just a few days. On BET, there was no war news, only one more voluptuous, half-naked dancer and another gaggle of wannabe thugs flashing their gold teeth at the camera, oblivious to the world falling down around them.

"Sorry, man," Jason said, tossing the remote down on the table then reaching to relight the joint. "I know that's the last shit you need to see tonight."

Opening his eyes, Baby Brother took the joint, inhaled deeply, and held the smoke as long as he could before blowing it out in one long stream. "Fuck it, man. It ain't nothin' I don't see over there every damn day of every damn week." He sat up and took a swallow of beer, enjoying the cool of it going down his dry throat. "How long you been gone? Four months?"

Jason nodded. "Give or take."

"Well, it's a lot worse than it was when you left. They got us doing shit now we ain't even trained to do. They're sending reserves over who ain't been in shape in twenty years. Big, fat motherfuckers, been working behind a desk or some shit. They sent a damn fifty-five-year-old woman over as infantry. She was so scared, all she could do was look at pictures of her grandkids and cry."

Baby Brother ran a hand over his face and rubbed his eyes. He hadn't meant to start talking about all this stuff, but watching that explosion had opened the floodgates. He took a deep breath and tried to calm down, but he couldn't.

"You know what they had us doing last week?"

Jason shook his head.

"Searching for roadside bombs and defusing them."

"When did they train you for that?"

"They didn't! That's what I'm trying to tell you. They just called us in one day and told us that was our new job. They had some sergeant show us the kinds of explosives these guys usually use and talk about how it could be in a car, in a truck, all by itself, just waiting for one of us to drive by or step on it. They even wirin' animals and dead babies and shit, but they didn't talk about that, so we weren't ready for it."

"That's some wrong shit."

"Tell me about it. The next day we rolled up on this old guy layin' across the road like somebody shot him and just left him layin' there. We didn't want to drive around him because that's where they put the shit, by the side of the road, remember?"

"I remember."

"So, the lieutenant told one of the new guys to go and drag the body out of our way. This brother was one of the reserves, hadn't been there two weeks. He didn't know no better than to jump down, run over there, and grab the dead guy's feet so he could move him."

Baby Brother shook his head as if to clear it of the pictures his own words had conjured up. "Motherfuckin' body blew up in his face, man. Literally. Took his head right off and we're sitting there watching it. The bitch with the grandkids really freaked out, but it didn't even surprise me. Nothing surprises me anymore."

His own voice was so sad and empty it frightened him to hear it. *What if he didn't survive this shit?* And if he did, what was he supposed to do with all the stuff he'd seen and heard and felt and done? Where was he supposed to put all that once he got home?

"You okay?" Jason's voice almost got lost in the intricacies of the latest Missy Elliott video. He reached for the remote, hit the mute button, and re-peated his question. *"You okay?"*

In light of what he had just described, the question was ludicrous, and Baby Brother's attempt at a rueful laugh came across more as a choking gurgle. He cleared his throat, looked at his friend, and stole a line from *Pulp Fiction.*

"Naw, man. I'm pretty fuckin' far from okay."

"I heard that," Jason said. "But you ain't there now, so leave it alone."

"How the hell am I supposed to do that?"

Baby Brother's voice suddenly had an edge of aggression that was not lost on Jason. Since there was no real answer to the question, any response would be the wrong one.

"What the fuck, man? How am I supposed to know?"

Glancing at his friend, Baby Brother stood up and walked over to the window. The quiet street was empty and Iraq seemed like a bad dream. Maybe that's all it was, a bad dream, from which he had finally awakened.

"Well, I know one thing," he said softly.

"What's that?" Jason was pleased to hear the calm return to his buddy's voice.

Baby Brother turned and looked at Jason. "I'm not going back."

"Now you just talkin' crazy."

"I'd be crazy to go back there." The idea was growing on him, taking hold, gaining credibility. "Maybe this is my mama's parting gift to her long-lost son, a chance to get my black ass out of there before I get my head blown off, too."

"You're not serious, so squash it."

"Do I look like I'm playin'?" Baby Brother spread his arms wide as if to issue a challenge.

"You can't just quit the army in the middle of a war." Jason frowned. "That's desertion. They get to shoot you for that, remember?"

"They can't shoot me if they can't find me." Baby Brother began to pace in front of the window, suddenly filled with the possibilities of this new idea. "I'll go to Canada or some shit like that. They still got people over there from the sixties. They don't even mess wit' 'em."

"You're not kidding, are you?" Still not believing what he was hearing, Jason was repeating himself.

"Damn, man, what I gotta do? Open a vein? I'm serious, okay? I'm done with all this shit *as of now!*"

Jason looked at Baby Brother like he had lost his mind. "What are you going to do, man? Just run away from the shit? Let everybody in your outfit down? Leave those guys even more shorthanded than they already are because you're too scared to be where you promised to be?"

"I didn't promise shit."

Jason stood up. "Yeah, you did. You volunteered. There ain't no draft. You stepped forward of your own free will and said 'I do.' It's too late to back out now. That's why they're calling up the reserves in the first place."

He was getting more worked up by the minute. "If I had to do my service for eighteen months, you have to do yours, too. *End of story.*"

Both men were aware that this was a dangerous moment. The positions they were staking out had no middle ground, and if they were going to spend the night under the same roof, they needed to find a compromise fast. Baby Brother blinked first. That wasn't surprising since he had the most to lose in the exchange. An argumentative houseguest is as unwelcome as a summer cold and it was too late to make other plans.

Looking at Jason's angry face, Baby Brother hoped he hadn't already gone too far. "Listen, man, I'm trying to tell you this shit is all wrong. It ain't about nothin' and it don't mean nothin'. I didn't promise to give my life for some bullshit."

Jason snorted contemptuously. "Don't try to make this something it's not. This is no political protest and you're no conscientious objector with a righteous cause. You're a *punk.* I got buddies over there that are never coming home, but at least they died like men. If you do this, you're a disgrace to everything they stood for."

Baby Brother saw no need for further discussion. Nobody could make this decision with him or for him. It was his choice and his alone, but right now it was time to go. He'd worry about where later. He reached for his jacket, knowing how little protection it would provide from the wind outside.

"Thanks for the beer."

"Fuck you."

He let himself out and heard Jason slam the door behind him. *Fuck you, too*, he thought. *Because your buddies didn't make it, I gotta shed my blood? It don't work that way.*

It was after midnight and the temperature had dropped significantly. He didn't have enough change for the metro, so he started walking back toward Dupont Circle in the hope that his uniform might generate a contribution from a patriotic citizen encountering an unlucky soldier on leave to bury his mama. It was a good plan, except that it was late and cold and there was no pedestrian traffic. Even the prostitutes had given up for the night.

Out of options, he turned up his collar, pulled that ugly GI hat down as far as he could, jammed his hands into his pockets, and headed toward Union Station. It was going to be a long, cold walk, but the train station was open all night, and if the uniform had any chance of generating a hot meal or a cold beer, that would be the place. All he had to do now was keep putting one frozen foot in front of the other.

He hadn't gone six blocks when a chocolate-brown BMW pulled up beside him and the driver, a well-dressed black man in his late forties, opened the passenger-side window and leaned over to make eye contact. Baby Brother knew that look.

"Need a ride, young brother?" the man said smoothly.

Soft jazz was playing on the car stereo and the blast of warm air from the heater warmed Baby Brother's cheeks as he stepped to the curb and leaned down to check the man out. He was expensively dressed and the interior and exterior of the car were spotless. The man was about his size and had closely cropped, salt-and-pepper hair and a neatly trimmed mustache.

"What I need is to get my black ass in out of the cold before I freeze my dick off."

The man laughed, leaned over, and popped the lock on the door. "Well, we can't have that, now can we? Get in . . ."

16

This is exactly what Juanita said would happen, General thought, sitting in the car outside Blue and Regina's house, waiting for sunrise. She had promised him a sign, one she said he probably wouldn't believe at first, and she had sure done that. He just wished he could be certain before he made a move. Was this little stripper with the heart-shaped birthmark and the supernatural behind really the medium Juanita was going to use to send him a message from *out there?* And if she was, just how close was he supposed to get to the messenger?

He smiled to himself, imagining Juanita looking down at him trying to figure this shit out. They used to laugh at how what they were doing would look from the outside. Juanita would tease him that he was barely legal and he'd call her his old lady. Mostly they would go to New Orleans or Atlantic City, rent a suite, and spend three days at a time making love, eating room service, and gambling.

Blue didn't like to gamble, but Juanita did, so General traveled with her as escort and bodyguard. They'd check into their separate rooms and then later she'd knock on his door, giggling like a schoolgirl at their elaborate subterfuge, but enjoying every minute. He did, too. They hadn't planned any of this adventure, but how could they? How do you plan for your best buddy's mother being the true love of your life?

At eighteen, what he knew about Juanita was mostly that Old Man Hamilton had been a cruel and domineering man, notorious for the frequency and brutality of his beatings. He'd attack his wife when Blue was at school or somewhere working, and then disappear for a week or two until she could talk Blue out of killing him. That's how it started for Juanita and General. Blue was at choir rehearsal. Mr. Hamilton was drunk. When his wife tried to leave the house to go to work, he accused her of having an affair, beat her, tore her clothes off, pushed her out into the street half-naked, and told her to run for her life.

General was coming home from football practice and had on his varsity jacket. It was just starting to get dark as Juanita stumbled off the porch and ran down the street in his direction. He remembered being too surprised to look away from her bare breasts and shredded panties, but he ripped off his jacket as she approached him, not sure if she would stop or keep running. Mr. Hamilton had gone back inside the house, but Juanita hadn't looked over her shoulder to see where he was. She was still running. General held out the jacket as she ran by so that if she wanted to, she could just grab it and keep moving.

When Juanita saw her son's friend dangling the jacket in front of her like a caution flag, she slowed to a trot then stopped in front of him, panting and trembling. That was when she looked over her shoulder to be sure her husband wasn't following her, then turned her terrified eyes back to General. He couldn't tell if she recognized him or not. Her teeth were chattering and her nipples were puckered up from the cold.

He hated himself for looking, *but Mrs. Hamilton was fine.* He had never realized it before. "It's me, Miz Hamilton, General Richardson from down the street. Take my jacket, okay?"

General draped it around her shoulders, careful not to touch her body. She clutched the jacket around her, opened her mouth to say something, but nothing came out. She took a few steps forward like she had to be on her way, but then her knees wobbled, and if he hadn't reached out and grabbed her arm, she would have fallen to the pavement. She slumped against him like a sack of flour, and even if he was eighteen, already six foot two, and in the best shape of his young life, he stumbled trying to hold up the sudden deadweight of her body.

A frantic glance around for assistance showed him only his own empty block. His parents were both working late shifts and Blue was nowhere in sight. He couldn't just leave her outside, the shape she was in, so he half carried, half dragged her to his house, dropped her on his mother's living-room couch, and stood there wondering what to do next. Juanita huddled on the sofa, weeping softly. His jacket only partially covered her bare breasts in the badly ripped bra and he was horrified to realize he was getting an erection looking at Blue Hamilton's mother's breasts!

He took the stairs two at a time and grabbed the top sheet off his bed and took it down to where she was still trying to cover herself with his jacket. She had clasped it around her chest, but her panties were barely covering her behind, much less her long, slender thighs. *Damn, she was fine,* General thought. *Mr. H. must be a damn fool!* He wondered how old she was as he handed her the sheet, which she wrapped around her body gratefully. A lump on her forehead was getting redder and angrier-looking by the minute. He always kept an ice bag in the refrigerator for after football practice and he went to get it now.

"Put this on your head," General said, handing her the cold pack.

She looked startled. "What?"

"You've got a knot there," he said, pointing. "The cold will keep down the swelling."

She reached for the ice bag and the sheet gapped enough for him to see the curve of her left breast against his jacket. He wondered if it would smell like her when he got it back.

"Thanks," she said, wincing slightly as she held it against her head obediently.

He didn't know what else to do, so he just stood there, looking at her, wondering if he should try to find Blue and tell him Juanita was hiding out in his living room. Before he could decide, Mrs. H. put the ice bag down and looked at him.

"What time is it?" she said.

He looked at his watch. "Twenty minutes to four."

"*Shit!*" she said, jumping up immediately. "I gotta get to work! If I'm late again that bitch will fire me for sure." She was still holding the sheet around her as she headed for the door.

"Wait, Miz H.," General said quickly. "You can't go . . . *like that.*"

She stopped and looked down at his jacket and the sheet as if she had forgotten they were her only attire, and then back at him helplessly.

"What am I gonna do?" she wailed. "He won't let me back in the house to get my clothes. He wants me to get fired. He's crazy! He's crazy and he's mean. One day he's gonna kill me and then what am I gonna do?"

He resisted pointing out that her options would be pretty much over at that point since she was right. Mr. H. was a mean drunk and nobody knew it better than she did. That's when she dropped the tangled sheet to the floor and started to cry like the world was coming to an end and she had to cry for all the losses and all the tears and all the pain there ever was anywhere. He had never seen anyone cry like that. It was a misery so deep the sound of it threatened to destroy them both.

He reached out and grabbed her before he knew he was going to, pulled her close, and just stood there with his big, young arms around her while she clung to him like he was the only thing standing between her and the end of the world. General's erection, oblivious to the details of the moment, rose to the challenge and urgently pressed itself against Juanita's body. If she felt it, she gave no sign. Even better, she made no move to step away. Gradually her sobbing stopped, but she continued to hold him tightly around the waist as if they were slow dancing to an old-school tune and she wasn't going anywhere until the song ended.

That was fine with General. When she began to rub her pelvis gently against his now-unavoidable erection, he responded in kind, but let her set the pace. He was not a virgin, but his sexual experiences had been limited to hurried moments with girls his own age, worried about getting pregnant or tarnishing their reputations. This kind of sex, if that's what it was they were getting ready to do, was something new. Something mysterious and desperate and wild. He reached down and ran his hand over Juanita's half-naked behind and the smoothness of her skin almost made him come right there in his favorite blue jeans. She moaned softly.

He knew Blue would kill him if he ever found out, but he'd never tell and he was pretty sure Miz H. wouldn't either. Especially when she reached down, unzipped his pants and reached in with her small, cool hand. General hoped he wouldn't do or say the wrong thing, because whatever they were doing was driving him crazy.

He leaned his head down until his lips were touching her ear. Her hand was still in his jeans. "Tell me what you want," he whispered urgently. "Tell me what you want me to do."

"Make love to me, General," she whispered. "Will you make love to me?"

The fact that she called him by his name only heightened his desire. "Oh, Miz Hamilton," he moaned. "I will."

He carried her upstairs to the bedroom where he had masturbated more times than he could count since crashing into puberty, laid her down gently on his twin bed under the poster of Pam Grier, and grabbed a condom from under the mattress, where he always kept one, *just in case.* There in the midst of his football trophies and shoulder pads and back issues of *Sports Illustrated,* he let her guide him into her body and made love to her with all the inexperienced, hopeful, fumbling sexual energy of his eighteen years. He tried unsuccessfully to keep up with the thrusting of her hips until she finally pulled him in so deep that all he could do was close his eyes and let her take whatever she wanted from him, even though he wasn't sure what it was.

When he rolled away from her, speechless and spent, a few minutes later, she sat up and smiled at him slowly.

"Now, General Richardson, do you think your mother has a dress I could borrow so I can get my ass to work?"

They used to laugh about that first time. Each confessed that they felt a strong connection even in the midst of all the drama, but figured this was a onetime moment. *What else could it be?* Juanita was married to a madman and her only son was General's best friend. They made no mention to Blue of what had happened, and when they passed each other in the street or at the neighborhood drugstore, they mumbled a greeting and hurried on, unable to meet each other's eyes. That went on for a month and a half.

Then Blue did a sold-out showcase that established him as a star on the rise at just shy of seventeen. He netted a minitour to ten clubs in Georgia and two just across the Alabama line. The producer asked him if he could start the next night in Macon, and Blue told him he could. Flush with success and their plans to go on the road for the first time, General and Blue burst into Juanita's kitchen to share the good news. They found her sitting next to the body of her husband, who was slumped over at the kitchen table with a butcher knife through his heart.

They didn't have to ask what had happened. That was the first time

Blue and General disposed of a body together. The next day, with General at the wheel of Mr. Hamilton's prized Buick, the three of them hit the road. Blue sat beside General in the front seat, Juanita sat alone in the back, watching the highway whizzing by, breathing easy for the first time in a long time.

No one who knew Blue's father reported him missing and no one was sorry when he stopped showing up at his usual haunts. There seemed to be a sigh of relief that he had gone somewhere—*anywhere*—else. No inquiries were made and no detectives came to call. Caught up in the whirlwind of their first tour, the three travelers let the memory of his evil ways fade from their minds like yesterday's news. Somewhere in the middle of that tour, General stepped into Juanita's life like Muhammad Ali stepping into the ring with George Foreman and she welcomed him with open arms.

Of course, General had been with other women since she died, but nothing serious. He was still in love with Juanita. His heart didn't really have room for anybody else. As far as General was concerned, the jury was still out on all that past-lives stuff, but he hoped it was true. He needed three or four lifetimes to love that woman the way she deserved to be loved. He needed at least *one* more just so they could come out of the shadows and proclaim their happiness to the world.

Just thinking about Juanita made his heart hurt. He took a deep breath.

"Is this the sign, baby?" he whispered. "Is she the sign?"

The night around him was so quiet he could hear the wind rustling through the leaves of the huge magnolia tree in Blue's front yard. As he watched, the breeze loosened one of the tree's big blossoms. In the darkness, the petals were an almost ghostly white as they fluttered to the ground. General felt the hair stand up on the back of his neck as that same wind blew the smell of honeysuckle into the car, replacing the smell of men and black leather with a sensual sweetness that was all female.

"All right, baby," he said softly, ignoring the tears that were prickling at the corners of his eyes. "I hear you."

At sunrise, he pulled the Lincoln slowly away from the curb and headed for Montre's.

17

General recognized Brandi immediately when the back door of Montre's opened and two women walked out, laughing and talking like city government workers on their way to the cafeteria for a sausage biscuit and coffee at the start of another busy day. He was relieved to see that she was actually fine. He hadn't been sure last night. It had been too dark in Montre's to tell. A lot of women look their best in low light, General thought, but this girl was made for sunshine. She had pulled her extensions back into a lazy ponytail, and when she turned in his direction, she looked like a kid. Without all the makeup, her skin glowed golden. He pushed the button and let the window down on his side of the car.

Both women noticed the car as they headed to a battered blue Chevrolet that had seen better days. Brandi recognized General at the wheel and touched her girlfriend's arm.

"This is the dude I was telling you about," she hissed. "Can you wait on me for a minute?"

"Sure, girl," her friend whispered back, casting an appraising eye at the car. "Handle your business."

Brandi wished she hadn't taken off her makeup. She wanted to make a good impression. At least she had on her favorite skintight jeans and some heels. She took a deep breath and pushed her breasts forward like a shield.

"You up awful early," she said, leaning down to grin at him through the open window.

"You working awful late."

The closer she got, the finer she looked. This girl was way too high-class for Montre's.

"Private party," she said. "We don't open until noon."

"I'm General Richardson."

She leaned a little farther into the window, resting her breasts on her crossed arms.

"Everybody knows who you are," she cooed. "I'm Brandi."

"Well, *Brandi*, would you like to have breakfast with me?"

"Breakfast?" Her voice was as incredulous as if he'd invited her to the rodeo.

"Paschal's all right?"

Brandi looked at General. "This ain't no freaky shit about my birthmark, is it?"

He shook his head and hoped his smile was reassuring. "You remind me of someone I used to know. A friend."

"How close a friend?"

"Close as you can get."

"Well, I'm a working woman," she said, running her tongue over her lips. "Is this a social call or a business arrangement?"

"I'll be happy to pay for your time. As you already know, I am a very generous man."

Brandi felt her stomach growl softly. She didn't give a damn if she reminded him of his dead grandmother if he was going to feed her. She waved to her friend across the parking lot, who waved back with a grin.

"Ah-iight, girl! Don't hurt nobody!"

Paschal's was a five-minute ride from Montre's. The restaurant offered only coffee and pastries in the morning, saving their culinary genius for the lunch and dinner crowd, but they made an exception for General and opened up the dining room. They had the whole place to themselves. He could tell Brandi was impressed as she slid into the booth and took off her denim jacket. Her breasts were bubbling out of her tight green halter top, but the waiter didn't break as he took their order. He knew who General was, too.

She ordered home fries, two eggs over easy, sausage, bacon, and a large orange juice. General looked on in amazement then asked for black coffee.

"I thought you wanted to have breakfast," she said.

"I wanted you to have breakfast," he said. "That doesn't mean I have to eat, too, does it?"

"Hell no, baby." She grinned. "I can eat enough for both of us. It's the dancing. It takes all the weight off of me if I'm not careful."

The waiter came back with a large, frosted glass filled to the brim with Florida's finest. Brandi gulped it greedily.

"How long you been dancing?"

She wiped the foam from her top lip, trying to decide whether or not to tell him the truth. For Brandi, that was always the question. *To lie or not to lie.* She looked at him and thought, *What the hell? Let's try the truth and see if the big man can handle it.*

"Since I was fourteen."

"How come you never got married?"

"Married?" Brandi snorted at the absurdity of the question. "Ain't no niggas around here lookin' for no wife. Besides, all the good ones are taken, *present company excepted.*"

"You think I'm a good one?"

"I know you are."

"How's that?"

"You feedin' me, ain't you?"

"Is that all it takes?"

"That's as good a place to start as any."

"Okay, then, can I ask you a question?"

"Sure." Her eyes were searching for the waiter. The juice had just whetted her appetite.

"What's your real name?"

She stiffened a little. "I told you my name."

"I'll bet you fifty bucks your mama didn't name you Brandi."

That made her smile. "That's a sucker bet. Okay, my mama named me Sarah after her grandmother. But when I started dancin' professionally, people kept tellin' me that didn't sound like no stripper. So the manager of the place where I was workin' named me Brandi. I told him I wanted it with an *i* not a *y* because I think that's classier." She frowned slightly. "You not gonna start callin' me Sarah, are you?"

General shook his head. "No."

"Good. I don't feel like no Sarah after all this time bein' Brandi."

"Brandi's fine," he said as the waiter emerged from the kitchen, holding aloft a tray crowded with her breakfast and a pot of fresh coffee.

For the next ten minutes, conversation was impossible. Brandi ate every last morsel of food on the plate nonstop in tiny little bites. He had never seen anyone eat so much so fast. He felt like a soldier who had rescued a starving child wandering in a war zone, seeking sustenance. Watching her didn't make him feel sexy. It just made him sad. *This girl was nothing like Juanita.*

She finished the last bit of bacon with a satisfied smile and a ladylike belch that she stifled with her napkin.

"Would you like anything else?" he said, wondering where she would put it.

"No thanks." She shook her head, then smiled seductively. *"Would you?"*

There was no mistaking the point of the question, but he couldn't have felt less like having sex with her. Trying so hard to see Juanita in Brandi had just made him miss the real one more.

"I've got some business to take care of," he said. "Can I drop you somewhere?"

She looked disappointed. "We didn't talk about your friend. The one I reminded you of."

"Next time." General stood up and dropped the money for the check, plus a generous tip on the table. He picked up his hat.

That's one thing about those Hamilton niggas, she thought. *They always clean.* In a sea of kids in baggy jeans and oversize white T-shirts, he looked like a grown man with prospects. She wasn't prepared to let him go that easy. Who knew when he might slide back into Montre's? Maybe tonight. Maybe never. She followed him out to the car.

"Where can I drop you?" he said again.

Brandi turned toward him. "What's the matter, baby? Did I eat too much?"

The question made him feel bad. It wasn't her fault that she wasn't who he had wanted her to be.

"You didn't do anything," he said. "I've just got business."

"Can you drop me at home?"

"Sure."

She gave him the address, hoping the ride over would give her a chance to figure out a way to make him come in when they got there. She was living in one of those residence motels where you pay by the week for one room because you can't save up enough for the deposit and the first month's rent on an apartment. She had moved in after Madonna started acting funny about her having company at the house, like she hadn't done her share of *emergency hookin'*. She hated the idea of taking a high-class *john* like General into that sad little room she was calling home, but she knew if she could just get him into bed, she wouldn't have to worry about him coming back. Brandi was a highly skilled exotic dancer, but her pole dancing was nothing compared to her dizzying array of sexual tricks.

General was familiar with the place where Brandi was living. It was right off the interstate and the downtown bus to Five Points stopped outside the front entrance. No longer a stopover for families on their way to Disney World or salesmen trying to crack Atlanta's market in one thing or another, it now housed people who were going nowhere fast. He felt sorry for her, living in a place like this. They pulled into a spot around the back and she pointed to the second floor.

"That's me," she said. "Number 227."

The door to 229 was open and he could see a television flickering in the gloom.

"Will you come up for a minute?" she said. "I know you got business, but I want to show you something."

He hesitated.

"No additional charge," she said, smiling.

"Okay." General knew it was probably a con, but he figured he owed her that much for trying to make her over into somebody else without her permission. He followed her up the stairs to her room, clocking the smell of curry and the sound of cooped up children.

"Excuse my mess," she said apologetically, pushing open the door. In truth, the place was anything but messy. The bed was neatly made with a leopard-print spread that was clearly her own decorator touch. There were no clothes lying around, no half-eaten cartons of takeout, no empty soft-drink cans. On the desk was a half-pint of cheap scotch and two clean glasses. There was, over the whole room, the lingering smell of strawberry incense, probably to cover the curry, he thought. The combination made him a little queasy.

Brandi dropped her purse and coat on a rickety-looking desk chair. "Want a drink?"

"What did you want to show me?"

She looked at him for a minute, then opened the drawer in the nearest bedside table and pulled out a framed photograph. She looked at it for a minute without turning to face him.

"When you asked me about my birthmark, I thought . . . well, I thought you might like to see this."

Brandi handed him the photograph and watched for his reaction. Putting two and two together, she figured his friend must have had a birthmark, too, and seeing hers brought back memories. Brandi wondered if the woman was dead or had just moved on. Wherever she was, if that mark had made him come back to Montre's at six in the morning, this picture ought to put a smile back on his face.

General didn't know what to expect, but even if he had, there was nothing he could have done to prepare himself. The photograph was a surprisingly artistic black-and-white nude shot of Brandi shaking her perfect ass at the camera and laughing over her shoulder like she knew exactly how good she looked. He could clearly see the heart-shaped mark that had first caught his eye, *and his heart.*

The whole ride over here, he had tried to focus on why Brandi wasn't his Juanita so he wouldn't have to keep remembering the one way that she was exactly like her. The one mark they had in common, same size, same shape, same place on their bodies, as if an angel had kissed them both and sent them on their way. There was no way he could continue to deny that this was the sign he'd been looking for all these years.

He sat down on the edge of the bed, overwhelmed by his own emotions. Brandi sat down next to him and reached for his hand.

"You okay, baby?"

All he could do was nod. General didn't know whether he was okay or going crazy. After all these years, *this was it!* The certainty of Juanita's presence in the same universe he was moving around in comforted and excited him in equal measure. As if she could read his thoughts, Brandi squeezed his hand gently.

"Was she your woman?"

General nodded again. His mind was whirling. *Would being inside Brandi feel like being inside Juanita?* The sounds of the kids downstairs and the television next door faded away and he heard a roaring in his ears.

"Yes." His voice cracked like a boy just entering manhood.

"Well, don't you worry," she whispered, giving his hand another squeeze and standing up to slip her jeans over her hips. "I'm gonna be your woman now."

In the semidarkness, he let her push him back against that faux leopard's spots and closed his eyes. Lying there, listening to the roaring in his ears, he could imagine it was Juanita's mouth giving him so much pleasure; Juanita's hands touching him, stroking him; Juanita's body that welcomed him back inside where he had thought he would never be again.

Minutes later, when he called her by another woman's name, Brandi wasn't even surprised.

18

Baby Brother's plan wasn't a very good one, but preparing for the future had never been his strong suit. After the well-dressed brother in the BMW had dropped him off at Union Station with two hundred dollars in his pocket, he realized there was no reason for him to be there at all. He had no place to go and no time to get there. The day stretched out in front of him with no design he could decipher, so he decided to focus on more immediate concerns.

He hadn't had anything to eat since yesterday afternoon and the smell of eggs and fried potatoes from a coffee shop already open for business made his stomach growl. He went inside, ordered a big country breakfast, which he polished off with dispatch. As he lingered over a second cup of black coffee, his plan began to take shape. *He would go to New York.*

When he left Iraq, the idea of not returning to his unit at the end of his leave hadn't even crossed his mind. He knew he didn't want to be there, but nobody with an ounce of sense would spend time in hell by choice. He knew the fear he felt was with him twenty-four hours a day because the enemy never, ever slept and every ordinary moment might be a soldier's last one. He remembered when they hit a mess hall a few months ago. Baby Brother had seen the pictures. Those guys were just on their way to breakfast, laughing and talking and shooting the shit and *BAM!* Game over, *jack.* No second chances.

Baby Brother sipped his coffee and made himself focus on his plan. He had showered and shaved, but he needed to get out of his uniform. If he wasn't going back, the sooner he stopped looking like a soldier, the better. He could probably get some jeans and a big white T-shirt with the money he had left from last night. Might even find a cheap pair of sneakers. He should have made that faggot give up one of those Italian suits he had lined up in his closet, Baby Brother thought. They were about the same size, but he didn't want to stir up a lot of questions about why he needed civilian clothes if he was on his way back to Iraq. Everybody in D.C. worked for the government one way or another. He didn't need a stranger all up in his business who might feel it was his patriotic duty to report a runaway soldier in an Armani suit.

The waitress refilled Baby Brother's coffee cup and gave him a dazzling smile as she bussed his table. Baby Brother smiled back, wondering if he could get her to give him a break on the check on the strength of his dimples. Her smile made him relax a little. *What was he worried about?* That guy was never going to report on him. He had more stake in keeping his own secrets than he did busting an army deserter he'd picked up only for sex.

The guy had requested that Baby Brother wear a condom, which was a first. None of the men he had been with for money bothered with protection, and since he wasn't the one on his knees, he figured it was every man for himself. This guy gave him a rubber that smelled like grape soda. The funny thing was that the condom was the only part of the exchange that made Baby Brother feel like a whore. He didn't like seeing himself as that kind of hustler, but the way things were going . . .

"Is this seat taken?"

Baby Brother looked up into the face of a young woman with a cup of coffee in her hand and a beautiful smile on her strikingly sweet face. She was tall and slender with caramel skin and the kind of big, curly, old-school Afro that people always hoped to find in the box with the blowout kit. Her eyes were big and green and her full lips and square white teeth sent his mind tumbling into fantasies where condoms were not allowed.

"No," he said, scrambling to his feet, wondering how long she'd been standing there. "Sit down if you want."

"Thanks." She slid into the chair across the table from him and stashed a small suitcase under her chair.

He watched her with a growing appreciation of how pretty she was. She didn't look like a prostitute, but women this fine didn't usually ask strangers in half-empty coffee shops if they minded company unless they were preparing to make a business transaction.

"I'm Zora," she said, reaching across the table to shake his hand firmly. *Even her fingers were fine*, he thought, releasing them slowly.

"My girlfriend is picking me up and she's running late. I just hate to sit in restaurants by myself, even if it's just for coffee. I don't know why, but I thought you might be that way, too."

This girl was no hooker. She looked more like a college student.

"I'm Wes," he said, following her lead and providing no last name.

"Nice to meet you, Wes," she said, tearing open four sugars and dumping them into her coffee. She followed that up with three small packets of hazelnut-flavored fake cream, and then stirred the whole thing vigorously.

Baby Brother watched her take a long swallow of this concoction and his expression must have mirrored his disapproval.

"What can I say? I like a little coffee with my sugar and cream," she said, grinning at him. "It's a Southern thing."

"I see."

From her accent, it sounded to Baby Brother like Zora was *a Southern thing* herself. She shrugged out of her coat and her breasts swayed under her sweater. It didn't look to him like she was wearing a bra.

"You coming or going?" she said, taking another sip of her sugar and cream.

"I'm going to New York," he said, immediately sorry he had told her the truth. *That was the problem with fine women. They could get all your secrets out of you just by being fine!* If he was going to be a fugitive, he had to learn to keep his mouth shut.

She draped her coat on the back of her chair. "What's in New York?"

Baby Brother tried to reclaim his cool by being vague. "I need to get lost for a while. New York's a big place."

She nodded slowly. "Won't your uncle be worried?"

"My uncle?"

"Your uncle Sam," she said, pointing at his uniform with one slender finger. "That's not a Halloween costume, is it?"

She was wearing a gauzy peasant blouse, and underneath, he could see a lacy camisole. He got so distracted, he forgot to answer her question.

"Should I put my coat back on?" she said, a little sarcastic, but kind of sweet, too. Truly fine women know what kind of effect they have on mortal men. This girl was probably used to it.

"It's just been a while since I've seen a woman as fine as yourself," he said. "Threw me off for a minute."

She tossed her head and her earrings made a little tinkling sound. "Oh yeah?"

He gave her his best movie-star smile. "Yeah."

"Then I've got a question for you."

"Shoot."

"I want to know where you've been that there weren't any fine women." She smiled to acknowledge the flattery.

"I didn't say there weren't any fine women. There's fine women everywhere. I said *as fine as you.*"

"That doesn't answer my question." She smiled back at him. "Where've you been?"

"Iraq," he said, watching her face for a response. "I've been stationed outside of Fallujah."

Her face grew suddenly serious. "You've been in the war?"

"That's what they tell me."

"Are you out now?" She sounded concerned.

He shook his head. "In my dreams. I'm supposed to be on my way back in a couple of days. I just got a pass to come home for my mom's funeral."

A combat soldier, home from the war to bury his mother. It was a perfect storm as far as sympathy sex was concerned. Her eyes were full of compassion. He made his face look properly sorrowful.

"Aren't you going back?" she said quietly.

That threw him a little and he immediately got paranoid. His eyes shifted nervously in his handsome face. "What do you mean?" he said. "Why wouldn't I be?"

"Relax," she said quickly. "It's just that you said, 'I'm supposed to go back.'" Her voice was gentle, but he was still wary.

"Yeah, so?"

"So the way you said it, it just sounded like you might not."

He narrowed his eyes. "Why do you care what I do?"

She leaned toward him and crossed her arms in front of her on the table. One slender wrist held five chunky bangles and the other sported a big old Timex watch with a fake gold band that was easily four sizes too big for her. She wore no rings.

"Because we're the same age and I know how I'd feel if they were trying to get me to fly around the world and kill people for them."

She got that right, Baby Brother thought. "How do you know we're the same age?"

"I'm nineteen. How old are you?"

She was right, but he just looked at her.

"I don't know what you're talking about."

"Look," she said, "I work with a group, African American Students Against the War, and we're always talking about what we can do about it, but we never talk to anybody who's really been there. When I saw you sitting here by yourself, with your uniform on and everything, I just thought maybe you could help me understand."

He looked at her lovely face and he knew she was clueless. Nothing she had ever seen or read or thought could possibly give her even an inkling of what he'd seen and done. Suddenly her innocence made him angry.

"You think I can help you understand?" he snapped. "Tell you some stories about the war to share with your girlfriends?"

She bristled at his tone. "It's not like that. We're just trying to help."

He rolled right over her objection. "I got some stories for you. How about a guy getting blown up on the day before he was scheduled to go home to his wife and kid? How about a guy getting shot in the head the first time he ever went out on patrol? How about guys dying over there every day, scared to death, crying like little bitches, shitting their pants? Ain't no heroes when you ridin' in a convoy and you see the truck right beside you blown to kingdom come and your buddy's brains all over the road and somebody holdin' what's left of their leg in their hand, screamin' for their mama, and the Iraqi kids standin' around, laughin', hopin' we all die so they can take what's left of what we got. And you know what else? That ain't even nothin' special. That's just an ordinary day, every day."

She was watching him intently. She didn't say anything, but her eyes were round as silver dollars. He leaned over then and grabbed her hands and she let him. It was as if they were alone in the midst of the early-morning commuters and camera-laden tourists from around the world.

Suddenly he felt nineteen, young and vulnerable and stupid for getting himself in this position in the first place.

"I'm not goin' out like that," he whispered between tightly clenched teeth. "If I'm goin' down, I'm goin' down for something I believe in."

"What do you believe in?" she said softly.

Baby Brother sat back slowly. "I believe in saving my own ass. *Period.*"

The chirp of Zora's cellphone startled them both. She fumbled in her coat pocket.

"Hello? . . . Yeah, I'm still here. Where are you? . . . Out front where? . . . Okay. I'm on my way."

She flipped the phone closed and looked at Baby Brother. "I've got to go. My girlfriend's here to pick me up."

He didn't say anything as she slipped her arms into her coat and picked up her bag. He could have gone to college. His father was always on him about it, but he never cared about the future. Not until he didn't see one. When she stood up to go, he did, too.

"It was good to meet you," Zora said, extending her hand again. "I hope I didn't upset you."

He took her hand and held it. "What do *you* believe in?"

"I believe in you," she said. "A lot of us do. If you decide not to go back. There are people who can help you."

"Help me how?"

"Legally, financially, whatever you need."

That sounded promising. "Oh yeah? So where are all these people who want to help me?"

"We're everywhere," she said. "I'm up here for a conference of other students from all over the country who are working for peace and I volunteer with a program in Atlanta that works with veterans."

"Do they work with deserters?"

Her cellphone chirped again. "Listen, I gotta go, but take this."

She fumbled in her backpack for a pen and a scrap of notebook paper, scribbled down a name and a telephone number, and handed it to him. Assuming it was her number, he took it gladly, but when he took a look, he frowned.

"Samson Epps?"

"He's in charge of the vet program I was telling you about. If New York doesn't work out, think about Atlanta."

"Is that where you'll be?" This woman was getting ready to walk out of his life and she was much too fine to let her go that easy. He needed more information fast.

"I'm in school at Spelman," she said. "I've got another year before I graduate."

"So I can't get *your* number?"

"If you get to Atlanta, call Dr. Epps. He'll know where to find me."

"So I gotta go through Samson to get to you?"

She smiled. "I have to go."

"Don't you trust me?"

"I don't know you."

"But don't I have an honest face?"

"You have a *baby face.* That's not the same thing."

Her cellphone chirp was getting more frequent and more insistent. "I really gotta go."

"I'll walk with you," he said, picking up her bag and tossing twenty dollars on the table to cover the check and tip the waitress whose inviting smile had faded from his mind the minute Zora had sat down across from him.

"Okay," she said, giving him another great smile.

They were about the same height, and as he allowed her to pass out of the restaurant before him, he glanced down at her behind to see if it was as exemplary as her breasts. It was.

"So when is this meeting you're going to?"

"This afternoon," she said. "Three o'clock at Ira Aldridge Theater on the Howard campus."

"Do I need a ticket to get in?"

Her hair bounced when she walked just like her behind.

"Tell them I invited you. I'll be there early since I'm on the program. If you have any trouble, tell anybody with an AASAW badge to come get me." She pronounced the acronym like it was a word.

"Aasaw?"

"African American Students Against the War."

"Right, right," he said as they stepped out into the fall sunshine. It was warm enough in the daytime. The *hawk* only seemed to come out at night. "Slipped my mind for a minute."

"There's my friend," Zora said, pointing to a young woman waving wildly in their direction. Homeland security in the nation's capital required cars around the station to keep moving and a frowning D.C. police officer was heading in her direction. They hurried over and Zora's friend popped the trunk so Baby Brother could toss the bag in.

"Hey, my sister!" said her friend, giving Zora a quick hug and eye-balling the young soldier who was accompanying her.

"Hey, Rita," Zora said. "This is my friend Wes."

"The more the merrier," Rita said. "Hop in."

"He's not coming with us," Zora said quickly. "We just had coffee."

"Maybe I'll see you later," Baby Brother said, wondering if it would be acceptable for him to kiss her in a friendly sort of promissory way.

"I'd like that," Zora said, leaning up to brush her lips lightly across his cheek before she jumped in the car beside Rita. "Take care of yourself."

Baby Brother grinned, and ran his fingers across his face where her lips had touched him. "Count on it."

19

Abbie was a fast walker. In excellent shape, she liked to move quickly enough to get her heart pumping merrily along like it belonged to a woman twenty years younger, although she didn't care anything about *looking* like she was twenty years younger. She wanted to look like who she was—a healthy, vigorous, sexually vibrant woman of almost sixty who was on the verge of taking a lover. Well, she thought, maybe a little further along than *on the verge. In the midst of* was probably a better description.

Being a man, Peachy had assumed that when Abbie suggested it might be time for them to have sex, she meant sometime within the next few hours. Over dinner, she had explained to him that she thought it would be better if they waited until she came back in two months for the harvest moon. The disappointment on his face at this suggestion was so comically tragic that for a moment, she almost reconsidered and led him upstairs to bed for a night of spontaneity and improvisation. But that would have been careless. It was trusting spontaneity that had gotten her into trouble the last time she had sex.

At this point in her life, Abbie knew miscommunication was a recipe for sexual disaster, but only if she didn't speak to Peachy honestly. Only if she didn't introduce him to her body with the loving care it deserved and then meet his with the same tenderness and willingness to laugh at the changes age always brings. After fifty, she knew, a sense of humor was as vital to good sex as privacy and a good mattress.

One of the things Abbie liked most of Peachy was his laugh. It was big and loud and rowdy enough to draw the startled gaze of those who heard it break out in restaurants where most people contented themselves with a discreet chuckle or two. She wanted to hear Peachy laugh *naked.* Just the thought made her smile. She was glad she had invited him back for breakfast.

The sun had broken through the morning clouds as she walked and the sky had gone from gray to brilliant blue. Abbie stopped to watch a tardy shrimp boat chugging up from the Savannah River channel and out to where the early risers were already hauling in the first catch of the day. The swoop and cry of the gulls over the gentle breaking of the waves made her heart almost ache at the beauty of the scene. She considered days like this gifts from a universe so bountiful with blessings that it could create these moments without requiring anything at all in return.

"Thank you," Abbie was saying out loud to whatever spirits might be listening. "Thank you."

"Well, you're welcome," Peachy's voice said behind her, "but I haven't done anything yet."

Turning to find him standing there with a smile on his face and a piece of driftwood in his hand like a walking stick, she laughed. "Good morning! I didn't hear you come up."

"I'm surprised you couldn't hear me huffing and puffing for the last half mile."

"Your knee again?"

He grimaced slightly. "I guess I can cancel the NBA as a second career option."

She smiled. "Were they under consideration?"

"The only thing under consideration is you, sweet thing," he said, smiling back. "Why else would I be walking my half-crippled ass this far down the beach?"

"You ready to head back?"

"I'm not sure I can keep up with your pace."

"I'll slow down for you," she said, linking her arm through his.

"Sure you don't mind?"

"Not a bit."

They fell into an unhurried stroll that didn't tax Peachy's knee. The sun on Abbie's face felt wonderful and she squeezed his arm a little tighter.

His elbow pressed gently against her breast. "You smell good."

"Patchouli."

He nodded. "I know. The other day, I stopped into a candle shop in town and they were burning some patchouli incense. The place was full of the smell of it and I had to leave or risk having a physical reaction that a gentleman tries to control in public so as not to frighten women and children."

"You mean you—?"

He nodded, grinning at her blush.

How long had it been, Abbie wondered, that just the memory of her smell had given a man an inappropriate erection?

"You better be careful." She laughed. "You'll be banned from the island for lewd behavior."

"I've got a head full of lewd behavior," he said, "but don't worry. I'm saving it all for you!"

"Promise me something."

"Anything."

"When we . . ." She suddenly felt shy as a schoolgirl. "When we make love, don't do anything that doesn't feel good. If your knee hurts, just tell me and we'll work around it."

He was so happy that she had said "make love" he forgot the throbbing in his knee for a second. "It's a deal."

"And I'll do the same," she said. "If it doesn't feel good, I'll let you know."

"I do have some experience with that," he said, a look she couldn't identify flickering across his face. "When Lillie was sick, sometimes she still wanted us to be . . . close."

Peachy was searching for the right words.

"Tell me," Abbie said softly. "It's okay."

"I wanted her so much, but I was afraid I might hurt her," Peachy said, looking out at the whitecapped waves sparkling in the sunshine. "So I didn't want to, but she told me she'd let me know if it didn't feel good, so I didn't need to worry about it." He turned back to Abbie. "Is that what you mean?"

She nodded. "Yes, that's what I mean, but you know what?"

"What?"

She leaned over and kissed him lightly on the mouth. "I'm not sick. I'm just sixty, and that's another thing all together."

As if to prove it, she stepped away from him, gave herself a running start, and did a perfectly executed cartwheel right there at the edge of the ocean. She ended with a big grin and outstretched arms like she was captain of the cheerleading squad and her team had just scored the winning touchdown. He was so surprised and delighted, all he could do was throw back his head and laugh in that loud, rowdy way that always made her laugh, too.

On the upper balcony of his beach house, Blue Hamilton lowered his binoculars and looked at his wife, who was staring in the same direction. "Did Miss Abbie just do a cartwheel?"

"Yes, I think she did," Regina said, amazed. They had just arrived from Atlanta to surprise Abbie and Peachy with their baby news. Finding the house empty, they had gone outside to scan the beach.

"You don't think she read our minds, do you?"

It was an ability Abbie shared with Blue, but Regina shook her head and grinned at her husband. "No, sweetie," she said, waving as Abbie and Peachy headed in their direction, walking arm in arm. "I don't think that cartwheel had a thing to do with us."

20

Precious Hargrove and Lee Kilgore were two of a kind. Smart and ambitious, they radiated the kind of confidence that comes with being at the top of your game and having enough sense to know it. Sitting in her large, light-filled office at Mandeville Maids, where she had served for the last two years as president and CEO, Precious was listening closely to Captain Kilgore. The two women knew each other only slightly, and this was the longest conversation they'd ever had.

Precious Hargrove's political ambitions were no secret to Lee or to anyone else in Atlanta who had been paying any attention at all. Precious had entered the arena as a young single mother, passionately indignant about the deterioration of her West End neighborhood. With no political experience but an abundance of energy, sincerity, and intelligence, she was able to handily defeat the incumbent and take a seat in the state legislature the day before her twenty-fifth birthday. At the swearing in, her son, Kwame, only seven years old, was proudly wearing his first dark suit and a tie he had learned to knot all by himself in honor of the occasion.

Since that first victory, Precious had worked tirelessly on behalf of her constituents. She had spearheaded efforts around the state on behalf of women and children and cosponsored a statewide voter registration drive with SonShine Enterprises that had signed up and energized over one hundred thousand new voters. Just two years earlier, speculation was high that when the popular Democratic governor finished his second term, Precious would run with his blessings and the full support of the party and its formidable statewide machine.

But then the national political winds changed and blew through Georgia with enough force to blow the Democrats out of control at the statehouse for the first time since Reconstruction and Precious had to be realistic. Her statewide plans were definitely over. She knew she was standing at a crossroads. *Was being a state senator from West End as far as she could go politically?* It was time to regroup and weigh her options. The opportunity to step in and run Mandeville Maids after its founder was sent to jail for her involvement in a multistate prostitution ring came at the perfect time. When Blue Hamilton joined the chorus of voices asking her to take the job for two years until the company could find a new chief operating officer, she agreed to do it.

Although his complicated position in the community often required that Blue play a less than public role in her political life, she considered him not only a friend but an adviser who had never steered her wrong. Of course, she knew the stories about Blue Hamilton having inhabited previous lives before he showed up this time around in Atlanta. One tale made him the leader of a far-flung empire who'd ruled with a just but unwavering hand. Another made him a Roaring Twenties gangster who'd been shot dead in the streets of Harlem. Another said he'd been a pirate, and the stories went on and on.

Even after almost twenty years of friendship, she still didn't know whether she believed any of the stories about Blue, and she still didn't have the nerve to ask him to explain. All she knew was that his political instincts were impeccable. She trusted him absolutely. Based on his advice, she'd stopped worrying about being the governor, and thrown herself into the daunting task of rebuilding Mandeville Maids.

She carefully reassured the company's regular customers that their high level of service wouldn't change and expanded employee benefits to include free, on-site day care. She instituted a package deal for busy young professionals that included cooking and cleaning at one low price and organized her workers into teams that allowed them more independence and greater productivity. It was an ambitious plan of attack, but Precious knew she had to make immediate changes that everyone could see if the business was going to survive. If it didn't, a thousand women would be out of work.

Precious had never worked harder. In fact, she barely had time to respond to the barrage of calls she got when Councilman Buford Long, the ambitious front-runner in the upcoming mayor's race, was named in a federal indictment for influence peddling and money laundering. The news did not take her by surprise. She had received a call from Blue the night before it hit the papers. He already knew about the indictment, although he didn't say how and she didn't ask him. When he inquired about her plans in the face of this latest development, she didn't hesitate.

"I intend to run," she said immediately.

"I hoped you'd say that," Blue said. "If you need my help, let me know."

"I always need your help. This doesn't change that."

"Just remember that when you get to city hall."

"Do you really think I can win?"

"If I didn't, I'd be talking to whoever I thought could beat you."

She laughed, but she knew he wasn't kidding. "Then I count myself lucky."

"Me, too," Blue said. "We've been working together a long time."

"Ever since I asked you to contribute to the uniforms for Kwame's baseball team."

"Is that how you remember it?" Blue's voice was amused. "I remember you strong-arming me out of a sizable chunk of real estate for the field, and an equally sizable chunk of money for the uniforms and equipment they needed."

She laughed. "Well, I'm in your debt for always being there when I need you."

"Don't worry about that," he said. "You just keep doing what you're doing, and so will I."

That wasn't hard. Precious had enjoyed the challenge of Mandeville Maids, but politics was where her heart was. She didn't know for sure yet, but she thought that was probably where Captain Lee Kilgore's heart was, too. The idea Lee wanted to discuss was a good one. She was trying to find funds for a pilot program to staff a police precinct entirely with female officers, specifically trained in domestic violence prevention and counseling.

The idea was that a woman already victimized by male violence might be further traumatized by having to call on other men she didn't even know for protection. An all-female precinct would eliminate the problem. Lee was hoping to open discussions with Precious about the possibility that Mandeville Maids could partner with the police department to create the first-ever *peace precinct.*

"It's a totally different approach," Lee was saying, "but I think that's the strength of it. We've tried everything else we can think of and the rate and severity of domestic violence are still rising."

Precious nodded. "We're getting more and more women showing up for work with black eyes or split lips. Things seemed to have calmed down last year, but now it's worse than it was before."

"Any of their guys veterans?"

Precious frowned, trying to recall the details about the men the victimized women were still going home to at the end of every working day. "I don't know. Why?"

"We're seeing a lot more problems with returning vets," Lee said. "There's not enough reentry counseling for them, almost nothing for their families, and they really need it."

Picking up a pen, Precious wrote the words *reentry counseling* on her yellow legal pad.

Lee smiled and reached into her slim, brown leather briefcase and pulled out a large envelope with *Peace Precinct: Confidential* printed discreetly on its left-hand corner. "You don't need to do that. I've pulled together some material for you to take a look at. It's all here."

Precious smiled and reached for the packet, recognizing someone who was as careful as she herself was about preparation.

"It would mean a lot to the success of the project if we could get you on board early," Lee said.

"It's an exciting idea," Precious said. "We have over a thousand female employees, as you know, and domestic violence is always an area where we're looking to do more. I'll take a look at your proposal and let you know if I see a place for our involvement."

"Thank you," Lee said, but she hesitated slightly.

"Was there something else?"

"There is one more thing," Lee said, choosing her words carefully. "I appreciate your time and I don't want to overstay my welcome, but may I have your permission to speak frankly on another issue that we haven't discussed?"

"Of course," Precious said.

"Senator Hargrove, I'm sure you know there is a great deal of speculation that you're going to run for the top spot. I'm not asking you to confirm or deny it. I know that kind of announcement has to be made carefully and in its own time."

Precious smiled.

"I just want you to know that if you do decide to run, I'd be honored to assist you in matters of public safety as well as personal security."

"I appreciate your offer," Precious said, and she meant it. If she was going to run for mayor, the police department was going to be a major challenge. Captain Kilgore would be a valuable addition to her team, and they both knew it. "And I'll be making a decision real soon."

"Well, I hope you decide in the affirmative," Lee said, standing up as she gathered her things to go. "I was really disappointed for you that the governor's race didn't work out, but it's like the old folks used to say."

Precious stood up, too, waiting for the punch line. According to how often we quoted them, she thought, the old folks spent so much time spouting wisdom, it was amazing they ever got any work done.

"The Lord never closes a door without opening a window," Lee said, holding out a hand to shake the one Precious offered.

"Amen to that," Precious said. "I'll be in touch."

"I'll look forward to it."

Precious closed the door behind Lee and went over to the floor-to-ceiling windows that allowed her to look down from her sixth-floor suite into the building's airy, plant-filled atrium. The colorful stained-glass dome above her was a constantly changing light show against the white walls. When she first started working here, she had been amazed that so many people hurried through the space every day without ever stopping long enough to notice the rainbows all around them.

As Precious stood there, admiring the building's beautifully restored architecture, Captain Kilgore emerged from the elevators and started across the atrium's marble floor toward the front door. Unaware that she was being observed, she stopped suddenly and gazed slowly up to where the sunshine was working its daily show. From where Precious stood in her office window, she could see Lee tilt her head back to enjoy the full view and then, with a brief private smile of appreciation, continue on her way.

Maybe there was something to that open-window thing, Precious thought. She couldn't wait to tell Kwame what had just blown in.

21

Baby Brother was kicking himself. He should have gone to that meeting with Zora. She had said he was welcome, but at the time, he thought he had some other shit working, so he didn't make it. But his boys had let him down. *Again!* Now here he was, back out on the street. He had spent the rest of the money the guy with the BMW had given him on a pair of jeans and some cheap sneakers, but there wasn't enough left over for a real coat. The cheap windbreaker he'd be able to afford wasn't much better than nothing. He never thought he'd miss the heat of the Iraqi desert, but he hated this cold almost as bad. If this was global warming, he didn't like it one bit.

The guards at Union Station had been tailing him suspiciously after two nights there, so he couldn't go back for a third time. He should have kept that damn uniform. Nobody would kick a soldier out of the train station in the nation's capital. Not when there was a war going on. But in his civvies, he just looked like another young black man who wanted something for nothing. Realizing with a tsunami of self-pity that he had absolutely no prospects, Baby Brother did what he'd been doing since he was fourteen. He used two of his last few dollars to catch the metro out to his sister's house. Just because she had married somebody who didn't like him didn't mean they weren't still *blood*. With his mother gone, she was his closest living relative. Maybe his only one. That had to count for something! She couldn't let him freeze to death just because they'd had their differences in the past. He was still her baby brother, and to his way of thinking, she still owed him.

He stared out the subway window and tried to make himself believe it, but he couldn't quite get the judge's angry face and words out of his mind. What if he walked up on the porch and his brother-in-law came outside and kicked his ass all up and down the street? Maybe it would be better, he thought, to wait until he could see Cassie alone. He'd wait until the judge went to work and then talk to his sister. The only problem was, *What was he supposed to do tonight?*

He stepped off the train at the stop for his sister's house and looked around. The cold wind went through his jacket like he wasn't even wearing one. Baby Brother shivered and realized he couldn't wait. If he was going to sleep indoors tonight, he was going to have to ask Cassie for a few bucks to tide him over until he could figure out a way to get to Atlanta. He hadn't realized that was what he was going to do until the thought popped into his mind fully formed. *Atlanta!* Of course that's what he should do.

Zora liked him. He could tell that at the train station. Plus, she knew somebody he could talk to about the army, too. He didn't know what he was going to do about deserting his outfit; all he knew was that he wasn't going back. She had given him some guy's number to call and he fumbled through his pockets, hoping he hadn't left the paper in his uniform. *There it was!* Written in her own neat hand: *Samson Epps, 404-344-8642. Ask for Zora.* That's what he intended to do, all right. But first he had to get his *broke ass* down there.

Lost in his new plan, he was almost in front of Cassie's place before he saw the front door opening. He ducked into the shadows of the big maple tree beside the house next door and watched his sister and her husband come outside, laughing and talking easily together. Even from where he was standing, he could see how happy his sister was and he felt a sudden, uncharacteristic pang of regret for the pain he'd caused her. He shook it off. This was no time to start feeling sentimental. Baby Brother watched them go down the walk, hand in hand, and get into a dark gray Lexus parked at the curb. That must be the judge's car, he thought. Cassie's Pontiac was parked in the driveway. They pulled away without ever seeing him.

It seemed to Baby Brother that no matter how hard he tried, he couldn't catch a break. He stood there in the dark, feeling sorry for himself, then he remembered something. He had hot-wired that Pontiac a thousand times as a kid. He even knew a way to jimmy the lock on the passenger side so he could get in without tripping the alarm. He wondered if Cassie had ever fixed it.

Glancing around and seeing no one, he slipped out of the shadows, hurried over to the car, and tried the door using his old trick. *It worked!* He slid into the front seat and quickly closed the door behind him. All he had to do now was cross a couple of wires and hope he hadn't lost his touch. The engine cranked on his first try and he almost shouted for joy. He clambered over into the driver's seat, checked to make sure she had gas, and put the car in reverse without a shred of guilt for stealing his sister's car *one more time.*

Let that nigga she married buy her another one, Baby Brother thought as he pulled off in the Pontiac. *This motherfucker is headed to Atlanta!*

22

Precious had almost finished her second glass of iced tea and was about to tell her server to go on and bring her Cobb salad when she saw Kwame pull up outside Murphy's, a popular lunch spot in the bustling in-town neighborhood of Virginia Highlands. Her tall, handsome son was dressed in a dark suit and tie, looking very professional indeed, she thought. She picked up the faint smell of his aftershave as he leaned down to kiss her on the cheek.

"I'm so sorry, Mom," he said. "I was at the planning-committee meeting down at city hall and I ran into Bob Watson."

"Bob Watson?" Precious forgot her pleasure in seeing her son and wrinkled her nose disapprovingly. "I can't stand him!"

"I'll keep that in mind," Kwame said, scanning the menu quickly.

His voice had an edge that surprised her. Their server glided up to take Kwame's order then refresh their water glasses.

"I'm sorry, Mr. Sensitive," she said, teasing him gently. "What was old Bob talking about anyway?"

"Preservation," Kwame said, mollified by her apology. He and Aretha had started the day arguing. He didn't have the energy for any more contentious exchanges with the women in his life. "He's interested in the West End Victorians."

West End boasted an impressive number of beautifully appointed, immaculately maintained Victorian homes, complete with wraparound porches and gingerbread latticework.

Precious smiled. "Your report is going to get a lot of people interested in those houses."

"You think?" Kwame had recently completed his exhaustive annotated inventory of West End's housing stock. It had taken him the better part of two years.

"Absolutely." Her son had done a good job and she was proud of him. "I read the whole thing last night, cover to cover, including the historical footnotes. That report is going to change the way West End is developed for the next thirty years, not to mention kicking up the price of those Victorians! Blue will love it."

"I hope so," Kwame said. "I want to end our association on good terms."

"End your association?" Precious said as their server arrived with her Cobb salad and his smoked turkey sandwich. "What are you talking about? You know Blue has work for you for as long as you want it."

"I know that," Kwame said quickly. "And this contract was fine, but I don't necessarily want to be on Blue Hamilton's payroll for the rest of my life."

Precious looked at him. "What does that mean?"

"Nothing," Kwame said, taking a bite out of his sandwich. "It's just that I'm feeling a little claustrophobic. My world has pretty much narrowed down to this one little neighborhood. I *live* in West End. I *work* in West End. My wife's *studio* is in West End. My daughter goes to *school* in West End."

He was getting more and more agitated, his voice rising just enough to draw a glance from the table closest to them. Kwame took a deep breath and gathered himself. His mother had been a public person since he was seven years old. He knew the drill. Personal business had to be kept just that: *personal.*

"What's wrong, son?" Precious said gently. "Are things going any better between you and Aretha?"

"Things are shitty between me and Aretha, as I'm sure she's told you, but that's not the problem." He sighed deeply. "The problem is, I am almost thirty years old and I am still living on the same block where I grew up. I'm four blocks from my mother. I'm spitting distance from every West Ender who remembers me when I was five or six or twelve or about to graduate from high school."

"Is that a bad thing?" Precious was confused.

Kwame sighed again. "I have to make some major changes in my life, Mom, and I have to do it *now*."

"What kinds of changes?" Precious said, feeling a knot of confusion and worry in the pit of her stomach.

"All kinds! Everything! To start off, I want to rent our house to some bright young faculty member from the AU Center and move my family to midtown or Virginia Highlands. I want to get a real job in a real firm where I can be an architect again, not just a glorified surveyor."

Precious knew her son so well she sometimes felt like she could read his mind. This was one of those times. "Are you going to work for Bob Watson?"

Kwame's eyes flashed. "He hasn't asked me, but Teddy mentioned that he was interested in me. So?"

Teddy Rogers and Bob Watson, Precious thought. Two of a kind, *both weasels*. "Did you ever ask yourself why he's interested?"

"Because I'm a talented young architect with a bright future who would be a great asset to any firm, even if his mother wasn't going to be the next mayor of Atlanta."

Looking at her son's angry face, she wished she could take back the question. What were they arguing about anyway? Whether or not he had to live and die in the neighborhood she had chosen for him as a child? Whether or not he should wash the dishes or expect his wife to handle it? It was dawning on Precious that she had crossed the line between being a loving, truthful mother and being a meddler who expected her son to agree with her plan for his life, his work, his family. She sat back in her chair and looked at Kwame, trying to collect her thoughts. Another apology was clearly in order.

"You're right," she said slowly. "You're absolutely right and I apologize."

"Apologize for what?" Kwame said warily.

Precious leaned across the table and took her son's hand. "For not trusting you to handle your business, personal and professional; for ruining our lunch; and for being the kind of mother I always swore I'd never be. Forgive me?"

Kwame relaxed then, raised her hand to his lips, and kissed it. "Of course I do. It's my fault, too. Things have been so crazy at home lately, I probably wouldn't have been the easiest person to talk to either."

"Crazy how?" Precious said, watching her son's face for clues.

He shrugged. "She's mad at me half the time. The other half, she acts like I'm not even there."

Precious took a deep breath. "It's none of my business, but . . ."

He gave her a very small smile. *"But?"*

"There's no other woman involved, is there?"

The irony of his mother's question, equal parts hope and dread, was not lost on Kwame. "No, Mom. There's no other woman. Whatever is going on between me and Aretha is something we're going to have to fix between ourselves. Okay?"

She nodded. "Okay."

"Good."

"Now will you promise me one thing?"

"Do I have any choice?"

"If you go to work for Bob Watson, don't tell him I said I didn't like him. It costs a lot to run an effective campaign for mayor, and this conversation aside, I'll be expecting a significant contribution from your new boss."

Kwame grinned at her. "He's not my boss yet."

"He will be. And it's okay. You've made your point, sweetie. Take the job! Move to midtown! Live your life!"

"Will you come visit us?"

"Try and keep me away," she said, grinning at her baby who had become a full-grown man without asking her permission. "I like midtown. I just wouldn't want to live there."

23

It was almost time for dinner and Peachy was cooking something special. Regina, already in the grip of the first trimester's overwhelming need for naps, was asleep upstairs. That gave Blue and Abbie a chance to walk down to the water's edge together. This was a shared pleasure. Whenever Blue had been away from Tybee, he always had to wet his feet in the ocean as soon as he returned. Abbie was the same way. They both thought it had something to do with the fact that in one of the past lives they had shared, they made their home by the sea. Sticking their feet in the same ocean they had known so long ago was a way of acknowledging, honoring, remembering.

Blue and Abbie talked about past lives the way most people talk about high school. It was disconcerting to people who didn't know them well, and truth be told, it sometimes startled people who knew them very well. Out of consideration, they refrained from such references as much as possible, but around each other, there was no such prohibition. They spoke freely, effortlessly moving back and forth between the centuries.

Blue had always accepted his past lives. Abbie had come to her understanding of this phenomenon later in life after she started having visions. Initially, she'd been a little nervous about this new gift, but when one of her visions predicted Blue's entrance into Regina's life so perfectly that even her sometimes skeptical niece could not deny it, she stopped being nervous and embraced her second sight with curiosity and enthusiasm. She printed up cards identifying herself as a "visionary adviser" and never looked back.

At this moment, Abbie was enjoying the quiet of Blue's company, the gentle pull of the water around her ankles as the tide receded, the perfect blue of the cloudless sky just before sunset splashed on the colors of day's end. She was delighted at the baby news, but there was a question she wanted to ask. Blue had been in other worlds, other places. He had been a full-grown man many times before he met Regina and Abbie had to know.

"Blue?"

Turning to her, he took off his sunglasses and she smiled. Something about those eyes made her feel happy. In beach light, they were somehow less startling. Reflecting sky and sea and sand, they seemed just one more natural wonder.

"Yes, Miss Abbie?"

Blue had affectionately adopted the Southern custom of adding *Miss* to her first name to show both love and respect.

"Is this baby your first one?"

"Yes."

She wasn't sure she'd been clear. "I don't mean just this time around. I mean *ever.*"

He smiled. "I know what you mean."

Abbie smiled back. "Good. I'm glad for Regina."

"Would it matter?"

"No," Abbie said thoughtfully. "I don't guess it would. It's just that you've already had so many lives, so many experiences. It's nice for her to be the first at something."

"Just like you were."

A trio of low-flying pelicans were scanning the waves for dinner possibilities and the shrimp boats were coming in with their usual escort of hungry gulls.

"Just like I was what?"

"The first at something." He hadn't replaced his glasses, but he was gazing out at the horizon again.

"Stop being so mysterious." Abbie dug her toes into the warm sand. "What are you talking about?"

"You were my first wife," he said, without turning in her direction.

Abbie felt herself blush. *His wife?* Even as a practicing visionary adviser, she had a hard time getting her mind around such an idea. She suddenly felt intensely disloyal to her niece.

"Where was Gina?"

"She was my adviser, my confidante, my conscience, my muse, although she'd probably deny that one."

"Go on," Abbie said.

"By the time she came to the palace, I already had three wives. It would have been greedy and scandalous to take another one just because I could."

"*Three* wives? I thought you said . . ."

"You were the first," he said. "Not the only."

"Typical king behavior." She laughed. "So what was my relationship to Gina? Did I know her?"

"She made you very nervous."

"Why?"

"Because she was a rebel. You were a wife."

"Couldn't I be both?"

"Not in those days."

Blue turned suddenly and looked over his shoulder as if someone had called his name. Abbie followed his gaze and saw Regina standing on the back deck waving a long blue scarf to get their attention. They waved back, and as she beckoned for them to come inside for dinner, the scarf she was holding blew out of her hand and fluttered out of reach. Carried by the wind, it undulated like a gossamer ribbon with a life of its own. Blue took two steps forward, and as the scarf fluttered just over his head, he reached up and plucked it out of the air like picking an apple off a tree. From the balcony, Regina applauded with delight like a child at the circus.

Abbie laughed and shook her head. "You two Negroes make such pretty pictures, you ought to be in the movies."

Blue grinned at her. "I thought this was a movie."

She linked her arm through his and they started back up to the house, knowing Peachy didn't like folks to be late for dinner. "Was I a good wife?"

"You were a wonderful wife."

"Then why did you take two more?"

He patted her hand where it rested on his arm, lightly, like the touch of a butterfly's wing. "I was trying to produce an heir."

She stopped in her tracks and looked up at him. "You're kidding, right?"

"The king was required to produce an heir." His voice was apologetic, as though he might still be held responsible for a two-hundred-year-old heartache. "We had been together five years and had no children. I had to take another wife. Then in five years, one more."

"And none of us produced an heir?"

"Or I didn't." He smiled and looped the blue silk scarf that still carried his wife's scent around Abbie's shoulders.

She started walking again, but she was clearly deep in thought. When they reached the back steps, they could smell the spicy seafood that Peachy had prepared and see Regina through the window, setting a bowl of flowers in the middle of the table. She was smiling. These days, Abbie thought, Regina was always smiling.

"Do you think this is the one?" she said, stopping again halfway up the stairs. "Is this your heir?"

Blue leaned over to kiss her cheek. "I'm not the king anymore. This time, I get to just be Daddy."

They both knew Blue was never just one thing. Abbie smiled, but she had one more question before they went inside.

"Have you ever told Peachy about me being a past-life wife?"

He laughed. "It never came up."

"Well, don't. I don't think he's ready for that particular piece of our personal history."

"No problem," Blue said, reaching for the sliding-glass door and winking at Abbie. "This time around, it'll be our secret."

24

Lee couldn't have been in a better mood. Her meeting with Precious had gone exactly as she'd hoped it would. The possibility of an innovative partnership with the new mayoral front-runner pleased the police-department brass and further burnished Lee's growing reputation as someone who could get things done. Add to that the bonus of having a chance to rub Bob Watson's nose in his recent political disaster and, to Lee's way of thinking, you had the makings of a perfect evening. She was looking forward to some spirited verbal jousting and then some equally spirited sex. The fact that she was planning to cut Bob loose soon didn't mean she couldn't enjoy what she knew would be one of their last few times together.

Driving slowly up the long, winding driveway to Bob's house, she wondered what Marian Watson would say if she knew that while she was away for a week at the most recent in a long line of spas she visited in search of the skin she'd had at twenty-one, her house was going to be the scene of her husband's infidelity one more time. Lee didn't care. She felt no loyalty to Marian and enjoyed the times she and Bob had the house to themselves. Her only concession was to refuse sex in the master bedroom. That was going too far.

She pulled around to the back of the house, cut the lights, and got out, smoothing her skirt over her hips. Lee had made Bob wait a year before she had sex with him. He'd raised the possibility almost immediately and she turned him down flat, saying she had no interest in being just another of the girls Bob Watson *used to fuck*.

"It's a very exclusive club," he had teased, gliding past his disappointment. "Don't knock it until you've tried it."

He wasn't sure exactly what made her change her mind. She wasn't sure either. Maybe it was just a moment when her curiosity got the better of her. They had dinner at her place one night to handle some business transactions, and after they had coffee, she put down her cup and asked him if he was still interested in having sex with her. He said *absolutely* and put down his cup, too. To their mutual surprise and satisfaction, they were good together. Bob was in his midfifties and she had expected one of those endless Viagra erections, but Bob was the real thing.

After that, they had sex regularly without the need to pretend they were in love or wanted to be. In fact, their relationship remained primarily that of co-conspirators and business partners. The sex was simply an unexpected bonus, but tonight Bob wasn't holding up his end of the bargain. His invitation had been explicitly sexual, but when she arrived, sex was the last thing on his mind. He was watching the eleven o'clock news and fussing. Standing in the beautiful living room of his perfectly designed, tastefully appointed house, sipping hundred-year-old brandy from an oversize crystal snifter, he was not happy.

"I despise that woman," Bob said, frowning as Precious Hargrove conducted another interview about her political future on his wall-size, flat-screen, high-definition television.

The interview was just a short feature on the local news and Lee was surprised at the vehemence of Bob's response. In past conversations in which Precious's name came up, he had been at most mildly irritated. This aggressive dislike was new. Maybe because a Hargrove candidacy suddenly had a lot more currency since Bob's choice, the former front-runner, had just been forced to withdraw on charges of massive corruption. In supporting the guy against Lee's advice, Bob had put his eggs in the wrong basket, and he knew it. Lee knew it, too.

"Despise her?" Lee sat down on the couch and hoped this mood was temporary. "Why?"

"She's bad for business," he snapped, like the answer was almost too obvious to suffer the question.

"Then why do you always give money to her campaigns and causes?"

"Because that's how Atlanta works," he snapped. "Haven't I taught you anything at all? We're both power players. I don't have to like her and she doesn't have to like me. All I have to do is give her money and all she has to do is return my call personally."

"What call?"

"*Whatever call I make!* All the money I've coughed up for her lousy state-senate campaigns and statewide voter education drives buys me a personal callback from the lady herself. It may not be worth much now, but who knows?" He groaned suddenly. "Jesus! Listen to me! I've already elected her just like they have! What are you drinking?"

"Perrier." Lee watched Bob pour the warm sparkling water into a glass without asking if she wanted ice or a wedge of lime. He handed her the glass and sat back down beside her as she took a sip of the tepid liquid. "The chamber of commerce doesn't seem to think she's bad for business."

"Are you talking about that quote in the paper this morning about how pleased they were that she was considering getting in the race?" Bob snorted with disgust. "That bunch of hicks and boosters! They wouldn't know a good deal if it bit them in the ass!"

He took a big swallow of his cognac and sighed. "I've had eight long years of this damn do-gooder drought. Mayor Franklin's so clean she practically squeaks when she walks. Now here comes Senator Hargrove, another Girl Scout. You can't even do business in this town anymore since the *bitches* took over."

Lee kicked off her heels and tucked her feet beneath her. His frustration amused her. "Maybe you just don't know how to talk to women."

"I do all right with you," he said, glancing over at her long, shapely legs and seeming to see her for the first time that night.

"Yeah," Lee said, "but I have a vested interest."

He touched her knee lightly. "What kind of vested interest?"

"I need you to help me get what I want."

He fell back, feigning shock and disappointment. "You mean you're using me?"

"Don't think of it like that." She grinned at him. "What are a few faked orgasms in the wider scheme of things?"

Bob winced. "Now you're just being cruel."

"Sorry."

Taking another swallow of his drink, he tried to let it go, but he was still annoyed at the sudden change in his political fortunes. "It's just that I've been here when the mayor didn't do business, like now, and I've been here when the mayor knew what time it was, and trust me, there's a difference."

"You're doing all right."

He frowned at her. "I have no interest in doing *all right.*"

"Stop worrying." She wondered what he would say if he knew she had already met with Precious and offered support.

"I always worry. That's why I'm rich."

"Well, what do you propose?"

"I need to find another viable candidate who can beat Precious Hargrove."

Lee raised her eyebrows. "Who did you have in mind?"

"There are other candidates in the race besides that fool who's on his way to the pen. Maybe one of them will step up."

"They're a sorry bunch of party hacks and clueless community activists and you know it," Lee said. "They couldn't beat Precious Hargrove if the election was five years away. If that's your plan, you need a better one."

He stood up and paced around the room. "Okay, you're right. None of them could beat her now, but what if her image got tarnished somehow?"

"Like how?"

"I don't know. What if she had a lover?"

"She's not married."

"How about a lesbian lover?" Bob looked hopeful.

"That's not really an issue anymore, remember?"

She wondered if he had forgotten that an openly gay woman had already been elected president of the Atlanta City Council.

"All right, then," he said, still pacing. "What about her relationship with Hamilton?"

"Blue Hamilton? How do you see that as a liability? He's as close as this town's got to Robin Hood. People love him."

"People loved Al Capone, too."

"But he couldn't sing and make your toes curl up."

"Spare me your sexual fantasies." Bob sneered.

"I'll remember you said that, but if Blue Hamilton is her only liability, you're *fucked.*"

"No, *we're* fucked."

"Speak for yourself," Lee said pleasantly. "You're the one who needs a new candidate."

"Last time I checked, you did, too."

"I've got one."

"Who?"

"Precious Hargrove, of course. I had an appointment with her today to talk about the peace precinct."

Bob was taken aback. First, because he had been scornful of the whole idea, taking the insane position that any woman who allowed herself to be abused deserved whatever she got. Second, because he didn't like surprises. "When were you going to tell me?"

"I'm telling you now."

"I see. Did you use the opportunity to kiss a little ass?"

Lee ignored that. "All I know is, she's going to be the mayor as sure as we're sitting here. If I play it right, I'll be a serious contender for the chief's spot."

"There's lots of guys ahead of you in line, remember?"

"Never underestimate the power of the sisterhood," she said, draining her glass.

He stared at her, then smiled slowly. "I admire your foresight, Captain Kilgore."

Men were forever underestimating her. Bob was no different. "Thank you."

"She's still bad for business," he said, touching her knee again, mollified now by the fact that Lee was already on the case. Maybe this cloud could still have a silver lining.

"Depends on what business you're in."

He ran his finger under the edge of her hem. "And what business are you in?"

"My own business." She didn't lean toward him, but she didn't move away.

"Still don't trust me, huh?"

"Never did, never will."

"I thought women couldn't love a man they didn't trust."

"Who said anything about love? Weren't we talking about business?"

"Just checking." He grinned, reaching over slowly to run his fingers lightly over the slippery silk of her blouse. "Where's your cop uniform?"

"In the trunk of my car."

"Go get it."

"Fuck you."

"*Exactly.*"

25

General had been in Montre's for the last four nights. He didn't even pretend to be doing business anymore. He was coming to see Brandi and they both knew it. With Blue down at Tybee again, General could set his own schedule, and for now, that schedule revolved around Brandi. Sometimes she'd dance for him. Sometimes he'd pay her just to have a drink. Sometimes he'd make arrangements to see her later. He always had money and he always gave her more than she expected. She rewarded him by being available whenever and wherever and by enthusiastically sharing her full repertoire of sexual tricks and treats with him.

Tonight, she saw him come in just as she was finishing up her pole routine. The stage was covered with dollar bills and two guys down front were on their feet throwing fives as she grabbed the pole, turned herself upside down, and shook herself silly in her trademark big finish. Her legs were open as wide as she could spread them. Her breasts were jiggling wildly and her butt was bouncing so fast it looked like it had a life of its own.

"Goddamn, girl, you shake that thing!" somebody shouted as she slid slowly to the floor, scooped up her money, and strutted off the stage to enthusiastic applause from the house.

She could have sold ten lap dances right then, but she acted like she didn't even see the men waving fives and even a few tens in her direction. She was headed for General's table. She got close enough for him to smell the sweat running off of her body and then stopped as if she'd just spotted him for the first time.

"Hey, baby! When you get here?"

"Just walked in," he said.

He caught a whiff of the musty-sweet odor of her sex wafting toward him. Stronger than the smell of cheap liquor and menthol cigarettes, it was primal and earthy and oblivious to the strange environment Brandi had found to exploit its magic.

"Want me to dance for you, baby?"

General looked at her and felt a slight stirring in his crotch. He would have loved a lap dance, but this girl was so fine she could make you come in your drawers like a fifteen-year-old kid in a whorehouse and he had a reputation to think about.

"No, I don't need a dance," he said. "Why don't you sit down and have that fool you work for bring me a bottle of real champagne?"

She looked around for Johnny, raised her hand, and pointed at General. He would know what that meant.

"Let me run to the little girls' room, baby. If I don't pee, you gonna get a show you ain't payin' for!"

He laughed and watched her walking quickly to the restroom. He wasn't naïve enough to think she loved him any more than a prostitute always loves a steady trick, but sometimes when she gasped and rocked her hips against him *just so*, he thought she might have loved him if their circumstances had been different. But they weren't, he always reminded himself. The best they could expect was an honest exchange where he got off thinking about Juanita, Brandi got paid, and everybody went home happy.

Knowing it would sound crazy if he tried to explain it to anyone, he didn't bother, but he felt closest to the essence of Juanita when he was having sex with Brandi. Maybe it was because when they were having sex, she didn't talk so much, except to ask him what he wanted or tell him how good it felt when they did all the things they did. And they did everything. Some stuff he asked for and some stuff he'd only dreamed about or seen in

porno movies. If Juanita truly had ordered Brandi up from the great beyond, she must have specified the top of their sexual line, General thought,
smiling to himself.

Johnny suddenly appeared beside him with a bottle of champagne and
two glasses. "Hey, my brother. How's it goin'?"

"It's goin'," General said, leaving no opening for further conversation.
Johnny opened the champagne, but didn't pour it, and eased nervously
away.

General didn't like Johnny. The sooner Brandi got out of this place and
into something better, the happier he'd be, General thought as she came
out of the ladies' room and sauntered back to his table. The eyes of the
hardworking men in Montre's watched her with a deep realization that she
was out of their league.

"That's better," she said, sitting down across from him. "I thought I
was gonna bust!"

"How you doin'?" He poured them each a glass of champagne.

"It's all good." Brandi sipped the champagne like she was on a date instead of at work. "Except that fool Johnny want to start advertisin' me."

"What do you mean?"

"You know, flyers and stuff with my picture on it to bring more customers in."

General frowned. "What did you say?"

"What you think I said, baby? I said, 'Hey, fool, I'm flyin' under radar
here, remember?' " She took another tiny sip of champagne. She'd have to
dance again in a few minutes and she didn't want to get bloated.

"You want me to talk to him?"

General's voice was quiet, neutral, but Brandi knew exactly what the
question meant and she appreciated it. It never hurt for a girl to have a
sponsor to look out for her interests.

"No, baby." She smiled at him. "Johnny's just trippin'. I can handle my
business. You know that."

"Don't let it be a problem, you hear?"

"I won't." Brandi put down her glass. "You sure you don't want me to
dance for you? I'm feelin' good, baby."

He smiled slowly at her. "I want you to do a lot more than that. How
soon can you get off?"

"You tell me."

He glanced at his watch. "An hour? My place?"

He stood up and pressed a folded hundred-dollar bill into her hand.

"I haven't done anything yet!" She grinned.

"Don't you worry," he said, heading for the door. "I fully expect to get my money's worth before this night is over."

26

The afternoon he had scheduled lunch with Kwame Hargrove, Bob Watson left his office at twelve forty-five. His driver met him downstairs. The 191 Club was only a few blocks away, but he always took a car. Presentation was half the battle. Everybody *and their mama* was riding around in Lincolns these days, but Bob was a traditionalist. He liked Cadillacs. *Black* Cadillacs. DeVille for business. Fleetwood for pleasure. Today was no exception and he was pleased to see that the car was so clean it practically gleamed in the sunshine.

The big sedan glided through Atlanta's lunchtime traffic like a shark on its way to the beach. Bob sat back to clear his mind. He had wasted the morning trying to find a new agent to handle the lease of the house he had designed and built in Ansley Park when his business had first taken off. Starkly modern in contrast to the rest of the homes around it, the house had caused quite a stir in its day. Several years ago his wife had decided she needed a more traditional space to host her endless round of dinner parties, receptions, and bridge games. Bob had acquiesced, under protest, but refused to sell the house, fully intending to move back into it one day, with or without his wife's approval.

The problem was the hassle of finding suitable tenants never ended. As soon as somebody got settled in, they'd get transferred, or decide to build their own house, or realize they didn't like the stark lines of the place as much as they thought they would. Tenants kept breaking their leases and leaving him in the lurch. Thinking about it was giving Bob a headache. He closed his eyes and took a deep breath. Right now he wanted to focus on the business at hand.

Lee's end run to Precious Hamilton hadn't gone down well with Bob. He had fumed about it for a long time after she left the other night, until he realized he, too, had an ace in the hole whose name was Hargrove—*Kwame* Hargrove. When Teddy Rogers had first mentioned Kwame over drinks a few weeks before, when bad weather left them stranded in LaGuardia without time to catch up, Bob had only half listened to the praise song his old friend was singing. Actually, he had been thinking about hiring a white female, but in the scramble of realignment that began immediately after the indictment of Councilman Long, Precious Hargrove had landed center stage.

Suddenly Teddy's enthusiastic promoting of her son, Kwame, seemed like a beacon in the darkness. Running into him in the flesh at the preservation hearing the other day only reinforced what Bob was already thinking. He had his secretary call the next day to set up a lunch. Bob's support for the disgraced councilman had been largely behind-the-scenes. The damage to his own reputation was containable. Hiring Precious Hargrove's only son would send a message that once again, he had landed on his feet. *It would practically make them family.*

The thought made him smile as the driver pulled up in front of the 191 Club and jumped out to open the door. At precisely two-fifteen, the same driver would return to drive Bob back to his office and the day's public presentation of *who* and *what* he was would be over. He would have arrived and departed in a style befitting any self-respecting power player in front of others of his kind. Atlanta was an O'Jays' kind of town: *People smilin' in your face, when all the time they want to take your place.* Bob knew that as well as anybody, but all those folks waiting for him to fall could just keep on *smilin'.* He wasn't going anywhere.

The 191 Club was one of those exclusive *members-only* establishments located at the top of one of Atlanta's downtown office towers. In addition to a main dining room, there were any number of private rooms, equipped with leather-bound books and fully stocked wet bars. The white-jacketed servers were known for their pleasant efficiency, the chef knew his way around a Southern kitchen, and the bartender was old-fashioned enough to make the mint juleps as strong at lunchtime as he did for happy hour.

On any given day, the mayor of Atlanta, the governor of Georgia, and an impressive roster of elected officials and corporate chief executives gathered there. This was a place where offers and counteroffers were made over drinks, careers were directed during the main course, and fortunes were invested over coffee. Bob Watson was a member of the board of directors. This was the official watering hole of the city's most active *movers and shakers* and everybody who came here knew it.

A firm believer in doing more than was expected during the early stages of a relationship, business or personal, Bob had reserved his favorite private dining room for lunch. He called this courting process "sweetening," but it was all about breaking down the other person's defenses by acting as if he or she had already been accepted into the rarefied realms where the Watsons of the world moved around so effortlessly. He intended to offer Kwame a position as a junior associate, and he wanted to show his young friend that if he came to work at the firm, everything about the experience would be *first-class.*

As he stepped off the elevator, the first person he saw in the small crowd around the hostess stand was Kwame Hargrove. Chatting as easily with Louis Adams, the editor and publisher of *The Sentinel,* as he had lingered to exchange ideas with Bob at city hall, the tall, handsome young man was at ease in a setting that might have intimidated someone less worldly. Watching Kwame talking and laughing with the club's regulars, Bob realized that this was beginning to look like a *win/win* situation. Those were Bob's favorite odds and he smiled as he approached the group.

"Who let the press in here?" he said, clapping Louis on the back and reaching to shake Kwame's hand.

"Don't tell my readers." Louis laughed. "My credibility will be shot."

"We are your readers," Bob said. "And have no fear. Your credibility is already shot."

"Love you, too, brother," Louis said, turning back to Kwame with a grin. "Make sure he picks up the check and give my best to the senator."

The woman had been out of politics for almost two years and they still called her senator, Bob thought. She was not only the front-runner. She was the *favorite*. He hadn't felt the political energy in this town so fully be-hind any candidate, announced or unannounced, since the possibility that Maynard Jackson could actually be elected mayor swept through Atlanta like a fever and carried him to victory on the power of the collective hopes and dreams of his people.

"I certainly will," said Kwame, turning back to Bob as Louis went off to join his party. "Pleasure to see you again, sir."

"I'm glad you could make it," Bob said, catching the eye of the smiling hostess, who picked up two menus and smiled even wider.

"If you'll follow me please, gentlemen?"

"I thought we could use a little privacy," Bob said as the hostess led them down a hallway lined with pictures of dead game birds and men on horseback. The carpet muffled their footsteps. "Sometimes when I come here for lunch, I spend so much time greeting friends, I can't get any busi-ness done."

"I understand," Kwame said, although he only wished he did.

The hostess opened the door to a small tastefully appointed dining room with a table set for two and the same spectacular view. A middle-aged black man with a round, pleasant face and a spotless white jacket entered the room and nodded to Bob as the hostess disappeared.

"Good afternoon, Roland," Bob said. "I'll have the usual. And for my guest?"

Bob knew this was a test of sorts. Kwame had no idea what *the usual* was. Hard liquor? A glass of wine? A beer? Coca-Cola Classic over ice with a slice of lemon? What if Kwame ordered a drink only to discover that Bob was a confirmed teetotaler? The moment presented a challenge for anyone without the courage of their convictions, but Kwame didn't blink.

"I'll have a Heineken."

Good choice, Bob thought. Nothing wrong with a beer at one o'clock in the afternoon. Bob was a member of the generation that always had a drink at lunch. Sometimes *two*. His *usual* was Meyer's rum on the rocks with a wedge of lime. Roland brought their drinks and took their lunch or-ders in one swift movement and left the two men alone.

"Sit down," Bob said, indicating a chair and taking one himself.

"It's a real honor to be sitting here with you, sir." Kwame brushed a nonexistent crumb off the crisply starched white linen tablecloth.

"Call me *Bob*."

"*Bob*." Kwame mentally ordered himself to banish the word *sir* from his vocabulary for at least the next two hours. "You're the reason I became an architect."

Bob always enjoyed anecdotes in which he was a source of pride, inspiration, or envy. He assumed this one would fall into the inspirational category.

"You gave the commencement speech when I graduated from high school," Kwame said. "I introduced you."

"That would make you the valedictorian." The honor of introducing the main speaker always went to the smartest kid in the class. That never seemed to change.

Kwame nodded.

"How was I?" Bob smiled.

"You were great. You said the challenge of our generation was to rethink the use of shared urban space." Kwame's voice was almost reverential. "You said there has to be a blurring of the distinctions between personal and communal space so that we begin to feel as protective and proprietary of our neighborhoods as we do of our living rooms."

"I still believe in that concept."

"I do, too."

The ice in Bob's glass tinkled softly as he sipped his rum. "Have you had a chance to check on those Victorians we talked about?"

"My information is that the owner isn't interested in selling any of them right now," Kwame said apologetically.

"Blue Hamilton is never interested in *selling*." Bob chuckled. "He's too busy *buying*."

Kwame just smiled, not confirming or denying Blue's ownership of a row of Victorian houses on Peeples' Street. They were worth millions of dollars already and their value would only continue to rise.

"My wife loves those houses, too," he said, hoping Bob didn't think he was being evasive. "She's had her eye on the big one in the middle of the block."

"Hamilton won't sell to her either?"

"It's not that," Kwame said. "I just think I'd like to try living in another neighborhood for a while."

"Are you really thinking of leaving West End?" An idea began to dawn at the back of Bob's mind.

"If I can convince my wife that there's life beyond Cascade Road. I'd like to find a place in midtown."

Bingo! Bob thought, delighted. Roland knocked on the door discreetly before entering with another server, who carried a tray with two covered dishes and a basket of homemade bread.

"Will there be anything else?" Roland said, whipping the tops off the food and releasing the smell of two perfectly grilled T-bone steaks into the air.

"Open us a nice bottle of Merlot," Bob said, "to complement these steaks, and I think we'll be set."

They chatted easily as the meal progressed. Bob asking questions so conversationally it hardly seemed like the interview Kwame knew that it was. He wasn't nervous as he told Bob about his experiences at Howard, his internship with Teddy, his move to Atlanta, and his most recent project. He wanted to present his best self to Bob Watson; a promising architect, a good son, a devoted husband and loving father. There was no need to confess that his mentor was also his lover.

For his part, Bob talked about his vision for the future of his company, their current expansion plans, and his confidence in the city itself.

"The next decade is going to be a period of unprecedented growth and development," he said over coffee, almost ready to seal the deal. "Watson and Associates is going to be a part of it, Kwame. We're going to be major players in reshaping this city for the next hundred years."

He leaned back and looked across the table as if waiting for an *amen.*

"It sounds exciting," Kwame said.

"It's damn exciting, and I'm inviting you to be part of it, too," Bob said. "Would you like to come and work with us at the firm?"

Kwame was momentarily speechless, overwhelmed at having his fantasy knock on the door and call his name. *Say something,* he scolded himself, *before the man reconsiders his offer!* "It would be an honor."

Bob smiled and extended his hand to Kwame, who shook it gratefully, hoping his palms weren't sweating, but convinced that they were.

"Good man," Bob said. "Welcome to the team!"

"Thank you, *Bob.*" That first name came a little easier now. "Thank you."

"I'd like to courier you over our salary offer and a benefits package in the morning. Take a look at it. Talk it over with your wife. I'll be traveling for the next four days, but I'll be back on Saturday morning. How about you and your missus—what's her name again?"

"Aretha."

"Why don't you and Aretha come by the house on Saturday night? I'll round up my partners and their wives, a few associates."

"I'd like that."

Bob stood up and went to the bar. "How about a brandy to seal the deal?"

Kwame wondered if Bob drank this much every day at lunch. He was already feeling a nice little buzz as Bob splashed the brandy into two snifters. But before they toasted, he turned back to Kwame slowly, the bottle still in his hand.

"There is one more thing."

Kwame practically held his breath like contestants do on game shows just before the host pulls back the curtain. Bob reached in his pocket and withdrew a set of keys. "I have a house I want you to take a look at."

Kwame sounded as confused as he felt. "A house?"

"When you said you were looking for a place in midtown, I couldn't help wondering if you'd consider Ansley Park," Bob said, sitting down again. "It's an ideal place to raise children. Big yard. Lots of space."

"I'm afraid we can't afford anything in that area yet."

"That's where the favor comes in," Bob said. "My wife and I moved three years ago, but I designed and built this house from scratch. It's my baby, so I can't part with it."

"You want me to *live* there?"

"Well, there would be rent, of course, but mostly I'm just desperate to get somebody in there who will appreciate it and stick around for a while."

He pushed the keys across the table toward Kwame. "It's empty. Go by and take a look at it. I'll write the address down for you."

"I know where it is," Kwame said, trying to fathom his good fortune.

"I think you and Aretha will love it. Take a look and let me know next Saturday when I get back to town."

"All right." Kwame slipped the keys into his pocket. "I will."

Bob handed Kwame a snifter, tapped it lightly with his own, tossed back the brandy in one big gulp, and stood up.

"I've got to go before I miss my flight, but that's no reason for you to rush your brandy," he said. "I think you're going to be a great addition to Watson and Associates." He extended his hand and grasped Kwame's firmly. "We're going to do business, young Hargrove. You wait and see. We're going to do big business."

27

It was Zora's kind of day. The spectacularly lovely Atlanta weather drove people out of their houses and into the streets. The West End Growers Association had enjoyed their first drought-free year in four summers, and even now, with the bountiful growing season officially over, the famous gardens were still bursting with sweet, impossibly juicy tomatoes, summer squash the color of sunshine, violet-hued eggplant, and sweet corn. The flower gardens were equally bountiful, overflowing with sunflowers, zinnias, assorted wildflowers, and all kinds of roses, from the palest amber to a red so deep it was almost purple.

Abernathy Boulevard, still the commercial heart of West End, was alive with shoppers and street vendors, all pursuing their small bit of the area's commerce with great enthusiasm. The West End Mall had as many people sitting on the pedestrian-friendly benches outside as it did window-shopping, but nobody seemed to mind. The twenty-four-hour beauty shop next to the West End News was full of patiently waiting women who knew this rare humidity-free moment would allow them to toss their freshly done hairdos around fearlessly for at least the next forty-eight hours.

There was a line inside and outside of the Krispy Kreme. Baseball legend Hank Aaron, the new owner, had destroyed a hundred people's dieting efforts by installing a drive-through where you could get a dozen dough-nuts in that flat, thin signature box so hot that you had to put them on the backseat to avoid burning your lap just carrying them home. The Ja-maican jerk-chicken specialists were in full swing next to the African cloth-ing store where merchandise had been hung outside to flutter up some paying customers.

Walking this route from her Lawton Place apartment to the University Center a few miles away was always an adventure for Zora. She enjoyed the crowded sidewalks, the spicy smells wafting from the restaurants on every corner, the greetings of the guys leaning in the barbershop door, waiting their turn. She even looked forward to buying a bag of fruit from the earnest young Muslim brothers on the corner in front of the bank who al-ways called her "Sister Zora" and invited her to services at the mosque.

Twice a day, sometimes more, Zora engaged in the street life of her neighborhood, but today, its charms were merely background. Her thoughts were focused on that soldier she'd met in D.C. She didn't know whether it was the unexpected beauty of Wes's face or the equally unex-pected vulnerability she'd glimpsed behind the macho facade, but Zora couldn't get him out of her mind. He was only nineteen and he was con-templating walking away from his post in the United State military in a time of war. If he got caught, he would be jailed or shot for desertion. If he wasn't caught, he would be forced to live as a fugitive. In that case, he would need all kinds of support, but would it even be legal to provide it?

Zora couldn't imagine Wes being a fugitive for long. He was so striking—"too fine" would be a more accurate description—to blend into the popula-tion easily. With those high cheekbones, big brown eyes, and impossibly long lashes, he was certain to draw admiring female glances wherever he went. All it took was one disgruntled girlfriend to blow his cover and his days as a fugitive would end with a trip to jail, or worse.

By the time she got to the Morehouse Medical School and took the steps to the tiny second-floor offices where Samson Epps ran his veterans' outreach program, Zora had dozens of questions she hoped he could an-swer. She'd been volunteering with Dr. Epps for only a few months, but she knew he was a walking resource guide to services available for vets and their families. If anybody would know how to guide Wes through whatever the military might throw at him, Dr. Epps would.

The door to the outside office was almost always open. A part-time secretary and two volunteers, plus Zora, shared the desk and the computer since they were rarely all there at the same time. But today, Dr. Epps himself sat at the desk, scribbling a note on a pink phone-message pad. His large head, old-school Afro, bushy beard, and broad shoulders raised the expectation of a much taller man, but Samson Epps was exactly five-six and one half inches tall. Zora had a good two inches on him. He had been divorced twice and Zora could see why. He was passionate about his work and dedicated to it, but in the name of being focused on a righteous cause, he was also overbearing, judgmental, unnecessarily brusque, and hard to please. Working for him was a challenge. Being married to him was probably a nightmare.

When he looked up and saw her, his habitually serious face lit up with a smile.

"There she is!" he crowed like she had just been nominated for an Oscar. "You just missed a call from *The Sentinel.* They're running Mr. Johnson's piece on our program in their weekend edition."

"This weekend?"

Dr. Epps nodded, tore the message off the pad, and handed it to Zora, still smiling. "They said Mr. Johnson especially wanted to thank you for bringing the program to his attention."

"I didn't expect it to be in the paper so fast."

"Frankly, I didn't either, but it couldn't come at a better time. This is exactly the kind of exposure we need."

The Sentinel was Atlanta's premiere black newspaper, with fifty thousand paying subscribers and a slew of Ida B. Wells Awards for journalistic excellence. A few weeks before, their investigative reporter, Burghardt Johnson, had done a terrifying story on the sudden spike in domestic violence and child abuse as the veterans of the Iraq war came home; confused, angry, disoriented, and disillusioned. The story painted a bleak picture of sad, violent, shell-shocked soldiers, long-suffering spouses, and frightened, helpless children.

It was a well-researched, well-written piece, but the conclusion offered no assistance or hope to those in the sometimes life-threatening situations the reporter had described, and Zora didn't appreciate it. She'd called the paper and invited Mr. Johnson to come and see what Dr. Epps was doing and write a follow-up story.

"Otherwise," she had said to Burghardt Johnson, "people are going to be left with nothing but fear and helplessness, and what good does that do?"

"None of this would have happened without you," Samson Epps said. "This is a real coup for us."

Zora smiled, remembering how nervous she had been before the interview.

"I probably shouldn't start counting our chickens," he said, heading back to his small office behind the reception area, "but come in my office for a minute, will you? I want to share something with you."

She followed him into his office. It was so full of books, magazines, and newspapers there was hardly room left for a desk and a chair for a visitor to squeeze into next to the door.

"Sit down, sit down."

He was reaching for a bright green folder on his desk. She could see the label on the outside said FUND-RAISING.

"Do you know what this is?" he said, lowering his voice conspiratorially even though there was no one in the office but the two of them.

Zora shook her head. It seemed too obvious to say "stuff about fund-raising?"

"This is a proposal that I've been working on for us to conduct a series of writing workshops for vets and their spouses. I've got some real interest from a few corporations, and with *The Sentinel* story, I'm sure we'll be able to get the funds raised in the next few months."

"That's great," she said, amused that he seemed to have forgotten she was the one who'd brought him the idea in the first place. "If there's anything I can do to help, I'd love to be involved."

Samson Epps nodded slowly, his hand still on the folder. "I knew you would say that, so I'm going to take you up on it." He extended the green folder. "I want you to review the preliminary work I've done and let me know if you think I'm headed in the right direction."

Zora was surprised and delighted. This was a huge increase in her role and responsibilities. "Of course. I'll look at it tonight and—"

He interrupted her pleasantly. "You don't have to do it that quickly. I'll be in Washington until Friday. Are you in on Monday?"

The schedule called for her on Tuesday, but that was the schedule for *interns.* She was now a *grant reviewer.* She could set her own schedule. "Yes."

"Good," he said, his attention already drawn to another folder before him. "We'll talk then."

"Okay," she said, getting up to go and suddenly realizing that she hadn't had a chance to ask him about Wes. "Dr. Epps?"

He looked up as if he was surprised to see her still standing there. "Yes?"

"I just wanted to ask you about . . ."

She hesitated. She couldn't just say, *I met this fine soldier who's thinking of dropping out of the war. Can we help him?*

"About what, Zora?"

"Last weekend when I went to D.C. for the student leaders' conference—"

"I've heard nothing but positive reviews of your participation."

"Thank you," she said, still casting around for the right words. "But while I was there, I met a soldier . . ."

"At the conference? I didn't know there were military involved."

She didn't correct the misunderstanding. Meeting at a conference sounded a lot more respectable than picking somebody up at a coffee shop. "He was on leave from Iraq. He had been there eight months. He's only nineteen and he's already seen so many of his friends killed or wounded that he's lost count."

Dr. Epps nodded, a sympathetic look on his face. He was a veteran of the Gulf War and understood the rigors of combat.

"And he said he was considering not going back."

Samson Epps raised his eyebrows. "What did he mean by that? Desertion from the field of battle?"

The way he said it, Zora instantly knew Dr. Epps didn't approve. She was sorry she had brought it up.

"I guess," she said. "He wasn't real specific or anything, but there are more and more guys thinking that same way and I was wondering if we were going to be offering any services to them."

"To deserters?" He sounded amazed that she would even suggest such a thing.

All she could do was nod. Dr. Epps just looked at her for a minute, a frown bunching his already bushy eyebrows even more.

"I'm glad you asked me about this, Zora, so we won't have any confusion about it later. This is a program dedicated to rebuilding the lives and families of men and women who have served their country honorably. We have no obligation to, and I personally have no use for, deserters. Do I make myself clear?"

Zora clutched the green folder to her chest, suddenly fearful he would grab it out of her hands for even bringing up Wes's plight.

"Yes, sir," she said quietly. "Thank you for clarifying that for me."

"You're welcome," he said. "I don't think our federal funding would last very long if the army found out we were aiding and abetting deserters, do you?"

She shook her head. "I understand."

"Good. Then let's get back to work."

She pulled Dr. Epps's office door closed behind her and sat down to collect her thoughts. She hadn't expected such a strong negative reaction. She understood completely, but that didn't mean she had to agree.

28

Leaving the 191 Club, Kwame immediately drove to Bob's empty house. A gleaming glass-and-chrome showpiece, it stood proudly at the top of a hill at the end of a tree-lined street crowded with stately old mansions and the large, rambling, perfectly restored homes favored by the city's younger traditionalists, who kept the facades but gutted the insides to add skylights, playrooms, entertainment centers, and home offices. Kwame had read about the opposition to Bob's house and it was easy to see why the neighbors had balked when the three-story structure began to take shape in their midst. The house grabbed your attention and held it. It made everything around it look stodgy and fussy and certainly not *of the moment* in any way that mattered. Bob said they had learned to love the house, but Kwame suspected they had simply made peace with it. This house was not looking for love. It was asserting dominance.

Using the key Bob had given him, he opened the front door, stepped inside, and took a look around. He could imagine himself living here. The vast open spaces and floor-to-ceiling windows in almost every room reflected Bob's design ideas, creating an environment that was as starkly modern on the inside as it was on the outside. Kwame liked the clean lines and the light. He admired the hardwood floors and what looked like a new coat of expensive ivory-colored paint. The kitchen was fully equipped with a Sub-Zero refrigerator and a stove that looked big enough to service a restaurant. The kitchen windows looked out on a large, startlingly green yard with a peaceful stand of hardwood trees rather than the ubiquitous Georgia pines.

The upstairs rooms were large and bright and featured a master suite with an opulent bathroom that boasted two showers, two sinks, a Jacuzzi, and a bidet. Kwame smiled. *This Negro is living,* he thought, wondering how many of the people who had been in this room had ever seen a real bidet, much less used one. The third floor was one large open space with a huge fireplace and a wall of built-in bookshelves. This was the room he would claim as his sanctum, he thought. The place to which he could retreat in the evenings for reading, reflection, creative contemplation. A man needed some personal space in his household, space he didn't have to share with his daughter's dinosaur collection.

Heading back downstairs, Kwame tried to imagine Aretha's reaction to this house. She would probably hate it at first. Looking out of the living-room windows at the terraced front yard, he knew this was a big leap from West End, but he was confident she could handle it. It wasn't really up to her anyway. *Not this time,* he thought. If Ansley Park could get used to Bob's baby, Aretha could, too.

He closed the glass front door behind him with a soft click and stood listening to the sound of what was soon to be his neighborhood. Birds. That's all he heard. No traffic. No sirens. No boom boxes blasting the latest offering from the hip-hop nation. *Birds.* Heading for his car, parked in what was soon to be his own driveway, he knew that was at least one thing Aretha would like about this place. She was big on birds.

As he pulled away from the house, stealing one last glance in the rearview mirror, he could hardly believe how much his life had changed in the last few hours. He'd been offered a great job and he had no doubt the salary would be competitive. He'd been handed the keys to a fabulous house in one of Atlanta's most prestigious zip codes and he'd been invited to bring his wife to meet the boss on Saturday night. If he had written down his hopes for the day, his imagination could never have come up with anything this perfect. It was, he knew, one of those moments in life when you have to just *go for it.* Even when it seems crazy to other people, even when those other people love you, you have to keep your eye on the prize and step out on faith. That's exactly what Kwame intended to do.

He pulled out his cellphone, threw caution to the winds, and dialed Teddy's number in D.C. After all, it had been his friend who had set all this in motion. It was time to share the good news.

29

Lee decided to reward herself for a job well done. She didn't like to work a room, but she was good at it, and if there had been any doubt, the last two hours were proof positive. She had been around long enough now to know that what she used to regard as hours wasted in meaningless schmoozing were in fact a wise investment in her own future. The event she had gone to tonight was a perfect example. After years in cramped quarters, the Feminist Women's Health Center had moved into a beautiful new facility and their many friends had come to offer congratulations, along with their continued and active support.

The center's director was already an enthusiastic supporter of the peace-precinct idea, and as Lee moved through the crowded reception she was gratified at the enthusiastic response she was getting from people who were beginning to hear about it and wanted to help. Lee knew this gathering would bring together in one room the very constituency she hoped to reach. Not only that, they were there to celebrate the survival of a pro-choice institution in a *no-choice* environment. Everybody would be in a good mood.

In dressing for the event, she had given some consideration to wearing her uniform. It was effective pro-police propaganda, but in overwhelmingly female gatherings, it intimidated some people. Besides, she wasn't attending as her *current self.* She was going as the woman who not only had a great idea, but the energy and connections to get it done. That woman's uniform was a well-cut suit, a good pair of pumps, and a purse big enough to stash her badge and her .38 and still look festive.

She had already greeted the host committee and dropped a twenty in the omnipresent fund-raising fishbowl, when she glanced up and saw Precious Hargrove headed her way.

"Captain Kilgore," she said, sticking out her hand like a good politician. "I put you on my call list for first thing tomorrow morning, and here you are!"

"Senator Hargrove," Lee said. "It's good to see you again so soon."

"I read your proposal for the peace precinct last night. That's why I wanted to call you. There's no question that Mandeville Maids will be involved."

"I'm so pleased to hear that!" This was an understatement. Lee was delighted. Precious brought instant credibility and a constituency that was already in place.

"It's a great idea," Precious said. "I'd like to work with you on it in whatever way would be most helpful. We can hash out the details next time we talk, which I hope will be soon."

"Count on it," Lee said, and they shook hands again before Precious moved away to greet another admirer.

Lee stayed around for another half hour or so, but as far as she was concerned, the party was over. *Mission accomplished.* She was a happy woman and it was only eight-fifteen. Cruising down Peachtree Street with no particular place to go, she decided to treat herself to dinner. Turning the car sharply at the next corner, she pulled into the valet parking outside Silk without giving herself time to second-guess the decision. She stepped into the soft, humid air of the fall night and loved the feel of the slight breeze against her face. She was glad she hadn't worn her uniform.

Silk was the kind of restaurant where they remembered your name if you came in more than twice. Lee was a regular. The smiling hostess seated her in a corner booth near the sushi bar, where the raw fish looked so fresh and inviting, she was tempted, but decided on the filet mignon instead. She relaxed into the serene beauty of the restaurant, congratulating herself on the decision to take a minute to enjoy herself. She had earned it.

Her salad hadn't even arrived when Lee heard the faint ringing of her telephone. The sound annoyed her. She was off duty and she intended to stay off duty. The phone rang again, softly but clearly audible, and a tall, fashionably thin woman with frizzy blond hair and artfully faded jeans, who was nibbling raw octopus at the sushi bar, turned around slightly and frowned her disapproval. Lee couldn't even be angry. She also hated cell-phones in public places. She reached into her bag and hit the mute button. That satisfied the blond woman, who turned back to her dinner. Glancing down, Lee recognized Bob's number on her caller ID.

"Hold on," she said, getting up. A ringing phone could be forgiven. A conversation was just bad manners. On the sidewalk outside, she stepped clear of arriving diners before she spoke again. "Sorry, I'm in a restaurant."

"Did you see the six o'clock news?"

"No, I was—"

He didn't let her finish the sentence. "There's been a murder. In the old fourth ward."

"Anybody we know?" The old fourth ward was the heart of their co-caine operation.

"How the hell would I know?" He sounded agitated. "I thought that was your job."

"Well, what *do* you know?" At this point, she needed details, not accu-sations.

"A couple of days ago this kid, high-school kid, disappears. His mom knows he's been hanging out with a rough crowd, so she's worried. She's asking people if they've seen Junior. *Where's Junior? Where's Junior?*"

"That's his name? Junior?" That didn't narrow it down. Half the guys in the neighborhood were called Junior by their mamas even if they'd never seen their daddies.

"Junior, Lil' Man, how the hell do I know?"

She resisted the impulse to comment on his tone of voice. "Go on."

"So she keeps poking her nose around, looking for Junior, and some of that bad crowd decided it was time for her to back off, so they sent her his dick home in a shoe box."

"What?"

"She stepped outside to get the paper and there was the box with a note that told her where to find the rest of her son if she wanted him."

"*Jesus!*"

"That's not all. They dropped his dickless ass body on the steps of his mother's church, which is where she found him."

The idea of a celebratory dinner suddenly seemed beside the point. This was dangerous. There hadn't been that kind of violence in the area in years. This was no time for it all to start up again. "All that was on the news?"

"Including the mother, live and in living color, demanding justice and accusing a rogue element in the police force of protecting the very cocaine dealers who killed her son."

Lee groaned. Murder and mutilation had never been part of the plan. "I'm on it."

"You should have *been* on it."

"You're right," she said, wondering why people wasted so much time in a crisis finger-pointing when *action* was required, not *recrimination*. "I'll call you when I find out what's going on?"

She snapped her phone closed without waiting for his good-bye. So this was why she hadn't been able to shake that bad feeling. This was what she had been trying to outrun and now here it was, knocking at the door and calling her name out loud. She took another step away from Silk's front door and punched in a number.

"Yo," the deep male voice answered roughly before the first ring was complete. "What up?"

"We need to talk," Lee said, skipping the formalities. She could hear loud music and people talking. "Where are you?"

"At Baltimore. Where you at?"

"I'm on my way. Have the valet meet me out front."

"You must have seen that crazy bitch on the six o'clock news."

Lee stopped him midsentence. She never trusted cellphones. "I'll come upstairs as soon as I get there. Don't make me have to find you."

"You ain't got to worry about that. I'm gonna be the first nigga you see in VIP, just like always."

She closed the phone without saying good-bye and sighed at this sudden change of plans. The last thing she wanted to do was meet T. G. Thomas and ask him what in the hell was going on in the area where he was supposed to be keeping order. Even worse, he was waiting for her at one of those Buckhead clubs where the music was always too loud and the frantic search for instant gratification was not simply the norm, but the universal cover charge. What she wanted to do was turn back the clock fifteen minutes, before she'd answered her phone.

Now she had no choice. All she could do was turn her attention to the business at hand. Her new life, and her steak, would have to wait.

B altimore was the second club to occupy the space on the corner of Buckhead Avenue and Peachtree Street. The first, a spot called Ellington's, had been forced to close after an unfortunate stabbing incident that had resulted in two deaths, a celebrity murder trial, and the unavoidable loss of the owner's liquor license. The new order had taken advantage of the location's notoriety by renaming it after the hometown of the superstar athlete who had been involved in the fracas, retaining most of the old staff and reopening almost immediately with a minimum of changes to the interior. Many patrons were unaware that the club had even changed hands.

Lee allowed herself to be led upstairs to the VIP area, although she knew exactly where it was. She had no doubt T.G. would be waiting for her inside. This was serious, and he knew it as well as she did. She stepped into the dimly lit area and glanced around. The room was furnished with several couches, some comfortable chairs, and stacks of big floor pillows arranged in cozy groupings or pulled up in front of the glass wall for an unobstructed view of the crowded dance floor.

Aside from T.G., whom she spotted immediately, there were several other men present, laughing and pointing at the dancers below. The music made it impossible to hear their voices, but their body language indicated an easy physical intimacy that made Lee suddenly focus on the fact that unlike her other visits to Baltimore, this time there were no other women around. One of the men looked vaguely family to her, but she looked away before he caught her staring.

T.G. watched her from a love seat tucked away in as quiet a corner as could be found in the place. He didn't get up as she approached, nor did she expect him to. This was not a social call.

"You drinkin'?" He indicated a glass ice bucket nearby where a bottle of Cristal was chilling. Tall and well built, he was attractive and slightly intimidating, a combination he exploited in all his relationships. His grandmother had given him the nickname T.G. for "tough guy" when he was seven.

"I'm *listening*."

"That nigga was stealing."

She narrowed her eyes and looked at him. "So you cut his dick off and send it to his mother?"

He shrugged. "Like I said, he was stealin'."

T.G. was twenty-eight, already old for the cocaine business. The murder of a small-time dealer was no big deal to him. Lee had to make him understand that it was a very big deal. Her look told him she was waiting for a more complete explanation of what had gone down.

"Look, his mama was pokin' her nose in all over the place. Knockin' on people's doors. Talkin' about goin' to the police with what homeboy had told her."

"And what did he tell her?"

T.G. took a sip of champagne and looked at Lee. "He told her the police were involved."

"What made him think that?"

"Niggas always talkin' about shit ain't none a they business. Who know where he heard it?"

"I want you to find out."

"What you think we was tryin' to do when we cut his shit off?"

"You know his mother?"

"Sure. She was always around trying to get him to quit hangin' out. She thought we was corruptin' him."

"Do you think she'll calm down?"

T.G. considered the question. The two men across the room had ordered their champagne and the tall one who looked familiar to Lee was doing the honors. The dance floor was filling up with brothers in baggy jeans and oversize T-shirts that would not have distinguished them from any other hip-hop heads except for the complete absence of women.

"I don't know," T.G. said slowly. "That nigga the only son she got ain't dead or already in jail."

The music was giving Lee a headache. She pinched the bridge of her nose.

T.G. put down his glass and leaned a little closer. "You want me to take care of it?"

"That's what started all this in the first place," she snapped. "I don't want you to do a damn thing until I tell you."

"Nuthin'?"

"Nothing at all. Let the woman bury her son. Nobody's going to talk for a while after what you did."

"That's why we did it," T.G. said, without any discernible shred of remorse.

Lee looked at him, her eyes as cold as his were. "Two things. If you ever do some psycho shit like this again, I'll send *your* dick home to *your* mama in a damn box."

He didn't flinch, but he knew she wasn't kidding. "What's the other thing?"

"How long has this club been gay?"

"It ain't gay," T.G. said, grinning. "This down-low night."

"I see."

"Don't worry, boss. I ain't no faggot, but just between you and me? Some of these brothers can suck a dick better than a bitch."

Obviously, she thought, his definition of what was and was not gay was more fluid than her own. It was time to go. Lee stood up.

"I'll be in touch. Keep your eyes open."

"Will do." In a sudden burst of gentlemanliness, he stood up, too.

"And, T.G.?"

"Yeah?"

"Use a condom."

"You know it, boss." He winked and patted the pocket of his oversize denim shirt.

Halfway home, Lee suddenly realized that the tall young man in the VIP room watching the dancers and pouring champagne was Precious Hargrove's very married son. She couldn't remember his name, but that was a small detail. The point was, the front-runner seemed to have a son *on the down low.* How the poor bastard figured he could pull off a double life in the relentless glare of the political spotlight was a mystery to Lee. VIP rooms at the club on down-low night aren't a very good place to hide, but he seemed oblivious. She picked up her cellphone and punched in Bob's number on the speed dial.

"Well?" He was obviously still nursing the same foul mood. His tone made her realize that she didn't want to share this latest tidbit with him. For now, she would simply report in and keep her own counsel.

"Everything is under control," she said, sounding like any good vice president charged with putting out a corporate fire.

"Are you sure?"

"I'm sure."

"You better be."

He hung up as abruptly as he had answered. Lee didn't care. She hadn't lied. Things were under control. The question was, *whose control?*

31

B y the time Baby Brother pulled into the parking lot beside the More-house Medical School, his sister's car was running on fumes. He'd driven the ten hours from D.C. straight through and arrived in Atlanta broke, exhausted, and annoyed at the insanity of the rush-hour traffic, as if the city had arranged it just to slow down his progress. He pulled off the freeway near the state capital and drove around for ten minutes, wasting gas and looking for a pay phone. He found two quarters in the loose change his sister, a nonsmoker, always kept in her ashtray, and called the number Zora had given him.

"Veterans Support Project," a male voice answered on the second ring. "Dr. Epps speaking."

"Can I speak to Zora?"

"She's not here," Dr. Epps said. "Can I help you with something?"

"Yeah, well, Zora said if I got to Atlanta to call you and you'd know how to find her."

There was a slight pause. "Are you a veteran?"

Technically, yes, Baby Brother thought. "Yeah, I'm a veteran."

"Are you driving?"

The questions were routine, but they annoyed Baby Brother. "Yeah, so?"

"Why don't you come by the office? I'll call Zora and tell her you've arrived. She'll probably want to meet you here. Do you need directions?"

That was the stupidest question yet. "Yeah."

Fifteen minutes later, Baby Brother was sitting in the project office, wondering where Zora was and being gently but firmly grilled by Samson Epps.

"I'm sorry about your mother," Dr. Epps said, after asking Baby Brother his current status with the army. He had seemed surprised that Baby Brother wasn't in uniform until he explained he was home on personal leave for a funeral. "How much leave did they give you?"

Baby Brother stood up, frowning. "Hey, look, man, I didn't come here for no counseling and shit. I'm just waiting for Zora, *aw-iiight?*"

As if on cue, before Samson could respond, Zora walked through the door, spotted Baby Brother, smiled, and stuck out her hand. Both men stood when she entered the room, either from politeness or simply because, as Baby Brother immediately recognized, *she was looking very, very good.* Her hair was pulled back from her face and her smile was as dazzling as he remembered. Her low-slung jeans were sexy without being obvious and he could glimpse the curve of her breast under her gauzy brown peasant blouse.

"Hey, Wes," she said, extending her hand to him. "You made it."

"Yeah, well . . ." He didn't know quite what to say. "Here I am."

"You met Dr. Epps?"

Samson nodded. "We've been getting to know each other."

Zora picked up the disapproval in Samson's tone and ignored it. "Good. Do you want to grab some breakfast before I have to go to class?"

"That's cool," he said, glad they were leaving this place. He was tired of answering questions.

"See you tomorrow, Dr. Epps," Zora said, leading the way out.

Baby Brother followed her happily, enjoying the view from behind. She wasn't driving, so she rode with him the few blocks to her apartment. He was glad he had enough gas to make it without asking her for money. She directed him to a parking space behind her building and he followed her through what looked like a great big garden and around to the bright blue front door. She reached into her pocket for her key and then turned to look at him with an expression he couldn't read.

He smiled what he hoped was a neutral smile. Who knew what the day would hold if he played his cards right and didn't act a fool.

She smiled back. "I don't know you very well, so I want to be really clear about things, okay?"

"What things?"

"I'm glad you came. I want to get to know you better. But this morning, all we're going to do is have breakfast and talk."

He grinned at her. "Damn, baby you slam the door in a brother's face before he even gets his foot in it."

"Call me Zora, okay?"

"Okay, *Zora*. This is just two friends talkin' over some bacon and eggs. Period."

"I'm a vegetarian," she said, but her smile widened.

"Okay, *bean sprouts* and eggs."

She actually giggled at that one and Baby Brother thought that even just breakfast would be a treat with a woman as fine as this one.

"I'll try and do better than that," she said, opening the blue door and leading him upstairs to her second-floor apartment. The inside door was unlocked and there were no burglar bars. She had a big old couch with a slouchy slipcover, a desk by the window, and a couple of well-used pillows stacked in the corner that were meant to substitute for chairs.

She dropped her book bag on the couch. "Come on in the kitchen," she said, clicking a CD to life on the small boom box on the desk. He recognized the voice of Alicia Keys lamenting the fact that some oblivious brother didn't even know her name.

"Sit down," Zora said, nodding at a tiny table and two chairs. "I'll make some coffee."

"I didn't know vegetarians could drink coffee."

"Where'd you hear that? The rule is don't eat anything with a face on it. That makes coffee beans fair game."

She moved around her kitchen easily, putting on the coffee, setting out cups, a small pitcher of cream, and an oversize sugar bowl. He remembered how much she had sweetened her coffee in D.C. and smiled to himself. She caught the look and smiled back at him.

"Sugar doesn't have a face either."

He laughed and she realized how different he looked when he smiled. Younger, cuter, *sweeter.* She reminded herself of the limitations she had imposed on their time together.

"How about an omelet?"

"Sounds good," he said, the words alone eliciting an audible growl of anticipation from his very empty stomach. "I'm starving."

"This won't take long," she said, cracking eggs in a bowl.

His eyes watched the gentle movement of her body inside her blouse. "You know something Zora?"

"What's that?"

"You even look good cookin'."

"You're just hungry." She laughed, reaching for the whisk.

"I ain't too hungry to recognize a fine woman when I see one."

"Thanks," she said, putting two slices of bread in the toaster. "Now why don't you tell me about your plan?"

Baby Brother was confused. "What plan?"

"Well, you came here, right?"

"Right."

She was putting out two plates, a couple of forks. She poured two glasses of juice. He immediately drank his.

"So what are you going to do now?"

She refilled his glass. The question hung in the air between them. Zora sliced some tomatoes that had been ripening in her kitchen window. He didn't have the foggiest idea what he was going to do. He had thought she would help him. Beyond that, there was no plan.

"Can't that program you work for help me?"

"I thought they could, but Dr. Epps won't help anybody who doesn't get an honorable discharge. He thinks it will jeopardize his grant money." She shook her head and slid a perfect omelet out of the pan. "He's being a real asshole about it."

The plate she set down in front of him held the best-looking meal he'd seen in months. Baby Brother decided that the fact the guy she worked for wasn't going to be of assistance hardly mattered. He was having breakfast with a beautiful woman, in her apartment, and he hadn't been in town three hours. So far, he seemed to be doing fine without much of a plan. He took a big bite of his eggs and beamed at Zora across the table.

"Eat your breakfast," she said. "We'll figure it out."

That *we* was worth the price of admission all by itself. When they finished eating, she stacked the dishes in the sink and poured them both some coffee. After adding enough sugar and cream to suit her, she suggested they move back to the living room. He sat down on the couch. She tossed down one of the pillows and sat cross-legged at his feet, her back as straight as a dancer's.

"Do you know anybody else in Atlanta?"

"Just you. That's why I came here, remember?"

"I know and I feel bad."

"Don't feel bad. Something will work out." He had no idea what that something might be.

"Things never just work out. The first thing we have to do is see what your options are."

He smiled and sipped his coffee. "Maybe I can just hang out for a while here with you until I get my bearings."

Zora raised her eyebrows slightly. "Well, you're homeless, jobless, and wanted for questioning by your favorite uncle, Sam. Seems to me like all you're offering is *a mouthful of gimmee and a handful of if you please.*"

He groaned. "Now you sound like my sister."

"Maybe you should have listened to her."

He didn't like the change in the conversational tone. "You're the one who told me to come here, remember? You said that guy Epps could do something for me. So now I'm here and all of a sudden he ain't down? What do you expect me to do? Live on the street? Start robbin' people?"

"Are those the only two options you can think of?"

Baby Brother put down his cup and stood up. "Hey, you know what? I don't need this shit. I don't know what game you're playin', but I don't have time for it, okay?"

Zora looked at him calmly, unfazed by his bluster. "Sit down and drink your coffee. All I'm saying is what about trying to get a job? What you do?"

He could have listed the skills he'd learned on the street—selling dope, stealing cars, shooting dice—but he didn't think those were the kinds of jobs she was talking about. "I been in the army, okay? But none of what they showed me how to do translates back in the real world. Ain't no tanks to fix around here. Ain't no bombs in the street that need to be checked out."

"You're right," she said, her face and her tone suddenly softer. "I apologize."

"Apology accepted," Baby Brother said, relieved.

"Look, I know a guy who can get you a job," she said. "It'll be off-the-books so the army can't come looking for you and he might even be able to hook you up with an apartment until you get yourself together."

"Another friend of yours like Epps?"

"Dr. Epps is an asshole about some stuff," she said, "but he does a lot of good stuff, too."

"So how do I know this other guy isn't going to act funny once you tell him I'm a deserter?"

"He won't care about that."

Baby Brother raised his eyebrows. "Oh yeah? Why is that?"

"He's against the war. He doesn't think anybody should fight in it."

"Well, that's a brother after my own heart. When can I talk to him?"

"Hold on, hold on. That's not how it works." Zora smiled at his sudden enthusiasm.

He frowned. "How what works?"

"You don't just go see Mr. Hamilton. You make an appointment."

"Okay, then make me an appointment."

"I will, but you need to understand that Mr. Hamilton is not a person who has any tolerance for bullshit."

"What's that supposed to mean?"

Zora smiled at him again. "It means you got a lot going for you, but you also got a lot of bullshit."

She sounded so sweet when she said it, he couldn't even get mad.

"Yeah, so what?"

"So don't try it with Mr. Hamilton. Just tell him the truth."

"Okay. I promise."

"I'll hold you to it," Zora said, picked up the phone, and dialed the West End News.

32

Blue had been at Tybee for almost a week. He and General had a lot of catching up to do. It was ten o'clock at night, but that was not unusual. After dinner until closing at midnight was always the slowest part of the day at the West End News. Morning was usually hectic with people trying to get their papers on the way to work and students coming off all-night study sessions looking for a hot cup of real espresso to kick-start their day. At noon, people came in with carryout meals from the area's many restaurants, looking for the latest celebrity tabloids to peruse as they sat in the park enjoying the sunshine and imagined living somebody else's life.

By three thirty, lunch was over and everybody was where they were going to be until five o'clock. Jimmy, the man behind the counter, would make fresh coffee, clean the cappuccino machine, and do a quick visual check to see what was running low so he could restock the shelves before their late-day customers started coming in for the evening paper and any neighborhood news they might have missed. Once this last wave cleared out, there were only a few regulars who came by to talk to Jimmy while he got things ready for the following morning. This was also the time when Blue and General tended to have their informal daily briefings. They often went their separate ways for big chunks of time, but once a day, they sat face-to-face and talked. Their routine since their days on the road had served them so well for so long, neither saw any reason to change it.

Blue's office was at the back of the newsstand, situated at the end of a short hallway crammed with back issues of a dizzying array of national and international publications and secured by a steel security door. In the technical sense, it wasn't an office. There were no telephones, computers, or office machines. Blue did all his real business by talking to people. Real estate transactions, royalty agreements, and tax preparations he left to trusted professionals, but all other business was conducted one-on-one. That cut way down on the possibility of any misunderstandings.

When people came to see Blue at the West End News, they found themselves in what had once been an old-fashioned ice-cream parlor. The large room with its traditional black-and-white-tiled floor had several small tables and a slightly larger one where Blue always sat, drinking one of the many espressos he consumed over the course of a day, listening to people ask for his advice, his help, his protection. General often sat in the room at a corner table, but he rarely ate or drank anything. He was too busy watching. Part of General's job was to sense fear or danger before it became a problem and he was good at it.

This morning, listening to the woman who had come to Blue asking for emergency housing because her husband had threatened her life, broken her wrist, and blackened her eye, General had felt himself wondering how long it would be before this same woman found herself sneaking off to see the same fool who had frightened her so badly she finally fled, fearing for her life. It had been happening more and more. They were having a serious problem with women sneaking these guys into the safe apartments Blue made available as emergency shelters. That put General in the impossible position of trying to patrol these women's houses like they were teenage girls suspected of violating curfew. He needed clarification about how to address the problem.

"Are you sure it's the same men?" Blue said after General explained what was going on.

"I'm sure," General said. "We've got pictures of all these guys so we can keep an eye out for them. When I got the call last night, I went around there myself just to be sure. It was him all right."

"Had he been warned?"

"He said she invited him, so he figured it was okay." General said.

"What did she say?"

"She said she didn't need anybody all up in her business and I could go to hell."

Blue slowly shook his head. His eyes had gone from robin's-egg blue to midnight in the space of a few short minutes.

"I told her she had until Sunday night to make other living arrangements, and that if I saw him around again, he wouldn't get off with a warning."

"How old is this one?"

"She's twenty-two. He was in Iraq for eighteen months. Turned twenty-five during the first bombing of Fallujah."

Blue nodded slowly. "I remember her. He was beating her so badly she lost a baby."

"She lost *two*."

Draining his espresso, Blue pushed the cup away. These women were exposing everyone to a danger they knew better than anyone else. He couldn't imagine what drove them back to the arms of these cruel men, but he didn't have to understand it. He just had to be sure it didn't undo what he was trying to do for them and their children.

"We've already warned these guys," General said. "The last official word they had from me was to steer clear of West End." He shrugged his massive shoulders. "I think we'd be within our rights to take care of it."

Blue knew what General meant and he shook his head. "This isn't that kind of problem."

"This is what you say it is."

What General didn't understand was that Blue's help had to be both *invited* and *freely given*. Tipping the balance based on who had *the right* to take it to the next level was counterproductive and ultimately self-destructive.

"You did the right thing, telling her she had to go and warning him again," Blue said, affirming General's good judgment, but clearly vetoing his suggested solution. "Make sure one of your guys offers her a ride if she needs it."

General nodded. He never argued with Blue, even when he disagreed. That wasn't the nature of the relationship and neither one ever forgot it.

"And keep me posted if it continues to be a problem," Blue said.

"It's going to continue to be a problem. You can count on that."

Blue knew his friend was right and suddenly he was weary of trying to save the race, *one crazy Negro at a time.* He decided to share some good news for a change.

"Are we through with this for now?"

"I got it covered," General said.

"Good. Then I've got one more thing to tell you."

"I'm listening."

"Gina's pregnant," Blue said with a proud smile. "I'm going to be a father."

General's joy couldn't have been more complete. He literally whooped, leaped from the chair, and hugged Blue, clapping him on the back and practically dancing him around in celebration. Somewhere, he knew Juanita was dancing, too.

"Oh, damn, man! *Damn!* Congratulations! I can't believe your black ass is going to be somebody's daddy!"

Blue laughed, his eyes twinkling happily. "You better believe it. I want you to be the godfather."

General's smile froze on his face. "You want *me* to be the godfather?"

"I think that's the way Juanita would have wanted it, don't you?"

"Yeah, man," General said, feeling the tears prickling behind his eyes. "I think that's exactly what she would have wanted. It's an honor, brother. A real honor."

"Good," Blue said. "I'll tell Regina."

General was watching Blue closely as if he wanted to say something but hadn't quite found the words.

"What?" Blue said.

"You ever think about letting this godfather shit go?" General said quietly. "Now that you're having a kid and all."

"When I accepted this responsibility, there wasn't any time limit on it," Blue said quietly.

General ran his hand over his close-cropped hair. "You think we'll be doing this when we're two old Negroes with bad feet and no driving skills?"

"Nothing changes but the changes."

They looked at each other, and if General was hoping for more clarification in Blue's eyes, he didn't find it.

"Then let's drink a toast to the next generation of you blue-eyed, past-life motherfuckers," General said, grinning as he headed for the bottle of cognac Blue always kept behind the ice-cream counter. "We need as many of y'all as we can get!"

33

Kentavious Robinson's mother looked around Precious Hargrove's office and felt small. Mamie Robinson knew everything about her looked wrong in a place where one chair probably cost more than everything in her whole apartment. The thought made her nervous and angry at the same time. She gulped down a few swallows from the icy-cold Coca-Cola the secretary had brought her when she first arrived, then stopped herself. Lord knows she didn't want to have to ask if she could use the bathroom.

Mamie wondered how long she'd have to wait. Her nerves were already bad, but she had no choice. She had to come here because of her child. It was wrong how they had killed her son and nobody seemed to be able or willing to do a thing about it. That's why she had put on her one good dress and a pair of heels, even if she didn't have any stockings left, and come down to see Precious Hargrove.

She knew it was a long shot. *What does this woman care about my Kentavious?* Mamie thought. Her beautiful, angry, *hurry-up* child. He'd done everything too early. Walked at eight months. Had almost all his teeth before his first birthday. She had to stop nursing him before she really wanted to because he'd bit her nipples until they bled. Now he had died too soon. *Fifteen years ain't no time to live a life,* Mamie thought. *You're still stupid as hell. Don't even have time to grow up and correct your shit and, BAM! You gone.* Like her child was gone. Forever.

Realizing there were tears running down her face, she wiped her eyes with the back of her hand, wishing she had a handkerchief. That's when the door opened and Senator Hargrove walked in carrying a briefcase.

"Hold my calls, please," she said to the woman in the outer office as she closed the door behind her, dropped her briefcase on her desk, walked over to Mamie, and held out her hand. "Mrs. Robinson? I'm Precious Hargrove. I'm sorry you had to wait. Can I get you anything?"

The woman looked a lot prettier in person than she did on television, Mamie thought. "No, I just . . . I saw your ads on TV during that campaign you had and you kept sayin' 'my door is always open.' So I figured I'd come by and see if you meant it."

That campaign was five years ago, Precious thought, sitting down across from Mamie. She knew all about Kentavious Robinson's murder. The brutality of the killing, the youth of the victim, and his mother's public collapse at the cemetery that almost toppled her into her son's grave had all propelled the story to the top of the six o'clock news for days.

Precious had reached out to the family right after the story broke, but the angry young man with whom she'd left a message had probably never relayed it to this exhausted-looking woman. It was hard to tell how old she was, but Precious placed her at right around forty. Mrs. Robinson looked like she'd been crying. That wasn't surprising, Precious thought. *If I was living her life, I'd be crying, too.*

"I was sorry to hear about the death of your son."

Mamie's eyes filled with tears and she shook her head sadly. "It ain't right. Kentavious wasn't no *gangsta* like his brothers. I know he wadn't no angel, but what did he do that was so bad? Sellin' a little weed to some of his boys? It mighta been wrong, what he was doin', but he didn't deserve to die for it. They didn't have to cut him up like that."

Looking at the heartbroken mother, Precious thanked her lucky stars one more time that she had been able to raise Kwame in peace, but she knew West End was only one tiny oasis. A few miles away, there was nothing but cruelty and chaos.

"Have the police arrested any suspects?" Precious asked.

"Suspects? They ain't got to look for no suspects. They know who did that to my boy. They *been* knowin'."

Precious frowned slightly, but her voice stayed even. "What do you mean?"

"I mean, they all in on it, too."

"The police?"

"Yeah, the police. They protectin' these coke dealers because they payin' 'em to look the other way. They were afraid my son might tell what he knew."

Precious leaned forward and took Mrs. Robinson's hand. It was damp with tears and sweat. "That's a very serious charge you're making."

Mamie didn't blink. "Why you think I came down here? Everybody else scared to help me or they takin' money."

"I don't really have any powers over the police department."

"I thought you was gonna be the mayor."

"That's a long time from now."

Precious wondered if Mrs. Robinson had ever voted. The charges the woman was making were explosive. The wiser course was probably not to get involved at all.

"So what was all that about the open door?"

"I was in the state legislature then," Precious said, knowing she might as well have said, *That's when I was living at the North Pole.* "But I still wouldn't have had any power over the Atlanta Police Department. The two governments don't work that way."

Mamie withdrew her hand and stood up. "Then I guess I wasted your time and mine by comin' here."

"I'm so sorry," Precious said. "But at this point, I don't know what you want me to do."

Mrs. Robinson lifted her chin. "I want you to do whatever you'd do if some niggas sent your son's dick home in a shoe box."

The two women looked at each other and in that look was all the information they both knew about the power of class and cast and gender; who was worth protecting and who was not. Precious's whole life had been dedicated to fighting for this woman's right to be heard, to be seen, to be respected. If she couldn't help a woman whose child had been killed so brutally, what good was all her talk about sisterhood and solidarity? If she started avoiding controversy now, the bad guys had already won.

"You're right," Precious said, ashamed at her initial hesitation. "You're absolutely right and I apologize. Please sit down and let's figure out how I can help you find out who killed your son."

Mamie began to cry again. "Thank you, Senator. Thank you!"

"Thank you for trusting me enough to come here." Precious picked up the phone. "Joann? Get me Lee Kilgore on the phone, will you?"

34

When Baby Brother arrived at the West End News, still wearing his baggy blue jeans, oversize white T-shirt, and 76ers baseball cap, he wasn't sure what to expect. Zora had made Blue Hamilton sound like some kind of godfather or something. That was cool, Baby Brother thought. He needed someone to watch his back until he got the lay of the land. Right now he needed a job and a place to live. Zora seemed to think this guy was good for both, so at the appointed hour, Baby Brother presented himself at the newsstand and asked for Mr. Hamilton.

The old man fiddling with the cappuccino machine looked him up and down, shook his head, and told him to take a seat. Baby Brother wanted to tell the old guy what he could do with that look, but he didn't want to get off on the wrong foot. Instead of picking a fight, he decided to use the time to look around. He had no idea what kind of place this might be. The shelves and racks were filled with newspapers and magazines. There was lots of foreign stuff with weird writing. It was like being back in Iraq, he thought. The people there read a million newspapers a day.

He wondered if they kept the porno in the back. There were a couple of people sitting around reading and drinking coffee and there was a pretty steady stream of folks coming in for the evening paper or the latest issue of

Jet magazine. He made eye contact with a slender, dark-skinned beauty who looked too regal for the sweats she was wearing. She smiled as she paid for her cappuccino and left. Atlanta was full of fine women, Baby Brother thought. *I think I'm gonna like it here.*

Momentarily distracted, he didn't see General come up behind his chair.

"Are you Wesley Jamerson?"

Baby Brother jumped about a foot in the air. "Damn, man! You scared the shit out of me!"

The big man just looked at him. "That's the last cursing you're going to do in here today, youngblood. Now I asked you a question. Answer it."

Being bold was one thing, but Baby Brother didn't have the nerve to say something smart back to this guy. "Yeah, I'm Wes Jamerson."

"Are you carrying any weapons or contraband of any kind?"

He felt like he was back at boot camp and he didn't like it one bit. "Naw, man. Are you Hamilton?"

"You're not here to ask questions, youngblood. You're here to answer them. Follow me."

Baby Brother walked behind the man down a short hallway full of more newspapers. At the end of the hall, the man pulled open a large metal door and moved inside to let him enter. Baby Brother found himself in a large room where a dark-skinned man in a beautiful black suit sat at a table drinking coffee in a little tiny cup.

General looked down at Baby Brother. "Stand until he tells you to sit, and when he tells you the meeting is over, the meeting is over."

"Cool," Baby Brother said, heading for Blue.

General grabbed his arm in a grip that made him wince. "Say 'yes, sir,' youngblood, and *pull your damn pants up!*"

Resisting the desire to rub his arm as he walked across the room, Baby Brother did as he was told. He stood awkwardly while Blue gave him a long, hard look. He was glad Zora had warned him about the eyes. Otherwise, he felt he never would have been able to withstand Blue's gaze. He had never seen a black man with eyes that color.

"What's your name?" Blue's voice was a low rumble.

"They call me Baby Brother."

Blue's eyes glittered in a way that made Baby Brother wish he'd just said "Wes Jamerson" like he had some sense.

"Well, *they* aren't here, so why don't you tell me what your mama calls you?"

Baby Brother swallowed hard. "My given name is Wesley."

"I'll call you Mr. Jamerson. You'll call me Mr. Hamilton."

Baby Brother wished he could sit down, but he knew better. *"Yes, sir."*

"What kind of work do you do?"

"Well . . ."

Zora said tell him the truth, but what was he supposed to say? *I used to browbeat my mother out of money, but she died. I hustled my father a lot, but he died, too. I guilt-tripped my sister. Stole from her, too. Sold a little dope to kids. Let the homies pay my way if they got it like that. You know, man, same ol' shit.*

That was the truth, but he was hardly going to say that to this blue-eyed stranger who had no sense of humor that Baby Brother had been able to detect.

"I've been in the army, sir."

"But you're not in the army anymore."

That was the one thing they could agree on. At least he wasn't in the army anymore. Baby Brother grinned at Blue. *"Word!"*

Blue's look was so disapproving, it sent a chill through Baby Brother. He hadn't meant any disrespect.

"Word, *sir.*"

"What are you going to do now?"

Baby Brother didn't know how to answer the question any better now than he had when Zora asked it, so he just stood there. Blue didn't move a muscle while Baby Brother shifted from one foot to the other and tried to think of something sensible to say. Failing that, he decided to throw himself on Blue's mercy and ask for some assistance.

"Look, Mr. Hamilton, *sir,*" Baby Brother said, choosing his words carefully, sounding suddenly more like the prep-school dropout he was than the pseudo-street-smart, wannabe hoodlum he was always pretending to be. "I saw things . . . I *did* things in Iraq that sort of messed with my mind. That's why I couldn't go back. Right now I'm just trying to find a job and a place to live while I figure out my next step. Zora seemed to think you might be able to help me, sir."

Blue watched Baby Brother morph effortlessly from one persona to the next and wondered why the one he chose most consistently was the one with no future. "Sit down."

Baby Brother took a seat across from Blue. Without being told, he pulled off the 76ers cap and placed it on the floor beside his chair.

"Since you don't seem to know what kind of work you can do, I'll find a job for you in West End. You'll be paid. It won't be much over minimum wage, but not working is not an option. Everybody works."

This was sounding more and more like the army. "Does everybody work for you?"

Blue's eyes glittered like black diamonds. "Everybody who's got any sense. Does that include you?"

"Yes, sir."

"Good. You'll share an apartment in one of our buildings until you find your own place. Mr. Mason will meet you there and tell you the rules."

Baby Brother felt like he'd jumped out of the frying pan into the fire. He hated rules. A flicker of annoyance passed across his face and Blue recognized it for what it was: defiance. He leaned forward and placed both his hands on the table. His long fingers were laced together like he was getting ready to pray. The cuffs of his white shirt were spotless.

"Let me explain something to you as clearly as I can. You are a deserter from the United States Army. You're not the only one, not by a long shot, and the army can't afford to let all of you just slip away. It sets a bad precedent. So they're going to be looking for you. If they find you, that's a problem for *you*. If they find you in West End, that's a problem for *me*."

Baby Brother didn't say anything. The last thing he wanted to be to this blue-eyed boss man was a problem.

"In order for us to avoid that moment, you have to stop acting like a damn kid who can't keep his britches up over his own ass and *be a man*." Blue paused to let his words sink in. "We don't tolerate violence toward women or abuse of children. We don't tolerate nonproductive people who want to live off their neighbors' hard work. We don't tolerate men acting a fool."

Baby Brother started to ask Blue for a more precise definition of *acting a fool*, but he knew better.

"West End is a unique community, Mr. Jamerson. There are lots of other places you can live in Atlanta where none of these rules apply. If you decide to do that, I will have nothing more to say about how you live your life. But if you stay in West End, you'll have to keep up your end of the bargain or I'll want to know the reason why."

The possibilities of what might happen if the explanation wasn't satis-factory was not something Baby Brother wanted to explore.

"Is that clear?" Blue said.

"Yes, sir."

"Are you sure you understand what I'm saying to you?"

"Yes, sir."

"Good." Blue stood up, and Baby Brother scrambled to his feet, too. Be-hind him, General was already opening the door. Outside, another man in a dark suit was waiting. "Then this meeting is over."

He held out his hand and Baby Brother shook it, feeling the strength of his grip without Blue having to squeeze too hard like men sometimes do to show how macho they are. Blue's strength seemed to flow down his arm and out through his fingers like a force Baby Brother could feel, but couldn't see.

"Thank you, sir," he said, backing away. "Thank you."

General stepped out into the hallway just long enough to introduce Baby Brother to Jerome Mason, who would take it from there. When he closed the door, Blue was already pouring himself another espresso. Gen-eral waited for Blue to speak first.

"What do you think about this kid?"

General didn't mince words. "He's trouble as sure as I'm sitting here."

"Keep an eye on him."

"Don't worry. I've got it covered."

35

Regina couldn't remember when her body had required so much sleep. Probably never. It was disconcerting at first. She'd be having lunch with Blue and all of a sudden she'd just start yawning in his face. She was mortified, but he found it funny. He encouraged her to listen to her body and do what it told her to do. She agreed and what it told her to do was take a nice long nap every day from twelve to two.

Once she surrendered to the naps, the house began to sprout suitable spots for her to enjoy them. The corner of the couch, with a jumble of pillows and the soft cashmere throw Abbie had sent her from India years ago, was as cozy as a cat's favorite basket. The bed in the guest room that was soon to be the baby's room was also a favorite. The nest that claimed her today was a tiny chaise longue that she kept on the sunporch off their bedroom. It was perfect for an afternoon nap and she was asleep almost before she laid her cheek on the plum-colored velvet cushion and pulled a light cotton quilt around her shoulders. For two hours, she dreamed of walking and laughing with her aunt on the beach at Tybee. At three-fifteen, she woke up, went downstairs for a cup of tea, and dialed Abbie's number in D.C.

"My dear girl," Abbie's voice sang out before the phone completed one ring. "I have conjured you up at last! I thought my much-sought-after powers were abandoning me!"

"We can't have that. What would your acolytes do without you?"

"They'd concoct a ritual for the return and revitalization of magic powers. These girls are serious believers in the power of burning sage and constructing altars in the woods."

"I wonder who taught them to do that?" Regina laughed.

Abbie had an active, if unofficial, relationship with the women's studies center at Howard University. Her classes and seminars were always full of earnest young women who needed to understand themselves and their world a little better. She also had a boisterous private clientele of *pre-*, *peri-*, *post-*, and *in-the-midst-of* menopausal women who flocked to her for advice and counsel. What had begun as Abbie's personal quest had become a collective journey of sisterhood.

"You sound great," Regina said.

"I feel great. How are *you* doing? Any morning sickness?"

"No, but I've been sleeping a lot more."

Abbie chuckled. "When your mother was carrying you, she used to go hide in her office between classes and grab forty winks."

"I've got that beat by half," Regina said. "So how are you? Any more break-ins?"

This was the question Abbie had hoped she wouldn't have to answer. She didn't want to worry Regina by telling her that there had been two more home invasions less than a mile from the house.

"Things have been pretty quiet lately."

"I don't believe you."

Trying to fool Regina had been silly. All she had to do was go to the Internet. Monday's *Washington Post* had carried a big story about the neighborhood being terrorized by a string of increasingly violent crimes. The victims had all described the perpetrators as two black males in their late teens, armed with a .22 pistol and a Boy Scout knife.

"Don't worry about it, dear. I'm always careful."

"Have you called that man about the burglar bars yet?"

"No, dear, not yet."

"Blue already paid for them!" Regina said. "All you have to do is schedule a time for the guy to come by and take the measurements."

Abbie hated the whole idea of putting bars on the doors and the windows. That was no way to live. She might as well be in prison if she was going to look through bars to see the sky.

"I just don't want to put bars on the house, Gina. I know it's your choice, but I don't think I could live here behind bars."

The last thing Regina wanted was for Abbie to leave the house. Last year she'd tried to give her aunt the deed, but Abbie wouldn't take it, pointing out that while her brother had been Gina's father, the house was her mother's legacy.

"Didn't you used to have a gun?" Regina said. "What happened to it?"

Abbie's laugh broke through the strange paranoia of the conversation like a ray of light. "How can you possibly remember that? It was a derringer, a very ladylike, pearl-handled derringer that I carried everywhere for years and never fired one time. I doubt if it would deter any thief worthy of the name."

"I wish you wouldn't make jokes about this. I'm worried about you."

"Don't be. I've been turning on the alarm every night and whenever I leave the house during the day."

"Really?" Abbie had resisted activating the house's ancient alarm system almost as much as she had installing the burglar bars.

"Really. Now stop worrying and tell me if you've laid eyes on my friend Mr. Nolan."

"Haven't you talked to him?"

"Every other day or so. Lately, he's been sending me letters."

"*Peachy?*"

"Don't sound so shocked, dear. As many spells as I've worked on that man, I'm surprised he hasn't shown up at my door."

"You better be careful. By the time you get back down here, you might blow his poor heart right up."

"If I've got enough magic in me to stop his heart, don't you think I've got enough to start it up again?"

Regina laughed. "You're terrible!"

"I've got to go, dear. There's a group arriving in twenty minutes for their journal workshop and I promised them fresh sangria. Tell your handsome husband I send enough love to last him until I lay eyes on you two in November."

"I will. And you be careful until they catch those guys."

"*They* better be careful. Woe be it to anybody who disturbs the peace of a postmenopausal woman at work!"

36

Three days after Mamie Robinson's visit to Precious Hargrove, Lee walked into the same office with a fat folder marked CONFIDENTIAL that contained the report she'd concocted and enough supporting documents not only to discredit Mamie Robinson, but to paint a picture of the Robinson family as a multigenerational crime wave. It wasn't hard to do. Mamie and her daughter had each been arrested for prostitution, passing bad checks, and various other ridiculously inept con games that always cost more in jail time than they ever paid off.

The husband and father of the household was in prison for life after stalking and killing a drug partner who tried to cut him out of a deal that went from bad to worse. Of the five sons he had with Mamie, two were in the same prison where he was housed, serving time for murder and minor drug trafficking. Two others had been killed by rivals several years before and Kentavious had been killed and mutilated in the same streets his father had been running all his life.

Before he died, Lee's report said, Kentavious, at fifteen, had already been to juvenile twice, dropped out of school, impregnated his fourteen-year-old neighbor, and begun a brief career as a small-time marijuana merchant. His mother's assertion that he was basically a good boy, Kilgore's report stated, was based on nothing more than grief and a mother's desire to generate sympathy and perhaps money in the wake of her son's death.

Precious listened to Lee while she looked through the xeroxed mug shots and long rap sheets that defined the state's interaction with the Robinsons. The two boys who were still serving time in the same prison as their father gazed defiantly out from their photos. Even in profile, they managed to convey their suicidal fearlessness. Their father, a long scar across his cheek and a dazed look in his eye, just looked tired.

"It didn't seem like a con," Precious said, looking at Mamie Robinson's rap sheet. Soliciting, shoplifting, stolen credit cards. "She seemed like a mother with nothing left to lose."

"That's all part of it," Lee said. "You're a well-known public figure now, Senator. People are going to come at you more and more with all kinds of schemes."

Precious closed the folder. She didn't need any more evidence that this was not a family you wanted moving in next door. "But do you think there's any truth at all to what she said about police officers protecting the dealers?"

Lee shook her head thoughtfully. "I didn't find any evidence of that."

Precious sat back with a sigh. "I don't know if I'm relieved or disappointed."

"What do you mean?"

Searching for the right words, Precious shrugged her shoulders. "I'd hate to think we've got dirty cops to deal with, but the truth is, I pride myself on being able to read people. I'm usually pretty good at recognizing when somebody's lying to me."

Not as good as you think you are, Lee thought. "These people are pros, Senator."

"I know, and I appreciate what you did," Precious said. "It's just that a politician isn't much good without a working *bullshit detector.* I hate to think Mrs. Robinson got past me."

"I understand. Do you want me to talk to her?"

Precious shook her head. "No, I'll call her myself."

Things had gone exactly as Lee had hoped they would. No candidate with any sense wants to emerge as the champion of people everybody wishes would just go away.

"I think the thing that really got to me about her story," Precious was saying, "is that I remember when my son was fifteen."

"These kids are nothing like your son," Lee said. "They've grown up with a level of violence most people can't even imagine, or don't want to. I saw it all when I walked a beat, day after day. I've seen what it does to them. They grow up mad and mean and ready to do whatever it takes to stay alive."

Precious was watching Lee closely. "We can't blame them for that, can we?"

Sure we can, Lee wanted to say. *Ask my dope-fiend parents. Ask my crack-head cousin. They're the ones making the bad decisions, ignoring the consequences, saggin' and shufflin' their way to oblivion.* Precious sounded to Lee like those *bourgie* Negroes who romanticize and rationalize the worst of the race's behavior as long as they don't have to get too close to it.

"I'm sorry, Senator. I don't mean to be talking out of school here."

Precious smiled a little. "I'm asking."

"The thing is, by the time most of these guys are the age Kentavious was when he died, they're already headed for the morgue or the penitentiary, which gives them just enough time to have a couple of babies by a couple of girls as clueless as they are."

The contempt Lee felt for the people she was describing came through clearly in her tone.

"You're not very optimistic, are you?" Precious said.

"I've seen what these guys can do to a neighborhood," Lee said. "The truth is, Senator, one more gone doesn't strike me as much of a tragedy." From the look on Precious's face, Lee realized suddenly that she had gone too far.

"I appreciate your candor," Precious said, standing up. Lee rose as well. "And I appreciate all your hard work."

"I hope I didn't offend you," Lee said. "Cynicism is the curse of the beat cop."

"You're not a beat cop anymore, Captain Kilgore," Precious said. "And you didn't offend me."

"I'm glad I could help," Lee said. "And please don't hesitate to call on me again if you need me."

"I will."

"I can show myself out."

Precious closed the door behind Lee, wondering what it was that left her feeling that perhaps Mrs. Robinson wasn't the only one trying to con her. She sat down, picked up the phone, and dialed Blue Hamilton's private number.

37

B lue had been trying to catch up with Aretha ever since he got back from the beach. When he looked out of the car window and saw her working in her garden, he leaned forward and spoke to General behind the wheel.

"Pull over at the house, will you?"

The house, in this case, was not the one he shared with Regina, but the apartment he'd had when they met and that he still maintained exclusively for his own use. In the perfectly maintained four-unit building with the blue front door, Aretha kept her studio upstairs across the hall from Blue's place. Zora lived downstairs on one side across from the guest suite that was always ready to receive short- or long-term residents seeking the privacy and safety that West End could offer.

General glanced at the clock as he eased the big Lincoln over to the curb. They hadn't had lunch and it was almost four o'clock. His stomach growled loud enough for Blue to hear it.

"Do you want me to wait for you?"

"Give me an hour," Blue said, as if he hadn't heard the rumbling. His meeting with Precious Hargrove had run long. It was almost dinnertime.

"I'll be back at five," General said, with visions of a trip to the Beautiful

Restaurant for some short ribs already dancing in his head. His stomach growled again as he stepped out of the car to open Blue's door. Aretha spotted them and waved.

"Fine," Blue said, waving back and heading in her direction. He heard the car pull off and chuckled to himself. General was getting ready to put a serious *hurtin'* on some lucky restaurant's afternoon menu.

"Hey, you!" Aretha said, pulling off her gloves and leaning over to kiss Blue's cheek. "Welcome back!"

"I've got something for you upstairs," he said. "How much more do you have to do?"

"I can finish up tomorrow," she said immediately. Aretha didn't see as much of Blue now that they had each married and moved into their own proper houses. Those moments were precious when both found themselves at the same place with time to visit. Aretha linked her arm through Blue's and grinned at her godfather. "I'm all yours."

"Well, I'm a lucky man indeed," he said, opening the blue door with a flourish so she could enter.

At the top of the stairs, she stood aside as he opened the door to his apartment and switched on the light. A fully stocked bar, black leather couches, and an entertainment center housing a blinking array of the latest audio and visual electronic equipment made this the quintessential male lair. Blue opened the floor-to-ceiling drapes and the late-afternoon sunshine filled the room, making it instantly more *visitor-friendly*. Aretha flopped down in a soft leather chair that cradled her like a protective mother's arms.

"Do you want a Coke or something?" Blue said.

He had met Aretha when she was seventeen and her aunt Ava had asked him to keep an eye on her as a naïve young girl from her tiny hometown, alone in the big city. Even though she was now a twenty-four-year-old wife and mother, he never offered her anything stronger than apple cider.

"I'm fine," she said. "What did you bring me?"

Blue walked behind the bar, opened an unseen drawer, and took out a small *something* wrapped in pale violet tissue paper.

"I'm really just the deliveryman," he said, walking over to Aretha and putting the package gently into her outstretched hand. "Regina thought I'd probably see you before she did."

Aretha peeled back the tissue paper and revealed a perfectly formed seashell in a shade of orange so vivid it looked like someone other than God had painted it.

"It's beautiful!" She touched it gently. "Is it real?"

Blue nodded. "I've never seen one this color. Regina hadn't either."

Aretha laid it back carefully in its tissue-paper nest, but continued to admire it. As a painter, she had spent years considering colors, and this was no ordinary orange. It practically glowed.

"There are lots of colors we haven't seen in the ocean," she said, "because nobody's ever been down far enough. It's like those transparent squids that they discovered a couple of years ago. Nobody even knew they were down there."

"Probably looked right through them," Blue said, teasing her.

"Make fun of me all you want," she said. "This shell is special. Tell Regina I said thank you."

"Why don't you tell her yourself? She'd love to see you."

Aretha sighed. "I've been missing her, too. Things have just been kind of crazy at my house the last few months."

The darkening of Blue's eyes was almost imperceptible. "Last time I saw Joyce Ann out with her grandmother, she didn't look crazy to me."

"All two-year-olds are crazy!" Aretha laughed. "They just learn to hide it from outsiders."

"How's Kwame?"

The tiniest pause before she answered was not lost on Blue. "He's fine. Busy all the time."

"Well, he did a great job on the project he just finished for me. You tell him next time he's looking for work, I've always got a place for him."

In that way, Blue let her know that if any of that craziness she was talking about had a basis in financial stress, she could rest assured her husband would always be gainfully employed.

"I told you he was a genius."

"So you've got a beautiful, sane child, a genius for a husband, friends who send you miracles from the sea, and a godfather who can't imagine his life without you." Blue's eyes were dark pools, but his smile was warm and curious. "Where's the crazy part?"

"Maybe it's all in my head," she said, with a wobbly little smile.

Blue nodded. "That's possible, but I don't think so." He was looking at her calmly from the other end of the sofa. "Do you?"

Aretha sat back and let out the air in her lungs with a soft sigh. She turned her head to look at him without lifting it from the leather. "Kwame wants to move to midtown."

Blue's expression didn't change. "What do you want?"

The question was so simple and straightforward, but it went directly to the heart of the matter and sat there, waiting for an answer.

"I want peace in my house," she said, surprising herself with the answer. She knew peace didn't have anything to do with place. Peace was a state of mind. She sat up, leaned toward him, and tried to explain. "I love living in West End, you know that. I've never been anything but safe and happy here." She felt disloyal even thinking about moving. "But I'm tired of arguing about it all the time. Maybe it's time for me to compromise a little, you know?"

"Compromise is fine," he said. "Just don't do anything you don't want to do."

"But isn't that the essence of marriage? That give-and-take?"

"I'm the wrong one to ask."

"Why?" she said, settling back into the chair's cozy leather embrace again. "You've been married four times!"

He laughed. "That should disqualify me as an expert witness."

"Well, what do you and Regina do when you have an argument?"

Blue's eyes twinkled in a way that had to be seen to be believed. "We don't argue."

Aretha raised her eyebrows. "Never?"

Blue shook his head. "Never."

"Did you argue with your other wives?"

"I don't argue."

Aretha wondered if that was why they had left him. Maybe what they needed was a good shouting match every now and then to clear the air.

"You're no help," she said.

"Because I don't argue?"

"Because you won't tell me what I ought to do."

"Nobody knows what you need but you," Blue said. "Not much I can do about that."

And that, she thought, was the whole problem. *What do I need?* "Can I ask you something?"

"Anything you can stand to have me answer."

"Do you ever miss singing?"

He smiled slowly. "I still sing."

"I mean, doing it full-time, every day. Traveling around, doing shows. Living your life as an artist instead of . . . what you're doing now."

"It was time for me to leave that life."

"Do you ever regret it?"

"I never regret anything."

The idea of living a life so fully integrated that second-guessing and the remorse that comes from twenty-twenty hindsight were nonexistent filled her with such longing that she could hardly keep from crying. But Blue was watching her and the last thing she wanted to do was burst into tears.

"What time is it?" she said, glad her voice didn't tremble.

"Almost five," Blue said without looking at his watch.

Aretha stood up, glad for a reason to escape before she said too much. "I've got to pick up Joyce Ann at Montessori. Can we continue this another time?"

"Of course." He picked up the shell in its violet nest. "Don't forget this."

She curled the paper back around it gently as he walked her to the door.

"Aretha," he said, pausing with his hand on the knob. "I want you to understand something."

"Yes?" Was he going to break down and give her some advice after all?

"What we've done here in West End doesn't mean you *have* to stay here. All it means is that if you do choose to live here, you'll always be safe."

"I know," she said, hugging him good-bye. "Thank you."

"Thank me by not being such a stranger."

"I promise," Aretha said, taking the stairs on the run. "Love you!"

Blue walked over to the window. General was back, leaning against the car smoking a cigarette. He tipped his hat to Aretha, who greeted him with a friendly wave and headed off down the street. Watching her, Blue knew she would be moving soon. He also knew this would be the first of a series of compromises if she and Kwame were going to stay together. Marriage was such a strange and complicated institution and it took a special kind of feeling deep in the hearts of both people taking the vows to make it work. He hoped his goddaughter and her husband had that kind of love to sustain them. In the meantime, Blue decided it couldn't hurt to stay close to Kwame.

38

Lee refused to give Bob a key to her condo, so when he came to visit, he had to be present himself at the desk downstairs to be announced, then take the elevator up to her floor, knock on the door, and wait until she let him in. Even if he had a key, he thought, today probably wouldn't have been the best day to use it. He wouldn't have risked sticking his head in the door and getting it blown off for his trouble. Lee was still angry about the way he had snapped at her the other day when he saw that kid's mother on the six o'clock news talking crazy. Bob had no reason to suspect Lee wasn't on top of things. Since the funeral, everything had been quiet. Whatever Lee had done, they were back to business as usual.

Once he cooled off, his plan had been to give her some space so she could, too. He was almost ready to make contact when she called him at the office, something she did rarely, and told him she'd like to see him that evening at seven o'clock at her place to discuss some business.

"Certainly," he said, aware that anyone in his office might be eavesdropping. "Is there a problem?"

"Nothing substantive," she said. "Just a communications oversight."

Oh, hell, he thought. *This is some more of her feminist shit. Some more of her "you will respect me as a woman and a police officer" crap.*

"Fine," Bob said. "I'll see you at seven."

He had a full day of meetings and a ten o'clock flight to Seattle later that night. The prospect of a confrontation with Lee before he left did not appeal to him. It wasn't that he didn't want to see her. He would have welcomed a preflight *quickie*, even if she didn't put on the uniform for him. But a discussion of a *communications oversight* was probably not going to wind up in the bedroom. On the other hand, with Lee, you could never tell. His luggage was already in the car and he definitely had time if she was so inclined.

The longer he thought about the possibility, the more excited he got. By six-thirty, he was hopeful enough of a positive outcome to their meeting that he stopped at the flower shop on the ground floor of his building and bought a dozen yellow roses. When he rang the bell at seven sharp, Lee opened the door and looked at him with undisguised antipathy. The flowers she ignored completely.

"Come in."

His hopes for an intimate exchange growing fainter by the second, Bob stepped in, turned to her, and extended the extravagantly gift-boxed roses. She glanced down like he had just extended a fresh turd in her direction. Of course she made no move to touch it.

"What the hell is that?"

Bob took a deep breath. He knew how to get through this moment. They'd been here before. The angry woman and the *semi*-contrite man.

"I'm sorry, Lee. I was an asshole on the phone the other night and I apologize."

"This is not a social call and I am not your girlfriend or your wife, so please don't insult me with your ridiculously transparent moves. The only way you'll be getting any sex here tonight is if you take it, and I don't think you can."

"Not my style," Bob said, preparing to let his mind wander while Lee got a chance to vent about men in general and him specifically.

"Why'd you bring the flowers?"

"When I'm wrong, I say I'm wrong. The flowers were just my way to say I'm sorry. I didn't mean to offend you."

She looked at him and he thought he saw something soften in her eyes, but he might have been imagining it. He decided to shut up until he could gauge her mood a little better and determine how angry she really was.

"Do you want a drink?" she said, still sounding pissed off, but a little less so, he thought.

"Thanks," he said, relieved at the unexpected invitation. *Maybe the flowers were working after all.* "Got any vodka?"

She always kept a bottle for his visits, but tonight he made no assumptions. It was safer that way.

"Come on in the kitchen," she said, finally picking up the florist's box. "Help yourself while I put these in water."

He went to the freezer and pulled out the frosted bottle of Grey Goose. Two ice cubes, a splash of tonic, and a twist of lime made him start to relax a little. He leaned against the kitchen sink and watched her lay out the flowers on the counter, cut the tips off the stems under cold-running water, and then arrange them in a cut-glass vase she had pulled from a top shelf on her tiptoes.

She had changed from her usual conservative work suit and heels into a pair of gray drawstring pants and a snug-fitting gray sweater that showed off her lean midsection. He sipped his drink and waited for her to make the next move.

"I like roses in the kitchen," she said, almost as if she was talking to herself. "It's a more private pleasure."

Bob sipped his drink and smiled.

"Sit down," she said, but she didn't smile back.

They almost never sat in the kitchen. Lee didn't cook and domesticity was not their style. Bob felt a little awkward pulling out a chair at her tiny breakfast table. She sat down across from him, so close their knees bumped gently, although neither one acknowledged it.

"When I called you this morning and told you to come over . . ."

"Told" you, he thought. *Not "invited" you.*

". . . I was prepared to read you the riot act because of how you were talking to me the other night."

"It was unforgivable," he said, breaking one of his own rules by jumping in before she finished.

She waved her hand to silence him. "Yes, it was, but we brought it on ourselves."

"We did?" He took another sip of vodka, unsure of where the conversation was going. "How did we do that?"

She leaned back in her chair and Bob concentrated on not looking at her breasts.

"We started having sex."

"I'm not sure I'm following you. I was upset with the situation, not with you."

"Exactly, so why did I take it so personally? Because we're having sex, so a part of my brain got confused about who we are and what we want from this arrangement."

"I want exactly what we've got," he said. "We're making a shitload of money on the coke. We're making all the right moves politically and we're having great sex with no strings attached." He put down his glass and looked at her. "What do you want?"

She didn't hesitate. "I want out of the coke. I want to make my own moves politically and I don't want to have sex with you anymore."

It was so cut-and-dried the way she said it, he winced. "Just like that?"

She shrugged. "I know it will take a little time to get things settled on the street after the murder, but once things slow down, I'm out."

"How long?"

"Three months, tops."

Bob frowned. "I've told you already, you can phase out in a year or so, after the mayor's race, when—"

Cutting him off abruptly, Lee's voice was harsh. "You don't tell me when it's time to make a move. I joined up with you on my own because we had common interests. Now I'm leaving on my own because those interests have changed."

Bob repressed a strong desire to toss the rest of his drink in her face. *Who the hell did she think she was? He had been calling Atlanta mayors by their first names since she was in kindergarten!*

"I see," he said.

"Good."

He could tell she was ready for him to leave, but his mind was racing. He couldn't force her to do what he wanted, but he didn't want to exit in a position of weakness. That wasn't his style.

"You might want to reconsider the politics," he said. "I think I've still got some ideas that might be good for both of us."

She raised her eyebrows. "Oh?"

Bob drained his glass and stood up. "I made Kwame Hargrove an offer to join the firm today as my newest associate."

The words were hardly out of his mouth when Lee threw back her head and laughed out loud. He wasn't sure what was so funny, but he didn't like the sound of that laugh. It was mean and hard and cold.

"What the hell is so funny about that?"

"Nothing. You just surprise me sometimes. You never even mentioned him before."

"You're not the only one with connections to Precious Hargrove," Bob snapped.

"I never said I was." She glanced at her watch like he had now truly overstayed his welcome. "Don't you have a plane to catch?"

"You're pretty sure of yourself, aren't you?"

"I had a good teacher."

"You think you've learned everything I can teach you?"

Lee gave him a small smile. "I think I've learned everything you're willing to teach me."

"What does that mean?"

She didn't answer and her silence infuriated him. They walked to the door, and when he turned to say good-bye, she gave him another flicker of a smile and extended her hand. He didn't know which irritated him more, the smirk or the handshake.

"I'm assuming," he said, trying to regain some semblance of the upper hand, "there will be no repercussions from the unfortunate mutilation incident."

"Don't worry," she said. "As my last official act of our partnership, I will make sure all of that goes away. I'm on top of it."

He wished she was on top of *him*, but those days seemed to be over. At least for now.

"Travel safe," she said. "And good luck with your newest associate."

"I don't need luck. I always land on my feet, remember?"

Nothing about this meeting had gone the way he'd hoped it would, and now, as he stood waiting for the elevator to take him back down to the building lobby, Bob could have sworn that behind her closed door, he could hear Lee laughing. Listening to the sound, he realized she had forgotten the first thing he'd taught her. She could laugh at everything and everybody, but not at him. *Never at him.*

39

Baby Brother had been standing in the shower for a long time. Eyes closed, head back, he was enjoying the feel of the hot water on his skin. It had been a long week and he was anxious to wash off the stink of all those tomatoes and collard greens and yellow squash. Hamilton had stuck him with a job delivering produce to West End restaurants from Soul Vegetarian to the twenty-four-hour Beautiful Restaurant, an offshoot of the self-described Perfect Church. That meant he had to get up at four in the morning to start deliveries at five since a lot of these places opened for breakfast at six.

His partner was a big country boy from Alabama who was just glad to be working and living indoors. He identified himself as Maurice Crockett, but everybody called him Davy, for obvious reasons. As the one with the experience and the seniority, Davy was the boss of their two-man crew, and as such, he got to decide what radio station they listened to in the truck. To Baby Brother's supreme annoyance, that meant right-wing talk radio. From Rush Limbaugh to G. Gordon Liddy to Don Imus and Atlanta's reigning Neanderthal, Neal Bortz, Davy listened to them all. From sunrise when they picked up at the Growers' Association warehouse down on White Street to the moment he dropped Baby Brother off at his apartment at the end of Peeples Street at just after one, the voices of America's angry white males filled the cab of the truck as it moved through a community where there weren't any white men for miles.

Sometimes Baby Brother wanted to just change the station to one of the city's hip-hop choices, but Davy was a big man. He had been a well-known prison boxer during the time he was serving for involuntary manslaughter because of a bar fight that got out of hand. Any physical confrontation he had with Baby Brother would be distinctly one-sided.

"Why do you listen to this shit?" Baby Brother had demanded on their second day together when he thought there was a chance for negotiating a change.

Davy tapped his temple with a thick finger. "That's how I find out how these crackers are thinkin'. Get inside their heads and shit. They can't get nothin' past me." After a week of such investigations, Baby Brother decided his first purchase when he got paid whatever piece of chump change they were going to throw his way would be an MP3 player. He'd stick that bad boy in the pocket of the beyond ugly uniform he had to wear and tune it all out with some Lil' John or the Ying Yang Twins.

But for tonight, the voices of angry white males were the last thing on his mind. He had accepted an invitation from Zora to go out to one of the Buckhead clubs he'd heard about, but if that didn't work out, he was prepared to pay for sex. Davy said the strip joint right across the West End line had five-dollar lap dances and sometimes for twenty, the girls would come out to your car for a quick blow job. That would be great, he thought, except he had to get rid of his car. He knew his sister's husband would have put out an APB, so he sold it for two hundred dollars to a guy who didn't ask about title and registration. Baby Brother pocketed the money and the guy slapped a "lost tag" sign in the back window and drove off a happy man.

He knew he couldn't bring anybody back to the apartment since Mr. Mason had told him that first day that no female company was allowed. When Baby Brother asked why, Mason said, "If you got money enough to be entertaining women, you got money enough to pay for your own place." Of course, if Zora was ready to *put out*, she had an apartment of her own, so he was home free. At the thought of seeing Zora naked, a wave of lust swept through his body. *Damn, she was fine!* But she didn't seem to be in any hurry to jump into bed with him, so he'd have to hope one of the dancers

Davy was talking about would take him home for a blow job, which was unlikely. Not for twenty dollars. He hoped he'd get lucky with Zora. She was definitely his first choice.

He was saving money from the sale of his sister's car to put down on his own place, but he spent half of his first week's paycheck on an outfit for tonight to maximize his chances of getting lucky with Zora. He got a haircut, too, and bought some new sneakers that didn't look like a Christmas gift from somebody's grandmother. He slipped on his baggy new Sean John jeans, another oversize white T-shirt, and looked in the mirror. He had bought a small gold hoop from a street vendor and been delighted to discover his pierced left ear had not closed up during the months he'd been in Iraq. What he saw satisfied him. However the evening went, he knew there was a woman roaming around out there right now who would think he was worth at least a second look.

Zora rang the doorbell right on time and Baby Brother grinned at his reflection. When he opened the door, his grin got even wider. Zora looked sexy as hell. She was wearing a black Gypsy skirt that was slung low on her hips and a silky white blouse that kept slipping off her shoulder. If she was wearing a bra, he couldn't see it. A pair of silver heels with what he guessed to be four-inch heels were gracing her pretty little feet.

"Hey," she said with a big pretty smile. "You ready?"

"Damn, girl," he said. "You didn't tell me to dress up. Am I okay for this place?"

"You're fine," she said. "I'm not really dressed up. It's just the skirt."

"Well, whatever it is, you look good enough to eat."

Zora laughed as they started down the walk. "My girlfriends love this place. That's the only reason I'm letting them horn in since we'd probably run into them anyway. *Plus*, Mickey has her brother's car."

Mickey, at the wheel of the red Lexus, was almost as fine as Zora. Beside her, the woman riding shotgun flashed him a dazzling smile as he climbed into the backseat with Zora.

"Hey, I'm Janice. Let me pull up a little bit to give you some legroom." She pressed a button and her seat eased forward with a gentle electric hum. "That better?"

"Thanks," he said, trying to calculate the odds that two of these girls could be talked into a threesome. It didn't even matter which two. They were all fine. "I'm Wes."

"We know," the other one chirped. "I'm Michelle."

Beside him, Zora sat close enough that their thighs were touching lightly. Maybe, he thought, he'd actually *died* in Iraq and was just now getting to heaven. Mickey pulled onto the freeway and headed north. It was ten thirty and Atlanta's Saturday-night traffic was already thick, but Mickey was a good driver—fast but careful. Baby Brother let his leg touch Zora's a little harder as they rounded the curve onto I-75.

"You girls ready for a good time?" he said, looking forward to a cold beer in the company of his new friends. He might even take one to the dance floor if he was feeling loose. He hoped he still had the moves.

"Oh yeah," Janice said, turning around in her seat and winking at Zora. "Are you?"

"Ladies," Baby Brother said, "I am the good-time man!"

40

It had seemed like a good idea at the time. General had stopped in at Justin's to do some business over drinks. After his associates departed, he decided to stay and have dinner. He was seeing Brandi at her place around midnight, but it was only ten o'clock and he was suddenly hungry. He checked in with Blue to let him know the meeting had gone as planned and asked the manager for a table. The place was filling up, but the tuxedo-clad brother showed General to a table in one of the restaurant's prime spots, accepted the fifty-dollar bill General pressed into his palm, and left him in the capable hands of the smooth-faced young server who identified himself as Randy. General half listened as Randy described the specials, took the drink order, and glided off with a promise to be right back.

One of several restaurants owned by entertainment and fashion magnate Sean Combs, Justin's had managed to maintain the high-quality service, creative cuisine, and eclectic brew of beautiful people, stars (real and imagined), tourists, and trendsetters that had first put it on the map when it opened six years before. Although there'd been a few isolated incidents, more often than not involving a visit from pop-singer-turned-reality-TV-star Bobby Brown, most of the time the hip-hop crowd mixed and mingled with a maximum of style and a minimum of confusion.

As General waited for his scotch on the rocks, a musical luminary he recognized, but couldn't have named, created the kind of stir that always swirls around stars. The manager embraced the young man. The model-thin hostess with the razor-sharp cheekbones and the sexy black dress turned up the wattage on her twinkle and the eyes of every woman in the place turned in his direction, staring unabashedly as he and his date, a cocoa-colored lovely in a sleek white suit with a bored expression, made their way to a table not far from General.

The young superstar held his companion's chair like a perfect gentleman before sitting down and earned an appreciative sigh from his captive female audience, who turned back to their dinners and drinks, wishing such behavior was the rule rather than the exception. From where he sat, General could see the light bouncing off of the large diamond studs in the young man's earlobes. He smiled to himself. There were so many people for whom such proximity might be the highlight of a day, or of a lifetime. For General, it was just another of Atlanta's young millionaires, out on the town.

Randy presented the scotch and took the order with equal aplomb, then left again as General felt his phone vibrating in his breast pocket. There were only two people who had this number, Blue and Brandi. He glanced at the caller ID and smiled.

"Hello?" he said quietly.

"Hey, baby." Brandi's voice was a sexy purr. "Is this a bad time?"

"Never a bad time. I thought you had to work. Where are you?"

They sounded more like lovers than two people who traded sex for money and called it even.

"Niggas started fightin' all up in the place. Somebody called the cops and they sent us all home, told us to come back tomorrow. Johnny was too pissed, but it wadn't nothin' he could do."

"You okay?"

"You know I know how to get out of a situation, baby!" She laughed. "I been around niggas fightin' all my life. If they ain't fightin' me, they ain't my problem."

She played so tough, he thought, and she wasn't big as a minute. "Where you at now?"

"In my car," she said. "I just wanted to tell you I was goin' home. You can come on by whenever you get ready."

"You eat yet?" he said as an idea presented itself to him.

"Not yet," she said. "You hungry? Want me to stop and pick up something for us?"

"I'm at Justin's," he said. "I just ordered. Want to join me?"

She hesitated. They didn't usually go out and the invitation surprised her.

"Hello?" he said.

"You mean join you for dinner?"

"It's a little late for lunch."

She laughed. "Hell, yeah, I'll join you! I'm just trippin' a little 'cause you so good to me, baby. That's all. I'm on my way."

He put the phone back in his pocket, already kicking himself. What was he thinking? He wasn't *dating* Brandi. He was *fucking* her. What had possessed him to invite her out to dinner? Was he turning into that foolish old man he didn't want to ever be? Lord knows what she might be wearing when she arrived. Looking at the stylish women around him, he hoped she wouldn't be dressed in a way that made it obvious that she was a hooker. Unfortunately, it was too late now for him to do anything about it. He signaled Randy, asked him to hold that steak, and ordered a bottle of champagne.

Fifteen minutes later, Brandi stepped in the front door dressed in a crimson micromini dress with a halter top that was hardly enough to cover her breasts, and a pair of five-inch stiletto heels, also red. Her hair was an upsweep of quivering ringlets and her makeup was more suited to stage lights than a candle's glow. The manager took one look at her and signaled the hostess, who began moving toward Brandi with a sense of purpose and an air of disdain. There was no mistaking what she was, he thought, but he'd invited her and he wasn't about to let some haughty little bitch in a black dress disrespect her. *Juanita would never forgive him.*

General stood up quickly and raised his hand in greeting. The manager caught sight of the gesture from the corner of his ever-watchful eye and reached out to intercept the hostess before she created an incident. He didn't need to worry. As soon as Brandi spotted him, she headed straight for his table without waiting for assistance. Twice in one evening, Justin's female patrons were treated to a man holding the chair of his dinner companion. The fact that this woman was clearly on the clock did not diminish their appreciation of the gesture.

"Hey, baby," she said, hanging her oversize fake gold purse on the back of her chair. "I didn't have time to change. I look okay?"

Only a true cad would have told her the truth. "You're the finest woman in here."

She giggled, pleased he had affirmed her own assessment. Randy appeared to open the Cristal with the appropriate *pop*, took Brandi's order for Justin's Caribbean chicken, and disappeared. They clinked their glasses lightly and General tried not to notice the other patrons smirking in their direction. Brandi took a long, greedy swallow of the sparkling golden liquid like it was a tall glass of red Kool-Aid on a hot summer afternoon. She was so young, he thought. Juanita was easily ten years older when they'd first gotten together. Brandi was a baby.

Draining her glass, she extended it for a refill. General repressed the urge to tell her she wasn't at Montre's now. She didn't get paid by how many bottles she sold.

"I used to dream about comin' in here," she said, looking around appreciatively. "This place is the *bomb*. Niggas always used to promise to bring me, but you know how shady people can be."

"So how do you like it so far?"

"It's perfect," she said, drawing out the word until it became a *purr* of satisfaction.

"Look behind you," General said, knowing she hadn't yet glimpsed the superstar whose name she would surely know.

"What?" She twisted in her seat to see the singer calmly enjoying his shrimp cocktail while his still-bored companion picked at her salad. She whipped back around in her seat so fast, General had to smile.

"Do you know who that is?" she whispered urgently. *"That is Busy Boy Baker!"*

The name conjured up media images of a local boy who'd hit the big time, but never forgot his roots. General vaguely remembered him promising to send a group of Mandeville Maids to college if they got their GEDs. It was a big story when the first group graduated.

"The one who started the scholarship program?"

"The one who got those supersexy abs on top of all those hit records," Brandi said.

The significance of the scholarship program was lost on her. She half turned around to sneak another look. Busy Boy was oblivious. He was probably accustomed to flustered females by now. That was how he made his money.

"Did you see those earrings?" Brandi shook her head in awe and took another gulp of champagne. "And what's up with Miss Thang? That bitch need to put a little pep in her step before somebody swoop on that man."

Randy reappeared with their dinners. They were both starving, and for a few minutes, Busy Boy and company had to take a backseat to a perfectly broiled steak and a half chicken slow-cooked the Jamaican way with plenty of spices. Maybe this wasn't going to be so bad, General thought. All he had to do was keep trusting his instincts. Juanita had said, "Don't talk yourself out of the truth of what you see, no matter how far-fetched it seems." He smiled to himself. You couldn't really get more far-fetched than taking a neighborhood stripper out for a nice dinner in the middle of Buckhead on a Saturday night. He bet Juanita was somewhere, looking down at him, laughing her fine ass off.

"More champagne?" he said when Brandi came up for air.

"Sure, baby," she said, but this time when he handed her the glass, she took a small sip and put the glass down. "You know what else I dream about?"

General was not a man who invited women he was paying for sex to share their dreams with him, but Brandi was different. He was still trying to figure out exactly how different. Maybe her dreams would give him a clue.

"What?"

"Vegas."

"You like to gamble?" The possibility flooded him with memories of all those weekends he and Juanita had spent in New Orleans, playing blackjack all day and making love all night.

"No, baby," she cooed. "I don't have that kinda luck, but out there, I won't need it. You know how much money a dancer can make in Vegas?"

"I have some idea."

"Well, so do I. And as soon as I can put my little coins together, that's where I'm goin'."

"Oh yeah?" He smiled at her determination.

"Absolutely. Atlanta's gettin' tired anymore. Even Usher moved to New York!"

He looked at her, sipping her champagne with her pinkie extended,

and wondered how the residence of another of the city's musical super-
stars had any relationship to any aspect of Brandi's life. Suddenly he felt
sorry for her. She wanted so much and had settled for so little. Las Vegas
would eat this girl alive.

General had taken Juanita to Vegas once. She'd been a big Sammy
Davis Jr. fan and he surprised her with a weekend trip when Sammy was
still playing the hotels on the strip. The day before they left, he treated her
to a shopping spree and she came home from Saks with a sophisticated
array of outfits that wedded class and sass to Juanita's personal style in a
way that made General proud to have her on his arm.

They saw Sammy's show twice. They made love in a suite with a mirror on the ceiling and a black marble Jacuzzi in the bathroom and ordered
room service. The only thing they didn't do was gamble. Juanita said water
was what brought her luck, so she wasn't about to waste her money trying
to gamble in the middle of the desert. General was used to playing blackjack by East Coast casino rules and found the Vegas way distracting. That
gave them more time for sightseeing, including a day trip to the Boulder
Dam because Juanita couldn't believe they had actually dammed up a
whole river just to be sure people in Vegas could flush their toilets.

He took a picture of her backstage with Sammy after the second show,
courtesy of a horn player who had traveled with one of Blue's tours years
earlier and was now part of the Davis ensemble, and got back on the plane
to Atlanta. They had a great time, but they never went back. New Orleans
and Atlantic City were more to their liking and a whole lot closer.

Everything he heard about Vegas today made him know it wasn't
for him. All those gigantic hotels and amateur, wannabe gamblers who
wouldn't know a real card game if they pulled up a chair and sat down to
it. Kids in the restaurants, old ladies at the slot machines, and bachelorette
parties at the crap tables. This was not a place he wanted to see again, *but
so what?* Brandi, he knew, had never been out of the state of Georgia. She
would have a ball in Vegas if they went there together. He'd call some of the
guys he still knew out there and get a nice weekend package. Limo, champagne, flowers in the suite, the whole deal. It would probably be the only
fantasy she'd ever have whose realization would exceed her expectations.

The intensity of his sudden desire to make this happen surprised him,
until he realized *this was another message from Juanita!* He'd been feeling

her presence all night, especially remembering that one great weekend in Vegas. Maybe she wanted him to go back. Maybe she wanted him to go back with Brandi.

"You know what I think?" he said, watching her wiping the corners of her mouth delicately with the white linen napkin and leaving bright red lipstick splotches behind.

"What's that, baby?" she said, reapplying her lipstick carefully. In front of her sat a plate filled with the bones that were all that remained of her meal. He had never seen anybody strip a chicken bone that clean with a knife and fork.

"I think if you're going to move there, maybe you ought to take a couple of days and look around first."

"How am I supposed to do that?"

"I'm going to take you."

Her mouth was a perfect *O* of surprise, but her eyes were wary. "Don't tease me like that, baby."

"Have I been teasing you?"

"You gonna take me to Vegas?"

She said it like he had just promised her a trip to paradise.

"I got some business I need to take care of first, but how does the first of next month sound to you?"

"It sounds *perfect!*" She let out a little squeal of pleasure. "Oh my God! That's only two weeks from now! Wait till I tell Madonna! She ain't gonna believe this!"

He chuckled, pleased at her enthusiasm, happy he had trusted that this was what he was supposed to do.

"What kind of clothes do I need to pack, baby? It'll be hot there, right?" Brandi was so happy she was almost squirming in her chair. Her right breast was about to pop out altogether and the complete inappropriateness of her outfit both embarrassed him and gave him an idea.

"There will be plenty of air-conditioning where we're going," he said, "but don't worry about that. I'll take care of everything."

She looked at him, unable to believe her ears. "You gonna buy me some clothes, too?"

"What are you? About a size six?"

She ran her hands over her breasts lightly, nudging the escapee back into place behind the dress's narrow ribbon of red silk. "Five petite on account of I'm so short and sometimes a three when I can find them." She grinned at him slowly. "I like stuff to fit tight on me."

That was an understatement. He was relieved that he had usurped her wardrobe planning so smoothly she never had a chance to take it the wrong way.

"I'll take care of everything," he said again.

Her eyes softened with gratitude and something else.

"Let's go home baby," she said softly, tossing her napkin down on the table and reaching for her purse. "I got some dessert for you."

"Is it sweet?" he said, laying down four crisp one hundred dollar bills to cover the meal, the champagne, and a big enough tip to guarantee him the same service whenever he came again.

"It's real sweet."

"Is it hot?"

"Hotter than that, baby." She ran her tongue lightly over her newly repainted lips and grinned at him. "Hot enough for Vegas."

41

Club Baltimore was pretty much an exact replica of a dozen other clubs within a five-block radius. The music was loud, the drinks were overpriced, the VIP section was off-limits unless you knew somebody, and everybody was real busy pretending they just flew in on a private jet from someplace more exciting than this could ever be. Even the valet parkers would tell you they were just doing the gig to keep body and soul together until some record company recognized their genius and got them into the studio. The bullshit was three feet deep and four across, Baby Brother thought. Of course he loved it.

Janice and Michelle did, too. They were clearly regulars. Everybody from the hostess at the door guarding her VIP list to the hot-dog bartender whose specialties were perfect cosmopolitans for the ladies and an endless supply of Cristal for the men who could afford it greeted the dynamic duo by name. They relished the attention as they eased through the crowd in their tight jeans and *Sex and the City* shoes, waving to friends, promising to call back, and pointing out the club's fine points to Baby Brother as Zora followed behind. It pleased him to notice that although Zora was completely comfortable, she didn't seem to frequent the place as often as her friends did. He liked that. He wasn't looking for a virgin, but he didn't want to be just one more in a long line.

Mickey and Jan proceeded upstairs to the VIP section without even stopping at the bar. Baby Brother had a sudden fear that since he was the only man in their group, he'd be expected to pay for whatever expensive drinks they ordered. These girls were not going to be satisfied with a glass of the house Chablis, if he could even afford three glasses of that and have enough left to buy himself a beer.

He didn't need to worry. As they settled into a cozy nook where they could see everything and enjoy the earsplitting beats pouring from the sound system without having to mingle with the crowd of *nobodies* downstairs, Zora leaned over and whispered in his ear.

"Don't worry about the drinks. Mickey knows the bartender. He always hooks us up."

Baby Brother knew why. It couldn't hurt a club to have these three beauties on the premises as often as they wanted to come. In reality, they were out of reach of most of the guys who caught a glimpse of them, but the hope that springs eternal in the male breast is part of what makes guys hang out in clubs in the first place. Zora and her girlfriends were the flesh-and-blood stuff of a brother's dreams, Baby Brother thought. Tonight, he was just lucky enough to be the one they chose to share their world.

"Cool," he said, and when the VIP room waiter came around with Mickey's cosmopolitan and Janice's champagne cocktail, he ordered Heineken and a shot of cognac for himself and a strawberry daiquiri for Zora, at her request. The service was fast, and within minutes, they were sipping their drinks and grinning around the table at one another.

"I think we should toast something," Janice said.

"Okay," Mickey said. "What?"

"I don't know. What about you, Zora? You got anything to toast?" And she rolled her eyes in Baby Brother's direction.

"I got somethin'," he said, raising his glass. They followed suit like good little schoolgirls. "To the three sexiest women in this whole club."

Mickey giggled and raised her glass. Jan rolled her eyes again as she clinked her glass against the others. "I'll drink to that."

"And the smartest," said Zora, taking a small sip of her daiquiri.

Janice groaned. "Speak for yourself. This is a night to get *stupid*."

Zora wondered how her genius friend, a straight-A premed major at Spelman, was going to accomplish that.

"You got that right." Mickey waved her perfectly manicured hand at the waiter for another round. It wouldn't be any easier for her to *get stupid* since she had just completed her junior year abroad in France and had already been offered a position as a teacher in the international school when she graduated in June if she wanted it.

Zora could tell both of her friends found Wes attractive. They acted this way only around men they'd be interested in having sex with sometime. Zora couldn't blame them. He was still fine, even without his uniform. She was glad he had gone to see Blue and moved into West End. Even though he bitched about the job, and even more about the housing, he wasn't going anywhere for a minute or two. That would give her time enough to see if there was anything to him worth exploring.

She knew she was physically attracted to him, but there was no rush to act on it right away. It took a long time for her to let a man get close to her sexually, and even when she did, she was so obsessed with safe sex that she limited her contact with her lovers to oral sex, with appropriate latex, mutual masturbation with fantasy, and role-playing. There was no need to tell Wes all that yet. Right now all she wanted to do was make sure he knew she was interested and let nature take its course.

"Do you want to dance?" she said.

Baby Brother looked at the VIP room, where couples and small groups of men and women were drinking and talking. There was a small dance floor, but it was empty. He'd been away long enough to be unsure whether his moves were still current. The last thing he wanted to do was jump out there with some tired old steps that would make him look foolish.

"Here?"

"If you want," she said, "but it's more fun downstairs."

He could just imagine that blouse slipping off her shoulder once she started dancing. This was no time to worry about looking foolish. He stood up, drained his beer, and held out his hand. "Then let's go where the fun is."

An hour later, they finally came back to the table, laughing and sweating, smelling themselves and each other like the sweetest perfume. She was a good dancer and so was he. Fast or slow, their bodies seemed in perfect sync. When they came together on a rare slow tune, she pressed herself lightly against him like a promise.

Janice and Michelle had joined two brothers at another table, but excused themselves when their friends returned and hurried over to signify.

"You didn't tell me you were auditioning for *Soul Train*," Mickey said.

"Go to hell." Zora laughed. "I haven't danced that much since high school."

"Me neither," Baby Brother said as a waitress brought him another beer and another shot without being asked. He took a long swallow of the beer and grinned at Zora. He had had two more drinks while they were downstairs and he was pleasantly high and feeling expansive. "We should come back here tomorrow."

Mickey giggled. "You don't want to do that, sweetheart. Tomorrow's DL night."

"What the hell is DL night?" He had been away only a few months, but the latest slang had already passed him.

"It's the one night of the week when all the *down-low* brothers come out to play. They spend all Sunday morning in church and all Sunday night at the club," Mickey was happy to explain, watching for his reaction.

"This club?" Baby Brother was surprised. He'd never heard of a straight club and a gay one sharing space. Most dudes on the DL were so paranoid about being *outted* they wouldn't go anywhere near a straight club with a man they were interested in sexually.

Jan giggled. "It's crazy, right? They don't even open the front door. All entry through the rear."

Zora wrinkled her perfect nose. "How corny is that?"

It didn't sound corny to Baby Brother. It sounded like *opportunity*. He knew he could always pick up a few dollars where men were looking for other men. That didn't make him a professional hustler. It was just a question of economics. Given a choice, he'd always rather have a woman, but he needed some cash fast, and hauling tomatoes at two hundred dollars a week wasn't taking him anywhere he wanted to go. Davy's right-wing radio fixation was already driving him crazy. Besides, he thought, draining the green bottle of the last of his beer, it wasn't like he'd never done it before.

"Too corny for me," he said, reaching for his beer. How many did this one make? Four? Or was it five? He couldn't remember. What difference did it make anyway? He wasn't paying or driving, and unless he was mistaken, Zora had something for him.

The DJ put on the latest hip-shaking anthem from Beyoncé and her girls. Zora stood up and held out her hand with a smile. "You want to give it one more try?"

He grinned at her, drained the last of the shot that came with the beer, and stood up to put his arm around her waist. His head was buzzing with the liquor and the music and the possibilities that lay ahead. "You ain't tryin' to hurt a nigga, are you?"

"Not me," Zora said, laughing. "I'm trying to *heal* one."

That dance turned into two or three more until Mickey finally said she was leaving, and if they wanted to stay, they could catch a cab home. It was time to call it a night and not a moment too soon. By the time Mickey dropped them off at Zora's apartment, Baby Brother realized he was way higher than he had intended to be. He hoped he wasn't too drunk to make love to Zora. Sometimes cognac put his penis to sleep and there was nothing he could do to wake it up until the liquor was out of his system. If that happened, he'd have to try oral sex, but even though he had been told he was good at it, that definitely wasn't his first choice.

He stumbled a little when he got out of the car and followed Zora up to the blue front door, weaving slightly as she searched for her key. She was one lucky girl to have hooked up with him, Baby Brother thought. She was in for the best sex of her life, *as soon as she got the damn door open.* He leaned forward suddenly, grabbed Zora's behind, and squeezed hard. When she whirled around, he stumbled against her, grinning and glassy-eyed.

"Are you drunk?" Zora said, a frown wrinkling her beautiful forehead.

"A little," he said, giving her a lopsided smile. "Are you?"

"I don't get drunk."

He noticed that she held her key in her hand, but was making no move to open the door. The urgent need to urinate suddenly overwhelmed him. "Can we go upstairs now, baby? I gotta pee bad."

Zora was incredulous. She couldn't believe he had gotten this drunk the first time they ever went out. He could hardly stand up. Any thought she might have had about inviting him upstairs vanished.

"Go home and pee."

"Can't make it that far, baby," he said, shifting from foot to foot.

"Try," she said, sarcastic as hell.

Baby Brother didn't appreciate her tone, but he couldn't really worry about that now. What she didn't seem to realize was that in about two seconds, he was going to pee all over her pretty little feet.

"Aw, baby," he whined. "Don't be that way."

"Go home," she said again, then opened and closed the door in one smooth motion, leaving him alone outside, too surprised and drunk to follow.

"What the fuck?" He really had to pee now. He looked around for assistance, but it was very late. The street was deserted and he knew nobody was going to let a drunk stranger in to use the bathroom. He had no choice but to knock on Zora's door, knowing she could hear it, even if she had already gone inside. "Zora! *What the fuck?*"

She didn't come back out, so he knocked again and called a little louder.

"*Zora!*"

The urge to pee was becoming imperative. *Shit!* She wasn't coming out again. That much was clear. He felt like he was about to explode. *What the hell was he supposed to do?* The large magnolia tree in front of the house seemed like the best option and Baby Brother stumbled back down the walk toward it, unzipping his jeans as he went. He didn't even notice the black Lincoln easing down the quiet street until it pulled over and stopped at the curb right beside him.

"*Jamerson!*"

Even drunk as he was, the sound of General's voice stopped him. He groaned, fumbling to zip his pants back up before he turned around. Baby Brother didn't know what was scarier. The fact that General had happened by or the fact that the man knew him by sight *and* by name.

"Yes, sir?" he said, trying not slur his words and failing.

"What the hell are you doing?" General's voice from inside the car was outraged and enraged, a dangerous combination for one o'clock on a Sunday morning.

"I just dropped off Zora," Baby Brother said, stumbling over her name.

"Did she tell you to pee in her front yard?"

"No, sir, I just . . . I had to pee and she wouldn't let me come inside."

"Why was that?"

"Because . . ." His voice trailed off. *Wasn't it obvious?* "Because I was . . . drinking."

"Because you're drunk."

"Yes, sir, I am." He would have confessed anything if General would just give him a chance to relieve himself.

"Get in the car."

Baby Brother resisted the urge to groan, climbed in the front seat, and pulled the door behind him. General loomed large in the seat beside him.

"If you pee in this car I will cut your head off," he said, locking the doors with a dull thud as they pulled away from the curb.

The two blocks to the apartment were excruciating. The car moved at a crawl and every small bump in the road was torture. When General pulled up in front of his apartment, Baby Brother wanted to fling open the door and run to the toilet, but General didn't click the locks. He looked at Baby Brother coldly, ignored the squirming, and spoke in a voice full of contempt and barely controlled anger.

"I recommended that Mr. Hamilton not make a place for you here, but he thinks you can grow the fuck up and be a man, so he's allowing you to stay. But know this, youngblood. I got my eye on you."

Baby Brother did not want General to cut his head off, but in about ten seconds, it wouldn't be up to him anymore. "Yes, sir."

General looked at him with undisguised contempt, then finally clicked the locks. "Get the fuck out."

Baby Brother half leaped, half stumbled out of the car. General turned out of sight at the corner, but it was too late. Before he could get in the house, *bad-ass Wes Jamerson* stood right there on the corner of Oglethorpe and Peeples streets, peed on his new Sean John jeans, and cried like a baby.

42

S unday was Regina's favorite day of the week. Blue made breakfast and squeezed fresh juice while she put on a pot of coffee, set the table, and found some music that suited them. Sometimes Blue would sing a little if something caught his ear. Regina would stop where she was and listen. His voice was still amazing even though he never sang professionally anymore. He was still sexy as hell, too, even just making pancakes. Maybe *especially* while making pancakes.

Sometimes they watched *CBS Sunday Morning.* Sometimes they went back to bed and made love. They always read the Sunday papers together. In addition to *The Atlanta Journal/Constitution,* they read *The New York Times, The Atlanta Sentinel,* and *The Washington Post.* Sometimes they would leaf through a paper printed in a language neither one could read or speak. Blue said it helped him remember how big the world was and that how smart you are depends on where you're standing. He read voraciously and was probably the most knowledgeable person Regina knew when it came to international affairs. Not many people were aware of this because Blue tended to keep his opinions to himself, preferring not to engage in emotionally charged discussions with people not nearly as well informed as he was and usually twice as opinionated.

Blue had never been a big talker. Regina sometimes teased him that he didn't need to talk as much as other people because he was such an expert mind reader.

"That should make me talk more." He laughed. "Think of the stories I could tell."

Regina could remember a time when the possibility that the man she loved had the ability to read her mind would have driven her into a frenzy of trying to think only the purest, most intelligent, admirable, compassionate thoughts possible, knowing her brain was at that very moment alive with fear, guilt, secrets, lies, and fabrications of all kinds. It was exhausting.

But she had no secrets from Blue. Even the idea of secrets was inconceivable. She wanted to get as close to him as she possibly could in every possible way. In order to do that, she had to be as light as a feather *inside.* She had to learn to just let people be, including her husband. Blue was not a work in progress. He was a fully formed human being and so was she. This had been a revelation, removing as it did the need to reform, refocus, nag, cajole, beg, wheedle, and weep. All she tried to do these days was stay in the moment and enjoy the life she was moving through *right now.* The one where she was sitting on the floor in her living room, surrounded by a disheveled pile of newspapers.

Blue was sitting in a big leather chair an arm's length away in a white sweater that made his skin look like dark chocolate, reading a story in *The New York Times* about the difficulty veterans returning from Iraq and Afghanistan were having trying to adjust to life back in the United States. He was reading the article aloud, his mellifluous voice as neutral as a network newscaster. The reporter chronicled the disastrous reentries of several young soldiers with young children and wives ill equipped to handle the volatile mixture of emotions these men were carrying like a virus. In each case, there was little help available, although the possibility for violence was always present.

He read the last sentence, a wistful quote from a young vet reacting to a friend's recent suicide by questioning his own desire to live, and looked over at Regina, listening intently and absentmindedly rubbing her belly.

"That's terrible," she said. "I can't believe the army doesn't routinely have counseling services in place for returning vets."

"They better do something fast." Blue folded the paper with a little frown, his eyes cloudy and distant. "It's already too late for some of these women."

Regina's hand now rested gently on her stomach. Blue's neutral voice had disappeared and his eyes became suddenly dark and cold.

"What do you mean? Too late for which women?"

She slid over closer and rested her hand against his knee. He stroked her hand slowly, lingering over each one of her long, slender fingers. Blue always chose his words carefully and she had learned to be patient. It was always worth the wait.

"You remember that woman they found cut up in her husband's apartment a couple of weeks ago?"

The extreme violence had been irresistible to the news media, which updated the story around the clock, including widespread speculation that the victim's missing husband was the killer. Regina remembered photographs of the woman's children at the funeral, huddling in a weeping little knot around their exhausted grandmother, their mother dead and their father nowhere to be found.

"I remember her."

"Her husband was in Iraq for a year."

Something in Blue's voice made Regina realize that this man, whom the police had been unable to find, had not been able to elude her husband's all-seeing eyes. A slight chill ran down her spine, but she shrugged it off and reached for *The Sentinal*.

"Did you see the piece B.J. did about the new veterans program at the Morehouse Medical School?" Regina asked.

Blue shook his head.

"It's aimed at easing the transition you're talking about. The guy in charge said it's a public-health crisis. Domestic violence, mental illness, post-traumatic stress. He says it's one big mess."

"He got that right," Blue said. "Is this guy a vet?"

"The director? I don't know." Her eyes scanned the article that ran alongside a photograph of a terrified-looking woman with an equally frightened-looking child in her arms, standing beside the man of the house, a huge Marine with a bodybuilder's physique and a recurring nightmare during which he beat his wife severely without ever waking up. "Does it matter?"

"Hard to relate to vets if you've never been to war."

Regina's eye found what she was looking for. "He was in the Gulf War. He didn't get any counseling when he got out either. That's why he started the program."

She handed Blue the paper. "It sounds like a good idea. Maybe you could help them."

He leaned back in the chair and smiled at her, his eyes clear again like a summer sky after the rain. "Help them?"

"Well, they're trying to raise money," she said. "And you agree it's a real problem. You've seen it yourself, right?"

"I have indeed."

"Well, this would be a way to address the problem without . . ." She felt herself beginning to flounder. "Without having to . . . do anything *directly.*"

"Not many things more direct than money."

"I just thought maybe . . . I mean, I know you can't stop doing what you do, but maybe you could step back just a little . . . from the day-to-day stuff . . . you know." She was in too deep to stop, but she hated herself for bringing it all up again. She took a deep breath and tried to take the edge off her voice. "Maybe try some other approaches."

He slid from the chair to the floor beside her and put his arm around Regina's shoulders. She turned to face him and he leaned over and kissed her, his lips warm against her own.

"Are you still trying to make an honest man out of me?" he said as she moved into the circle of his arms and cuddled against his chest. He kissed the top of her head.

"You're the most honest man I know."

"Then what's the problem?" He raised her palm to his lips, his mustache a soft tickle.

"No problem." She sighed. "I think I might volunteer for that program over at Morehouse."

"That's good," he said, kissing her fingertips. "You're not starting today, are you?"

She laughed and slipped her other hand under his sweater. His skin was as warm as his mouth. "No, baby. Not today."

43

Monday was always slow at Montre's. By late afternoon, Brandi had been at work almost two hours and had made exactly three dollars in tips. She was as bored as the two guys at the bar who were nursing their lukewarm beers. All the weekend money had been spent and payday was still four days away. Brandi slithered around the pole without enthusiasm. Those guys didn't deserve a full show, she thought. They weren't going to tip anyway.

General had said he was coming by later, but that usually meant after midnight. That way if he wanted her to leave with him, she could get off a little early without hearing a lot of grumbling from Johnny. Not that Johnny ever said anything to General. His place was over the West End boundary, true enough, but that didn't mean he wanted to be on the wrong side of Blue Hamilton. These days, if the big man wanted her for a private dance at his place, Brandi kicked back something to the other girls who'd have to cover for her on the pole and *kept steppin'*.

To Brandi, General was the best thing that had happened to her in ages. He liked pretty straightforward sex and he was in great shape, so she didn't have to do all the work. She hated rolling around with the fat guys, or even the ones who weren't fat, just *soft*. They wanted those gymnastics they saw in the porno movies, where a woman could take on two guys at the same time while standing on one foot and giving a third man a blow job. General wasn't looking for all that. He liked to get in the bed, turn out the lights, and take his time. That was fine with Brandi. The bed was always the easiest place to drive a man crazy and she was trying to do just that so General wouldn't forget his promise to take her to Vegas. She couldn't get away from Montre's fast enough, and with him as her sponsor, there was no telling what might open up.

She looked around the almost empty room and sighed. It was time for her to try to get some lap dances, but the two sad-eyed men at the bar were busy staring into their half-empty beer bottles. She knew approaching them would be a waste of time, so she decided to do one more set and, if nobody came in, take a break. *Ain't no point in killin' myself up here,* she thought. *I ain't gonna be here that much longer no way.*

The sound system was blasting Lil' John and the East Side Boys just like it did when the place was full and something in the music made Brandi decide to really dance. The fact that Montre's patrons didn't know how to appreciate *real class* didn't mean she had to stoop to their level. She hooked her arm around the pole and shook her breasts like she was trying to wake them up. *I'm gonna do this one for me,* she thought. *I'm gonna do this one like I'm already in Vegas!*

Closing her eyes, she began to move to the music. Her sudden energy hit the guys at the bar like a splash of cold water and they looked at each other and then back toward the small stage. Brandi was twisting herself around the pole in a series of positions that amazed and excited them. They clutched their beer, hoping she wouldn't stop. Johnny, behind the bar, grinned at their reaction and, in a sudden burst of uncharacteristic generosity, handed them each another cold beer, on the house.

"Tell your friends what kinds of girls we got in here," he said, enjoying the shock on their faces.

Their unexpected good fortune, plus the shaking, shimmying vision of feminine pulchritude *dancing her ass off* only a few feet away, took them by surprise. They thanked Johnny, assured him they would tell everybody they knew, and moved to a table down front, determined to make the most of whatever other good fortune came their way. Brandi ignored them. In her mind, she was dancing at the Paris Casino. So focused was she that she didn't even notice the new guy at the bar ordering a rum and Coke.

He noticed her, though. Baby Brother had spent the weekend trying unsuccessfully to get laid. Since his drunken scene at her front door, Zora was no longer a possibility. He woke up Sunday with a hangover and a hard-on and walked over to Montre's only to find out that they were closed for a private party. Over the bouncer's head, he could see a fine woman with a tiny little waist and a beautiful behind doing things with a strip pole he'd seen only in X-rated movies. Something in the way she was moving produced an instant erection and he tried to draw out the conversation as long as he could, but the bouncer slammed the door in his face.

That night, all he dreamed about was that stripper, twisting herself around that silver pole. He'd spent the morning making deliveries and wondering if she'd be working there tonight, too. Since he hadn't had to pay for any drinks on Saturday night, he had a couple of dollars left to play with. Even if all he got was a lap dance from a woman that fine, he thought, he'd be a happy man.

It took his eyes a few minutes to adjust to the dim light in Montre's, but he spotted her instantly. She was working that pole again, to the amazement of two guys down front, but otherwise he had her all to himself. He took a table near the stage, but as far away from the dynamic duo as possible. He didn't want her to think he was with them. They looked even broker than he was.

On the stage, Brandi was winding up with her trademark upside-down *rump-shaker* finale. In her mind, she was already breathing desert air and learning to play blackjack. When she slid to her feet and looked around, a new guy she hadn't seen come in held up a five-dollar bill and smiled. She smiled back and headed over to him. Keisha, late for her shift again, passed her with a wink.

"Make that money, girl!"

Brandi did not consider five bucks cause for celebration and she was tired of Keisha always showing up late. "Get a damn watch, bitch," she snapped, brushing past the woman.

Baby Brother watched Brandi head his way. She wasn't as fine as Zora, but she was fine enough.

"Hey, baby," she said, plucking the money from his fingers. "You want me to dance for you?"

"Oh yeah," he said, sliding down in the chair and opening his legs a little wider. Touching the dancers was not allowed, but if a girl knew what she was doing, you didn't have to touch her to get off. Brandi was a pro. She danced so close to him he could feel the heat coming off her body and smell the sweat running down between her breasts. From the way she was moving, he thought she might be getting turned on as much as he was. He hoped she was. He had ten dollars left. Maybe that would be enough for a little something extra.

The song ended and Brandi unstraddled his leg and smiled at him like she'd just had the best time of her life. He had no way of knowing her Vegas fantasy was still in full effect. She was pretending he was Busy Boy Baker and he'd come to the Paris and asked for her exclusively.

"How about another one, baby?" she cooed. "I can make it special."

"How special?"

She slid back into his lap and bounced up and down slowly. "How much you got, baby?"

This was the moment of truth. She hoped he had some money. He was young and kind of cute. Looked like he might have a few bucks on him. At least he was clean. So many of these guys smelled like sweat and urine. He smelled like soap.

"I got ten dollars," Baby Brother said, still smiling, trying to make it sound like a hundred.

Ten dollars. That pretty much blew Brandi's Busy Boy fantasy. He probably didn't carry anything smaller than a fifty. *Who was she kidding?* This was a long way from Vegas, but she was still at work and ten bucks was still ten bucks.

She sighed. "Let me see it."

He reached into his pocket and pulled out his last ten-dollar bill. She took it without looking and smiled at him again.

"Thank you, baby. I'm gonna give you something really special."

Brandi closed her eyes and tried to conjure up her fantasy again. She turned around in his lap so Johnny couldn't see her initiating contact and put Baby Brother's hands on her breasts while she rocked and rolled her hips against him. On the stage, Keisha was just going through the motions, but Brandi was pulling out all the stops. She rocked her behind just like she did onstage, and when Baby Brother groaned, she pretended it was Busy Boy she was driving crazy.

"Oh yeah, baby," she said, feeling his excitement and her own. As long as she kept her eyes closed, this *was* Busy Boy.

Baby Brother groaned again, realizing he was about to climax right there sitting at that little scuffed-up table in this hellhole of a strip joint.

"Come on, baby." She urged him on, moving faster and faster. "You know you want to."

No longer caring about the rules, he held on for dear life until Brandi arched her back, threw back her head, and did something that felt so good to him that he did come. *They both did.* Baby Brother groaned once more and it was over.

Brandi couldn't remember the last time she'd had a real sexual response to a paying customer. She opened her eyes and stood up. That's when she saw General watching her from the dark end of the bar. Something about the way he was staring made her nervous, although there was no reason for it. She was at work. If a guy paid five dollars, he got a lap dance. If he paid ten, he got a little extra.

"Come back and see me," she said, moving toward General without a backward glance, leaving Baby Brother plucking at his sticky clothes and trying to think of something to say.

A couple of more guys had come in and Keisha was giving one of them a lap dance that didn't seem to be doing much for him or her. Johnny was talking on the phone and General was sipping his scotch.

"Hey, baby," she said. "What you doin' in here so early? Want me to dance for you?"

"You going to give me the same dance you just gave that yellow nigga?"

Brandi froze. The harshness of his tone surprised her. "What you mean, baby? You know I'm at work."

"That didn't look like work to me."

How General recognized a real orgasm from the fakes she usually served up in his bed, she didn't know, but she just played it off. "That's because I'm good."

He jerked his big head in Baby Brother's direction. "How long you been knowin' this guy?"

"I don't know him," she said, getting more annoyed by the minute. "He's a nigga with fifteen bucks to buy my time. This is my job, remember?"

General knew that as well as she did, but he was getting tired of seeing this young fool everywhere he went. He hadn't been in West End for more than two weeks and he had already overstayed his welcome. "Well, maybe you need to find another one."

"What's that supposed to mean?"

He put down his drink. "It means I don't want you doing any more lap dances. You stick to the stage from now on."

"You got no claim on me," she said. He was acting like a jealous husband, and if she'd wanted one of those, she'd have gotten married. "I'll do whatever the fuck I please, and anytime you don't like it, *you can kiss my black ass.*"

She turned away to illustrate her point and there it was. Juanita's birthmark right there at the small of Brandi's back. *What was wrong with him tonight anyway?* It wasn't her fault she was doing this for a living and it wasn't his job to make her feel bad about it. His job was to give her a better option.

He reached out and grabbed her arm before she walked away, but she shook him off like a bad kid defying the principal.

"Get off me!"

The few other patrons were all down by the stage waving money at Keisha. Only Johnny at the bar was watching General and his star dancer out of the corner of his eye. He hoped Brandi's smart mouth didn't write any checks that beautiful ass couldn't cash.

"I'm sorry," General said, dropping his hand. He had to admire her spirit. She wasn't scared of him even though she probably should have been.

She rubbed her arm, pouting now. "You should be sorry. I ain't doin' nothin' but workin' and here you come, actin' all crazy."

"Did I hurt you?"

"What you think?"

"I think we both need a vacation."

Her eyes searched his face for a clue as to what he was talking about. "What you mean?"

"I mean I made some calls and put some things in place."

"What kind of things?" She was smiling again, hopeful.

General smiled back at her. "The things a brother needs to show a lady Las Vegas for the first time."

"*When?*" She was barely able to contain her excitement.

"Two weeks from today."

"You not just sayin' it 'cause I got mad before, are you?"

"No."

He wanted her to turn around again so he could see the mark on her back, but she squealed and threw her arms around his neck and kissed him on the mouth right there in the middle of Montre's. At the end of the bar, Johnny let the no-contact rule slide, relieved at a happy ending.

"Oh, baby, I can't wait! You too good to me, you know that?"

He smiled and finished his drink in one long gulp. She didn't move away from him, just stood there smiling like all was forgiven.

"Am I gonna see you later?"

"How about now?" he said, suddenly not wanting to wait for her. Suddenly wanting to hold her body close. Wanting to sex away the image of her bouncing Juanita's mark around in that young *nigga's* lap.

"Now?" She glanced at Johnny, who was back on the phone.

"Right now."

Brandi grinned. Obviously, Johnny was not a problem. General had it covered, and as long as she was his woman, she had it like that, too.

"Let me get my coat," she said. "I'll meet you out back."

By the time she came outside, General was sitting in the car with the motor running and Baby Brother was gone.

44

K wame dropped Joyce Ann at school and doubled back for coffee and conversation with his wife. As she poured them each a steaming cup strong and black like they both preferred it, he knew it was time to tell her about the house. He had been procrastinating for a week, and tomorrow night, they were due at Bob's house for cocktails and Kwame knew that at some point in the evening, Bob was going to turn to Aretha, smile, and say, "So how did you like the house?" and Aretha was going to smile back and say, "What house?"

That would not be the optimum way for her to hear that moving to midtown was a fait accompli, not simply a topic for another of those endless, interlocking conversations where the real story of any marriage can always be found. The move was going to happen. The best thing to do would be for him to tell her about Bob's offer of the house, apologize for not telling her sooner, drive her over to see it, apologizing all the way across town if necessary, and then lobby like hell until she finally acquiesced and started packing.

At first he thought his nervousness about whether or not she would like the house was making him put off telling her about it. Then yesterday, he realized that wasn't it at all. The problem was, he couldn't figure out how to present the house as if it was up for discussion when it wasn't. He had already committed them. When she understood that part of it, he knew she'd be angry and that was absolutely the last thing he wanted. The peace in their household lately had been a real blessing. He didn't know if the job offer was responsible for the change in her, but he knew the difference it had made in him. He felt like he was in the process of reclaiming the life he'd been born to live.

"Thanks," he said as she put the mug down in front of him and curved her graceful fingers around one of her own. The aroma of freshly brewed coffee and the lingering scent of the morning's blueberry waffles were soothing and familiar, just like the cozy room in which they were sitting. He tried to imagine Aretha making waffles in her elegant new kitchen as she took the chair nearest to him and smiled.

"Will we still be able to do this when you're downtown working for the big shots?"

"Working *with* the big shots, okay?" He smiled back. "Give me a little credit. I'm not exactly coming in as an entry-level draftsman."

"You got that right," she said. "Not with a salary like that."

Bob Watson's offer had been almost twice what Kwame had expected and included a schedule of merit raises and a generous benefits package. Even Aretha "I never think about money" had been impressed by all those zeros.

He put down his mug. "There's more."

She raised her eyebrows. "More money?" Her voice was incredulous.

"No. There's a house."

"A house?" She put her mug down, too. "What house?"

Kwame took a deep breath. "I told Bob we were considering a move to midtown and it turns out he has a house in Ansley Park that he wants us to take a look at."

"He wants to sell us his house?"

"It would be a long-term lease, actually. He designed the house himself and he doesn't want to sell it."

"He wants us to rent his house?"

"More of a lease situation, but I think he'd sell it if we really like it."

"You're not making any sense, Kwame."

Dragging it out was only making it worse. "The house is a showpiece, Ree, but his wife got tired of it or something, so they moved into a bigger place. He's prepared to let us have it dirt cheap and I know he'd really appreciate having someone in there he could trust."

Aretha was frowning. "Is this part of the package? If we don't agree to rent his house, you don't get to join his firm?"

"No, baby, no! Nothing like that. He didn't even mention it until I told him we were looking."

Her frown stayed where it was, but Aretha couldn't deny she had agreed to look at some houses in midtown.

"We *are* looking, right?"

"Have you seen it?"

He nodded slowly, not sure if that was good or bad. "Yes."

"When?"

"The same day Bob and I had lunch."

"You're just now telling me?" She sounded more hurt than angry.

"I'm sorry. I was trying to figure out a way to make you see what a good thing this is. I guess I didn't do such a good job."

She smiled a little when he said that. "Not so hot, no."

He clung to the slim promise of that half smile as she leaned across the table toward him.

"You don't have to treat me like I'm some kind of crazy woman, you know? You can tell me stuff when it happens. I won't go off. I'm an adult, remember?"

He took her hand. "I don't think you're crazy."

"You sure?" She laced her fingers through his.

"I'm positive."

Then she surprised the hell out of him by leaning over and giving him a big wet kiss. When they came up for air, she was smiling.

"You don't have to work today, do you?"

He grinned at her. "I'm all yours."

"Good," she said. "Then why don't you show me this fabulous house so I can decide if it's fit for my family to live in."

Kwame felt a weight lift from his shoulders. "Thanks, Ree."

"Don't thank me. Get your keys."

So he did.

45

Samson Epps was shorter than Regina had expected him to be and louder. He was one of those people who can shatter your eardrum on a cellphone as well as informing everyone within a six-foot radius of a matter you had hoped to keep confidential. His picture in *The Sentinel* had given her the impression of a tall man, and when she called to schedule an appointment, his big voice had suggested an imposing personality that she had mentally translated into physical size. She was surprised when they shook hands and looked at each other eye to eye.

"Mrs. Hamilton. Please come in," he said, ushering her into his office and closing the door behind them. "Sit down."

Regina took a chair and Samson Epps went back to sit behind his desk. Something in his manner made her feel like she was imposing, although he himself had chosen this time for their meeting. She had said she'd like to explore some fund-raising ideas that might get the neighborhood involved and he had been enthusiastic. Now he seemed to have no memory of her or of their positive telephone exchange.

"I appreciate your time," Regina said. "I'm sure you're busy."

His smile was restrained. "We're always busy, but I do appreciate your interest in our program. What can I do for you?"

"As I mentioned on the phone, I'd like to support the work you're doing with returning vets and their families. The piece in *The Sentinel* made such an impression on me."

At the mention of the Sunday story, which had been full of praise for his program and his vision, the slight smile flickered again briefly. "That was well done, wasn't it?"

Regina waited for him to say more, but he just looked at her.

"Yes, it was," she said. "It made me want to get involved instead of just complaining. I live in West End, where we're already feeling the consequences of what's happening, and since you're right here in the neighborhood, I thought this would be a good place to start."

He placed his palms together under his chin and an expression she couldn't read flickered across his face.

"To start what?"

"I beg your pardon?"

Samson Epps shook his head disapprovingly. "Mrs. Hamilton, there is no need for either of us to continue this charade."

Regina felt her cheeks flush, although she had no idea what he was talking about. "If you have something to say to me, Dr. Epps, I encourage you to say it. I came here to talk about helping you raise funds for your program. Your tone is inappropriate."

He pushed his chair away from the desk slightly. "*Inappropriate?* I mentioned to one of my colleagues that a neighborhood woman who had seen our recent press coverage had called to explore a possible fund-raiser to support the project."

Regina hated the way he described her as "a neighborhood woman." It was the way people talked about the human beings they had decided to think of generically. A *native* woman. A *Palestinian* child. A *homeless* man. The more he talked, the more she didn't like him.

"My colleague was pleased, but when I told her your name, she kind of laughed and said, 'Don't you know who that is?' "

A sudden realization made her cheeks flush. *This was about Blue!* The article had said Samson Epps had been in Atlanta for only a year, but how long did it take to meet the community that was the campus's nearest neighbor? How long did it take to notice how different that community was and ask somebody *why?*

But there was another voice in her head arguing the other side almost as strongly. That part of her wanted to know why she was blaming Samson Epps for not knowing that in some circles, her husband was regarded as less than respectable and, when crossed, undeniably dangerous. That part of her wanted to know whom she was really mad at, Samson or Blue. Regina sat silent, not knowing what to say next.

"Mrs. Hamilton, you must be aware of your husband's reputation," Samson Epps said.

"Go on," was Regina's answer. *Aware of it?* She thought. *I live with it every day.*

"Then you must know that there are certain trade-offs for the lives we choose."

He was talking to her like she had come to him for pastoral counseling.

"I respect the choices your husband has made and I'm asking that you respect mine. This is a government-funded program, Mrs. Hamilton. I can't accept money from *gangsters.*"

He said the word with such contempt he almost spit it at her. Regina tried to compose herself before she responded. She wanted to find the words to explain how careful Blue was never to take his role lightly or use the power he had irresponsibly. She wanted to say it weighed on him. She wanted to tell Samson Epps about the women and children whose lives were saved by Blue's willingness to defend them. She wanted to witness for the brothers who had been transformed by working with her husband in West End. She wanted to tell him how they had become men who could be loved and trusted without fear. She wanted to tell him that her husband acted out of absolute love for his people and a definition of manhood that did not depend on any commander in chief other than the one he saw in the mirror every morning, gazing back through his own blue eyes.

But she didn't tell him any of that. *What was the point?* Besides, she didn't think she would be able to get the words out without crying. She stood up, gathered her things, and walked out of Samson Epps's office without uttering another sound. She had nothing to say to him. The person she needed to talk to was Blue.

46

Precious was not looking forward to this meeting. She had liked and trusted Lee Kilgore, *but no more.* The things Blue had told Precious made it impossible for her to even consider keeping Lee around as part of her team. It was Precious's intention to be in and out in fifteen minutes, *tops.* There was really nothing to discuss. Blue had not only confirmed what Mrs. Robinson had said, but had identified Kilgore as part of a network of dirty cops and corrupt civilians who were making millions with little or no danger of arrest.

Before she had fully digested that news, Blue also shared a rumor he had not personally verified yet that Bob Watson had a hand in it, too. That was the part that had really thrown Precious for a loop. She had no idea how she could tell Kwame that his new idol had feet of clay. Taking a deep breath, she pulled into the visitors' lot behind the Atlanta Police Department's downtown headquarters and tried to compose herself before she confronted Lee Kilgore.

Police headquarters was always crowded. Police officers and perpetrators, people being charged and discharged. There was a grim determination in their faces. Everybody knew that once you walked inside those doors, everything that happened was going to be serious. Precious knew it, too, but she still smiled back at the young female police officer at the security desk inside the front door who directed her to a tiny cubicle on the second floor.

When Precious knocked on the door, Lee's voice answered with the edge of someone who doesn't want to be disturbed.

"It's open!"

Somehow, Precious had imagined Lee in grander surroundings. This small, airless space was barely large enough for a desk and a tiny bookcase. A chair for visitors was wedged in the corner almost as an afterthought. Lee's annoyance at being interrupted was immediately replaced by her surprise at finding Precious standing in her doorway.

"Senator Hargrove." She stood up and came around to extend a hand. "What a pleasant surprise. Sit down."

Precious stepped in and closed the door behind her without a handshake.

Lee frowned. "Is something wrong?"

"I'll get right to the point, Captain Kilgore. As part of my investigation into the death of Kentavious Robinson, I've been given some information by a completely reliable source that not only confirms his mother's suspicions about police involvement, but points to you specifically as one of those protecting the dealers. Is there any truth to what I've been told?"

Lee sat back down behind her desk. She tried to keep her face impassive. This was the moment she had been trying to outrun. *Remain calm,* she thought. *Just remain calm.*

"I'm shocked that you would ask me such a question."

Precious didn't blink. "That's not an answer."

"No. There is no truth to it at all."

The two women looked at each other for a minute, each taking the measure of the other. Finally, Precious spoke quietly. "I don't believe you."

Lee's left eye twitched slightly. "These rumors always follow a cop who tries to bust the dealers, Senator. You should know that."

"You're a talented woman," Precious said quietly. "I admire some of your ideas, but I can't ask you to be part of my team. Not anymore."

Lee felt her future drying up like Georgia crops in a summer-long drought, but she didn't flinch. "I'm sorry to hear that, Senator."

"I won't be pursuing these allegations personally at this time, but I think it's only fair to warn you that I will be passing on what I've heard to your superiors, and one more thing." Precious stood up. "When I'm elected, cleaning up the police department will be job one."

Lee's eye twitched again. "I understand."

"Good." Precious picked up her purse.

Lee stood up, too. "Do you mind if I ask you one question?"

"Go ahead."

"Are you really destroying what we both know could be a productive partnership based on the word of a bunch of crackheads and con artists?"

"No." Precious opened the door. "I'm dissolving our association because it's still working."

"What's still working?"

"My built-in bullshit detector."

47

Kwame turned the car into a long winding driveway that brought Aretha to the front door of the three-story, blindingly white house. She was shocked. Its glass-and-chrome exterior was glittering in the mid-day sun and she could only imagine how bright the interior of the house was with all those windows everywhere. The old adage about people who live in glass houses not throwing stones came immediately to her mind. Sitting there, so dramatically different from its neighbors, the structure didn't look like a house as much as a museum extension or the offices of a once very hip architect with a chip on his shoulder.

"Wow!" was all she could say.

"I told you it was a showpiece," Kwame said, coming around to open her door.

She stepped out and followed him up the front steps into the small entryway that opened quickly into the great room with its high ceiling and glittering chandelier. The windows were even more dramatic than she had imagined and the sunlight streaming in everywhere was bright enough to make her squint. Kwame, who was watching her closely, flipped a wall switch and what looked like flat silk or linen venetian blinds hissed into place without disturbing the clean lines of the place.

White walls? Floor-to-ceiling glass? Linen blinds? Bob had clearly not designed the place with an active two-year-old around. Aretha's motherly eye clocked the potential dangers as Kwame walked her through every room, including the giant kitchen and the master suite, which boasted a tub big enough for the whole family to enjoy a soak. *Could I live here?* she asked herself at the doorway to each new room. *Could I be myself here?* The house felt so cold she almost shivered.

At the end of the tour, they went back downstairs. There were no chairs. Kwame hugged Aretha gently and tried to read her reaction in her face.

"So what do you think?" he said. "Can you stand it for a year or two until we decide what we really want to do?"

From the circle of his arms, she looked around. It helped to think of it as temporary. She could stand almost anything for a year or two.

"Are you sure this is really where you want to live?"

He nodded and tightened his arms around her. "This is where I want *us* to live."

"All right," she said. "Then this is where we'll live."

"I love you," Kwame whispered, leaning down to kiss her, relief flooding his body. *And he did love her.* The part of him that needed more didn't have anything to do with his wife. That was just who he was.

Aretha kissed him back, reminding herself that Kwame had changed his whole life for her and Joyce Ann. She knew this job and this house meant a lot to him and maybe she owed him a little compromise to make it work. That was part of love, too, wasn't it? Learning to meet the beloved halfway? She couldn't deny that he had been a different person since accepting the new job. When they made love, it almost felt like it used to before they started fighting all the time. She tightened her arms around him.

When they came up for air, she grinned at Kwame. "You think Bob would let me add some color to these walls?"

"Probably not," Kwame said, so happy at the outcome of the morning he decided to take a chance. "Maybe there's another way we can warm it up."

As he spoke, he slid his hand under her skirt and caressed her gently. She leaned into his hand and felt herself tremble slightly. He felt it, too, and kissed her again, softly, sweetly, with no demand implied. Just an invitation.

She put her lips against his ear and teased him. "What are you doing up here in these people's house?"

"I'm making love to my wife," he whispered back, loving the way her breasts felt against his chest. *Teddy was right,* he thought. There was no reason he couldn't have everything he wanted. *This was only the beginning!*

"I don't care where we live," Aretha said softly, leaning back to look into his face. "I just want us to be okay."

"We're better than okay." He kissed her again. "We're doing just fine."

He caressed her with growing passion and she responded the same way. He nibbled her neck, the base of her throat.

"Kiss me *there,* baby," she whispered. "Will you kiss me *there?*"

Kwame lifted her skirt to her waist and lowered himself to his knees, pulling her toward him and burying his face in her softness. Moaning softly, she surrendered to the waves of pleasure that weakened her knees, closed her eyes, and slid to the floor, pulling him closer, playing the role this strange house required, and pretending she could make it real just because she wanted it to be.

48

L ee hadn't spoken to Bob in a week. There had been no contact since their last meeting when she told him their partnership was in its last days, but Precious had really shaken her up. The last thing Lee wanted was an official investigation into anything. She needed a way to cut this off at the pass and the only person with as much to lose as she did was Bob. He would have to help her contain this situation. She didn't intend to go limping back to Macon in disgrace, or worse, serve time in jail for drug trafficking.

She needed Bob to use that special access to Precious Hargrove he'd bought with all those campaign contributions. She needed him to vouch for her integrity and help her nip this in the bud before it ruined everything. It was his fault she had stayed in the business long after she wanted out. He owed her this much and she intended to make sure he understood that, too.

Bob greeted Lee at the door in his shirtsleeves. "Aren't you a sight for sore eyes. Come in."

"Where's your lovely wife this evening?" Lee said, looking around to be sure they were alone.

"She's at a spa in Santa Barbara, thanks for asking." Bob led the way into the den.

"Like I give a damn."

His lips curled into a smile that was more of a sneer. "Exactly. Drink?"

"Rum. On the rocks."

Bob splashed the dark, fragrant liquid over ice and handed her the Tiffany cocktail tumblers with which Marian had outfitted the bar. "Are we celebrating or commiserating?"

Lee took a swallow of her drink and the rum burned its way down her throat. "Precious Hargrove said she has it on good authority that I am one of a cadre of dirty cops protecting the cocaine trade, including the murderers of Kentavious Robinson."

"Jesus," Bob said beside her, and took a swallow of his scotch and soda.

"She also said that she's going to turn the information over to my superiors, and when she gets elected mayor, my ass is grass."

"Jesus!"

"You already said that."

"Did she say anything about me?"

Lee looked at him. "As I recall, your name never came up."

"Good."

His obvious relief annoyed her. "That doesn't mean it won't."

Bob raised his eyebrows. "You're not threatening me, are you?"

"Of course not. But we're still partners, remember?"

"Oh, that." He smiled that sneering smile again. "Didn't I tell you?"

"Tell me what?"

"We're not partners anymore. I'm out. Turns out T.G. already had a guy lined up who wanted in immediately. Nice guy, too. Record producer. Lots of available cash. He made me a nice offer for my share of future earnings. Couldn't have come at a better time, actually. I'm too old for all that mess."

Lee willed her face to remain neutral. She hadn't expected Bob to move so quickly, but she couldn't fault him. This was business and she was the one who'd told him to make other arrangements. That was exactly what he had done.

"So you don't have to worry about me, sweetie," he said, his voice oozing insincerity, "but I do appreciate your concern. For old time's sake and all that, but I'm back to being just another hardworking black architect with a few political connections. So, what can I do for you? Freshen your drink?"

"I don't need a drink," Lee snapped. "I need you to make that call."

"What call would that be?" Bob got up and poured himself another splash of cognac.

"The one you bought with all your contributions to Precious Hargrove. The one you're always bragging about."

"Oh, you mean my emergency phone call."

"You know damn well what I mean."

"I'm not sure I do," Bob said, still standing at the bar. "Can you be a little more specific?"

Lee wanted to throw what was left of her drink in his face. She forced herself to speak calmly. "I need you to call Precious Hargrove and vouch for me."

"Vouch for you?"

"Tell her I'm innocent of the charges she's heard, no matter where she heard them."

He nodded slowly like he was considering her request. "And what if she asks me how I can be so sure?"

"Tell her you've known me for years and you have no doubts whatsoever regarding my integrity."

"I see. And what if she remains unconvinced of your innocence?"

Lee took a breath. She hoped it wouldn't come to that, but she had already considered the possibility. "Then tell her I want to be allowed to resign and pursue my professional options elsewhere."

"So let me get this straight," Bob said. "You want me to use my one phone call to save your ass? You want me to call the next mayor of Atlanta and tell her to please back up off my friend the dirty cop who promises to leave town immediately and return to whatever sad little Southern fork in the road spawned her?"

Lee looked at Bob and suddenly wished she'd never come here. There was no way he was going to help her and she knew it. "Fuck you, Bob."

"Too late for that, baby," he said. "Looks like you made your move too soon. Remember I used to tell you how treacherous Atlanta can be? How the same Negroes who were grinning in your face will forget they ever knew your name? Well, now you're going to see firsthand what I was talking about."

Lee had two choices. She could stay there and trade insults with Bob or she could remember Robert Kennedy's famous advice to a friend who had just been royally screwed: *Don't get mad. Get even.* There were no other options and the longer she sat there pretending there were, the longer she delayed making some hard decisions. She was on her own, but she still had one piece of information that might buy her a call back from a concerned mother, even if she was running for mayor. Maybe that information would even buy her one more meeting with the good senator, where Precious could get that self-righteous tone out of her voice and get a dose of her own reality.

It was time to make a move. Lee stood up.

"Leaving already?" Bob said, sipping his drink. "Well, good luck, darlin'. I think you know the way out."

"You're right," Lee said, heading for the door. "I think I do."

49

"What do you say when people call you a gangster?"

Blue and Regina were lying in an oversize hammock that he had hung between the two sweet gum trees that dominated their backyard. Set in a secluded part of the property that rendered them invisible to their neighbors or passersby, but gave Blue an unobstructed view of everything, the hammock had become one of their favorite places to be outside together. They had been lying there in silence for almost an hour, her ear against Blue's chest as the sway of the hammock and the steady rhythm of his heart soothed her like walking beside the ocean.

One of the things she liked about Blue was that he could be silent without being disconnected. She often felt like the most complex conversations they had were nonverbal, depending instead on their physical intimacy to carry the weight of the exchange. Lying in his arms, she remembered Samson Epps's characterization of her husband as a *gangster,* and her own inability to respond. Her ride home had been filled with snappy comebacks and withering put-downs, but they were all too little, too late. In the face of the accusation, the best she could think of was a strategic retreat. She knew there had to be a better response than that.

"What?" Blue sounded surprised.

"When people call you a *gangster.* What do you say?"

"No one has ever called me a gangster."

She half sat up so she could look him the eye. *"Not to your face."*

He smiled and rubbed his hand lightly over her back. "I'm not required to respond to people who don't say it to my face, am I? How would I know?"

"Well, if you *did* know, what would you say?"

Blue looked at her. "Did you hear somebody talking about me?"

She sat up slowly so she wouldn't tip the hammock and swung her legs over the side, her toes just touching the soft grass beneath them. Blue stayed where he was, one arm behind his head, one hand still stroking her back. His eyes were gleaming gray in the twilight.

"I went over to Morehouse today to see Samson Epps about the vets program."

Blue was watching her, but he said nothing.

"I told him we would be interested in doing a fund-raiser since they needed money and he told me . . ."

She hesitated, looking at her husband's dark handsome face. She had never seen him angry; had never witnessed him raise a hand to another human being. Would Epps's accusation make Blue angry? she wondered. The thought caused her hesitation. She thought Samson Epps was a condescending, judgmental bastard, but she didn't necessarily want to place him in the way of her husband's wrath.

Blue gripped both sides of the hammock for balance and easily swung his legs over the side next to Regina. "What did he tell you, baby?"

There was no way to say it but just to say it. "He said he couldn't take money from you because you were a gangster and he was afraid it might jeopardize his federal funding."

For a second, Blue didn't say anything, then he laughed out loud and shook his head. "These Atlanta Negroes never change. The world is coming apart and the doc is worrying about me messing up his grants." He laughed again, genuinely amused, with no undertow of anger or outrage.

Regina was surprised. "I was afraid you might be mad."

"If I got angry every time I ran into a scared Negro, I'd be one mad black man." Blue chuckled.

"But you're not a gangster."

Blue smiled at her. "Absolutely right."

"You're a businessman."

"Right again," he said, still smiling.

"Don't say it like that."

Blue pulled her closer, steadying the hammock with his feet so she could curl up against him again. "Listen, Gina, I'm not a gangster. *I'm a free black man.* That's all I am. The problem is that we are such a rare and dying breed in these United States that sometimes people don't recognize us when we show up, so they call us gangsters, or vigilantes or other things that miss the essence of the answer to their question, which is that I am *first, last, and always* a free man, and I'm prepared to do whatever it takes to stay free and to keep my family safe from harm."

She looked at his eyes, blazing turquoise and golden, and she knew he was telling her the truth. She knew who he was and what he was and *Samson Epps could go to hell!*

She smiled slowly. "Why didn't you just say that in the beginning?"

"I did," he said. "I've been saying it for at least three lifetimes that I can remember, not counting this one."

"How long did it take me to get it the last time?"

"As long as it took for me to figure out how to say it right."

The perfection of his answer pleased her enough to tease him. "So you're not going to *go legit?* Even for the sake of our child?"

"Well, I'm a successful businessman. I'm active in political circles, respected in my community, and I pay my taxes on time. *I'm too legit to quit!*"

The idea of her ever-cool husband quoting the ever-manic MC Hammer brought forth a giggle from Regina that Blue smothered with a kiss. They cuddled close, enjoying the hammock's gentle sway.

"Our child is going to be fine," he said softly. "Trust me."

"I do trust you."

"Good. That's all that matters."

And that was that.

50

aby Brother was on a mission. He had tossed those pissed-out jeans and used most of his check to buy some new clothes. Saturday he played cards with Davy and his idiot friends and picked up a hundred and fifty bucks cheating them at blackjack. On Sunday, he spent the day sleeping and watching whatever games were on TV. At ten o'clock, he walked up to the intersection of Abernathy and Ashby streets and caught a cab to Club Baltimore. When he got there, he went around to the back, paid the ten-dollar cover, and walked in like he did it every night of the week.

He stood at the bar, sipping a beer since he was off cognac for a while considering his disastrous last outing, and looked around. This was a high-end place, no doubt about that. Straight or gay or somewhere in between, the people who came to Club Baltimore were black and beautiful and un-apologetic about the money they spent on cars and clothes and magnums of Cristal. There were only two groups of people allowed in places like this, he thought. *The ones with cash and the ones with beauty.*

Baby Brother considered this a trial run, but he knew he had *the look.* Baby face and a *gangsta* style always attracted the *wannabe bad boys* who wouldn't survive on the street for ten minutes without bodyguards. No way he couldn't pick up a hundred bucks now and then in a place like this.

Even in Iraq, there had been plenty of guys willing to pay to play. Sometimes when he needed cash, he'd let them. That didn't mean he was gay. At those moments, all that went down was that he was on the receiving end of a blow job in a place where any sex was rarer than a day without anybody dying. Besides, once he closed his eyes and pictured Lil' Kim kneeling in front of him, it didn't matter that it wasn't a woman at all, only a terrified young soldier with a secret.

At first, when guys started hinting around, he wondered why they kept assuming he would do it. He didn't *look* gay. In civvies, his classic hip-hop style of baggy jeans, oversize T-shirt, and spotless tennis shoes screamed "straight" as loud as if he'd had it tattooed on his stomach like Tupac had *thug life.* He'd asked a couple of them to explain why they had approached him, but they would just mumble something about a certain feeling; a certain way he looked at them. After a while, he stopped worrying about it. The truth was, he didn't give a damn what people thought about him. He was here tonight to make some money and if he had some fun in the process, that was all to the good.

The crowd was already picking up and he was glad he had found a place at the bar that gave him a view of the whole room. Everything sounded and looked and even smelled just like it had the other night when he'd been here with Zora. The only difference was that there weren't any women. Not on the dance floor. Not at the tables. Not at the bar. Not even *behind* the bar. Tonight, Club Baltimore was all about *the brothers.*

"You look like you could use another beer."

That was almost as weak a pickup line as "do you come here often?" but the bottle of Heineken Baby Brother had been nursing was about to give up the ghost and the offer was right on time. He turned to look at whoever was making the offer. Good face, good body, expensive silk shirt, well-cut suit, and a big smile.

"Thanks," Baby Brother said.

The man smiled and signaled the bartender. "I'm Kwame."

"Wes," Baby Brother said, thinking this guy looked more like a Kevin than a Kwame.

The bartender put down two more beers and grinned at the guy. "These are on the house. Welcome back, brother."

"Thanks, J.P.," Kwame said, tipping him twenty bucks for two beers that would have cost twelve.

"My pleasure," the bartender said, heading back to his post. "Just let me know what you need. Denny's downstairs tonight."

Baby Brother took in everything about the exchange. Kwame turned back to him with the same big smile. "Well, I guess that pretty much ruins any chance I had of claiming to be a first-timer."

"You some kind of big shot around here or something?"

Baby Brother knew what he was doing. The thug persona he was wearing tonight didn't allow for much chitchat.

"Or something," Kwame said, taking a swallow of beer. "I got to know some of the guys when I designed their renovation."

"That makes you an architect?"

Kwame nodded. "Guilty as charged. How about you, Wes?"

Baby Brother looked at Kwame. *Punks flirt. Gangstas fuck.* "Why don't you show me what's up downstairs?"

He knew that would be where the kind of action he was looking for took place. The faster they got down there, the faster some money would change hands. The way the guy responded to Baby Brother's directness would indicate whether or not he was serious or just fooling around.

"Is that what you want?" Kwame said.

Bingo! Baby Brother drained the beer and put down the bottle. "No, motherfucker, that's what *you* want."

Kwame wasn't smiling anymore. He had that look these guys always got when they knew it was really going to happen. If Baby Brother had looked more closely, he would have seen a combination of desire and despair that might have triggered some compassion in him, but it was too late for that. Or too early.

"It's nothing much," Kwame said, his voice already thickening with anticipation. "Sometimes a man needs a little privacy."

This was almost too easy, Baby Brother thought. "So you gonna show it to me or what?"

Kwame looked at Baby Brother while he seemed to be making up his mind, then he raised a hand at J.P., who was handing two cosmopolitans to a couple of guys who looked like they should have been out to dinner with their wives or their bosses.

"What can I get for you?" he said, coming over as the men touched their glasses in a toast.

"Ask Denny to bring me the usual," Kwame said. "Tell him to leave it outside."

"You got it," J.P. said with a professional smile.

Baby Brother followed Kwame through a door at the end of the bar and down a narrow stairway that opened into a dimly lit hallway. The very last door required two keys. Kwame had both. The room was small with a big white leather sofa, a wet bar, a huge TV, and not much else. Kwame closed the door behind them, picked up the remote, and pointed it at the screen. Rapper 50 Cent, the quintessential video thug, swaggered into view doing the same song they had been playing upstairs. Baby Brother wondered what 50 would think watching a bunch of brothers dancing to "In Da Club."

"Got any porno?"

Kwame clicked the remote and two well-built white men in cowboy hats appeared on the screen, enthusiastically engaged in anal sex.

"Not that fag shit," Baby Brother snarled. "*Real* porno."

Kwame complied by switching to a channel featuring a woman with no visible gag reflex giving oral sex to a man whose nickname was probably "Jumbo." If the *fag-shit* comment bothered him, Kwame didn't show it. He knew what came next just like Baby Brother did. All they were doing now was making themselves comfortable. A soft tap on the door let them know Denny had left *the usual* outside as he had been instructed.

Sometimes Kwame went to the VIP room upstairs if that was required to get everybody in the right mood, but he was always afraid he'd be recognized up there. Always afraid someone would come up and ask him if he wasn't Precious Hargrove's son. He preferred the privacy of this space, which he had included in his design in response to the owner's request for a personal playroom. A happily heterosexual man, the owner never came in on DL night. He said being around that many *faggots* made him nervous, although, as J.P. pointed out, that didn't stop him from taking their money.

Kwame opened the door and brought in a bottle of expensive champagne in a silver bucket while Baby Brother got comfortable on the sofa. He had already tossed his jacket aside and was rubbing his stomach under the big white T-shirt while he watched the woman performing fellatio on Jumbo with a bored expression on her face as if her mind was a thousand miles away. Kwame poured them each a glass of champagne and went to sit beside Baby Brother. This was the moment Kwame hated most. *The moment when the power changed hands.* The moment when he wanted something bad enough to risk everything to get it. He reached over and unbuckled Baby Brother's belt, hoping they wanted the same thing.

"Are you as good as she is?" Baby Brother said, pointing to the woman on the screen.

Kwame grinned and slid over a little closer. "I'm better."

When the two men exited the club together an hour later, neither one saw the woman in the dark gray sedan snap their picture before they drove away in Kwame's car. Lee noted the time in her notebook and headed out behind them.

51

When Brandi opened the door to find General standing there with his arms full of black garment bags, she clapped her hands like a kid on Christmas morning who'd just discovered that new bike under the tree tied up with a big red bow. Her delight was exactly what he'd been hoping for when he put himself in the hands of the smiling young man at Stephan's Vintage Clothing who said his name was Terrance and who had no trouble translating General's vision of a Rat Pack–era Vegas wardrobe into a dazzling array of outfits, all carefully selected in Brandi's size five. He had asked them to leave the clothes on the hangers to avoid wrinkling and tipped Terrance like he was an Atlantic City blackjack dealer.

Brandi's spontaneous applause was the perfect response. She flung herself against his body and kissed him passionately, wrapping her arms around his neck and pressing her warm body against him, even though he couldn't return her embrace without dropping his purchases to the floor. He laughed and stumbled backward slightly.

"Hold on, girl! You ain't gotta knock me down just because you're glad to see me!"

She laughed, too, locking the door behind him. She was wearing a transparent minidress, a silver thong, and five-inch patent-leather heels. To General, she looked good enough to eat.

"What you expect me to do?" she said, prancing along beside him, her dark eyes shining in anticipation. "You come in here loaded down like Santa Claus or some shit. I lost my head for a minute, baby, that's all!"

"What makes you think any of this is for you?" he teased her, walking in the bedroom and spreading the bags across her bed. With his help, she had moved out of the extended-stay motel and into her own apartment, but she had kept the animal-print bedspread at his request. He liked it.

She grinned at him, pulled her tiny dress over her head, and tossed it to the floor. "What makes you think any of *this* is for you?"

He came to her and wrapped one big arm around her waist, loving the feel of her skin, the slightly musty smell of her sex. She glued her mouth to his and teased his tongue in a kiss.

"I'm just kiddin' you, baby," she said. "You know this ain't for nobody but you."

It was a mark of how deeply attached to her he had become that he almost believed her. *Almost.*

"Well, you keep it that way," he said. "Now come on and try these clothes on before I take them back to the store."

"You ain't got to tell me twice, baby," she said, carefully unzipping the first garment bag. It stuck halfway down and she tugged at it. "You bought all this stuff for Vegas?"

"Any law against that?"

"*Hell, no!*" she said, her fingers working the zipper excitedly. "You just so good to me, baby, sometimes I don't know what to do."

The zipper finally surrendered and she reached in eagerly to pull out a classic sixties sheath dress in navy blue with white trim. It was accompanied by a small bolero jacket, also trimmed in white. Brandi froze, her face suddenly filled with confusion and disappointment.

The look was not lost on General, sitting on the edge of the bed. "What's wrong? Did I get the wrong size?"

Ignoring his question, Brandi rapidly unzipped the next bag, revealing a bright yellow day dress with a full skirt, accompanied by a white cardigan sweater. The next bag held a black cocktail dress with a high neck and a deep V in the back, not quite low enough to show the birthmark, but close enough to excite him. He waited for her to squeal like she had before, but she was quiet. *Too quiet.* Something wasn't right. Brandi's silence grew with every new outfit she uncovered until she turned to him after unzipping the last one with eyes full of questions he probably couldn't answer, even for himself.

"Well, aren't you going to try them on for me?" he said, trying to recover the celebratory spirit that had swirled around them when he'd first walked in.

She looked uncomfortable as she reached for the first outfit and held it up in front of her body, careful not to actually touch the fabric to her skin. He had asked the clerk to remove all sales tags so the dress looked like she had just taken it out of the closet, but it wasn't Brandi's closet he had recreated. *It was Juanita's.* Next to Brandi's contemporary urban fashions, these clothes, which had looked so right in the store surrounded by padded shoulders from the forties and poodle skirts from the fifties, now looked just plain *wrong.*

General wondered suddenly what he had been thinking when he bought all this stuff, but he really knew. He had been shopping for Juanita. Brandi wasn't even in it. The problem was, how was he going to explain all that to a girl who hadn't even been born last time these clothes were in style?

"Go ahead and put it on," he said with a big smile, trying to dissipate the strange mood that had settled over them.

Still silent, Brandi slipped the dress over her head and winced as it slid over her hips to end just above her knees. She glanced down at it and then looked at him again with the same confused expression.

"Come on over here, girl, and let me zip it up."

She backed away a few steps, plucking at the dress like somebody had smeared spaghetti sauce on it. "Look, no offense, baby, but this is some old-time shit you got here."

General was stung. He looked at her and his eyes narrowed. "I didn't ask you to critique it. I asked you to try it on. Can you do that?"

"I'm tryin' it on, baby," she said, her voice taking on an unpleasant wheedling tone. "But it just ain't me."

He knew he had gone too far with the fantasy. Trying to turn Brandi into Juanita was a fool's errand. *And an old fool at that.* But maybe he could still rescue the moment. Maybe she would cheer up if he reminded her that they were getting ready to take their relationship to a whole new level.

Maybe she just needed to hear how fine she was, all wrapped up in a grown man's fantasy of a dead woman's style.

"Come here," General said.

She went and stood in front of him slowly, the new/old dress hanging from her shoulders like a broken promise.

"Listen, baby," General said, stroking her arm gently. "Vegas is the big time. You're going to meet some of my associates. These are high-class people and their women are high-class women. I don't want you to look like somebody's country cousin from Atlanta."

She just stood there.

"Turn around now and let me zip you up so you can see how it looks and don't worry. You're going to be the finest woman these niggas ever saw."

He zipped up the dress while she gazed disapprovingly at her reflection in the mirror.

"Where you get this stuff anyway?" she whined.

General was staring at Brandi with his own critical eye. When Juanita had worn a dress almost exactly like this one, she had looked like *pure class.* They had gone down to New Orleans for the weekend while Blue was in Canada on his second honeymoon in five years, and everywhere they went, General remembered the envy in other men's eyes. She was a queen and she looked every inch the part. Brandi, on the other hand, somehow managed to make the outfit look like secondhand news.

"What do you care where I got it?" he snapped at her. "All you got to worry about is how to wear it."

"It just don't look like me is all I'm sayin', baby. That's all."

She reached behind her, unzipped the dress awkwardly, and stepped out of it. That annoyed him even more. What had made him think he could make her into anything other than what she was? A small-time stripper with no style and no future.

"Hey!" she said suddenly. "Are these clothes *used?*"

She was looking at the side seams of the dress with the practiced eye of a veteran mall shopper. Her tone accused him.

"They're *vintage,*" he said, sounding defensive to his own ears.

She knew what that meant and she didn't appreciate it one bit. "You bought some *used* clothes up in here?"

Without another word, he stood up and began to gather the bags, stuffing the clothes inside roughly. "Fuck this. You ain't ever got to go to Vegas with me. I ain't the one who's never been there."

Brandi watched him with alarm. She didn't want to lose him, but what was the deal with these frumpy old clothes? *Had they belonged to somebody else he knew?* The thought made her feel creepy. *Maybe they belonged to that bitch whose name he always called out when he came,* she thought. *Juanita. Were these her clothes? Was this like one of those old horror movies where the guy kills his wife and then tries to make somebody else look like her by wearing the dead bitch's clothes?*

General was stuffing the clothes back in their bags angrily and Brandi grabbed his arm in desperation.

"Wait, baby!" she said, grabbing his arm, seeing her trip to Vegas disappearing before her eyes. "I just—"

"Shut up," he said, shaking her off. "You ain't got nothin' else to say to me."

Suddenly her desperation felt more like anger. She hadn't done anything wrong and now he was walking out the door. *It wasn't fair!*

"How come I ain't got nuthin' to say?" she shouted as he walked out of the room with the bags over his arm. "Because I won't wear Juanita's old clothes?"

General dropped the bags he was holding to the floor, closed the small space between them in one swift motion, grabbed her arm, and lifted her off the floor like a rag doll. She was too terrified to scream. His face, only a few inches from her own, was a hard mask of rage. She saw him draw back his hand and closed her eyes against the blow. She hoped he wouldn't beat her up too bad. She couldn't work all beat-up.

Then, to her surprise, he released her arm and half dropped her to the floor. She staggered and then steadied herself before she opened her eyes and saw him standing with his back to her, obviously struggling to regain control of his emotions. Brandi remained motionless, hardly breathing.

"How do you know Juanita?" General's voice was an ominous rumble of pain and confusion.

"You say her name," Brandi whispered, trembling in her G-string.

He turned to face her, his face a terrible thundercloud, his eyes like lasers boring into her soul. Brandi swallowed hard and said a little prayer. At this moment, the question wasn't whether or not to lie, but whether or not the truth would save her or seal her fate at General's hands.

"I say her name *when?*"

"When we . . . when you *come.*"

The frown on General's face relaxed almost imperceptibly, but it emboldened her just enough for her to continue.

"You been doin' it the whole time we been seein' each other, baby."

The energy seemed to leave his body in a rush and he sat down on the edge of the bed like an old man. Brandi slowly, very slowly, sat beside him. She kept her knees slightly apart so he could smell her sweetness, but it was obvious that sex was the last thing on General's mind right now. He sat with his head in his big hands as if she wasn't even there.

"You ain't got to tell me nuthin'," she said softly, as if speaking any louder might set off a response that would endanger her. "I'm just . . . I'm just not down for no spooky shit, okay?"

He didn't move. She could see his big shoulders rising and falling with his breathing, but his sudden stillness was beginning to frighten her more than his anger. Shouting matches were familiar territory. Silence was an unknown danger, which is why it frightened her even more.

"You feelin' okay, baby?"

In response to her question, he spoke so softly at first, she wasn't sure if it was only a sigh. "I'm sorry."

She leaned closer. "What you say, baby?"

"I'm so sorry."

He repeated his apology as he raised his ravaged face. The pain she saw there frightened her, not for herself, but for his ability to bear it.

"What you got to apologize for? Good as you been to me, you can call me any name you want to call me."

General looked at her sweet face and she could see that he was searching for the words to make her understand. She waited for him to explain what was going on, touching his thigh gently.

"You can tell me, baby," she said. "You can tell me anything."

He sat quiet and rigid and she began to stroke his leg slowly with no hint of sexual promise, only comfort.

"Tell me."

General took a deep breath. "Juanita was the only woman I ever loved. She died ten years ago."

"I'm so sorry, baby."

"Before she went, she told me she would . . ."

Brandi's hand on his leg never stopped stroking. He took another deep breath.

"She told me she would send me a sign."

The hair stood up on the back of Brandi's neck. "What kind of sign?"

He shrugged his massive shoulders. "She didn't say exactly what. She just said it would be something only I would recognize."

"And did you?"

He nodded slowly, never taking his eyes from her. "Yes. When I saw *you.*"

"*Me?*"

He nodded again. "She had a birthmark just like yours. Same shape. Same place on her body. That first time I saw you at Montre's, I didn't know what to think, but there it was."

"So you think I'm like her *reincarnated* or something?"

He smiled. "Nothing like that. Just that . . . seeing you . . . seeing that mark on you . . ." His voice trailed off.

"You still love her?" Brandi wasn't scared anymore, but she was intrigued. She thought this kind of stuff happened only in the movies.

"I'll always love her." General whispered.

Suddenly she felt bad for him. The lie that had seemed routine when she told it came back like a bad dream. *He thinks he got a signal from his true love,* she thought with a pang of guilt, *and that mark on my ass isn't even a real birthmark.* This was getting way too complicated. Brandi stood up and looked down at General.

"Want a drink, baby?"

"Yeah."

He stood up and followed her into the kitchen. She poured them each a shot of scotch.

"I didn't mean to call you by her name."

"Forget about it." She smiled, handing him one glass and taking a small sip from the other as they headed back to the bedroom. She was still naked except for her high heels and the silver thong.

"And for the record," he said, sitting down again on the side of the bed, "those weren't *her* clothes. They're from that vintage store in Little Five Points."

"Thanks for sayin' it," she said, sitting beside him, "but I knew you had too much class for some shit like that."

He smiled at her and sipped his scotch. "So now you know my secret. What about you?"

She shrugged. "I ain't got no secrets, baby. What you see is what you get."

He didn't say anything. He just leaned over and hugged her with such tenderness that she felt guilty again. Tenderness was more unfamiliar than silence, so she leaned her bare breasts against his chest and waited for him to make the next move. His massive arms suddenly seemed the safest place on earth for her to be. If there had ever been a time to tell the truth, this was it. There was no room left for the lie. She leaned back and looked into his face. He smiled, his big hands moving down her shoulders, caressing her lightly.

"What is it?"

"Well," she said, "since we're confessing and shit, I have to tell you something, too."

"All right. Tell me."

"That ain't no birthmark on me. I had a nigga's name tattooed on my behind because he liked to do it doggy style, and when we broke up, I had it lasered off, but it left a scar."

General didn't say anything for a minute and she was afraid that telling him the truth had been a bad idea. Her mother always said the stupidest thing a woman could do was tell a man the truth. "They can't handle it," she'd say, sucking her sunken cheeks hollow trying to get *the goodie* out of whatever she was smoking. "They think they can until they hear it, then they lose their whole minds." Brandi hoped General wouldn't lose his whole mind, or his interest in her. He was a good, steady john and he definitely had connections. He was old enough to appreciate her, young enough to satisfy her, and there was something about him that she was starting to really like.

Maybe it was how he always treated her like a lady, or maybe she just admired a man who could love a woman as strong as he loved his Juanita. Brandi wished somebody would love her that hard. Maybe General was the one. She hoped her mother was wrong.

"What was his name?" General said after what seemed to Brandi like a two-hour pause to digest her confession.

"His name?" Brandi's mind went blank. It had been so long ago and there had been so many since then. She felt a sudden flush of embarrassment. She had cared enough to tattoo his name on her skin and now she couldn't even remember who it was. "I don't know. Ain't that a bitch? I don't even know."

She tried to laugh, but it came out more like a gurgle. That's when she realized General didn't look mad or sad anymore. He was sitting there grinning at her like a Cheshire cat. She grinned back, more relieved than she would have admitted. That's when he started to laugh. Not just a little chuckle to show he wasn't pissed. He was laughing so loud her neighbors could probably hear it.

His delight, although mysterious, was contagious and Brandi's own laugh bubbled out of her like clear water in a mountain stream. There they sat, the great big man with the bald head and the broken heart and the pretty little woman whose tight butt and bouncing breasts paid her rent each and every month, laughing so hard they finally had to just sit there and breathe deeply to get control of themselves. He took her hand and she squeezed his thick fingers, lifted them to her lips, and nibbled his knuckles gently. He watched her.

"Well, all Juanita said was she'd send me a sign," he said. "She didn't say anything about whether it had to be a real birthmark or not."

She looked up at him. "So you ain't mad?"

He shook his head and smiled slowly. "A sign is a sign, right?"

She nodded. "You got that right, baby. A sign is a sign."

He reached for her and she moved into his arms in one smooth motion, pushing him down on the bed and straddling his hips, rocking herself against him, feeling his response and her own. He closed his eyes. Her braided extensions brushing against his belly felt more like horsehair than human tresses, but it didn't matter. She was a gift from his beloved, the living proof that what they'd had on earth was still present in the universe; that Juanita was somewhere, *out there*, watching him, waiting for him, wanting him as much as he still wanted her.

"Say her name!" Brandi panted.

He hesitated for just a heartbeat, but Brandi would not be denied.

"Say her name!"

General heard himself groan and then he couldn't hold it back anymore. It was a cry, a prayer, a penitent's confession, and a believer's testimony. *"Juanita!"*

Then it was over.

52

B aby Brother was pissed. It had been a week. He'd been calling Zora on Davy's cellphone, the same number he'd given Kwame, but neither one had called back. Or maybe they had called back and Davy hadn't heard the ring over Rush Limbaugh's latest harangue. The topic of the week was the war in Iraq and how what every red-blooded American needed to do was get behind the president, no matter what fool thing he decided to do next.

After a day of having to listen to all that crap, Baby Brother wanted to tell the people who were calling to argue that they ought to spend a week or two in Fallujah before they made any final decisions. By the time a woman who proudly identified herself as a white Southerner without having been asked stated that she thought they should empty out the jails by sending all the prisoners to work off their sentences as frontline soldiers, he wanted to scream. The caller credited her husband with the bright idea and urged the station's listeners to write their congressmen.

"You see what I'm talkin' about?" Davy said as they finished their last delivery and climbed back in the truck for the ride home. "That's how they think."

"Yeah, so?" said Baby Brother. "A lot of niggas think that way, too."

"Yeah, but they just talkin' shit. These crackers ain't kiddin'."

Davy indicated a left at Lawton Street and Baby Brother realized they were going to pass right by Zora's bright blue front door. Maybe he could catch her at home and just drop in long enough to see if she was still mad at him for having had a little too much to drink the other night. He'd paid for it by peeing all over himself, but she had no way of knowing that. He'd paid for it tell her. Maybe she'd laugh and feel a little sorry for a soldier, a long way from home. Sympathy sex was some of the best sex around and he was overdue. That guy he'd met at the club had given him two hundred bucks and a blow job, but that was business. For pleasure, Baby Brother needed a woman.

"Hey, man," he said to Davy as they turned toward the corner. "Pull over for a minute."

"For what?"

"Just pull over, okay? I need to check on something."

"On somebody, you mean." Davy pulled up in front of Zora's place and grinned. "You better leave that woman alone. She ain't thinkin' about your broke ass."

Baby Brother had made the mistake of telling Davy he might get a call from Zora on his cell. He hadn't mentioned a possible call from Kwame. That wasn't anybody's business. Davy had initially been impressed, but after several days went by with no contact, he began to tease Baby Brother for having delusions of grandeur.

"Your cheap-ass phone probably ain't even hooked up," Baby Brother said, jumping out of the truck and heading up the walk. He rang the bell above Zora's name, but got no response. Annoyed, he pushed it again, laying on it longer.

"Come on, nigga. Even if she's there, she ain't home to you. Can't you take a hint?"

Before Baby Brother could respond to Davy's taunt, the blue door opened and a tall, good-looking woman with a little Afro and a kid in her arms almost bumped right into him. She was talking to someone over her shoulder, and if he hadn't reached out to stop her, she would have walked right into him.

"Oh! I'm sorry," she said, her hand moving to the child's back protectively. "I didn't even see you."

"No problem," he said, but he was looking at the man standing behind her. No doubt about it. It was Kwame from the club. "Excuse me."

"Are you looking for someone?" the woman said pleasantly, stepping out of the open door. The man returned Baby Brother's gaze, but said nothing, perhaps hoping that without his voice, his identity might still be in question.

"I'm a friend of Zora's," Baby Brother said. "I was passing by on my way home from work and I thought I might be able to catch her."

The woman shifted the baby on her hip. "She's not here right now. You want me to tell her you stopped by?"

In the truck, Davy had turned down the radio long enough to try to eavesdrop on the conversation.

"Yeah, sure," Baby Brother said. "Tell her Wes came by."

"Wes?" She was waiting for him to say his last name.

"Wes Jamerson."

"You working with Davy?" She waved, and from the truck, Davy waved back.

"For a minute."

She grinned at him. "I heard that. I'm Aretha Hargrove. I have a studio upstairs. This is my husband, Kwame."

Baby Brother held out his hand and Kwame shook it. "Whazzup, brother?"

"Whazzup?"

"Me, Mommy!" the little kid said. "Tell him *me.*"

"I'm sorry, baby." Aretha smiled. "This is Joyce Ann."

"Ice cream," the little girl said. "Ice cream, Daddy?"

Kwame had no choice but to respond in correct fatherly fashion. "After you have your dinner, remember? Then we'll have ice cream."

"Ice cream!" she said again, and hugged her mother's neck.

"I'll tell Zora you came by," Aretha said, heading down the walk.

"Yeah, thanks," Baby Brother said, locking eyes with Kwame so there would be no mistake. "Good to meet you, man."

"You, too."

The three of them got into their car, complete with a baby seat in the back that Baby Brother remembered from the other night, and drove away with Kwame at the wheel. Davy was watching, too.

"That's one lucky nigga," Davy said as Baby Brother hopped back into the truck.

"Oh yeah?" he said, wondering how much this fool knew. "Why's that?"

"He's married to that fine-ass Aretha, he's working for Blue Hamilton, and his mama is gonna be the next mayor."

"*Of Atlanta?*"

"No, nigga, of Macon. Of course, Atlanta. What you think?"

"When?"

"As soon as the next election comes around. Next year or some shit."

Baby Brother wanted to holler. He felt like he had just hit the lottery. This guy wasn't just somebody on the down low with a few dollars to spare. This guy was a gold mine.

"So what you got on my forty?" Davy said, thirsty for a cheap malt liquor because that's all he could afford.

"Fuck that," Baby Brother said, feeling expansive. "Let's get a six-pack. Of Heineken."

"You ain't got to tell me twice," Davy said, pointing the truck toward Mr. Jackson's liquor store. "What are we celebratin' all of a sudden?"

"That nigga ain't the only one who's lucky."

"Oh yeah? What kind of luck you got all of a sudden?"

"You gonna be drinkin' good. What the fuck you care?"

Davy laughed. "You got that shit right!"

Baby Brother didn't care what Davy was drinking to celebrate. He knew his celebration was because his ship had just come in big-time. And not a moment too soon, he thought. Not a moment too soon.

53

The last session of Abbie's Introduction to Altars seminar had been one of those moments that made her realize one more time how grateful she was to be doing this work with these young women. They had all shared a potluck supper, another of Abbie's traditions, cleared away the dishes, and gathered in their sisterhood circle to say a formal good-bye to this moment they had shared.

"I want to thank all of you for being willing to explore your spirits," Abbie said, smiling around the circle. "For being so open to new ideas about yourselves and about each other. It is my hope that you will regard this seminar as only one small step on a journey that will take you a lifetime. Take care of yourselves. Take care of each other. *Be peace!*"

Then they all hugged. Some of the more sentimental ones cried a little, but by nine-thirty, they had all gotten themselves together and headed home. Abbie spent an hour cleaning up, but it was still too early to go to bed. She didn't feel like reading or watching televison, so she stretched as tall as she could then leaned over to touch her toes while she considered her other options. That's when she realized what she wanted to do was get into a nice hot bath and think about Peachy.

Their *date* was only a few weeks away and her imagination was working overtime. Lately, she had been considering the possibility of sex toys, although she wasn't really sure about that yet. Her experience had been that when men thought of sex toys at all, their imaginations ran more toward voluptuous young women rolling around naked while pleasuring themselves and one another with an oversize dildo that would strike fear into anybody who wasn't getting paid to stuff the thing into every available orifice. She had tried to introduce a vibrator into the proceedings once with a widower whose prostate cancer had left him wanting sex as much as ever but unable to sustain an erection or make peace with oral sex on any kind of regular basis. Abbie had suggested that a vibrator might be the most pleasurable and practical solution and he had responded by calling her a whore for suggesting such a thing and never calling again.

Peachy was certainly more worldly than that, she thought. From the conversations they'd been having and the letters he'd been sending her, Abbie knew her *almost lover* was open, adventurous, and as excited about their upcoming exchange as she was. They hadn't had phone sex yet, but the last few times he'd called late at night, they had walked right up on it before she pulled back. She didn't want their first time together to be long-distance. The first time, she wanted to feel his body against her own. She wanted to hear him call her name . . .

Down, girl, Abbie admonished herself as she turned out the lights and headed upstairs. She glanced at the clock in the hall. It was almost eleven and the neighborhood was surprisingly quiet. She was glad. The home invasions seemed to have stopped. Even though the police had never made any arrests, everybody was breathing a little easier. She lit a fat scented candle in the bedroom at the top of the stairs and started the water in the tub, pouring in enough sweet oil to make things both fragrant and slippery. In the bedroom she stepped out of her clothes and hung them neatly in the closet, listening to the CD she'd been playing all week, *The Very Best of Solomon Burke.* His unashamedly *mannish* tones filled the room and she smiled, listening to his heartfelt plea for some attention from a faraway lover.

A love that runs away from me.
Dreams that just won't let me be . . .

Abbie walked naked into the steamy bathroom, singing along like Solomon had invited her to join his backup trio.

So far away from you
And all your charms . . .

The water was high enough and hot enough, so she turned off the faucet and stepped in carefully. Solomon's voice from the other room was urging a brokenhearted damsel to bring him her troubles.

Don't you feel like cryin'?
Come on, cry to me.

Crying was the last thing on Abbie's mind as she slid down into the water up to her shoulders. The girl Solomon had been talking to must have finished with her crying because he had slowed things down and now he was promising not to stop loving her until she told him everything was all right.

Can't nobody kiss you, little girl,
Like I'm kissin' you . . .

Abbie took a deep breath, closed her eyes, and ran her hands over her breasts, her stomach, the soft prickle of her wet pubic hair. She touched her body gently and thought of Peachy's hands, Peachy's mouth, Peachy's desire for her as a woman, and hers for him as a man. Solomon Burke was crooning that *tonight was the night* and she closed her eyes, let her legs fall apart a little farther there in that candlelit room, and sighed. That's when she heard the glass breaking downstairs.

54

In his breast pocket, General was carrying three thousand dollars in cash. He hated credit cards, and anytime he could use real money, he did. This was one of those times. Things had been so quiet in the neighborhood lately, Blue and Regina had gone to Tybee for the weekend and General and Brandi were booked first-class on a midnight flight to Vegas.

He couldn't wait. Things between him and Brandi were going so good, sometimes it almost scared him. Since they'd had that conversation about the sign he'd been looking for, it even seemed like more of Juanita was coming through in things about Brandi. *Personal things.* Things that were more intimate than a birthmark or a tattoo. Things only he would know. He knew it might sound crazy if he said it out loud, but the truth was, the last two times he had been inside her, Brandi's body felt exactly like Juanita's. He didn't know how that could happen and he didn't even care anymore. The first time, he asked her if she was doing something different. She said she was always doing something different so he wouldn't get bored. But the next time, it happened again and he realized it wasn't anything she was *doing.* It was something he was *feeling,* and that something was *Juanita.*

That's when he decided they should get married. It was time for her to stop working anyway. Every time he went into Montre's and saw her on the pole, upside down, shaking her ass for anybody who walked in the door, he wanted to go up there and carry her away like those macho guys do in the movies. The lap dances were even worse. She was so good at it, half these young fools came in their damn baggy pants. They tried to play it off, but he could always tell. She was that good and General was tired of sharing. Especially now that Brandi was carrying Juanita's *essence* inside her.

The idea of marriage came to him as he was trying to figure out how to tell Blue he was going to Vegas with Brandi for the weekend. Because of the nature of the roles they played in each other's life, part of their deal was that they always knew who was where at any given moment, but he hadn't even told Blue he was seeing her, much less that things were so serious. General couldn't just disappear for three days and expect Blue not to worry.

On the other hand, he was a grown man, and if he wanted to take a lady to Vegas, he wasn't required to get a second opinion. Besides, even if Blue got a little pissed off, General knew once he came back with a wife, all would be forgiven. He and Brandi could get married in Vegas, come back here, and make a real life together. She could live like a little queen and never have to work again. He had more than enough money to support a wife. *All she'll have to do,* he thought with a slow grin, *is shop and eat good and let me love her all I want to.* He knew Juanita would approve. He was, after all, doing it for her.

He reached for his cellphone, but before he could punch in Blue's number, it rang in his hand. On the other end, Blue's voice was all about business.

"I've got to go to D.C. tonight. Some young fools broke in on Gina's aunt. She's in the hospital."

General felt a wave of anger wash over him. He liked Abbie and he knew Blue was crazy about her. "How bad is it?"

"We're not sure. No rape, but they tied her up and trashed the place. I need you to put the car on the road and meet me in D.C. tomorrow. I'll get a plane in Savannah."

"Done. Do the cops have any leads?"

"Not yet, but somebody knows something. Maybe we can shake loose some information to help the investigation along."

It was almost ten-thirty. D.C. was eleven hours, barring traffic jams, accidents, and road construction. "I'll be there by noon."

"Meet me at the house."

General had been there for Blue and Regina's wedding two years earlier. He didn't need an address. "Done."

Blue didn't say how long they'd be in D.C. and General didn't ask. He knew the answer. *As long as it took to do what needed to be done.* His matrimonial plans would have to be put on hold for a few days. He knew Brandi wouldn't appreciate the change, but this was the life he had chosen, and as his wife, she'd have to get used to it. *As his wife.* The words made him feel good. Now that he'd realized what he wanted to do, he could hardly wait. As soon as they got to Vegas, he'd tell the limo driver to take them to that cheesy little chapel where the movie stars go for their quickie weddings. She would love that and he would love having her, *and the part of Juanita that lived in her,* all to himself.

But first he had business to take care of in D.C.

55

I t hadn't been hard for Baby Brother to get Kwame's phone number. He waited until Old Man Mason was at work, then typed his name into Mason's ancient PC. It spit out two phone numbers and an address that was three blocks away. It also referred him to lots of information about Precious Hargrove that confirmed what Davy had said yesterday about her being elected mayor next time around. Baby Brother turned off the computer and picked up the phone.

At the first number, a woman's voice asked him to leave a message for Kwame or Aretha. That would be his wife. *Aretha.* He wondered if she could sing. The second number rang twice and a familiar voice answered. "Good afternoon. This is Kwame Hargrove."

"No shit," Baby Brother said. "Who do you think this is?"

Kwame had been dreading this moment ever since he started sneaking off to the down-low nights at clubs all over town. He knew it was only a matter of time, but now that he was in the middle of the moment, he couldn't say a word.

"You can't talk, nigga? I said who the fuck do you think this is?"

"I know who it is," Kwame said, trying to sound firm.

"So how come you didn't call me, nigga?"

"I was going to—"

"Save that shit. My boy Davy told me who the fuck you are and I already know what you like."

"What do you want?" Kwame heard his own voice as if he was calling from the bottom of a well.

"What you got, nigga?" Baby Brother's laugh was hard and mean. "Why don't we start there?"

The nightmare was knocking on the door and there was still no plan forming in Kwame's mind. There was only a big black hole of fear and guilt. *What the hell was he supposed to do now?*

"We need to talk, *brother.* Your place or mine?" Baby Brother smiled at his own wit.

"You can't come here," Kwame said quickly. "Can you meet me at Baltimore? Tomorrow night around—"

"Hell no, I can't meet you at no Baltimore. I ain't got no damn car and this ain't no damn date." He tried to sound as mean and hard as he could. It would save time later. "You got that?"

"I got it."

Kwame sounded scared, which made Baby Brother feel bold.

"Yeah, well, you better get it or I'm gonna blow your shit sky high. *Faggot!*"

Kwame held the phone and closed his eyes. He tried to imagine how Baby Brother would do that exactly. Tell his mother? Tell his wife? Tell his new partners? Take the story to the newspapers? Tell Blue Hamilton? That thought actually made Kwame's heart skip. Blue was Aretha's godfather and he adored her. He couldn't let Blue find out about this. That meant they couldn't talk in West End. Blue had eyes everywhere in the neighborhood. There was only one place close by where Kwame could be sure they'd be alone; the loft that nobody knew about but him.

"All right," Kwame said. "I know a place where we can talk."

"Good."

"Do you know Peters Street?"

"No, nigga, I don't know no damn Peters Street. I know my ass is gonna be standing in front of Montre's in fifteen minutes so you can pick me up and take me where I need to go so we can get this shit straight. You got that?"

"I'm driving a gray Accord," Kwame said miserably.

"I know what you're driving, fool. I saw you with your family in it yesterday, remember?"

Kwame knew he would never forget that moment. "I remember."

"Don't keep me waiting."

Kwame took the admonition seriously. He was pulling up at the club at the same moment Baby Brother crossed the street against the light outside the MARTA station. He jumped into the front seat next to Kwame and they took a right at the corner where the Wachovia Bank was still hunkered down hoping for gentrification, and headed north. On the way over, Baby Brother was so busy talking, and Kwame seemed to be so busy listening, that neither one saw the charcoal-gray Intrepid cruising along a half a block behind them. Neither one of them noticed Lee enter a date and time in a small notebook lying open on the seat beside her.

They had no way of knowing she'd been tailing Kwame regularly ever since she landed on Precious Hargrove's *shit list.* They had no way of knowing their little tryst was the payoff for all those long boring hours of tagging along behind him when the most interesting thing Kwame did was spend an hour picking out fruit at Whole Foods or browsing in the Barnes & Noble. Lee kept a safe distance as the two men turned down Peters Street, parked in front of a partially renovated loft, and got out, Kwame leading the way.

As he opened the door with a key, Lee raised her palm-size digital camera and, as she drove by, snapped a series of pictures with no sound and no flash. Kwame looked up as she passed, but in the rearview mirror, she could see that it was only one fast, furtive glance before he followed Baby Brother inside and closed the door behind him.

56

Brandi still thought these were some ugly outfits, but she had promised, so here she was, getting ready to fly to Vegas for the first time looking like somebody's out-of-step auntie. She had taken everything to the Vietnamese alterations lady at Greenbriar Mall, but General didn't want her to change much, so all she'd done was take the hems up a few inches. *Well,* she thought, *there's nothing I can do about it now.*

Aside from the clothes, everything was perfect. They were going first-class all the way. Looking at herself in the little black cocktail dress he had asked her to travel in, she had to admit there was something classy about it. She had started to jazz it up with some big earrings, but now she thought she'd just leave it plain. General was the first real *sugar daddy* she'd ever had, and if he wanted her to wear some weird-ass clothes every once in a while, she could do it.

When the phone rang, she assumed it was General calling to say he was on his way, and didn't even check the caller ID.

"Hey, baby! Where you at?"

"Hello?" said a voice on the other end that she didn't recognize. "Is this Brandi Harris?"

"Who is this?" she said, frowning.

"You don't know me," he said. "Well, not my name anyway. It's Wes, Wes Jamerson. You danced for me the other night. I thought—"

She interrupted him. "How did you get this number?"

"One of the other dancers gave it to me."

Probably that bitch Keisha, Brandi thought. The girls never gave one another's numbers out. Too many psychos running around these days to get careless.

"Well, maybe you should call her."

"I got two hundred dollars for a house call," he said quickly before she could hang up. "I was hoping I could talk to you."

Two hundred dollars? "What kind of house call you got in mind?"

"Nothin' freaky," he said. "Just straight-up fuckin'. I just moved into a new place. I want to celebrate."

That wasn't a complete lie, he thought. In less than an hour, Baby Brother had made Kwame give up the keys to the loft and the two hundred dollars he had on him as down payment on the five hundred a month he was going to charge to keep his mouth shut. *And that was just for starters.* He had given Kwame until the following night to bring him the rest of the money, but Baby Brother had already moved in. As he stood in the living room alone, his first thought had been, *All I need now is a woman.* That's when he called Brandi.

"I danced for you?"

"Yeah. Took me ten minutes to clean up enough to walk home."

"Are you light-skinned?"

"Yeah, that's me."

She remembered him. He was the one who'd reaped the rewards of the Busy Boy fantasy. This conversation sounded promising, but she was flying to Vegas tonight. It would have to wait.

"I'm sorry . . . what did you say your name was?"

"Wes."

"I'm sorry, Wes, but I have a date tonight. Why don't you give me your number and I'll call you when I'm free."

"You goin' out with that big bald-headed motherfucker I saw you with at the club?"

Brandi bristled. "You payin' for pussy, not my personal business."

"Don't get mad," he said, giving her the number at the loft. "I just felt something the other night when you danced for me. I thought you might have felt it, too."

That was true. She had felt something. He was pretty as a little girl and his eyelashes were a foot long. A lot of girls didn't like the yellow boys anymore, but she had never seen a rule that said a man couldn't be light-skinned *and* fine. Not fine enough to do him for free, but *almost.*

"Nigga, are you trying to sweet-talk me into not charging you?" she said, half teasing, but all the way serious.

"No, no. I got the money," he said. "I just wondered if you felt something, too."

She sighed loud enough for him to hear it. "Listen, sweetie, I am a businesswoman and pussy is my only product. I don't give it, loan it, send it, or forget to take it in for regular checkups. If that's what you lookin' for, I'll call you sometime and maybe we can have a date next time I'm free. But it's business, okay? As long as you remember that, we'll be cool."

"Don't make me wait too long," he said. "I got something good for you, girl."

"I know you do, baby." She clicked off the phone. *If I had a dollar for every nigga that said that,* she thought, *I could retire to Vegas and never have to shake my ass again. Not for money anyway . . .*

She slipped on her jacket as General rang the bell, threw open the door, and twirled around in her four-inch heels so he could fully appreciate her faithful re-creation of the look he wanted. She had even asked her stylist for a flip with some bangs instead of her usual extensions. He just stood there staring at her. *It must be working,* she thought. *The man is speechless.*

"How'd I do, baby? Is this classic Vegas or what?"

She looked exactly the way he'd hoped she would and her happiness was bubbling out of her like a kid at her first birthday party. He hated to tell her they weren't going.

"You look great, baby!"

Brandi heard the disappointment in his voice before he had a chance to say another word and immediately assumed the worst: *they weren't going.* After she had been bragging all week to the girls at the club. After she had begged the time off from Johnny. After she had gotten her hair done, her nails done, her eyebrows arched, and a bikini wax? After she had packed up all those ugly clothes?

She stepped back. "What's wrong?"

"Nothing's wrong," he said quickly. "Something's come up. I've got some business to take care of in D.C."

"In D.C.? What you mean *in D.C*? We goin' to Vegas!"

"I'm not saying we're not going. We just can't go tonight."

She looked at him and her eyes narrowed. Her lovely young face hardened before his eyes until he saw her twenty years from now, an angry, disappointed woman with nothing but bad memories and bad men to keep her company.

"We were never gonna go, were we?" She spit the words at him, too angry now to even try to understand.

"You saw the tickets, baby. Remember?"

"Where are they now?"

He reached into his pocket and pulled out two Delta Airlines ticket folders.

"Let me see them."

Her voice was even harder than her expression. He handed them to her, wanting her to know he had been serious; that he was still serious; wanting to tell her he had a wedding in mind.

"I was on my way, baby, but I got a call and—"

He stopped himself in midsentence, hearing himself trying to explain. He didn't have to explain his comings and goings to anybody, especially not her.

"And now we can't use 'em, right? 'Cause you got something better to do?" she said.

"I have *business*." He underlined the word with his voice. All he wanted to do was calm her down so he could get on the road. There would be time later for explanations, but Blue would be expecting him in D.C. at noon and he intended to be there. That was his job.

Brandi looked at the tickets in her hand, but she was so mad, just holding them did not mollify her.

"Well, fuck you, then," she said suddenly, tearing up the tickets and letting the pieces flutter to the floor. She grabbed her purse. "I got business, too."

He took a sideways step, placing his considerable bulk directly in her path to the doorway. She looked up into his face and put her hands on her hips. She let out a long, exasperated breath.

"Let me tell you something. I've been out here a long time. I've been hustled every kind of way and I've done my share, but I think we got some-thin' for each other." She swallowed hard, realizing she was getting a little emotional. "I don't know if it's your fantasy trip or my every other kinda trip, but we might do okay for a minute, you know what I mean?"

"I know what you mean." He was happy she had calmed down.

"But if you don't really mean to take me to Vegas, don't tease me with it, okay? My heart been hurt too many times." *Now that's the truth,* she thought. *At last.*

He walked over to her then and put his arms around her. "I'm not teas-ing, baby. We're going to Vegas and we're going to have a ball when we get there."

"You promise?" She wanted to believe him, but she wasn't sure she did.

"I promise." He gave her a gentle squeeze. "I've got a lot to offer a woman who wants to go places."

"I want to go everywhere."

"Then roll with this, baby. I gotta go to D.C. No choice. But when I get back, we gonna sit down and talk about the future. You and me, okay?"

She gave him a little smile, calm again, at least for the moment. "What-ever you say, baby. You know that."

He looked at her, ready for the trip in her little black dress, and he felt sorry for trying so hard to make her someone else. "You know what else?"

"What?"

"I know you ain't Juanita and you ain't got to wear those clothes if you don't want to wear them."

She grinned at him, glad they were back on track. "Don't worry about it, baby. I'm startin' to kind of like 'em."

He laughed and squeezed her behind one time before he headed out, wishing he had more time; knowing he didn't. "I'll call you when I get back."

"I'll be here, baby."

Suddenly, when she said the words, he realized that was exactly where he wanted her to be. He wanted her to be waiting for him to come back, like Regina always waited for Blue. He wanted her to *feel* him like that. To *need* him that strong. Maybe it was Juanita coming to the surface more and more. Maybe it was that dress, or maybe, this was the real damn thing. Maybe he was going to get another chance to love a woman down deep in his soul. *Maybe.*

"You not working this weekend, are you?" he said.

"I gotta do somethin' to pass the time," she said. "And make that money."

He reached into his pocket and pulled off ten one-hundred-dollar bills. "Don't work this weekend. I want you to stay home."

She raised her eyebrows and smiled. "And be a good girl?"

"You're always good, baby, you know that," he said, wishing he could make love to her, but it was a long drive and he was the only driver. He still had to get the Lincoln ready for the road and throw some things in a bag. There just wasn't time.

She tucked the money into her bra delicately and smiled up at him again, wondering if it was too late to call that pretty little *nigga* with the two hundred bucks in his pocket. Twelve hundred bucks in one night would be a personal best. "Thank you, baby. *I love you, too.*"

It was a throwaway line, just a grateful woman thanking a generous man, but the sound of her voice saying those words lingered in General's ears as he went about his normal *getting ready for the road* routine. *I love you, too.* He wondered if it was possible that she really did care for him. That there were real feelings between them. Once he got back to his place, he checked the bag he always kept packed for this kind of business trip and tucked the .38 he was legally licensed to carry into his pocket. Whatever else he needed for the task at hand he'd get once he got where he was going. Post-9/11 America was no place to be riding around with a trunk full of weapons.

He drove the big black Town Car through an all-night car wash even though it was already spotless, picked up another road atlas, and headed for the freeway, but her voice was still whispering in his head: *I love you, too.* The thought of holding her in his arms, loving her the way only he could love her, was like a fever in his blood. He glanced at his watch. If he stopped back by her place for an hour, it wouldn't really throw him off. He was riding at night, so it would be him and the truckers for long stretches of road. He could make up the time easily, he thought as he swung the car around and headed back toward Brandi's. *I love you, too.* Maybe he would even propose when he got there instead of waiting until they got to Vegas. *No time like the present.*

When he didn't see her car, it surprised him. He had been gone only a couple of hours. Where could she go that fast? She wouldn't go to work.

Not when he had just handed her a grand to just take it easy until he got back. Maybe she'd gone to get something to eat. He checked his watch again. She never ate this late at night. He pulled up in front of her place and sat there. What was he getting so agitated about anyway? They had said their good-byes, everything was cool, and when he got back, they'd head for Vegas on the first plane out. She had even dressed up like he wanted, so what was he worrying about?

The truth was, General knew exactly what he was worrying about. *That young nigga he'd known was trouble from the very beginning. That young nigga who had moved out of Mason's owing everybody money and talking plenty of shit. That young nigga who'd gotten a lap dance he didn't deserve from a woman who didn't belong to him.* General tried to remember where *that young fool* had told Mason he was moving to when he left West End. Was it some loft over on Peters Street near the U-Haul? That was all he could remember, but that was enough. He drove straight there, turned the corner, and saw her car parked out front of one of the warehouses that were being redeveloped for residential space. He parked down the block in the shadows, cut the lights and the motor, and waited.

An hour and a half later, Brandi came out, still wearing the dress he'd bought her for the trip, still wearing the high-heeled shoes, got in the car, and drove away. General's heart was beating so hard he thought it would come through his chest. *That yella nigga was fuckin' Juanita!* He stepped out of the car with the .38 in his hand, reached for his gloves, and walked quickly around to the back of the building without making a sound. Through the open window, he could see Baby Brother in a pair of red silk boxers, leaning into the refrigerator and talking on the phone.

"Yeah, well, I don't give a damn what I said about tomorrow. You better bring me my money tonight or I'm gonna have to make some phone calls." He reached in for a carton of Chinese takeout, opened it, and sniffed delicately. General's mind was chanting the same words over and over. *This yella nigga was fuckin' Juanita!*

"You're damn right you'll bring it," Baby Brother said, deciding on a beer instead. He popped the top and closed the refrigerator door without replacing the Chinese food.

General eased up the fire escape more gracefully than might have been expected for a man his size and flattened himself against the outside wall closest to the window. Baby Brother had turned off the light in the kitchen and wandered off into another room. General slowly opened the window, slid his massive body through the space without any visible strain, and entered the loft unobserved.

Baby Brother had turned on the television to pass the time until Kwame arrived with some cash. After that, he was going to call Brandi and tell her they could hit the clubs hard. He knew Brandi was a pro. Their earlier session at the loft had proved that, but he didn't care. *Hoes need love, too,* he thought, chuckling at his own humor. He was still in the mood to celebrate his unexpected good fortune, but she had been real clear: *no pay, no play.*

That's when he called Kwame. She had declined to wait, telling him instead to call her when the cash arrived and she'd see what she could do. He wanted to see what else she could do, too, he thought, strolling into the kitchen for another beer without ever seeing General waiting for him in the shadows. As Baby Brother reached into the refrigerator, General raised the .38 to the back of his head and pulled the trigger twice.

Nobody was around to hear the gunfire, but General wasn't taking any chances. He left the loft the same way he came in, walked quickly back to his car, climbed in, and pulled away without turning on the lights until he rounded the next corner and headed for the freeway. If he was going to make D.C. by tomorrow noon, he didn't have any time to waste.

57

Lee hadn't even been looking for Kwame. She was on her way home from a community meeting and stopped in at the West End News for a paper. She ordered a cappuccino to go and picked up a copy of the new *Essence* magazine. She almost never read the articles, but she couldn't resist the pretty pictures. It was almost eleven thirty when she came outside and saw Kwame's car at the light, headed north. It wasn't hard for her to guess where he was headed. Either to the club or to what she had taken to calling *the love nest*. No other reason for a married man to be headed out alone this late.

Careful to stay out of sight, Lee pulled in between two parked cars almost half a block down the street. She had invested in a telephoto lens to minimize the risks of this kind of surveillance. It came in handy now, bringing Kwame in close enough for her to see the worried expression on his face as she clicked off three or four shots as he entered the building with his key. There was already a light on upstairs. She got a long shot that showed his car in front of the building and a close-up that showed his license tag clear enough to read it. Reaching into the glove box for her small notebook and a pen, Lee recorded the date and time.

She hadn't heard anything else from Precious since she received a very formal letter withdrawing Mandeville Maids from the peace precinct, but she knew it was only a matter of time. There was no way it would be over until Precious had forced Lee to resign or Lee could force Precious to back off. These pictures of Kwame and his lover were her best defense. Nobody who wanted to be mayor of Atlanta could afford this kind of scandal. By the time she needed to use them, these pictures would be worth their weight in gold.

Suddenly, less than two minutes after he went inside, barely long enough for her to record the activity, the door literally burst open and Kwame came running out of the building like it was on fire. Lee grabbed her camera. Through the eye of the telephoto lens, his face was a mask of terror. She kept clicking as he jumped into his car and sped away without closing the building's outside door behind him.

Once the sound of Kwame's fast retreat faded away, the street was silent. There were no other residents in the building and the other warehouses in the area were still awaiting the kiss of gentrification to bring them back to life. It appeared there was no one else around but Lee. She sat for several minutes to be sure, and to guard against what she regarded as the very remote possibility of Kwame's return. The way he had left, like a bat out of hell, she didn't think he was coming back anytime soon.

Ten minutes seemed long enough to wait. Lee got out quietly, her camera around her neck and her police-issue magnum in her hand, walked into the building and up the stairs to Kwame's apartment. That door was open, too. *What the hell was going on?* Lee's cop radar was sounding the alarm and she cocked her gun quietly and held it at the ready position as she stepped into the space. Nothing seemed amiss in the living area. The television was on and there was a light coming from what she assumed was the kitchen. She walked slowly, silently, toward the doorway.

Still hearing nothing, she stepped quickly into the lighted room, which was indeed the kitchen. It had a stove, a refrigerator, and a half-eaten carton of shrimp fried rice on the counter. The only problem was, it also had a dead body lying in the middle of the floor. Shot in the head. *Clean.* She leaned down to take a look. From the looks of the body, it had happened within the last hour. Two hours, tops. But she would have heard gunshots if Kwame was the murderer and she had heard nothing but the roar of his engine as he *hauled ass.* She stood up and looked around. The possibilities were endless, but all she knew for sure was that somebody had left a body in Kwame Hargrove's love nest and she was the only witness who could place him at the crime scene. She holstered her weapon and reached for her camera. She didn't need her telephoto lens for this one. If she got any closer, she'd have to kiss the body.

A few blocks away, back at home, Kwame awakened Aretha like a man on fire and made love like someone who never will again.

58

B lue was on the phone when Regina walked in the front door and tossed her keys on the table with the mail. He smiled and held out his arm to her. Exhausted, she walked into his embrace, wrapped her arms around his waist, and took a deep breath. Blue smelled like lemon and she closed her eyes and leaned against him. *Thank God for you,* she thought, her cheek against his chest. *Thank God for you.*

And a voice that seemed to come from inside her own head, but sounded exactly like her husband's rumbling baritone, replied, *And for you, my love. Thank God for you.*

She opened her eyes, but Blue was still engaged in his conversation. He couldn't have murmured such an endearment without thoroughly confusing whoever was on the other end. *Telepathy,* she thought. *I must be getting better at sending and receiving.* Abbie had told her this would happen and Regina wished she could call her now and apologize for ever doubting that it would. She owed Abbie so many *thank yous* for so many things, but now was not the time for *thank yous.* Now was the time for rest and care and healing.

"Thanks for keeping me informed, Lieutenant," Blue said. "Call me at any time."

He clicked off the call and put the phone down so he could give Regina a real welcome-home hug. She hugged him back, realizing he must have been on the phone with the D.C. police.

"Any news?" she said as he drew her down beside him on the big white sofa in front of the window. It was just after sunset and they could see their neighbors going about their evening routines, but Regina paid no attention. She needed to hear that warrants had been issued, arrests had been made, justice was being done.

"They've got a couple of guys in custody for another robbery two blocks away. They think it might be them."

Regina's heart beat a little faster and she unconsciously folded her arms protectively across her belly. "When will they know?"

"They're faxing down mug shots for Abbie to take a look at. They're hoping she can identify them informally. If she thinks these are the guys, they'll put them in a lineup and see if she can pick them out."

"How's she going to do that from here?"

"She'll have to go back to D.C.," Blue said gently.

Regina shook her head. "You know she can't do that. She won't even come out of the apartment."

"That's why they're sending the pictures. To give her a little more time."

Regina looked at Blue like he had taken leave of his senses. She had spent all afternoon with a frightened, damaged creature that bore little resemblance to her vibrant, beautiful aunt. When they went to D.C. immediately after the break in, the police had already taken Abbie to the emergency room. The young woman doctor who met them at the hospital said there had been no rape, but the young thieves had both urinated and masturbated on Abbie after they tied her naked to the antique four-poster where Regina's mother had been born. After that, they trashed the house, took what they could carry, and left her there, still bound. One of her students came by and found her the next afternoon.

At the hospital, Abbie had refused a sedative and asked that no visitors be allowed except Blue and Regina. Although Peachy had flown up with them from Savannah, she refused to see him or to fly back with him on the same plane. Reluctantly agreeing to her wishes, he had driven back to Atlanta with General and moved into Blue's apartment on Lawton Street. Abbie had put up no resistance to Regina's plan to take her back to Atlanta, but had drawn the line at staying at the house, as she always did when she visited. *This was not a visit,* she insisted quietly. At that point, Blue offered her the unoccupied apartment downstairs from Aretha's studio and told her she could stay there as long as she liked. Abbie had thanked him, gone inside, and shut the door.

She barely tolerated Regina's daily attempts to visit and the meals she delivered in covered dishes went untouched while fresh fruit withered in the bowl. Peachy's presence upstairs at Blue's place, where he waited anxiously for a chance to see Abbie, to hold her, to console her, she ignored completely. Urging her to talk about her ordeal had earned Regina an invitation to leave and not come back unless she promised to never, *ever* speak of it again. Regina, terrified of the pain she saw in Abbie's eyes, promised. There was no way that promise left space for her to go knocking on the door with some mug shots or, worse, proposing a trip back to the scene of the crime to see the suspects live and in the flesh, separated from Abbie only by a pane of one-way glass.

This is a nightmare, Regina thought, her eyes filling up with tears. "She can't do it, Blue. It will kill her."

"Come here, baby," he said, reaching out and gathering her in close.

She clung to him, afraid that she was right and Abbie would not survive. Blue rocked her in his arms and she let him, thinking to herself that this would never have happened in West End. She knew her husband made sure women were safe and children were cared for and old people could walk in peace. What she wanted to know was why this neighborhood was the exception, not the rule.

"You okay?" Blue said gently.

"It feels different when it happens to somebody you love," she whispered.

Blue kissed the top of her head. "Everybody's somebody's somebody."

"How come you know that and nobody else seems to?"

"I used to be the emperor. I have to know it."

She smiled a little at the easy way he said it, like saying *I used to live on Willis Mill Road.* "Do you really remember how it feels to be free?"

"I don't have to remember it," he said. "I'm still free."

Outside the window, the big Lincoln pulled up and General got out. Regina watched him coming up the walk and looked at Blue.

"General and I are just going to have a drink," he said quickly, answering the question she hadn't asked out loud. "I'm not going anywhere."

She was relieved. This was not a night she wanted to spend alone.

Blue put his hand on her belly. "Don't worry."

She covered his hand with her own. "Why? Because it's bad for the baby?"

"Because it's bad for *you*," he said, and kissed her gently. "And you know I don't allow that."

59

On the phone, Captain Kilgore had said it was routine, but Kwame felt like he was trapped in a bad episode of a TV cop show. The police had, of course, questioned him when he called to report finding the body on a routine check of his property. He told them he had been having a problem with squatters since the loft wasn't his primary residence and *no,* he explained, he'd never seen the victim before.

They seemed to buy it, and one of the detectives told him it was always a problem with areas that are gentrifying. Kwame had explained that he used the place off and on as a studio since it was hard for him to work at home with a small child. He went on to say that he hadn't needed it as often lately since his daughter was not in day care and, he supposed, that was why the guy was able to use the place without Kwame knowing about it. He had even joked with the cop about being lucky to have had such a neat squatter since nothing much was out of place and nothing stolen. The captain agreed, took his phone number in case they needed him, and that was that.

For the next three days, he picked up Joyce Ann at school. He made love to his wife. He conferred with his mother about campaign strategies and accompanied Bob Watson to a luncheon with a potential client. From the outside, he looked like an ambitious young man just hitting his stride, but in the back of Kwame's mind was the expression on Baby Brother's face when he'd found him lying there on the kitchen floor, *dead, dead, dead.* He shuddered every time he thought about it. *Who could have killed him and why?*

Kwame scanned the paper nervously every morning and watched the local news every night, but a shoot-out at the courthouse dominated the media and there was only one small item about a homeless man's body being found in a newly gentrified area near downtown. He hoped that would be the end of it. He was afraid his name would have to appear in any major news coverage of the crime and that wasn't how he wanted Aretha to hear about his loft.

On the way to Captain Kilgore's office, he tried to calm down, telling himself it was probably just routine. She had said she had a few follow-up questions about the murder and could he drop by her office around six? He had agreed immediately, of course, and spent the rest of the morning and half the afternoon worrying about what questions she might have for him. He had met her once before at a function he attended with his mother and he knew Precious admired the captain's ideas on domestic violence prevention. He hoped the association would make her move sympathetic to his current predicament. If worse came to worst, at least she would understand his desire for discretion.

By the time he arrived at police headquarters, he had a sudden premonition that he was about to be arrested. Beyond that, his mind went blank. He couldn't remember what he had told the first investigator. He couldn't remember exactly how Captain Kilgore sounded on the telephone. He couldn't imagine what it was like to be arrested for murder. The possibilities were too awful to imagine. He forced himself to enter the building and ask for directions to her office.

When he tapped on her door and she opened it, Captain Kilgore's appearance was reassuring. She was not wearing a uniform and, to Kwame's panicky eyes, looked more like a hip social worker than a cop.

"I appreciate you taking the time to come down, Mr. Hargrove," she said, offering him a chair and taking a seat behind her desk. The space was small and impersonal. He wondered if this was an interrogation room like the ones on TV, where there is always weeping and denial, sometimes violence, and then confession.

"No problem," he said, deciding not to mention Precious unless she did. "Have you found out anything else about the guy?"

"I was hoping that's where you might be able to be of some assistance."

The knot in his stomach tightened a little. "I already gave . . . the other officer . . . a statement."

"The story about the squatter?"

He didn't like the way she called it a *story*, but he nodded. "That's right."

"You stated that you'd never seen the deceased before he somehow ended up on your kitchen floor?"

"Yes."

She looked at him and frowned slightly. "Mr. Hargrove, we'll get along a lot better if you tell me the truth."

"I . . . I am telling you the truth." He wondering suddenly if he was being taped.

"Well, if that's your story," she said, reaching into her pocket to produce a stack of snapshots that she slid across the table in his direction. "How do you explain these?"

On top of the stack was a photo of Kwame and Baby Brother standing at the front door of the loft the first time they'd gone there. The knot in his stomach tightened a little more. If this one was on the top, what kinds of pictures were next? Kwame couldn't make himself pick them up to see.

As if on cue, Captain Kilgore leaned over and spread the photos out like a deck of cards. There he was at the loft that first night. There they were sitting in the car together. There he was picking up Wes in front of Montre's. *And there was that dead, dead body lying on his kitchen floor.* He stared at the photographs, aghast; speechless; terrified.

"Mr. Hargrove?"

He looked up into her eyes, a frightened man, out of options. "Yes?"

"I'm a busy woman, so I'm going to try and minimize the bullshit in our exchange."

The profanity startled him. He felt like he was going to throw up, but Captain Kilgore didn't seem to notice. She reached out, picked up the photographs, and slipped them back into her pocket. He wondered if they were going to handcuff him now and take him to jail.

"I understand," he whispered.

"Your squatter story doesn't really make much sense, but you're a respectable guy with a beautiful family and a famous mother, not to mention friends in high places. The victim is a small-time hood with a record dating back to his overprivileged adolescence. He's also an army deserter who abandoned his unit in Iraq and was known to frequent Club Baltimore, which is where he met you."

She looked at Kwame without a shred of pity for his predicament. She didn't look like a kindly social worker anymore. She looked like a pissed-off police officer interrogating a sweating perpetrator.

"Are you with me so far, Mr. Hargrove? Would you like some water or something?"

"Yes," he croaked. "Thank you."

She handed him a small bottle of tepid water from a neat row on her bookshelf. He opened it and drank gratefully. The water felt good going down. His mouth had been dry as cotton.

"The way I see it, you and Mr. Jamerson had set up a love nest, and when things went wrong, you shot him." She shrugged. "Classic lovers' quarrel. Where'd you stash the gun?"

"*I didn't kill him!*" Kwame's voice was a muted cry of anguish. "You've got to believe me! *I didn't kill him!*"

She looked at him. "Well, maybe you did and maybe you didn't, but these pictures, plus my testimony of how you came flying out of the crime scene that night like a bat out of hell right before I discovered the body, is going to make it hard to convince anybody that you didn't have a little something to do with it."

Kwame felt like she had kicked him in the stomach. "What do you mean?"

Her eyes narrowed a little like she was running out of patience and her voice was harsh, commanding. "I mean if you don't want to be arrested for the murder of your little boyfriend, you better get yourself together and listen to what I have to say."

Kwame took a deep breath. "I'm listening."

"Your mother has some information that could be damaging to me, personally and professionally."

"Leave my mother out of this," Kwame said quickly, as if he was in any position to make demands.

"I'm not the one who put her in it," Lee snapped. "*You* did, and now you're the one who's going to get her out."

Kwame swallowed hard. "What kind of information?"

"That's none of your business," Lee said. "The point is, I want her promise—in writing—that she will never pursue a case against me for any crimes she imagines I committed."

"I can't ask her to do that." Kwame's head was spinning.

"I think you can, Mr. Hargrove, and do you know why?"

He didn't know anything anymore. All he wanted to do was go home, crawl into bed, and hope it would all go away. "Why?"

"Because if she doesn't, I'll be forced to do my duty as a police officer and file a report about this whole thing."

She paused to let her words sink in. "That fool at the courthouse bought you a few days' reprieve from the media and the department. If nobody comes forward, the victim's sister will come to claim his body and you'll be home free. But all that can change."

He knew what that meant. "How long have you been watching me?"

"Long enough."

"Why?"

"Because you have secrets, and in this town, secrets are better than money."

"But I didn't kill him!" Kwame's voice was an anguished cry.

"I know that, and you know that, and after a long, messy trial, the jury may believe it, too. But in the meantime, these pictures will be on the front page of the paper and all over the Internet. Your mother will have to withdraw from the race. You'll lose your job and your wife will almost certainly divorce you and take the baby. What's her name?"

"Joyce Ann," Kwame whispered.

"Well, you think about the effect of her daddy's murder trial on Joyce Ann." Captain Kilgore paused to let the idea of his daughter being caught up in this whole mess sink in before she spoke again. Kwame leaned over and put his head in his hands. "And then you explain to your mother that I need her answer in twenty-four hours."

Kwame sat up and stared at Lee. "Twenty-four hours?"

"How long do you think I can withhold information regarding an ongoing murder investigation? It's already been two days. Twenty-four hours is the best I can do, Mr. Hargrove. Are we clear?"

What choice did he have? Kwame nodded.

"Good. Call me when you've got an answer from your mother." She handed him a piece of paper with a number typed on it, but no name. "And don't be late."

The meeting was over, but Kwame didn't know how he got out of the building. He walked the two blocks to his car in a daze. Twenty-four hours to try to convince his mother to compromise herself because he was caught up in some madness that could put him in jail for life. *Or worse.* How could he even begin to have such a conversation with Precious? He didn't have a clue, but he knew he had to try, *and right now.* The clock was running and Precious held his future and the future of his family in her always capable hands. He picked up his phone and speed-dialed her number, knowing wherever she was, she would respond to the sound of the Ohio Players.

When you're hot, you're hot,
You really shoot your shot,
Fi-i-i-re!

60

E ven though they had been back from D.C. for almost a week, Blue and General hadn't had much time to talk. The personal trauma of Abbie's experience with urban violence was mirrored citywide in a panic after a shoot-out at the Fulton County Court House left three people dead, five wounded, and a fugitive at large somewhere in the metro area. There were cops everywhere, and West End was no exception. They had sought Blue's assistance, but he had no leads to share, so they did a quick pass through the neighborhood and moved on. Once the guy had finally surrendered, exhausted and out of options, things returned to a more normal pace and Blue asked General to stop by for a drink.

He poured his friend a scotch and a cognac for himself. Anyone watching the two men would have observed them chatting easily about the events of the day, but General knew this was no ordinary catch-up session. They could have done that at the West End News. The reason Blue had invited him here was still a mystery, but somehow General knew it had something to do with the death of Baby Brother. He hadn't told Blue what he had done and the lie of omission floated between them like a malodorous cloud.

"Anything else we need to talk about?" Blue said as he refreshed their drinks.

General shook his big head slowly. "Not that I can think of."

Blue sat back down, swirling the cognac slowly around in an oversize snifter, and looked at his friend. "You moving to Vegas?"

Thrown for a loop by the directness of the question, General tried to keep his voice steady. "You know I don't like Vegas."

"I know. That's why I thought there must be a damn good reason. You want to share it with me?"

General sipped his scotch, tried to remember the last time he had lied to Blue's face, and couldn't. He could keep a secret as long as the question was never broached directly. That was one level of deception. Looking into Blue's strange eyes and outright *lying* was something else altogether. General knew he had to tell Blue about Brandi. He just couldn't figure out how without making himself look as foolish as he felt.

"I've been seeing this woman," he said carefully. "She's a dancer . . . at Montre's . . . and we just kind of . . . hit it off."

Blue was looking at him with no readable emotion on his face. General plowed ahead, the words coming slowly as he tried to explain.

"She's young, man, and *fine*." He heard himself attempt a small laugh, a *man-to-man* laugh, to pave the way for a lighthearted exchange about the inscrutable ways of women, but Blue's expression didn't change. General decided to cut the chitchat and lay his cards on the table. "She's never been to Vegas. I told her I was the man to take her."

Blue's eyes began to darken imperceptibly. Their sky blue was becoming inkier by degrees. General knew from experience that silence was always on Blue's side. He could sit still and quiet longer than anybody had a right to. If that was the contest, General conceded defeat without a struggle.

"Just a visit, man. I'm not moving anywhere."

Pouring himself another splash of cognac, Blue nodded. "Her cousin came to see me."

That surprised General. *What did Madonna have to do with it?*

General reached out for the scotch. "Oh yeah?"

"She was worried because some guy her cousin was seeing got shot last weekend, and all of a sudden Brandi's talking about moving to Vegas. She asked me to check into it for her. That's her name, right? Brandi?"

So that was it. Brandi had blabbed to Madonna about that dead *faggot* and then said she's moving to Vegas. *Damn!* he thought. *Couldn't she just keep her mouth shut?* "Yeah, that's her name."

"When her cousin said she was going away with you, that made Madonna feel better, but she wanted to check with me because she's convinced her cousin is a pathological liar."

General felt the ground shifting beneath his feet.

"I asked Madonna if Brandi had given her a name for this guy, the one who got shot. She said his name was Wes Jamerson." Blue watched General, whose studied nonreaction told him what he needed to know. "You remember him, don't you?"

"That nigga who came here looking for Zora?"

"That's the one."

Feigning surprise, General shook his head. "I always knew he was going to be trouble. You remember I said it first off."

"I just don't want his trouble to become my trouble," Blue said.

"You can't control what happens to every punk who passes through West End."

General wanted to change the subject, but he hadn't introduced it and it wasn't his place to try to move on. He sipped his scotch and waited.

"Are you in love with this girl?"

General had to bite his tongue to keep from blurting out the truth. *I'm in love with the part of Juanita that lives in her!* "No. I'm just seeing her, that's all."

They both knew that what Blue was really asking was how a man of his age and position in the neighborhood could get so deeply involved with a stripper who trailed trouble behind her like a full-length mink. There was no answer but the truth that would even begin to explain his behavior, but that was an impossibility. This was no way to reveal a secret he'd been sworn to keep for twenty years. Suddenly General was flooded with anger at Blue for asking him these questions like he was a child. Like he had to justify who he took to Vegas and why. If the best defense is a good offense, General decided to go for broke. He put down his glass.

"Tell me again why this is of concern to you."

"Because," Blue said calmly, "I'm only supposed to hear that you're considering a move out of West End from you."

General took a deep breath, sat back into the soft leather of the big chair, swallowed his pride, and spread his arms in a gesture of supplication and surrender, his eyes downcast to avoid Blue's glare.

"You're right," he said softly, hating the words he was about to offer in his defense. "You're right, brother. I'm an old fool chasin' some young pussy that don't belong to me."

"So you still owe this girl a trip to Vegas?"

"Yeah, I guess I do," General said.

"When do you intend to take her?"

"Maybe this weekend if I can get things set up."

"You'll be back by Sunday?"

"No problem."

"Good."

The two sat looking at each other for a moment, glasses empty now, hearts and minds full of history and the complexity of their overlapping lives. Then Blue stood up to signal that the meeting was over. General stood up, too, and they embraced like brothers.

"You can be an old fool," Blue said at the door. "You were a young fool, so I'm used to it."

"Fuck you, too." General smiled, glad it was over and that Blue hadn't pressed him any further about his relationship with Brandi.

"The important thing is that we're still brothers," Blue said. "I trust you with my life and the life of my family."

General wanted to look away, but the intensity of Blue's gaze caught and held him. "You can trust me. You *know* you can trust me."

"Good," Blue said, nodding slightly and stepping back inside. "Take it slow."

Relief flooded General's body as he walked to the car, even though he knew this was probably not the last of it. Blue wasn't careless or stupid and there were questions still to be answered. He drove to the corner without looking back and turned the car toward Montre's. He needed to talk to Brandi.

61

As soon as she heard his voice, Precious knew Kwame was in trouble. "What's wrong?"

"You busy?"

"Of course not. Come on by. I'll put on some coffee."

"I'm on my way."

"You all right?"

"I been better."

"Okay. I'll put some rum in that coffee."

His laugh was dry and mirthless. "Sounds good."

He knocked on the back door five minutes later and she was shocked at his appearance.

"You look terrible!" she said. "What the hell is going on? Are Aretha and Joyce Ann okay?"

"They're fine." He sat down at the table and took a long breath.

"Did something happen?"

"It's a long story, Mom. Can I have that cup of coffee first?"

"Of course you can." Precious poured them both a cup and added a dollop of the Captain Morgan she kept from one Christmas to the next for eggnog. "Now tell me everything. Whatever it is, we can handle it."

"I don't know where to begin. It's complicated."

"Just start anywhere," she said. "I'll keep up."

"Well . . . I . . . I own a loft."

"A loft?"

He nodded. "Over on Peters Street. I bought it last year as an investment."

Precious sipped her coffee, wondering why he'd never mentioned it, but knowing this was not the time to ask. "There's a lot of development over there, that's for sure."

"A guy got killed in it."

"*What?*"

"I went over there a couple of days ago to work on the place a little, and . . . I found the body in the kitchen."

"My God, Kwame! How awful!"

"It was terrible." His eyes filled with tears.

"Did you call the police?"

"Of course. They sent two detectives over. I told them I'd had a problem with squatters."

"Is that who they think he was? A squatter?"

He looked up at his mother again. "That's what I told them."

The difference between her question and her child's answer was not lost on Precious. She looked at her son. There was something he wasn't telling her. *Something important.* "Do they have any suspects?"

Kwame looked around the kitchen where he had sat so many times, in this same chair, talking to his mother, swapping stories, sharing a meal of a tall glass of iced tea. Every inch of this table was familiar to him and every memory of this room was a good one. Now he was going to destroy all that. He didn't know if he had the strength.

Precious watched the conflicting emotions playing across Kwame's face and leaned over to take his hand. It felt so cold and clammy she was frightened. "What is it, son? Just tell me."

Her face was so concerned, so worried. It was cruel to make her wait for such terrible news.

"What I told the police . . ." Kwame hesitated.

"About the squatters?" Precious said encouragingly.

He nodded. "Yes, well, they think . . . not all of the . . . but one of them thinks that . . . well, they . . . *she*, it's a woman . . . seems to believe that I . . .

that *they* should talk to me about it more because . . . she had some . . . pictures that made her start speculating that he . . . might not have been a squatter."

Kwame had always been a terrible liar. Tonight was no exception. The words he was speaking were tumbling out in an indecipherable jumble.

"Then what was he doing there?"

"She thinks maybe he was . . . maybe I knew him."

"Did you?"

It was a simple question with a very complicated answer. "Yes."

Precious was now thoroughly confused. "Then why did the police think he was a squatter?"

Kwame stood up and walked over to the sink. Through the kitchen window, the barest sliver of a new moon was not enough to dispel the shadows in the yard. He turned back to his mother. It was time to tell the truth. She was his brilliant, beautiful, strong, sensible mother. If he could just tell her the nightmare he had made of his life, he knew she could help him fix it. *She had to help him fix it!*

"Because I met him . . . at a club."

"You met the squatter?"

"Well, he wasn't a squatter when I met him, but when he found out who I was, he started blackmailing me. That's why I took him up there."

"You're not making any sense, Kwame. Blackmailing you about what?"

There was no way to say it but to say it. The captain's clock was still running. "Sometimes, Mom . . . sometimes . . . I have sex . . . with men."

He hated himself for saying it that way. *Sometimes.* He should have said *every chance I get.*

"You what?"

At least she didn't jump up and throw him out of the house. He sat back down, and this time, he reached for her hand. She didn't take her eyes off his face.

"Sometimes I have sex with men."

"For money?" She whispered the words, unable to comprehend what he was saying.

"No, no," he said quickly. "I don't do it for money. I do it . . ."

He didn't know how to finish the sentence. *Because I like it? Because I can't not do it?* They sat looking at each other across the small table, neither one having the words to say all they felt, or feared.

"I don't know why I do it," Kwame said quietly.

Now Precious took both his hands and gripped them so hard it was painful. "Did you have sex with the man who was murdered?"

"Yes," he whispered. "Yes, I did."

She squeezed his hand so tightly he wanted to jerk his fingers free. "Did you kill him?"

"*No, no, no!*" he said urgently, needing her to believe him. "I didn't kill him. He was dead when I got there, just lying on the floor." He shuddered at the memory of that face, those eyes. "But they don't believe me."

"Why?"

"Because they have pictures! They have pictures of me with him in the car and at the loft."

"Pictures of you doing what?"

Her voice rose alarmingly at the end of the question, a terrible mixture of confusion, disappointment, rage. Kwame hung his head. There was no room for him to be self-righteous about the nature of her questions. He had never felt so ashamed and helpless.

"Talking in the car, going inside. But she said it gives me a motive and that she . . . she was there the night I found the body. She had pictures of me leaving. I was . . . running."

"Who took the pictures?"

"I don't know. She did, I guess. I saw them. They're real."

Precious closed her eyes. She couldn't bear the sight of this stranger's face, but it was too late to run. It was time for truth.

"Have you been charged with anything?"

He shook his head. "No, but Captain Kilgore said—"

The tiny hairs on the back of Precious's neck stood up. "*Captain Lee Kilgore?*"

"Yes."

"She had the pictures?"

"Yes."

"How long has she been watching you?"

"I don't know."

"She said she hadn't shown them to anybody and that they were prepared to go with my squatter story, but she . . . she . . ."

He hesitated again, but Precious was tired of coaxing the story out of him. "*Dammit, Kwame, stop stuttering and tell me what you know!*"

Startled by the harshness of her tone, he blurted out the rest of his sorry story.

"She's prepared to turn over the pictures to us and never mention any of this again if you agree to absolve her of any crimes."

"What?"

"She said you have information that could damage her career and that if you don't agree—in writing—not to use it, she'll have me arrested for first-degree murder. She gave us twenty-four hours."

Precious stood up and walked out of her back door without another word. She sat down in her favorite porch rocker and tried to make sense of what she was hearing. She knew that putting something like that in writing would give Lee the power to blackmail her forever. She could never run for mayor with something like this hanging over her. The drug charges must be pretty close to home for Lee to resort to blackmail, Precious thought. Lee had to be really scared to risk coming after family. There were probably millions of dollars at stake. Rocking slowly, rhythmically, Precious realized this was all about *business*. But it was more than that. This was personal. Very personal.

Precious stopped the chair's motion and turned to Kwame, standing in the doorway. "Have you told Aretha?"

He ducked his head like a ten-year-old kid with a bad report card. "About the murder?"

"About who you are!"

He winced at her angry tone. "I wanted to tell you first. It's your future they're trying to snatch."

"This isn't about politics," Precious said, hearing the anger in her tone and unable to mute it. "You can't run away from what you've done."

"I didn't kill him!"

Precious stood up and walked quickly back inside. Kwame backed away as if he thought she might strike him. For several minutes, she just looked at him, then she took a deep breath. She realized he was hoping she could make it all go away. He was hoping *Mommy could fix it*.

"That's not what I'm talking about," she said quietly. "First you have to tell Aretha *everything*. Then I'll call Hank Lumumba and see if he can represent you."

Kwame's shocked face told her this possibility had never entered his mind. "Represent me?"

"You're going to need a good lawyer."

"You're going to let them arrest me?"

"I'm not going to compound one lie with another."

It was dawning on him that she was not going to do what Captain Kilgore wanted. She was going to hire him a lawyer and stand her ground. The only problem was, as she stood there, his life would be slipping away like a California mud slide. He'd be arrested. His private life would be public knowledge. His job would evaporate. His marriage would disintegrate, and even if he was acquitted—and that was a big *if* since innocent men and women went to jail every day in America!—the sordid details of the case would follow him for the rest of his life.

"Do you know what kind of publicity there will be if you let this go forward?" he whined.

"I have some idea."

"Do you know what that will do to Aretha?"

"Do you care?"

He sat back down suddenly and tears filled his eyes. "That isn't fair."

"Go home and talk to your wife."

Kwame buried his face in his hands again. "This will kill her."

"No, it won't. *It can't.* Somebody has to think about your daughter."

At the mention of Joyce Ann, Kwame began to moan softly. He buried his face in his hands. The sound of such misery in her only son made Precious want to weep, too, but it was too late for tears. She reached out and touched his head gently, hoping he understood that his sexuality was not the problem, his lies were. He reached out and encircled her waist with his arms, his head burrowed into her belly like there was still safety to be found there.

"My beautiful boy," she whispered. "What have you done to us all?"

When he didn't look up, she knew he could never tell Aretha the whole truth. He probably didn't know it himself, and twenty-four hours wasn't enough time to find out.

"Did Captain Kilgore give you a number for me to call with my answer?"

Kwame nodded, fumbled in his shirt pocket, and handed her a crumpled piece of paper.

"Mom, please . . ."

"Call your wife," Precious said, dialing Lee's number.

Lee answered on the second ring. "Senator Hargrove," she said, reading the caller ID. "What can I do for you?"

"You can't do anything for me," Precious said evenly. "My son told me about your offer and I don't need twenty-four hours. You can have my answer now."

"Your choice, Senator."

"That's right, it is. Let me make this as clear as I can. You can go to hell, Captain Kilgore. I intend to see the mayor first thing tomorrow morning to share my concerns about your role in all of this, and I mean *all of it.* You're a disgrace to your uniform and the people who died for your right to wear it."

"I don't have to listen to—"

"Yes, you do. You've got to listen long enough to see if I'm going to let you hold my child's fear of who he is over my head like a stick. But I've never been afraid of the truth and I never will be. You know my son is innocent of murder and so do I. If he has to go to court to prove it, I'll be right beside him every step of the way."

"I see," Lee said quietly. "I think it's only fair to warn you that I'll have to turn everything over to the proper authorities."

"You're supposed to be the proper authorities, Captain Kilgore. *Remember?*"

Precious hung up before Lee could say another word, glanced at her son still weeping in his chair, and punched in her daughter-in-law's number.

62

In the dream, it always begins with the sound of breaking glass and muffled voices, cursing as they climb the stairs. Tonight was the same. Abbie awoke with a start and ran to the bathroom. After the dream, she always vomited. She had stopped eating to prevent this final indignity, but it didn't matter. Her stomach would still flip and cramp and retch, bringing up nothing but bile and bitterness. Afterward, she splashed water on her face and gazed at her reflection, hardly recognizing herself in the pale, wild-eyed woman staring back.

This is what I am now, she thought. *No voices, no visions, no sound of the sea inside my head.* Now when she closed her eyes, all she heard was their angry voices and all she smelled was her own terror. In the mirror, she watched her left eye twitching and wished they had burned the house down around her. That house and the safety it had always promised was a lie. She knew that now. There were no safe spaces no matter how many prayers she prayed and spells she cast. She was alone.

Abbie wondered if other people saw the world as she now perceived it. She wondered if they saw the same mean, vicious, ugly place that waited just outside her blue front door. Maybe this was how other people saw one another, as capable of such casual evil that there could be no words to describe it, no charms to dispel it, no explanation to allow the mind to understand, the heart to forgive, and the soul to continue its journey. She closed her eyes and wept.

It began as a long, low groan and then rose to a high, thin, anguished wail. She made no attempt to control the sounds suddenly issuing from her body. She just leaned against the sink and let herself cry for all she'd lost and for whatever she had now become. She felt at that moment that if she stopped herself, she might die from the effort. Even more frightening to her, she wasn't sure that wasn't what she really wanted. If the rest of her life was to be lived in this dark pit, she was ready to let it go and try the next one. It had to be better than this.

In the hallway outside Abbie's apartment, Peachy pressed his ear to the door and listened. He could hear her sobbing and the sound broke and rebroke his heart until he thought he would go insane. She had no idea that he was sitting outside her door that midnight, just as he had done every day and every night since she arrived. She had no idea that he left his self-appointed post only long enough to eat and catch a few hours' sleep when her niece was there.

Regina had told him he didn't have to sit there and promised she would come upstairs and get him the minute Abbie gave her permission, but Peachy just thanked her and said it was no trouble. What he meant was, there was no way he was leaving Abbie alone. Even if she thought that was what she needed, he wasn't going anywhere. He remembered when Lillie had tried to tell him she didn't want him to come to the hospital anymore after the cancer had robbed her of everything but her spirit. Something about not wanting him to see her *that way.* It had taken him the better part of a day to explain that he wanted to see her any and every way he could for as long as he could because he loved her, and unless she was going to have the police come and haul him away, he was there for the duration. After he said that, knowing how much he hated the police, she knew he was serious and she stopped trying to make him go away. Later, she even told him she was sorry she had tried and he kissed her little bald head and told her that was okay. He knew she didn't mean it.

He knew Abbie didn't mean it either, but she was still a free woman, and even though he was her chosen man, he had to respect her wishes. Not going to her was one of the hardest things he ever had to do. But she had decided to walk this part of the road by herself and he had to go along with that. Just like he had to believe that when she was ready, she would know that his love could hold her and heal her and lead her back to who she really was, *no matter what those fiends had done.*

So Peachy stood there listening until her sobbing stopped and he heard her walk back toward the bedroom. Then he sat back down to wait, because he knew that one night, maybe not tonight, but soon, she would open that door, *slowly, slowly,* and when she did, he would be there.

63

Her car was in the lot, but when General walked into Montre's after he talked to Blue, Brandi wasn't on the pole or finishing up a lap dance. Johnny told him she was up next, but he wasn't in the mood to wait, so he told Johnny to go get her. Not in the mood for random contact either, he sat alone in Johnny's sad little excuse for an office. There was a broken-down desk, a couple of rickety-looking folding chairs, a couch that looked like it had absorbed its share of fluids, bodily and otherwise, and a calendar from the year 2000.

The dime-store corkboard above Johnny's desk was crowded with snapshots of tired-looking naked women, along with their names, vital statistics, and phone numbers. As if there was no photographic evidence to the contrary, most of the measurements the women were claiming added up to perfect hourglass figures. General turned away from their sad eyes and cellulite-dimpled thighs. All he wanted to do was talk to Brandi.

Why had he ever questioned her about that young fool? That one lapse in judgment meant that she was the only person who could connect him to the murder. The way she'd been blabbing to Madonna, he knew it was only a matter of time before she said too much. It was time for her to go to Vegas. When he got back, he'd tell Blue she liked it so much, she decided to stay.

They'd have a good laugh about how a man his age should have known better and that would be the end of it.

"Hey, baby!" she said, coming into the office and hugging him quickly. She had thrown on a thin robe, but underneath it she was still naked. "Johnny said you was in here. *'Bout time!* I thought you was never gonna come see me!"

"I been busy."

Something in his tone made her nervous. Ever since Keisha had shown her the news item in the paper about Baby Brother, she'd been looking over her shoulder. The police didn't have any suspects, and until they arrested somebody, she was being extra careful. She'd had a john die of a heart attack once, but nothing like this, and Brandi was scared. General being out of town hadn't made her feel any more secure. He'd called her a couple of times since he returned from D.C., but he hadn't been by to see her but once and then he didn't even stay long enough to get a dance.

Of course, she was glad to see him back. The problem was, she still couldn't tell him how frightened she'd been while he was gone. She couldn't confess that she'd been with Baby Brother in that loft the same night he got killed. General had given her a thousand dollars and told her to stay home, but she just had to go make that extra money! She couldn't just do like he said, *like she promised,* and now look what she'd gotten herself into.

"What's wrong, baby?"

"Why don't you tell me?"

In the small room, General suddenly seemed like a giant to her. She felt sweat forming under her breasts. "What do you mean, baby? Ain't nothin' wrong with me now that you back."

He looked at her so hard that if he hadn't been standing between her and the door, she would have tried to make a run for it.

"I saw you."

The sweat began to run down her body in small rivulets, but she didn't notice. "Saw me do what?"

"I saw you leave that nigga's place the night I went to D.C."

Her frightened, guilty look made him feel sorry for her, but she was going to be a lot more frightened before he was through. He had to scare Brandi enough to make her shut up before she blew everything wide open just by talking too much.

"What you mean? I wadn't at no nigga's place that night."

"I saw you come out wearing the dress I got you for Vegas."

The idea made her feel weak with fear. She sat down heavily on the nasty couch. "You were watchin' me?"

"I watch everybody."

She broke down immediately. "He just said he wanted some company, baby, and you had left me already."

"With a thousand dollars of my money in your pocket."

"Don't be mad, baby. He don't mean nothin' to me. I only saw him a couple of times at the club and then that one night."

"Did you kill him?"

She groaned. "Don't say that, baby! Don't say that! You know I didn't kill nobody. I ain't even got no gun. I didn't even have no beef with that guy. He paid me my money and I left. He wanted me to go out to the club, but I didn't go, baby. I went home like you told me. I swear I did!"

That much was true. She had taken all the cash Baby Brother had and his promise to raise more did not impress her. *Call me when it's in your hand,* she'd said over her shoulder on her way out the door.

"You think the police are going to believe that bullshit?" General growled.

Her eyes opened even wider. "What police?"

"The ones that are going to be looking for you."

"For me?"

"You're a suspect."

"*Oh my God! Oh my God!* How do you know?"

"Don't worry about how I know. You better be trying to figure out what you're going to do when they start asking around about who knew him and who saw him last."

Tears were rolling down her face and her mascara was smeared around her eyes like a raccoon. General knew there'd been no witnesses to the murder, but she was so terrified, if he'd told her there was a videotape, she probably would have believed him.

"Oh my God," she said again, jumping up suddenly and throwing her arms around his neck in desperation. "You gotta help me, baby! You gotta help me!"

He pulled her arms away. "You should have thought of that when you took my money and went looking for a nigga who didn't have no better sense than to get himself killed."

She was crying harder and harder and her eyes implored him. "I'm so sorry, baby. I was wrong. I'll never do it again, I swear to God, but you gotta help me! You gotta believe me!"

He let her stand there, shivering with fear for long enough to make his point. "Are you going to do everything I tell you?"

"Yes, baby! I swear I will! Whatever you tell me is what I'm gonna do. Just help me. Please help me!"

That was what he needed to hear. "You have to get out of town until things cool off."

"Out of town?" she said. "Where am I gonna go?"

"Vegas. Just like we planned."

"Vegas?" Relief flooded her face, but her tone was incredulous; still scared to believe him.

He nodded. "I've made some calls. We'll get you a job. A place to stay. A couple of months, this will all blow over and you can come back."

"I gotta go by myself?" she whimpered.

She sounded so scared, he felt sorry for her all over again. This wasn't her fault. She was caught up in something she didn't even understand. He reached out then and pulled her up tight against him. She collapsed into his arms.

"You know I'm going to take better care of you than that," he said gently. "I'm leaving tonight to get everything set up. There will be a ticket for you at the airport, and when you get to Vegas tomorrow, I'll meet you with a limo and everything else you need."

"Thank you, baby," she whispered, burying her face in his chest, trembling like the last leaf on the tree. "Thank you."

He reached into his pocket and handed her all the cash he found there. She clutched it in her hand miserably. He knew she was afraid to fly by herself, but he had to go on ahead to put some things in place. Everything had to look absolutely cool when she got there so she wouldn't even suspect that she wasn't ever coming back. He just couldn't risk it.

"You okay?"

She nodded.

"Good. Now go do your show and make it a good one."

"Why, baby?" Things were moving so fast she felt dizzy.

"Because this is the last time you're going to have to shake your fine ass in front of these broke-ass niggas."

That elicited a shaky smile. "You promise, baby?"

"I promise."

"I'll see you tomorrow night. In Vegas."

He kissed her once quickly and left her standing in Johnny's office alone. It wasn't until after she had finished her shift and started for home that the thought crossed her mind that General knew exactly who had killed Baby Brother. *And so did she.*

64

Regina was sleeping. Her body was curved so closely against Blue's that they were now breathing in perfect sync. His arms were wrapped protectively around her, and in the first rays of early morning light, his eyes were wide open and shining like sapphires. Blue lay down with Regina every night, but he rarely slept. His mind seemed to prefer nighttime for the processing of information. He had spent the last seven hours holding his wife's soft, warm body and thinking about what he always said were the only two questions worth asking: *What is?* and *What is next?*

Lying there in the darkness, he thought about the world into which his child would be born and he was filled with joy at the creation of new life from the love he shared with Regina, and despair at what his people had become. He was filled with rage at the destruction of a whole race, who'd gone from being free men and free women to being called slaves in the time it took those evil ships to cross the Atlantic Ocean. He knew few of his brothers had survived that Middle Passage with manhood and sanity intact. The ones who did were quickly identified and destroyed, since manhood is an easily recognizable state of heart and mind that can never coexist with a system of slavery.

The few intact men who made it through are still under siege by those who would be their masters, Blue thought, or their destroyers. He knew their numbers were dwindling. He also knew what life would be like in African American neighborhoods once the predators reached the necessary numbers to take full control. In many places, it had already happened. In West End, he knew all they were doing was holding a finger to the dike, but he believed that history required only that each one play the role that is assigned. Blue had always known that. General was about to learn it.

When the phone rang at just after six, Regina murmured softly and turned in her sleep. Blue picked it up and slipped out of bed in one smooth motion. "Hello?"

"Blue? I'm so sorry to call this early, but I need your help." Precious sounded tense and tired.

"You have it," Blue said. "This is a safe line. What can you tell me?"

Precious took a deep breath and said it all in a rush. "Kwame is a suspect in a murder case."

"Where are you now?"

"I'm at his place with Aretha and Joyce Ann. He stayed at my house last night."

"I'm on my way."

"Blue?"

"Yes?"

"Is there any way Regina could come with you? I think Aretha's going to need all the sisters she's got to get through this."

"We'll be there in twenty minutes."

When Blue walked back into the bedroom, Regina was already up, pulling on her robe. She tied it snugly across her gently rounding belly. The sun through the window behind her head outlined her body in a soft-focus glow and Blue thanked the gods as he always did for finally bringing this woman to his side.

"Precious says Kwame is a suspect in a murder case."

"What?" Regina's voice was full of shock and disbelief.

"I'm going over there to get the whole story. She's with Aretha. Can you come with me?"

"Of course," she said, heading for the shower. "Give me ten minutes."

"I'll put on some coffee."

"Blue?" She turned at the bathroom door.

"Yes, baby?"

"Do you think he did it?"

Blue shook his head. "No. Kwame's not a killer."

She looked relieved. "Good. I didn't think so."

He waited until he heard the water spring into life before he picked up the phone and dialed Zeke's number. Blue knew it wasn't too early. Zeke didn't sleep much either. He answered on the first ring.

"Brother Hamilton, you're up early this morning."

"Can you make a run with me to Vegas tonight? Just out and back."

"Our plane or one of theirs?"

"Ours."

"Done."

65

B lue was at his office getting ready to go to the airport when the call came from Lee Kilgore asking if she could see him immediately. His early-morning conversation with Precious fresh in his mind, he agreed and told her to come by his office at the West End News. She arrived a few minutes later, looking tense but determined. He had no idea what she wanted, but he had no doubt she was there to tell him.

"Thank you for agreeing to see me, Mr. Hamilton," Lee said, sitting down across from Blue.

His famous eyes were partially hidden behind tinted glasses, but still impossible not to notice.

"I don't have much time," he said, and his voice was cold. "What can I do for you?"

"I realize I'm in no position to ask you for a favor, but I—"

"Precious Hargrove is a good friend of mine," he interrupted her quietly. "Her son is married to my goddaughter. I'm aware of your ultimatum."

"Yes, I know," Lee said. "That's what I wanted to talk to you about. I'm sure she told you about—"

"She told me everything, Captain Kilgore. Now what are *you* trying to tell me?"

His directness took away any opportunity to present context, and at that moment, Lee felt context was everything. She knew she had done wrong, but it hadn't started out that way. In the beginning, all she wanted to do was stop the dealers from shooting up the neighborhood. Sure, she had selfish reasons for trying to make peace, but the end result was the same, wasn't it? She had never intended for things to get so out of hand that people were killing and mutilating one another. That had never been part of the plan.

"I'm trying to say that I'm sorry for my part in some of the things that have happened recently in regard to Senator Hargrove and her family."

"What about Kentavious Robinson and his family?" Blue said.

Lee sighed. He wasn't going to make this easy. "I've made some bad decisions and I'm prepared to pay for them."

"That's usually the way it works."

She flushed and decided to stop hoping he would understand. It wasn't important if he did or not. She wasn't here to offer apologies. She was here to try and buy a little time.

"I'm leaving town tonight," Lee said, reaching for the big manila envelope she had been holding in her lap. "I'd appreciate it if you'd give this to the senator."

She slid the bulky package across the table in Blue's direction, but he never took his eyes from her face.

"All the photos and notes from my surveillance of Kwame Hargrove are there. I didn't make copies, so she won't have to worry about anybody else contacting her. My notes from that night make it clear he wasn't the shooter."

"I'm sure she'll be relieved to hear that."

"There are some tapes in there, too," Lee said. "Audiotapes."

Blue frowned slightly. "What's on the them?"

Lee shifted in her seat and leaned forward, lowering her voice out of habit more than necessity. "Bob Watson and I did a lot of business together during the last five years. I've taped a number of our phone calls and conversations."

"Insurance?"

"Look, Mr. Hamilton," Lee said. "I know I have to answer for what happened to Kentavious Robinson, but there's enough blame to go around. I'm hoping my long-distance cooperation will buy me a little slack from your friend the senator."

Blue touched the envelope lightly. "You know you'll be called on to testify if any charges are brought against Bob."

"This is a great big world, Mr. Hamilton," Lee said. "I intend to get lost in it to make sure that doesn't happen."

"They'll come looking for you."

"No, they won't," Lee said. "If there's an investigation, Bob will be enough to hold them. He'd be quite a prize for any ambitious prosecutor, or candidate."

Blue looked at her for a minute. She had nothing to lose by looking right back. He stood up. "I'll make sure the senator gets this immediately. Now I have other business to attend to."

"Thank you." Lee stood up and turned away. She suddenly felt the urge to get on the road right away. Blue was probably right that the authorities would come looking for her, and it was always harder to hit a moving target.

"Captain Kilgore?" Blue said quietly just before she reached the door.

"Yes, Mr. Hamilton?"

"That peace precinct was a good idea."

"Thank you," she said, surprised. She wished she could wash away the last five years and start again. "You can have it."

66

General lay down across the room's king-size bed to catch a few hours of sleep before Brandi's plane got in at midnight. The limo was picking him up at eleven-fifteen to meet her plane. Even as scared as she probably was, he knew she'd relax when she saw that he'd gone all out for her arrival. He'd even told the driver to put a bottle of Cristal on ice and get some roses. It wasn't her fault that things had to end this way, but there was no way around it. At least her one memory of Vegas would be a good one, he thought, rubbing his eyes with exhaustion.

He still hated Vegas. The short ride from the airport to his hotel had confirmed his worst fears about *the new Vegas.* When they got off the freeway, the glittering golden Mandelay Bay Casino almost blinded him with its unapologetic excess. The New York/New York Casino boasted a fake Brooklyn Bridge and a hotel tower the shape of the Chrysler Building. The Boardwalk Casino had games of chance, cotton candy, and a roller coaster, but no ocean. It was like driving through a child's idea of a city. Everything about it seemed to be dedicated to encouraging people to do things they'd never do at home. That wasn't how it was for General. He was getting ready to do exactly what he did at home, but this time he was on his own.

When the cabdriver turned in at The Paris, he took a right at the fake

Arc de Triomphe and pulled in under the legs of the fake Eiffel Tower. Inexplicably, there was a huge brightly colored hot-air balloon out front, competing for attention with giant jumbotrons and the shadow of the huge, green MGM pyramid with the fake lions crouched out front. He hated the whole thing, but he wasn't here for pleasure. He was here to do a job and go home with his secrets intact and his life back under his own control.

The doorman directed him to check in and he entered the building by stepping onto a fake cobblestone street the likes of which had probably not been seen in Paris since the 1800s. Over his head, a fake sky twinkled with fake stars and fake trees cast their shade over the entrances to shops selling Cartier watches and the *National Enquirer.* The gaming tables and slots almost seemed to be an afterthought.

He checked in under the name he'd told Brandi to use if for any reason he couldn't meet her plane as two big-breasted women in teeny bikinis and diamond earrings chatted with the clerk at the next station as if they were in line at the grocery store. General shook his head. Vegas was the only place in America where you could order room service with a side of hookers.

When he got to the room, General hung the "Do Not Disturb" sign on the door and stretched out, closed his eyes, and sighed deeply. He hoped Blue would let this one moment of madness slide. Wes Jamerson had been a bad seed from the start and he'd deserved what he got. But all Blue ever required was the truth, General thought, and here he was, *knee-deep in lies and bullshit.* When he got back, he'd have to figure it all out, but not right now. He was too tired to think. He closed his eyes and tried to rest.

When he woke up with a start an hour later, he glanced at the clock to be sure he hadn't overslept. That's when he saw Blue sitting in the dimly lit room. It had never occurred to General that Blue would come to Vegas. This was a surprise, and in their business, surprises were never a good thing.

"Turn on the light," Blue said.

General sat up and swung his long legs over the side of the bed. He had loosened his tie and draped his jacket on the desk chair. He leaned over and flipped on the bedside lamp closest to him. Blue was wearing a dark suit, white shirt, and tie. His black homburg was balanced easily on his knee. There was no way to know how long he had been sitting there.

"What's up, brother?" General said, trying not to look directly into those strange blue eyes. Trying to sound *normal.*

"You tell me," Blue said, his voice as cold as his eyes.

General wished there was some way to know how much Blue knew and who had told him. He needed time to think. "Tell you what? I told you I was coming to Vegas. Here I am."

"The police are getting ready to charge Kwame Hargrove for the murder of Wes Jamerson."

"No shit? I didn't even know they knew each other." *That much was true.*

The expression on Blue's face didn't change. "Brandi Harris thinks they've got it all wrong. She thinks you killed him."

General's heart and mind were racing. *How could he have been so stupid?* "Is she a liar?"

Blue's voice cut through his jumbled thoughts. "What?"

"If she's lying, then she's the problem. If she's telling the truth, then you are."

"She's a whore."

Blue just looked at him. "She said you were jealous because she was seeing Jamerson at the same time she was seeing you."

Hearing such a commonplace description of what had been for him such an intensely passionate moment shamed him and angered him in equal measure. Blue was sitting here asking him if he had killed a man for sleeping with a woman he himself described as a *whore*. General felt his shoulders sag. There was no longer any question about it. He had become the most foolish of foolish old men. He had not only killed another man over a woman who reminded him of someone else, he had allowed the police to suspect another man of the crime. *A capital crime.* How could he possibly explain? He took a deep breath and tried.

"I know this doesn't make any sense, but I thought she might be . . . somebody else."

He waited for Blue to ask him who he thought she might be, but Blue didn't say a word. His expression never changed. His eyes glittered like black diamonds in the moonlight.

"I thought somebody sent her to me, you know? Like you found—"

Blue's voice cut him off. "Before my mother died, she made me promise her one thing."

General felt his heart skip and flutter in his chest.

"She made me promise to look out for you. No matter what."

Sweet Juanita, General thought. She had tried to guard against this moment in perpetuity by binding them both to the same promise.

"That's the only reason you're still alive," Blue said, as calmly as he might have said he was going to pick up a newspaper.

General flushed. He had heard that tone many times and he knew what it meant. *But he wasn't going out like this!* He called up whatever scrap of indignation he could muster. "My life is in danger now? For what? Taking out that sorry piece of shit?" General knew he was begging for his life and he heard the panic around the edges of his voice. It didn't matter how many guns he'd stashed around the room. He couldn't face Juanita in heaven and tell her he had killed her only son.

"The only way what we do is part of the solution and not part of the problem is if it's *never personal.*" Blue's voice was so quiet it was almost a whisper. "It can only be about order and honor and truth. Nothing else. *Ever.*"

General was guilty as charged and they both knew it. Blue stood up and settled the homburg before he spoke again. "You lied to me. That can't happen."

Everything they did was based on mutual and absolute trust. One lie can break down a thousand truths. The reasons don't even matter. It was over. All he could do now was wait for his instructions.

"I've got a car downstairs," Blue said. "We'll fly out in an hour."

General stood up, too. There was just one more thing he had to take care of. Brandi was on her way to Vegas. Somebody had to meet her.

"I need to stop downstairs to leave a message at the desk for my lady friend."

Blue looked at him with no sympathy in his eyes. "She's not coming."

Just like that. Of course she wasn't coming. That was all in the past. *Just like that.* General reached for his coat and slipped it on, straightened his tie. In the mirror, he didn't recognize the face of the tired old man looking back at him. He hoped his beloved wasn't looking down on him right now. He didn't want Juanita to see him like this. So he squared his broad shoulders and turned back to face her son.

"Ain't no point in sayin' I'm sorry, but I am."

If General hoped for a moment of forgiveness between them, he was disappointed. Blue reached for his hat as if his old friend hadn't uttered a sound. *So be it,* General thought, but there was one final piece of housekeeping he needed to take care of before they headed out into the neon of the Las Vegas night. He spoke the words they always used to indicate it was time to collect any weapons that had been strategically stashed around and about in case the negotiations in question took a turn for the worse.

"I need to clean the room."

"Zeke's going to take care of it," Blue said, opening the door. Zeke was standing outside alone.

"What's up, brother?" General said, stepping out into the hallway behind Blue. Zeke nodded a greeting, walked into the room, and closed the door.

Forty-five minutes later, the three of them stepped back into the Gulf Stream for the return trip to Atlanta. General watched the spot of man-made illumination that is Vegas being swallowed up in the deep darkness that is nature and tried not to think about all that would come next. Even if he didn't get the death penalty, this was no time for a middle-aged man to be in prison with those young fools who don't give a damn about dying since everybody they know is already dead. The fact that his status as Blue Hamilton's right-hand man would make him a tempting target for any *wannabe gangsta* looking to establish a reputation as a badass would only make things worse.

He leaned back and closed his eyes. First he'd have to get through the trial. He'd have to listen to Brandi describe his obsession with her. He'd have to sit there while she told them about him thinking the botched tattoo on her ass was a sign from his dead girlfriend. He'd have to hear her say Juanita's name in a courtroom full of strangers. The thought made him feel nauseous. There was no way he was going to let that happen. *No way he could.*

He opened his eyes and looked around. On the small table beside his seat there was a bottle of water, a pint of scotch, a legal pad, a pen, and a small shaving kit. *Why hadn't he noticed all that stuff before?* He picked up the pad slowly, an idea dawning, and at the top he wrote the date, glanced at his watch, and added the time. That was the easy part. The hard part was figuring out how to say what he had to say as clearly and as dispassionately as possible. He remembered that old television show from the fifties where the guy says "just the facts, ma'am, just the facts." It would be easier if he just stuck to the facts.

"On the night of October 5, I broke into the home of Wes Jamerson and shot him to death with two bullets to the back of the head. This act was the result of . . ."

His hand hesitated above the page. *The result of what?* The facts, he reminded himself. Just the facts.

". . . the result of me being jealous over a woman named Brandi Harris."

Another pause. He had to make it clear that none of this was her fault. He wrote a little faster.

"Miss Harris was not involved in any way. Neither was . . ." What should he call Kwame? *The accused?* "Neither was Kwame Hargrove. He is innocent of all charges against him."

Was that enough? He wanted it to be enough. He wanted this to be the end of it. If he confessed, they didn't need to have a trial and Juanita could continue to rest in peace without their business being dragged through the streets of Atlanta.

"I swear on the Bible that this is my true and real testimony," he wrote, more slowly now, wanting to get it right. "Nobody is forcing me to say this."

He signed his name at the bottom and put his address and phone number like he was filling out a job application. Then he put the pen down and looked up. Although he hadn't heard him approaching, Blue was standing there watching him, and for the first time that night, General saw a flicker of empathy in his eyes. He so wanted to see it there. Blue was as close to a brother as he had ever had and he loved him. He knew what to do. Tearing the page carefully away from the pad, he folded his confession neatly and handed it to Blue, who slipped it into his left breast pocket without a glance. In the silence, the plane's engine hummed.

"I got one more thing to say," General said.

"Go ahead." Blue stood there looking down at him.

General took a deep breath. "I was in love with Juanita for twenty years. No other woman ever meant a damn thing to me. She made me promise not to tell you, but I don't want any more secrets between us. I loved her, man. I always will."

"She loved you, too," Blue said quietly.

General's eyes filled with tears for so much wasted time. "You knew?"

Blue nodded. "I always knew."

The peace that comes with no more secrets washed over General like a warm dip in the Caribbean Sea.

"We'll be there in under an hour," Blue said. "Why don't you get a shave before we land?"

The suggestion might have seemed a little odd, except the shaving kit was sitting right there. General picked it up. He felt very old and very tired.

"I think I will."

Blue nodded. "Good."

"I love you, man."

"I love you, too, brother."

The night was clear and the small plane was cruising effortlessly along toward Atlanta without even a hint of turbulence. General stepped into the bathroom, twice as large as the ones on most commercial planes, but still cramped quarters for a man his size. He closed the door and that same world-weary brother who had gazed back at him in Vegas had beat him to the mirror and was looking back with what seemed to be a new expression on his face. *Was it resignation or relief?* General couldn't tell. Maybe a little of both.

Of course there were razor blades in the shaving kit. He pulled one out and laid it gently on the edge of the sink. He took off his jacket, hung it on the door, closed the top of the commode, and sat down. It was a squeeze for such a large man in such a small room, but he didn't seem to notice. He turned on the hot water and let the sink fill halfway as he rolled up his sleeves carefully. The mirror was clouded with steam, but he had no more interest in his own face. The face he wanted to see next was the face of God. *And then Juanita.* He drew the razor three times across each wrist quickly. The blade was as sharp as a surgical scalpel and for a second he just watched the six cuts as they began to ooze crimson. Then he plunged his arms into the hot water and closed his eyes.

By the time the captain came on to tell them to fasten their seat belts for landing, General was gone.

Epilogue

Regina was waiting for Blue. The others had already gone back to the house to prepare dinner, but she wasn't ready to go in yet. The sound of the gulls following the shrimp boats in soothed her as she walked, at peace for the first time in a long time. Driving to Tybee from Atlanta, Blue had called a few hours before with the news that the suspects in Abbie's case had made bail two days ago, stolen a car that same night, and been killed instantly when they crashed it against an antiterrorism security barrier three blocks from the White House. Abbie offered a prayer that in their next lives the two young predators would get to come back as human beings. Peachy said *amen*, and Regina offered up a silent *thank you* to her husband for being everything he was.

Their little group had been holed up at Tybee for almost six weeks. Aretha and Joyce Ann were there, too. General's confession stood up in court and Kwame had been cleared of all charges, but Aretha wasn't ready to see him yet. She needed time to deal with everything that had happened. Her friends understood. They gave her space when she needed it and company when she wanted some. Blue came down every weekend and spent hours walking with her on the beach. They didn't talk much, but Regina could see Aretha getting stronger as the days went by.

The mayor had announced a citizens' committee to begin looking into allegations of police involvement in the city's cocaine trade and named Precious Hargrove to head it up. Just yesterday, Abbie's apprentices had called to report that they had cleaned her house from top to bottom and installed a set of sky-blue burglar bars that, according to their report, didn't look the least bit prisonlike. They had also burned enough purifying sage for a thousand Thanksgiving turkeys. Abbie thanked them and promised she'd be back soon. She wasn't ready yet, but every night she spent sleeping beside Peachy and listening to the ocean made her know she would be ready soon. Her dreams had already returned. She knew the visions would be next.

It was a time for healing and they all knew it. They needed these six peaceful weeks to find a way back from the places their lives had taken them. They needed time to understand the price of freedom, the inevitability of pain, and the presence of lies from which there can be no turning away.

But lots of things are stronger than lies, Regina thought, watching the sand crabs emerging from their holes in the deepening twilight. *A new baby on the way is stronger. A little girl for Aretha to raise is stronger. A love that found itself that night Abbie finally poked her head out and saw Peachy waiting to take her back to the beach before she missed one more sunset was stronger.* Last night there had been the sound of laughter in the house again and this afternoon, dozing in her favorite chair, Regina had had a sudden vision of her daughter, a chubby chocolate drop of a girl, standing by the window, watching for her daddy. When she turned to smile at her mama, her eyes were cornflower blue. Regina smiled to herself, remembering. She couldn't wait to share the news with her husband.

That's when she'd turned toward the house and there he was, standing on the deck, gazing in her direction. She raised her hand in a welcome-home wave and started walking quickly toward him in the growing darkness. The waiting was over.

"Come on, baby girl," she whispered to her daughter. *"Daddy's home!"*

PEARL CLEAGE is the author of *Babylon Sisters*, *What Looks Like Crazy on an Ordinary Day . . .* , which was an Oprah's Book Club selection, *Some Things I Never Thought I'd Do*, and *I Wish I Had a Red Dress*, as well as two works of nonfiction: *Mad at Miles: A Black Woman's Guide to Truth* and *Deals with the Devil and Other Reasons to Riot*. She is also an accomplished dramatist. Her plays include *Flyin' West* and *Blues for an Albama Sky*. Cleage lives in Atlanta with her husband, writer Zaron W. Burnett, Jr.

ABOUT THE TYPE

This book was set in Photina, a typeface designed by José Mendoza in 1971. It is a very elegant design with high legibility, and its close character fit has made it a popular choice for use in quality magazines and art gallery publications.